Splendor of Dawn

Splendor of Dawn

PART ONE
OF
THE JEWEL OF LIFE

RYAN D GEBHART

Copyright © 2015 Ryan Gebhart

Library of Congress Control Number: TX 8-173-586

Hardcover ISBN 978-1-7326355-0-0

Paperback ISBN 978-1-7326355-1-7

Distributed by Ingram Publisher Services

Printed in the United States of America

Cover design by Fiona Jayde Media

*To my parents
and their unending faith in me.*

TABLE OF CONTENTS

Acknowledgements

Shortly after I finished my undergrad studies, a story revealed itself to me. It was very shy at the beginning but as the months stretched on, it became bolder and impossible to ignore. Like the story, I too was very shy and hesitant to share it with others, without the encouragement of my dear friend and brother, Will Tarraza, I doubt I would have ever had the courage to invite others into this story.

From that summer of 2012 and onward, my heart grew determined to let go of the story and share it. I completed the original manuscript in 2013 and hastily made it available electronically, thinking it was complete. However, I made an unexpected friend on Twitter, Wendy Oleston, a friendship that placed me on a path toward a more professional publication. Several years later, another Twitter friend, Melissa McPhail, entered the scene, and it's been through her guidance and encouragement that I've pursued self-publication. Melissa also put me in contact with an editor, Micheline Brodeur, who was set on retiring and not taking on any new authors. Fortunately, she agreed to tackle this odd writer from Delaware and her constant care and attention has polished and refined what was once a rough manuscript into this completed book.

There are dozens more people who have been influential and supportive throughout my writing this book, and to name you all and the individual reasons for my appreciation of each of you would require an entire chapter. Know that I am forever grateful for your role in my life and in my writing.

I will personally thank Fred Cabras though, thank you for jumping into that pool and saving the only copy of the first chapters of this book, handwritten on my yellow note paper. I still have them and they are still crinkled but no longer smell like chlorine.

Dear good and gracious reader, I hope the story which follows fills you with the same joy and excitement that I had while writing. This story has come to life, quite literally, across the country over the past six years, beginning in Philadelphia, PA then on to Victoria, KS; Santa Ynez, CA; Washington, DC; Wilmington, DE; Pittsburgh, PA; Middletown, CT; and finally, Richmond, VA. The pages of this story are filled with enchanting characters, mythical races, wondrous lands, and of course, magic. I've included a glossary for your convenience, because my imagination ran rampant as this story unfolded and it became a necessity. To help with any confusion that may occur, I've listed the days of the week and the months below.

Days of the Week

Gwynthaen–Thenaen–Uraen–Ramaen–Lerenaen–Saraen–Karaen

Months

Spring – Marenth, Aurenth, Delenth

Summer – Dynenth, Meridenth, Reventh

Autumn – Kyrenth, Vespenth, Orenth

Winter – Estlenth, Borenth, Lierenth

Ryan D Gebhart

September 2018

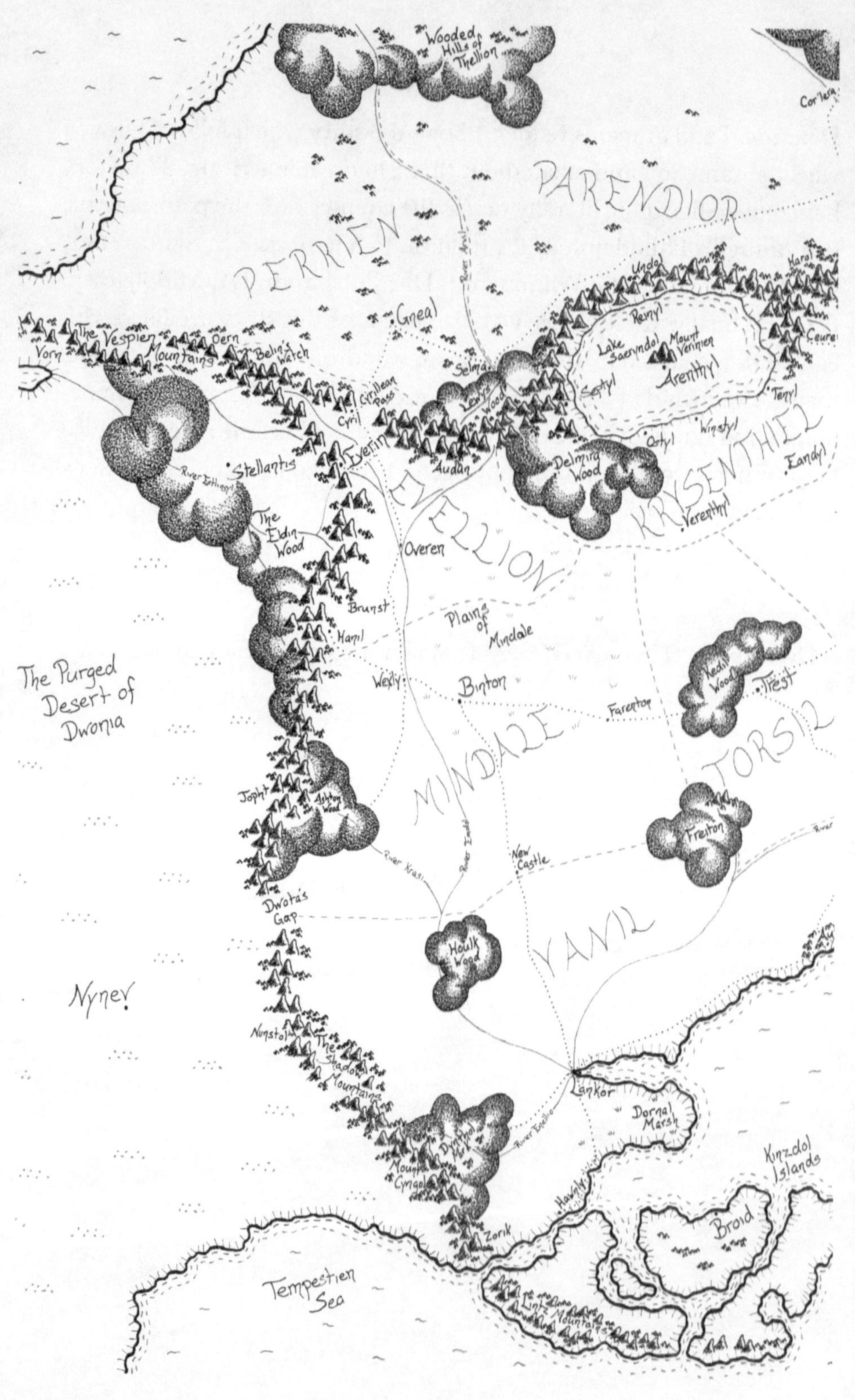

PARENDIOR
PERRIEN
Wooded Hills of Thellion
Corlesa
Ungol
Karol
Renyl
Lake Saeryndol
Mount Verinien
Arenthyl
Ceure
Gneal
Septyl
Tenyl
Vorn
The Vespien Mountains
Oern
Belin's Watch
Selma
Lexyr Wood
Winstyl
Ostyl
KRYSENTHIEL
Eandyl
Cyrillean Pass
Cyril
Eyerin
Audun
Delmira Wood
Verenthyl
River Ethiand
Stellantis
EYELLION
The Eldin Wood
Overen
Nedhil Wood
Trest
Brunst
Plains of Mindale
Hanil
Wexly
Binton
Farenton
TORSID
The Purged Desert of Dwonia
MINDALE
Freiton
River
Jopht
Ashton Wood
River Iredil
New Castle
River Krasi
Dwota's Gap
Houlk Wood
VANIL
Nyner
Lankor
Dornal Marsh
Kinzdol Islands
Nunstol
The Shadow Mountains
River Emelno
Broid
Drathlor Hills
Mount Cyngol
Hawglin
Zorik
Tempestien Sea
Linz Mountains

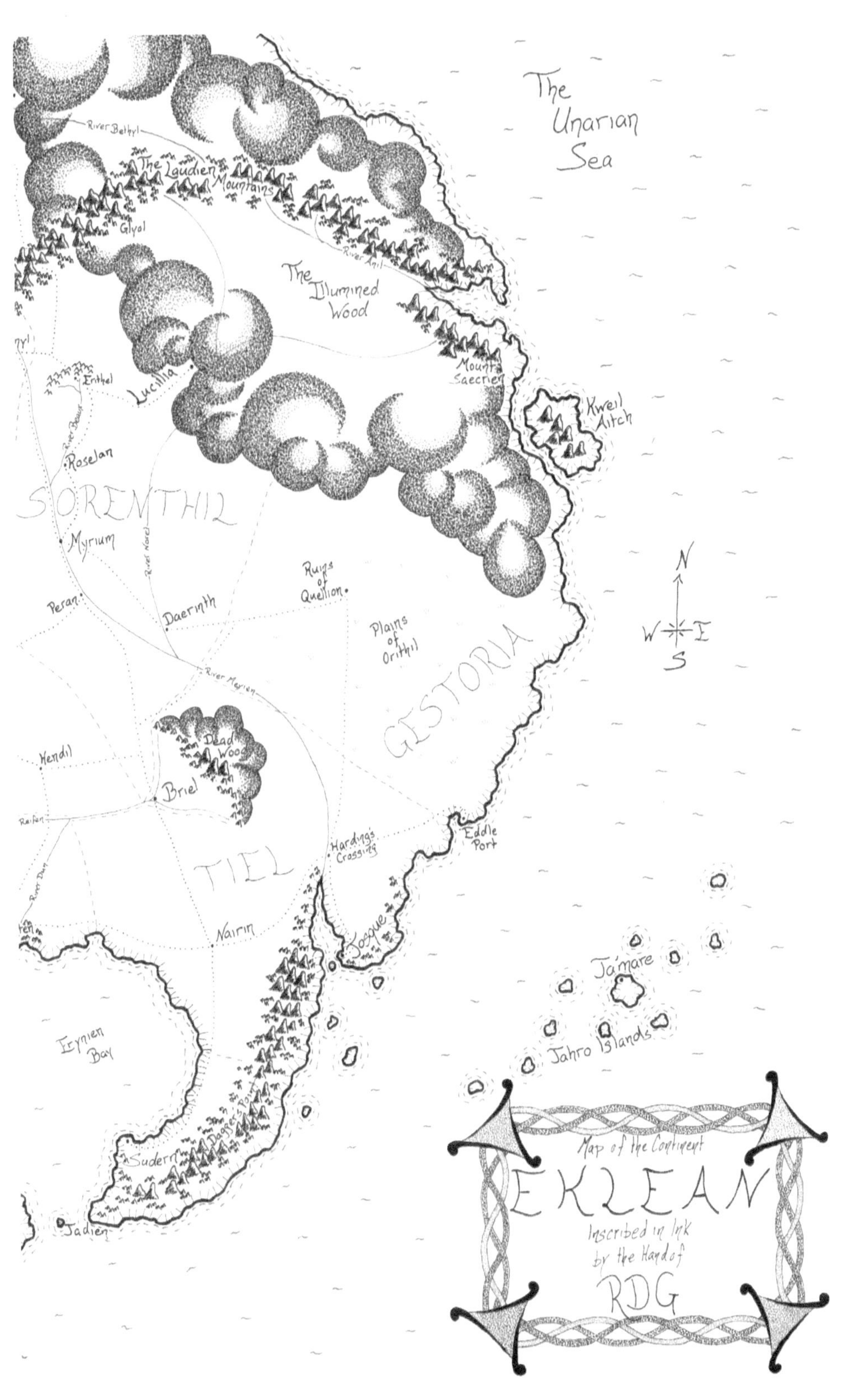

The Unarian Sea
River Bethyl
The Laudien Mountains
Glyol
The Illumined Wood
River Anil
Mount Saecrien
Kweil Aitch
Enthel
Lucilla
Roselan
SORENTHIL
Myrium
River Noril
Peran
Daerinth
Ruins of Quellion
Plains of Orithil
GESTORIA
River Marien
Dead Wood
Hendil
Briel
Raifen
River Daru
TIEL
Nairin
Harding's Crossing
Eddle Port
Josque
Jamare
Jahro Islands
Erynien Bay
Dagger's Point
Sudern
Jadien
N
W E
S
Map of the Continent
EKLEAN
Inscribed in Ink
by the Hand of
RDG

THE LINE OF FEOLYN

Backs against the setting sun, Velaria and Arlyn approached the small, yet expanding village of Cor'lera, the narrow River Bethyl just behind and the end of their northward journey just ahead.

"Before we enter," said Arlyn, bringing Velaria's attention to the narrow gate and the man standing guard with foreign soldiers closely behind, "remember that the people here must not learn that you are training with the Ei'ana. Unfortunately, the rumors of whole villages tossing out anyone they suspect to be wielders are true; it wasn't all that long ago when the villagers here exiled the neighbors they considered suspicious."

Velaria nodded and kept a steady pace to avoid raising suspicion from the guards. They had dismounted after crossing the rickety bridge over the river, partly to rest their horses, but also to provide a less threatening approach.

A simple wooden wall shielded most of the small village, while buildings erected within the last thirty years stood outside the walls, evidencing recent growth. A dozen buildings were paused in partial completion and work would presumably resume when the snow melted, and the land thawed in the spring. This far north, they might have to wait until Delenth in late spring. Since it was now only Borenth, winter was in full swing and spring still two months off, so construction wasn't resuming any time soon.

Farms scattered in every direction beyond the village. At the start of their voyage, Velaria had gazed on them with fascination, but as their travels drew on and the distance between villages increased, the scenery became repetitive. Now, she longed to return to Ceurenyl or even better, to her home city of Lucillia.

Velaria's thoughts drifted to the wooded structures of her home, the buildings simply grown from the very trees, the domed buildings, and the magnificent walls, but above all, the royal palace resting atop the crest of the sloping hill holding Lucillia. Each building held its own identity, yet they all belonged and complemented each other. Even the common buildings shared the same attention to beauty. The twining wood gave a fluid motion to the city; Velaria half expected to see the buildings move on their own one day.

As lively as the buildings were, her people were the true heart of Lucillia. They shared an eagerness to enjoy life and possessed an impeccable energy toward living every moment, a quality which had dimmed with every town they passed in their journey north. In village after village, the people grew gloomier; the greater the distance grew between them and Lucillia, the greater the despair and fear evidenced.

"Halt!" the guard at the gate ordered as they approached.

He was unlike the rough soldiers behind him; instead he shared the features common to the people of this region. His age could be no more than thirty, yet the greasy shine of the visible parts of his body along with his disheveled appearance made Velaria think otherwise. Most appalling was the hatred in his eyes and Velaria looked away from it. Even their color was not memorable; she thought them brown, like the mud currently holding her attention, but they could have easily been blue. She felt him glare at her with evident disdain.

"Quickly state your purpose," his lips formed a snarl as he spat out the words, followed by a wad of phlegm that landed just before their feet. No mistaking that the voice belonged to its owner; it was as foul as his mood. "It's Lerenaen, and I don't want to keep this gate open longer than needed."

Velaria had not the slightest idea what impact the day of the week had on the openness of a gate, even if it was late in the week.

"My daughter and I are simple travelers seeking a pleasant home to the north, far enough away from the growing turmoil in the south." Arlyn spoke quickly before the guard could refuse them admittance. The guard eyed them suspiciously before he responded.

"You look to be of wealthy stock. Why would you desert your lands for the cold north? Turn out those pockets while you're at it, let me see those crowns you're hiding; there's a gate tax." The guard snapped, his mouth curling.

"I have no lands to the south. It could be said that I've been stripped of them and my possessions do not surpass what we carry." Arlyn turned out his pockets, upending the contents of his light purse into his palm. Copper lewts and iron angots spilled from the purse, but only one silver jent.

Velaria stared blindly at him in disbelief. *I thought he wasn't allowed to lie.*

"A man should have a firm grip on his property." The guard glanced toward the jent, lewts, and angots, visibly disappointed to not find any golden crowns. He snatched the jent, daring Arlyn to protest the gate tax. "Move on, I don't care to hear the rest of your pathetic story. If it's north you're heading, set out before dawn and be gone from our village," he instructed.

He grimaced toward Velaria in visible disgust. "We don't appreciate your kind, witch. All you ei'ana witches are the same, thinking you're higher than nobles. I hope it's out of wisdom that you flee north to be rid of them; wouldn't find me sticking around." With no more than that, and without pointing them toward an inn, the guard stepped aside and permitted the pair to guide their horses through the small gate.

How did he know?

The foreign soldiers just inside the gate gave Velaria pause. The hatred in their eyes somehow managed to surpass that of the guard. Without stopping, they walked past the cluster of men and into the village. It had a pleasant look about it, and surely at an earlier time, the neglected buildings of either rough stone or timber topped with thatched roofs had been well-cared for.

Rubbish littered the streets and the trees and plants in the gardens looked neglected. The few villagers found outside their homes gave off the same suspicion and anger as the guard, but no one stopped to question the two strangers, preferring to whisper among themselves.

Velaria picked up only their tones without hearing the words, but it was evident that they distrusted the newcomers.

She walked warily next to Arlyn along the cobbled streets until they reached one of the better-maintained buildings in Cor'lera, an inn toward the edge of the village. It included a stable to the rear. *I recognize this building,* she thought, *but why? Where have I seen it before?*

"Welcome to the Cor Inn, or as it is more commonly known, the King's Inn," said Arlyn.

The familiarity struck home. The inn resembled those structures she knew all too well in Lucillia, except of course this building looked to have been built by elven or human hands and not molded from the very forest. The details and the masterful carvings could not disguise the inn's origin. Delighted with her discovery, she shared it with Arlyn.

"You learn quickly; I had grown accustomed to lecturing the same point on several occasions before my students remembered."

Velaria received the praise from her teacher with a beaming smile.

"It's said that the builders of this inn came from your beloved home, and inspired by Lucilla's beauty, they replicated the architecture. This inn also happens to be the namesake of the entire village."

"Remarkable; I feel closer to home already."

"As do I." Arlyn seemed to recall an unspoken past.

Before they moved on to the stable, Velaria asked the question she had withheld since passing through the gate, "Why did you lie back there? *How* could you lie back there?"

"Where, tell me, did the deception dwell? Was not every word I spoke truthful?" inquired Arlyn, looking every part the teacher and Velaria the student.

"Well, for one, you called me daughter."

"Do you not address me as father? Is not daughter a loving term for a pupil? Especially in relation to an ei'ceuril steward."

The answer to the riddle was plain, yet she still could not hide her amazement.

"Remember, all of Eklean does not need to hear your whole truth, let alone the rest of Teraeniel."

"All right." Velaria paused a moment to look around before continuing in her hushed tone. "Should I be concerned about the guard?"

"I doubt he would have named you ei'ana if he wasn't certain, despite you not professing the counsels yet. I didn't think anyone in this small village would recognize a wielder, but he must have spent time in a larger city where ei'ana are a common sight. We'll have to be cautious. Refrain from wielding, lest we stir anything here."

"Where do you suppose the family lives?" asked Velaria, only just realizing how many questions she asked. "None of the villagers seem eager to speak with us."

"I've been here before, in a time that seems a lost memory. It was before I entered the Temple of Ceur all those years ago."

Velaria found it difficult to imagine Arlyn as a teenage boy, traveling to the Temple of Ceur as a kien wielder, to spend the rest of his days locked within. She thought it a shame that men could not wield safely; if she'd been restricted, she would have run away. Restraining from wielding even for only a single day was difficult; there was little she did that did not involve wielding. Granted, the kien wielders could inadvertently cause grave damage, and the temple was not a bad place to live, considering the alternative.

"And as to the family, Evellyn was only a girl at the time, and the Shadow had just begun to creep into this village. She has all the qualities you would expect and more. She won't be difficult to recognize," said Arlyn.

Velaria and Arlyn left their horses in the care of the cheery stable boy with silver-grey eyes. Velaria could not tell whether he was an elf like herself and Arlyn, or only part elf like many of the inhabitants of Cor'lera. He gladly accepted the horses and led them into the stable as they entered the inn through a finely carved wooden door.

Relieved to escape the harsh wintry chill, Velaria hurried inside to breathe in the warmth.

The common room was comfortable with a fire roaring in the hearth on the far wall. Tables and chairs were scattered throughout in an orderly fashion and several couches invited them to rest and warm themselves in the room's welcoming atmosphere where the regular patrons enjoyed a meal, a drink or two, or simply the warmth.

As they stood in the entry, Velaria felt them peer covertly toward Arlyn and herself. A fellow standing behind a counter to the left of the entry was the only one who showed a genuine interest in the newcomers.

He's probably only interested with what lines our purses, thought Velaria, suddenly happy that all they had were lewts and angots.

Closing the distance between the entry and the man at the counter, she noticed that he was genuinely happy. His grey eyes radiated energy under neatly combed black hair with hints of red. Over the past month, she had grown accustomed to thinking that care about personal grooming was a quality that belonged only to Arlyn and herself. The startling surprise wiped away her previous assumptions as the merry man greeted them.

"Good day to you, fine travelers. Would you be interested in a room this cold evening? We have mighty fine rooms, some better than others, mind you," said the man before quickly adding, "there's a nice stew for supper if you haven't other obligations; only an angot per bowl. Nothing better than a hot stew next to the fire after a day of traveling in this weather. It's cold for Borenth this year."

"That would be most welcome. Would you mind showing us to our rooms first though? It would be nice to rest a bit before supper."

"Certainly, let me just call my eldest boy from the stables to keep an eye on things here," the innkeeper replied with a broad smile before opening the door and hollering out for his son. "Liam. LIAM! Quick, come here, son! Those horses can manage without your eyes constantly on them."

Shortly after, Liam came through the front door bringing with him a chilled breeze and a questioning look. The breeze had ruffled his hair so that his pointed ears struck through the jet-black hair highlighted by a few strands of red.

"Close the door, you'll let all the warmth out," said the innkeeper. "I need you to look over the common room while I show our guests to their rooms."

"All right."

"Please, just this way. I'm Dolan Telvin," he introduced himself and led them up the stairs behind the counter. "Fine young man that boy of mine is, and he knows it too, bless the lad! Reminds me of his mother, he does. It's a shame he didn't have the chance to meet her. Passed during childbirth, she did. Fortunately, my wife, who I married some years after returning from Gneal, embraced Liam as her own. He was only nine at the time. It's she who runs this fine inn, of course."

Dolan continued cheerfully the entire way up to the third and highest floor of the inn and stopped before a pair of adjacent rooms. "Here we are, some of the finest we have."

He unlocked the door and Velaria was pleased by a glimpse of a modestly sized room with intricately carved yet sturdy furnishings. Dolan had spoken truthfully when he'd described the quality of the rooms on their journey up the stairs. Before Velaria could take advantage of the comfortable mattress to rest and soothe her back from the constant motions of riding horseback, Arlyn addressed Dolan.

"Sir, I'm Steward Arlyn. We've not met before, and truly that pains me. We traveled from Ceurenyl through Lucillia to speak privately with your wife, Evellyn. It's of critical importance—no eager ears."

Dolan's mood dampened slightly, but he took the news in stride and responded. "Arlyn—I thought you looked familiar. How could I miss it? Your face and those eyes of yours. Please, forgive me, steward, this way. My family lives in the private quarters behind the kitchen."

Velaria trailed behind as Dolan led Arlyn down the narrow servants' stair. Wondrous aromas tickled Velaria's nose as the kitchen came into view. A single cook stood by the stove, watching over the contents of the bubbling pots and sending two waiters in and out of the kitchen with the appropriate dishes.

Dolan led them through a beautiful wooden door, just as masterfully crafted as the front door to the inn, and into the private quarters. The massive door easily swung open onto the parlor and Dolan called for his wife.

Before she had an opportunity to respond, two children came sprinting toward their father.

Dolan's face broke into a smile, bracing himself as they collided into him. He looked down and asked in a surprisingly stern voice, "Does your mother know you're out of bed?"

The two shook their heads in denial.

"You know she will blame me for your late night, don't you?"

Again, the two shook their heads in denial.

"Do you really want me to get in trouble with your mother? She'll toss me out in the cold if you two lose a minute of your precious sleep."

The children began protesting and declaring all sorts of promises to shoulder the blame.

Before they got too far, a female voice called from deeper in the quarters, demanding that the children return to their beds.

"You two had better listen to her or else I'll be the one in trouble. But, first, please greet our guests. This gentleman is Arlyn, he's a steward with the ei'ceuril. And this young lady here is…I'm sorry miss, but I never got your name. Pardon my manners."

"That's no fault of yours, Master Dolan." Velaria bent down to the children's level. "My name is Velaria. And might you tell me yours?"

"I'm Leilyn," piped up the girl. "But I'm not so little. I'm already six years old." She held out her hands, three fingers on each hand pointing to the ceiling.

The younger boy struggled to form his own words, too young to manage more than a stuttering syllable which sounded like 'deb.'

"This is Devlyn. He's not even two yet. Much more littleler than me," said Leilyn, the last part spoken on her tiptoes.

"Oh, what lovely names." From the rooms beyond, the voice called again for the children. This time they hurried away without further debate, calling goodnight as they went.

"What lovely children," Velaria complimented Dolan. They were, without question, the most beautiful children she had ever seen. Their hair held hints of red, blond, and black woven through the dominant golden-brown and their sparkling eyes resembled Arlyn's with a silver iris shifting to a stunning green around the pupil.

Before she could comment further, a gentle voice replied to the compliment.

"They are beautiful, aren't they? As their mother, I might be biased, but I can't help admiring them." Velaria, Arlyn, and Dolan turned toward a woman of remarkable beauty, the children's features clearly gifts from this woman. "I am..."

"Evellyn—I can't begin to say how much I've longed to see you again." Arlyn crossed the room toward the woman, arms open for an embrace.

"I've missed you too, brother," Evellyn replied as their arms wrapped around each other tightly.

Velaria's mouth dropped in astonishment. Incredible as it was, the connection between the siblings was obvious. Both had the same golden-brown hair with hints of blond although Arlyn's showed some silvery threads, most prominent at his temples. The brother and sister complemented each other's beauty. Velaria assumed the children would grow to resemble their mother and uncle. All four of them had the same remarkable, almost shimmering eyes, a jubilant silver giving way to a forest green encircling the pupil.

Surely, thought Velaria, *such eyes are only found among the royal line of Lucillia.* As the two women's eyes met, Evellyn ended the silent connection by saying, "You behold my eyes in the same manner as one would the queen of Lucillia."

Unprepared for such an assertion, Velaria stammered as she struggled to find the appropriate words. "I do apologize ma'am, but you and Queen Vernal, descendant of King Roendryn the Great himself, share the same eyes." Unable to restrain her growing enthusiasm, she added, "Surely a common relation must exist between you and the Aryl of Lucillia."

"His name is Feolyn. And it's an old story and the connection you refer to just as old." Evellyn gestured the guests toward couches. "Please, have a seat if you would. The tale is not a brief one and you could both benefit from a comfortable seat. There's tea if you would like a cup."

Without waiting for a response to the offer, she gathered four cups onto a tray and poured a fragrant hot liquid into each from a glass teapot. She brought the tray over to a small table between the couches. "Nothing better than a hot cup of tea after a cold day in Borenth. Cream and sugar?"

They all answered gratefully and received their now-overflowing cups with appreciation.

DAWN'S STRANGER

The sun hung low in the western sky and Devlyn waited for it to sink below the horizon, but the evening kiss between sun and land never approached. The golden rays of the setting sun colored the sky in assorted shades of triumphant reds and oranges tinted with the first hints of somber purples. The clouds caught in the rays swirled and danced about the sun, reflecting colors more vibrant than the trees of the wood sprawling below. Looking closer, Devlyn perceived something that wasn't usual. It didn't move like clouds do, nor did it dance about like the golden light, but the form belonged to and complemented the twilight sky.

From the evening sun just above a knoll, a woman of unsurpassed beauty materialized and glided toward him. As the lady slowly approached Devlyn, the object dancing in the sky drew closer as well. The lady's hair was golden, and she appeared to be clothed in the light of the sun himself. A magnificent bird danced around her, its feathers shifting with the various spectrums of color from the setting sun; amid the lesser colors, a vibrant gold outshone them all. While the bird reflected the sun, it also had a light of its own. Devlyn felt a familiarity with the beautiful bird, yet he could not imagine why. As it fluttered closer, Devlyn noticed that the stream of golden fire flowing from the bird faded away behind it.

The lady and the bird of light were just a few strides away now but just as the sun refused to set, so too the lady and the bird of light refused to close the gap. Her legs glided elegantly above the ground and the wings of the bird fluttered through the air, yet no closer did they come. As he maintained eye contact, Devlyn recognized the longing in their eyes that reflected his own.

Unable to endure the separation, Devlyn extended a single foot forward to greet the pair and join with them at last. But as the gap between them closed, the sun fell at last below the knoll and the evening light faded, taking the lady and the bird of light with it.

Devlyn woke from his dream and opened his eyes. The room was dark, and he heard the familiar steady rumble of his cousin Alex's snoring on the far side. As he listened, the rhythmic sound tempted him back to his own dreams.

Rolling onto his side to gaze out the low window, Devlyn looked out to the sky above the quiet village of Cor'lera nestled along the edge of the Illumined Wood. The sun was still a few hours away from bringing forth a new day as night blanketed the land beyond his window; stars still twinkled above. The moon hid somewhere in the sky; she always did just before the new month started. Devlyn liked the new moon; it allowed the stars to shine brighter in the night sky.

With still-sleepy eyes looking east, Devlyn thought he saw a star dancing in the night sky. It twirled about among the other stars illogically, rising and falling with a will of its own.

Was he still dreaming? *Stars don't move like that, not even the few that fell to Teraeniel.* Despite his grogginess, he recognized his own consciousness.

Determined to identify the small light, Devlyn sat up in his bed and strained his eyes beyond the tower window.

The star danced playfully about in the sky, dipping into the leafy canopy of the Illumined Wood and rising to soar above the trees before diving once again.

That can't be a star, Devlyn thought as he watched the acrobatic light. *It might be a bird? Perhaps the one from my dreams?* Devlyn strained to recall the dream bird. *What kind of nonsense is this? Birds don't fly about the sky as if set aflame like a...*

Before his thought fully realized, the features of the bird magnified as his eyes adjusted. Although it was leagues away, it seemed as if it flew just before his window, not a glowing speck in the distance. The bird continued to draw closer, and before Devlyn could blink, the bird's golden eyes engulfed him.

Looking from another's perspective, a lighted perspective, Devlyn saw the village, forest, and surrounding country filled with light. Leagues to the west, he saw himself in a tower window from a pair of eyes other than his own. His hair was disheveled, all in a tangle, and pointing in every direction. As he looked into his own eyes, he no longer saw the silver fading to green he was accustomed to seeing in a mirror or a pool of water. Tiny golden lights shot out of his eyes, their intensity diminished by the light emanating from his chest.

Chills washed through his body. He tried to look away but had no control over his vision.

His other vision drew closer to his body, growing brighter the closer he drew. The light from his chest forced Devlyn to shut his eyes.

Heart pounding, eyes shut, Devlyn could feel his bed beneath him again. Lifting a single eyelid, Devlyn risked a peek beyond his window, relieved that he once again saw from his own eyes. The sudden dimness replacing the bird's light-filled vision of the room and the landscape beyond the window left him feeling dark and empty—blind, as if he should see more.

What was that?

Devlyn rubbed his hands over his still-heaving chest, feeling his skin beneath his fingers. *Was that real?* he thought, trying to understand. Looking out the window, he searched for a trace of the bird of light, but it had disappeared.

The bird, or more likely the speck of light, brought the dream he had woken from to the surface. While the dream was common, the frequency of its recurrence over the past weeks made Devlyn wonder. He had never been able to draw so closely to the silver lady and the bird of light as he had this time. Typically, once he moved that first foot forward, the dream sun would wake him. This time however, he had drawn close enough to see their golden eyes, close enough that he felt them in himself, beating in his heart, calling to him.

Knowing that he would not fall back to sleep, he forced himself from his bed and gazed out the window again, his eyes falling to the ground he still could not see in the dark at the tower's foundation. The first of Marenth marked the beginning of spring, yet the ground remained frozen. *Why have spring start this month if there's still snow on the ground?* he thought idly before deciding that he might as well get an early start on his morning chores rather than spend the next couple of hours thinking in the dark about whether what just happened really did happen. *Before Abbot Entiel can breathe down my neck on my birthday.* The abbot of the abbey school of Cor'lera treated Devlyn very poorly yet seemed most concerned that Devlyn complete his lengthy list of daily chores. Devlyn often wondered whether the poor treatment or the concern about chores were normal for a ward of the abbot, but now was not the time to be thinking too deeply about it.

He tried to be quiet but, certain that he slept in the oldest bed in the school, he found it impossible to rise silently as a series of loud squeaks announced his slightest movement. Devlyn looked over toward Alex and saw him roll onto his stomach before pulling his pillow over his head.

Devlyn moved across the room to his clothes conveniently discarded last night on the dresser next to Alex's bed.

Alex rolled over once again, his bleary eyes squinting at Devlyn from under the pillow.

"Sorry, I tried to be quiet, but you know what that bed is like," whispered Devlyn.

Alex grunted something unrecognizable in return.

"Those weren't words, were they?"

"Oh, don't be smart so early." Alex enunciated every word as he pulled himself upright.

To Devlyn, Alex and he shared little resemblance. Only a year younger than Alex, Devlyn's greater height and leanness contrasted with Alex's broader shoulders and more muscled arms. Still, Devlyn was happy that they were evenly matched whenever they wrestled. Always insecure about his height, Devlyn tended to slouch to make himself appear shorter. His height, common to his Lucillian ancestry, was mocked among the pure and shorter Perrien villagers of Cor'lera.

While their builds differed significantly, Devlyn thought the differences in their hair and facial features were even more distinct. Devlyn's mostly brown hair held hints of black, blond, and red, while Alex's hair was entirely blond, and his eyes were blue and had none of the angled features that marked Devlyn as a Lucillian with elven blood. Even more curious a difference was that Alex had rounded ears like everyone else's in the area, not the pointy ones that went with the angled eyes.

"I said, what are you moving about so early for? The rooster won't crow for at least an hour; closer to two by the looks of it."

"I thought I'd get an early start on the day. Besides, how often am I given an hour or two without Ents breathing down my neck? It can be his birthday gift to me, although don't mention it to him, he might try to steal it back."

"Oh." Alex yawned. "That's right, I forgot about that." He rose from his bed with considerably less noise than Devlyn's attempt. He made his way to his own clothes, also discarded in a pile atop the dresser. "Well in that case, I'll give you some company. Consider it my gift to you; I can't imagine our dear uncle, the abbot, doing one better. Happy thirteenth birthday, Dev."

The cousins dressed quickly and quietly before making their way down from the squat tower, out of the dormitory, and through the abbey school.

Freezing air greeted them as they stepped outside, and Devlyn wrapped his arms about his chest hoping to keep as much warmth in his body as possible. His bed and blanket were suddenly very appealing.

A gate separated the abbey school from the rest of the countryside, but there were no additional walls enclosing the grounds, making the gate rather useless.

Walking toward the barn and stables near the gate, Devlyn mentioned that he'd woken early because he'd had *that* dream.

"Again? I still don't think it's as unusual as you're making it sound; beautiful women visit my dreams all the time."

"Never the same one though, in your case," Devlyn retorted. Alex grinned and shrugged his shoulders in reply as they continued toward the school gate.

"Anyway, that's what I thought at first, just a normal dream, but something's weird about it, not to mention its reoccurrence. It feels…real. And that lady! There's something about her; she looks like a queen." No need to mention his encounter with the bird of light, both in the dream and whatever it was that happened after, in case it would make Alex wonder about Devlyn's mental state. His height and pointed ears made him different enough.

"So, let me get this straight. Not only are you having vivid dreams, but you think there's a queen out there destined to fall in love with you?" Alex's right eyebrow raised skeptically.

"Never mind. It's only a dream." Devlyn regretted saying anything.

"Maybe I'll find myself a noblewoman and we'll run off to Gneal together." Alex's eyes glazed over as he looked past the gate.

"Don't you want to go somewhere other than Gneal?"

"Why bother? Our family's from there. I still don't understand why we moved here in the first place."

"Probably to get away from that wretched council."

"Shh." Alex turned back toward the school, returning a heated glare to Devlyn. "One of these days, old Ents will hear you. Remember what happened to the last student he heard say something negative about the Council of Perrien? Detention. For a month! You know Ents doesn't care that you're his nephew," he hissed. Devlyn nodded and they continued in silence, reaching the chicken coop next to the gate as the stars faded in the promised light of the dawning sun.

Holding the egg basket he'd grabbed earlier as they'd passed through the doorway of the school, Devlyn held the door to the coop open, about to enter, when Alex, looking down the eastern road leading to Cor'lera pointed to an approaching figure shrouded in the early fog.

"There's a man on a horse."

Curious about the traveler and well aware that his eyesight was much sharper than Alex's, Devlyn squinted down the road too.

"It's not a man, it's a woman." At Devlyn's words, Alex squinted harder, to no avail. He trusted Devlyn's better eyesight though.

"Maybe it's your noblewoman. But if she falls in love with me first, you'll have to accept and support us."

Aware that he needed to be in the abbot's good graces, Devlyn turned back to the chicken coop to collect the eggs while Alex remained at the gate, watching the approaching traveler. Several more minutes passed before the rider was close enough for the boys to hear the *clip clop* of the horse trotting on the crunchy snow, drawing Devlyn back to his cousin's side.

"She's coming to the abbey school; she just passed the last side road leading to the farms."

Placing his basket of eleven eggs on the snow, Devlyn stood next to Alex and looked past the gate. He could see her simple blue riding cloak and caught a glimpse of what looked like leaves cascading from the sleeves of her garment, unhindered by her riding cloak. Long, fiery red hair fell from beneath her hood.

As she drew near the boys, the leaves seemed to disappear up her sleeves, taking away the incongruity of their appearance in a wintery scene. Devlyn thought that while Alex probably noticed the red hair, it was unlikely he'd also noticed the disappearing leaves.

"Good morning," she said with a small smile. Her silver-grey eyes seemed impossibly knowing, as though they could read Devlyn's soul.

"Welcome to the abbey school of Cor'lera, my lady," Devlyn and Alex responded simultaneously with a bow in the proper manner instilled by the ei'ceuril at the abbey school. The proper manner of response also required them to introduce themselves, although the lady had not done so yet.

"I'm Alexander, son of Clyde and Vine Vaerin, student of the abbey school of Cor'lera."

"My name's Devlyn, son of Evellyn and Dolan Telvin."

Devlyn caught a spark of recognition in her eyes, a look he frequently noticed at the shops in the village when someone had found what they were looking for but did not want the merchant knowing their interest, hoping for a cheaper price. Devlyn felt uneasy with the similarity. His shoulders tensed reflexively.

"I notice, Devlyn, that you mention your mother first. There isn't a reason behind that, is there?"

What does that matter? Unprepared to answer such an obscure question, Devlyn found himself saying, "It's how everyone talks of my parents, my lady, as Evellyn and Dolan." He did not want to say more about his parents. While having a deceased father was common enough, a mother branded as a criminal was more complicated. The lady would probably hear the gossip in Cor'lera soon enough, if she was that interested.

"Still, it's curious, in Perrien nonetheless," she commented, and again with an odd look on her face.

She knew more than she said. He had seen that look in Ents' eyes at least five times a day. "Let me guess, my lady, you already heard the villagers gossiping."

"The villagers? No. As you can see, it's still early, and I have not yet reached the village. Guards tend to not trust travelers who arrive before the sun does. But, I am aware of Evellyn and Dolan's tragic story. My name is Velaria Treyven, and I assure you, I am not of noble birth, so you need not address me as lady. Also, this is not the first occasion that the waves of time have witnessed our meeting, Devlyn."

Devlyn shared the disbelief he caught on Alex's face, but her claim of having met Devlyn before was harder to accept than her claim that she did not belong to a noble family.

"Well, you're obviously not from Perrien; you don't look like anyone else here. But, maybe from the kingdoms to the south?" Alex pressed on. "After all, you are riding a horse at leisure."

A small smile made its way across Velaria's face.

"I have not enjoyed a time of leisure, as you say, Alexander, for several years now, let alone the past months. I've been traveling at great speed and with inadequate rest."

"I prefer to be called Alex." Few, other than his mother, referred to him as Alexander, and even that occurred too often for him. Devlyn knew that the quickest way to get a bruised arm was to call him Alexander.

"What could be so urgent for you to travel through Perrien in winter? Is Abbot Entiel expecting you? Surely all the mountain passes have been blocked by snow and ice, since Orenth most likely." Alex's annoyance with her use of his full name was reflected in the sharpness of his questions. And oddly she did not seem to mind the onslaught.

"It's certainly dreadful to travel this far north during the winter. And yes, it's common for passes to be blocked as early as late fall, and weeks beyond the first of spring," Velaria replied politely. "Fortunately, not every pass was barred. The urgency comes from the Ceurtriarch, the Seven Chairs of Septyl, and the Aryl of Lucillia who have sent me on this task."

"What's an aryl, and why are they important?" asked Alex.

Devlyn did not think his cousin intended to be rude, but it certainly sounded that way. Devlyn knew that the Ceurtriarch was the head of the Ei'ceuril, but he had never heard of the seven chairs of septyl or an aryl.

Velaria's eyes drifted south, and Devlyn imagined he saw something resembling regret in them, perhaps sadness, as the slanted lines angled downward.

"An aryl is two people who are the united head of an elven house; they act as one in carrying out the duties of the office. Queen Vernal and King Harnyl Roendryn are the Aryl of Lucillia." Before either Devlyn or Alex could respond, Velaria continued. "I was sent to the eastern province of the kingdom of Perrien, once called Parendior, to inquire about a particular Cor'leran family, Evellyn's family."

UNSPOKEN TALE

A confusing array of emotions crashed over Devlyn at hearing his mother's name. *Perhaps it's a different Evellyn,* he told himself, desperately trying to still his confusion, frustration, and sense of abandonment. He cast the thought aside immediately to focus on the gravity of a situation requiring the attention of the Ceurtriarch, a king and queen, and whatever those chairs were. Devlyn's greatest concern was that he represented the last of that family remaining in Cor'lera, and he had a hunch that this pointy-eared Lucillian woman knew that.

"I'm sorry, but all I know about my mother is what I've been told from others, and it's nothing that is worth the inquiry of a foreign king and queen." Devlyn choked on his own words. "And all I've heard are horrendous accounts connecting me to a dreadful woman." Only two people had chosen not to condemn his mother, Brother Bernard and Walei, but neither had lived in Cor'lera at the time of the incident.

"It saddens me to hear Evellyn reduced in memory to the word dreadful by her youngest child. Do not believe all you were told; we live in an age of deception." Velaria swung herself off the horse and stood before the boys.

They stared at the woman, in awe of the first person to ever denounce village gossip as a lie. The ei'ceuril at the abbey school preached that those who did so were the true deceivers.

"Would you like to hear the truth?"

"How could I take what you say as truth, when you so quickly condemn others for lying?" Devlyn wasn't going to be taken in so easily.

"Even a lie can imitate the truth, but it cannot replace it. Only the truth can expose a lie. If the truth is unknown, and remains unknown, the deception endures. Does that make the deception true?" asked Velaria in a matter-of-fact way.

He looked unwillingly into her silver-grey eyes.

"What do they say of Evellyn, here?" asked Velaria.

Devlyn felt his stomach twist in uncertainty. Despite a small glimmer of hope that everything he had been told about his mother and father was a lie, he couldn't help his immediate reaction. *She abandoned me! Now I'm a ward of a school and my uncle, the abbot, hates me!*

The little hope Devlyn reserved toward a belief in his mother's innocence vanished at the reminder of his status as orphan and ward.

"The villagers thought my parents odd; they say their family life was barbaric. Only greed fueled them. They say that the struggle reached its climax when my mother had had enough, and in her vile nature murdered my father and mutilated my sister. Witnesses saw my sister screaming and running from town toward the Illumined Wood leaving only a trail of blood behind. They say that someone her age had no chance of survival within the forest.

"My mother vanished into the night with my half-brother, along with all her relatives, leaving me here, crying on my father's body. Abbot Entiel and the other ei'ceuril at the abbey school say that my father wrought his own fate by wedding Evellyn and later having children with her. They said he did it to collect the profits of the Cor Inn. They said that he paid the ultimate price for marrying one of Evellyn's kind, and that he should have stayed in Gneal with his motherless son after leaving Cor'lera in the first place. And the abbot, my father's own brother, says that I'm no relative of his. Even among my remaining family, I'm a stranger!" Devlyn found himself panting and paused to settle his breathing.

"Is that what you believe?" The question was soft, but firm.

"How could I believe otherwise? There's no reason for me to doubt my entire village, even if Walei says differently." Devlyn could feel the anger rising.

"What has Waleisius told you?"

"Walei only says that she didn't do it." The tiny reserve of hope he had for his mother flared.

"And why don't you believe him?"

"He did not live here then, how could he know?" His mind and heartbeat relaxed, his voice steadied.

"True, but like myself, he knew your mother and father, and knows the account fed to you was fabricated to disguise the actual crime."

Devlyn had asked every villager in Cor'lera, and except for Walei and Brother Bernard, was told the same ugly story. Whenever he asked why his mother had done such a thing, everyone said that it was her vile Lucillian nature—his nature, tainted with elven blood. Always trying to understand why, he probed different villagers whenever he had the chance, and had run out of new villagers to ask just last year. He had asked them all the same questions and had learned nothing different. Every story was the same, nothing new, and nothing left out, as if they read the story from a book word for word.

That small part of him buried deep within ached to hear of his mother's innocence, even though it would not return his father from his early grave.

"Would you like to hear what I have to share with you?"

A few moments passed before Devlyn nodded yes.

"Shall we go for a short walk then? The invitation is open to you as well, Alexander."

"I'm not sure. We have chores to do and our uncle isn't the most for-giving when it comes to tardiness. And please, call me Alex."

"The choice is yours, Alexander." Velaria ignored the repeated re-quest to shorten his name. "I do think you would benefit from the conver-sation if you joined us."

Her phrasing led Devlyn to think that she referred to something oth-er than simply listening.

Alex's struggle was clear. Should he follow orders or continue to listen to this stranger who claimed to possess knowledge no one else in Cor'lera seemed to have? His family, especially on his mother's side, was known to value skepticism.

"Come on, Alex. It would be nice to have another set of ears." Devlyn hoped his support for continuing to talk to the woman would prevent Alex from abandoning him with this stranger. "She might be fabricating a wild story, but maybe it is the truth! You know how much I want to understand what happened all those years ago. Everything is so fogged over as it is."

Eyes downcast under a set brow, Alex considered his options.

"Most of the eggs are already collected anyway," Devlyn pressed, "and besides, Ents will hold me to blame over you any day."

"Fine, because it is still early, but you know he won't be happy if we're late for breakfast. You're lucky it's your birthday, Dev."

Velaria had waited patiently as they bickered about chores until deciding it had gone on long enough.

"Well, if it's all settled, how about that walk." She turned and led her horse away from the road. Clearly, she expected them to follow.

Devlyn and Alex caught up with her quickly. *Good thing she's no longer on that horse*, Devlyn thought as he eyed its beautiful coat appreciatively.

Velaria led them quietly west through the snow toward the Bethyl River, hidden from the abbey school and the village of Cor'lera by a stunted hill. The river was still frozen even though spring officially arrived today.

"Well?" asked Alex after they had gone a fair distance. Velaria seemed amused by his impatience.

"Well, to begin, you should know that Evellyn is no murderer. Simply imagining her committing such a crime is unthinkable and murdering her beloved husband even less so."

Devlyn's small reserve of hope grew by the second, even though he did not necessarily trust Velaria, a complete stranger. Although she had so far not provided proof, a memory of a graceful voice sprang in his mind, saying his name affectionately, a voice heard long ago.

Noticing his expression, Velaria continued, "Yes, it truly is wonderful news, isn't it? I too find it spectacular, even though I've never considered otherwise. I can only imagine how welcome it is for you. Surely, you sense the truth behind it."

"I suppose so, but how could you know this when no one else seems to?" asked Devlyn.

"Yes, how do you know this? The villagers and the ei'ceuril at the abbey school say that no one was present except those involved. And Devlyn here is the only eyewitness left in the village, and he was only two then." Alex crossed his arms, skepticism clear.

"Regrettably, I too was not present. Surely if I had been, history would have been recorded differently," Velaria replied somberly before turning to Devlyn with compassion brimming in her eyes. "And you would still call the Cor Inn your home, filled with family and mirth aplenty," she added in her more usual authoritative manner.

"The Ceurtriarch, the Seven Chairs, and the Aryl of Lucillia have cause to believe that the stories spreading through Cor'lera were nothing more than a hoax, a deliberate act to keep anyone from asking too many questions. While I could tell you how I believe the events played out, I know someone whose account you might trust above my own, so I'll allow him to explain instead."

Devlyn looked to her, a single eyebrow raised. He'd been hoping to hear her tell the story and now she wanted him to wait to hear it from some one else? "And who might that be?"

"Your half-brother, Liam."

Devlyn's heart froze in his chest. He knew he had a brother, just as he knew from the stories that he had a sister, but from what he'd been told, Liam was part of the conspiracy. "And how might I hear his account?"

"We believe that your family, all thirty-four of them, were abducted the night you were left behind and taken to the cells of Gneal, including your mother and brother. We hope that Evellyn is still in Gneal, but we also doubt that they would have left her there all this time. However, we have reasonable cause to assume that Liam and the rest of your family never left those cells." Velaria turned and gazed eastward.

Devlyn found himself staring in the opposite direction. He knew little of geography, but from the few maps he had seen, he knew that Gneal lay far to the west, across the River Arvil.

"Let me get this straight," said Alex. "You think our entire village was fed a hoax, a package of lies, and you want us to travel to Gneal so Devlyn can hear a different account from a murderer?"

Velaria remained silent, her back to them.

Enflamed by her silence, Alex took up his rant again. "This is nonsense! We wasted our morning and an early start on our chores. We're leaving." Alex turned to walk back to Devlyn, only a handful of paces away.

"Devlyn would be stricken if you decided not to accompany him to Gneal." Velaria continued to gaze eastward.

Alex gasped in disbelief as he turned. "Are you out of your mind? Ask anyone in our village and they'll tell you what Evellyn did. There's no way Devlyn believes that rubbish you spat at us. And to follow you to Gneal? You'll only increase his nightmares now, his waking in cold sweats. Is that what you want?"

"Perhaps, you should ask him before continuing to place words in his mouth. I believe he is quite capable of speaking for himself, Alexander."

Devlyn turned to them, noticing that Alex struggled to hold something back. "You're certain they're there, in Gneal? I'm tired of living in the shadows of lies."

"You believe her—this stranger?" Alex couldn't believe that Devlyn was giving credence to Velaria's story.

"Don't you understand what this could mean? I can find my family and find out what really happened."

"I'm your family, and I believe our neighbors, you know, the people we grew up with. The ones who have taken care of us our entire lives. I've no reason to doubt them! And neither do you."

"What if they don't know what really happened? They might not be actively deceiving us, simply repeating gossip, passing on what they've heard. All they truly know is what they saw, and what they saw was a little boy, me, crying on my father's corpse and my mother's family vanished in the night."

"But, to leave Cor'lera for Gneal! Ents would track us down before we made it to the closest village. Not to mention the distance; we won't get there for at least a month."

"Two and a half moons actually," interjected Velaria.

Devlyn pressed on but looked to his feet rather than at Alex. "I have no one else to ask. The entire village looks at me as the son of a murderer. There's no future for me here, you know that."

"You're more interested in running away from Cor'lera than whatever falsehoods this stranger is feeding you."

Devlyn's face reddened. "You said you wanted to go to Gneal."

"Not with a stranger."

"The choice belongs to you alone, Alexander," said Velaria, interrupting again. "You don't have to decide now, but I don't intend on remaining in Cor'lera more than three days."

"How will we let you know what we decide?" asked Devlyn, eager to hear what actually happened from his brother.

"I won't leave without hearing your decision. If you do decide to go to Gneal, it's best that you pack what you might need sooner than later." Eyeing them both, she added, "The clothes you're wearing are fine for travel in the snow. Horses would be useful, but they've grown sparse in this region in recent times, so we'll have to do without. Our pace will regrettably be slower than I had hoped, but nothing can be done about that. Saying any farewells could prove disastrous, so tell no one. Whatever you decide, I will leave after the sun sets, while the village sleeps, in three days.

"With that, I must go now. I have some errands to see to in the village. Take care and good morning. Oh, and Devlyn, you really shouldn't slouch; it's bad for your back and quite unbecoming." With that she remounted, turned the horse east and rode off.

Left speechless, more from her last comment than from the entire encounter, Devlyn turned back to the school where his chores remained incomplete and with his back straight. *At least the eggs are collected.* Alex followed, the two walking quickly to avoid being late, and not discussing their encounter or whether they would go to Gneal.

Making good time, they arrived shortly following the rooster's crow. From the barn door they watched the sun climb above the Illumined Wood, casting wondrous colors across the eastern sky, reflecting off the trees below and marking the start of a cold first of spring, a new year, and Devlyn's birthday.

"And to think, we haven't had breakfast yet. I never thought so much could happen before the sun rose! You're lucky it's your birthday, Dev. You owe me when mine comes around." Alex shoved Devlyn playfully.

And as they spent the first sunlit hour of the day feeding the hens and milking the cows, Devlyn's mind churned with thoughts of his mother, his family, and what he might discover in Gneal. Not least too, was the possibility of never returning to the abbey school and the awful Abbot Entiel.

Once they finished the chores, they walked together back to the abbey school for breakfast, carefully carrying the eggs and two very full pails of milk.

Cor'lera

The pompous Abbot Entiel waited for them at the side entrance, his pristine white robes without a single wrinkle. Ents was clearly ready to scold, although it was also obvious that he had no intention of trudging through the snow to deliver that scolding. He first looked at his nephew, Alex, and then to his other nephew, Devlyn, less-than-family, and lastly to the eggs and milk carried between them.

Abbot Entiel seemed disappointed at the lost chance to hassle Devlyn before breakfast, but he managed to contrive something to pick at anyways.

"Well, since Alex had pity for and aided the poor pointy-eared Lucillian this morning, you can start by following me to the kitchens," he said. "But since it *is* a special day, Devlyn, you need only stay a short while. Alex, you may go once you have left the milk."

Devlyn dared not inquire why he was needed in the kitchen, nor why it would be only a short while, but followed the abbot through the kitchen door, focused on not spilling any of the milk or eggs. Alex quickly deposited the pail he carried on the counter and slipped back out to the hallway before disappearing up the stairs to the dormitory.

"Now, several items must be collected from town for this evening's party," Abbot Entiel instructed, managing to make it sound like a lecture. "Since we must remain here and see to final preparations, you are the only one available to run to town and back. Before classes begin, of course."

Devlyn placed the eggs and milk atop the counter as Abbot Entiel rambled on.

The abbot's tone changed remarkably, his excitement showing as he described in fine detail the luxuries that would be served at the party and listed some of the guests who had been invited. Devlyn interrupted to ask why the party was being held.

"Bloody Lucillians!" the abbot spluttered. "Never have I known one so discourteous. One would think that an extended residence at an abbey school under ei'ceuril guidance would have taught some manners," he snarled, making it clear that Devlyn was more of a ward of the school than a student or nephew.

"Natures such as yours, I'm afraid to admit, simply cannot be corrected, even after years of reformation. You really are fortunate that we agreed to your staying here, in spite of all our failed attempts to properly educate you. How could we have known you would turn out the way you have, even without your mother's influence—you were only a toddler. While such failure weighs heavily on us, we know the fault is not ours. Your mother's blood simply runs too thick through your veins.

"As for the party, my brother, General Lex, will be stopping by our modest village this afternoon on a routine inspection of Cor'lera. As he was born and raised here, the Council of Perrien agreed that he would best serve Perrien with the protection and security of the entirety of Parendior. My dear sister decided that we should hold a party, truth be told. Once she learned that Lex was returning to Cor'lera for a routine visit, not a moment passed before she began preparing for a party of sorts."

Devlyn stopped listening when the abbot failed to consider that through his father, Devlyn was also the nephew of General Lex and their party-planning sister and shifted his focus on putting the eggs and milk in their proper places.

"Is this the same general that hunted down that murderous Lucillian, Evellyn, and her family?" asked Magister Elias as he entered the kitchen, interrupting the abbot mid-sentence.

Rather than being bothered by this interruption, the abbot seemed delighted, especially since the event mentioned was his favorite of his brother's achievements.

"Oh yes, he's most recognized for that bit of justice served. He was the head of the village guard at the time and organized them on that awful night when Dolan was murdered, not that anyone really missed Dolan after he died. He also led the hunt for that wretched woman and her vile family."

"Pah, they should've taken this one as well. Leaving a toddler to be cared for by ei'ceuril! What was that brother of yours thinking?" asked Magister Elias.

I bet you would have liked that, Lex leading me off to Gneal in chains with my family, Devlyn thought as he turned away from the now stored eggs and milk toward the other two, catching the smirk on the abbot's face, as if he'd heard Devlyn's thoughts. And from the look in his eyes, Devlyn realized that there was nothing the abbot wanted more than to see him locked in a cell.

Rather than voice his longing desire though, he spoke with an emotionless voice. "No, Perrien is far too preoccupied to concern itself over insignificant boys. He will simply have to remain with us and we can only hope that his foul nature will realign while under our protection. Speaking of which, why are you still here, boy, you'll be late for class as it is."

Abbot Entiel drew a piece of parchment from a pocket deep in his robes and held it before Devlyn's face. "Not one item is to be overlooked. My sister prepared this list. She'll have only the best for our dear brother, so remember that if one item is not up to par, you *will* make a second trip following your lessons." The abbot punctuated his words by waving the list in short sharp strokes before Devlyn's nose. From another pocket he drew out a bulging purse and handed it over with a threatening glare that said what he really thought more fiercely than words could ever convey. Devlyn had never held a purse so heavy, the copper lewts and iron angots jangling in his palm through the leather. Old Ents would never trust him with a full golden crown, let alone a silver jent.

A single glance at the list was enough to overwhelm Devlyn. It was an unbelievable length; who could require so much for a simple party? "There's no way I'll be able to haul all of this back from town," he said, not daring to mention the amount of time it would waste.

"Always complaining. Very well, you can take the donkey and cart if you must. Now get on with yourself."

"Yes, hurry along. And you're not to be late for my lesson either," added Elias.

"Yes, Magister Elias. Is there anything else, Abbot Entiel?" asked Devlyn, his tone cautious as he paused for the answer. Receiving no response, he left the kitchen, list and purse in hand.

"I wonder if it's the shape of their ears; perhaps they hear differently." Elias's voice carried clearly from behind the closed door.

Although Devlyn did not hear the abbot's response, he doubted he would need a lot of creativity to imagine the vulgar reply.

Happy to be away from those two, he headed through the snow again toward the stables. Without wasting any time, Devlyn led the donkey from the stall and hitched him to a cart and was soon guiding it to the village in the winter-cold first day of spring morning.

Thoughts coursed through Devlyn's mind as he traveled across the snow-packed road to Cor'lera, particularly of his uncle, General Lex. His involvement eleven years ago had made him quite famous in Perrien where everyone considered him a hero for his leadership in the apprehension of Devlyn's mother and the rest of her family. Rumors were that Lex had personally dragged them before the Council of Perrien for trial in Gneal, resulting in their permanent incarceration.

What Velaria had told him earlier about his mother troubled him greatly. If Velaria's account was true, then Lex was anything but a hero. Despite the conflicting stories, he worried about the coincidence of the arrivals of both Velaria and Lex on the same day. It seemed unplanned and simply unfortunate, which Devlyn highly doubted; it was all too convenient.

Even with the novelty of being allowed to take the donkey and cart, the clopping of the donkey's hooves and the high-pitched squealing of the rusted wheels faded as his mind raced.

The road required little attention; he traveled it often and knew it better than most, especially during the winter months when few willingly braved the cold and snow-covered road connecting the abbey school and many of the farms to Cor'lera. And the donkey needed little guidance on a road he too had often traveled.

Lost in his thoughts, Devlyn paid little attention to his surroundings as they rolled along. He kept his head down and his hood drawn, shielding his face and neck from the frigid wind. The road that stretched from the abbey school to the village was rarely used. The farmers who lived between the two did take their produce in to the village for sale, but they rarely left their lands during the winter months. And with the main road to Cor'lera coming from the south and leading to other villages and eventually west across the River Arvil, travelers had no need to use the road to the abbey school.

Before reaching the west gate of Cor'lera that would take him to the shops within the original village, the many buildings more recently built outside the walls came into view. Every time Devlyn visited the village on various errands for the abbot, he saw a building that had not previously been there. Cor'lera was growing quickly and who knew when, or if, construction would cease.

Is everyone in Gneal trying to get away from that council? Devlyn asked himself, imagining how horrible it had to be in the capital city.

Heavy galloping from behind interrupted his thoughts. Since it didn't seem that the horse was slowing at all, Devlyn steered the donkey and cart to the edge of the narrow road and continued at the donkey's slow and steady pace.

The rider paid no attention to Devlyn as he passed swiftly by but was easily recognized as a Perrien soldier by both his grey cloak with a white emblem and the large grey courser he rode on.

Once, the iconic grey coursers of Perrien and Parendior had been horses commonly available to all. However, over the past several decades, the Council of Perrien confiscated all the grey coursers and reserved their use primarily for soldiers and, of course, anyone else who could afford a new premium tax allowing their use.

The Perrien crest derived from the beautiful horses: a grey rider on a grey courser galloping on a field of white, much like the soldier that had rushed past. The strong grey coursers of Perrien were objects of envy to the southern kingdoms, where their steeds never compared favorably.

Devlyn reached the edge of Cor'lera, the part that stood outside its walls, too newly constructed and too ever-expanding to have a wall of its own. At the pace the village increased, who could tell when or even where the new wall would have to stand? The original section of the village sat mostly level atop the hill, leaving the slopes as the only option for new construction, some sections steeper than others. The part of the village outside the walls was now larger than what stood within. The new residents had traveled across the River Arvil into Parendior shortly after the Council of Perrien claimed the vast land east of the Arvil as their own, doubling the size of Perrien.

Most of the buildings outside the old wall were the homes and shops of the newcomers because there simply was not enough room within to house them. They had brought much wealth to Cor'lera and Devlyn always found it odd how the buildings outside the walls housed the wealthiest of Cor'lera's villagers, whereas in nearly all the other villages and towns, the wealthy occupied the inner walled area. In looking to maintain their economic status, these wealthy newcomers sought to monopolize the ice grapes known to only grow between the Bethyl and the Illumined Wood. So far, many of the vineyards still belonged to their original owners rather than to the newcomers. Devlyn knew this infuriated the newcomers, forcing them to purchase the ice grapes from the vineyards. Most of the shops in this district sold the much valued, much sought Cor'leran Blue ice wine.

Devlyn's list included items available only in this district, so the cart already held a number of packages by the time he reached the gate where an aged man stood guard. Well-known by the guard due to his many trips to Cor'lera on errands, he was readily granted entrance, although the man seemed a bit unsettled. Devlyn could only assume it related to the soldier who galloped up to the gate—perhaps he had passed through without slowing or stopping?

The buildings on the street opposite the gate were the typical Cor'leran structures with thatched roofs and plastered wooden walls. Devlyn located the first of the shops he needed, just a few buildings away from the gate. Since the west gate was originally intended for farmers in the surrounding area, most of the shops along this road offered ideal locations to sell their wares. The road eventually crossed the main street, where the two formed a spacious square.

Devlyn managed to put a small dent in the abbot's list before reaching the village square. A thrum of noise reached his ears before he saw the gathered crowd. *What's this all about?* he wondered, knowing that Cor'lerans spent little time in the harsh chill.

Among the usual sounds of a crowd, Devlyn could hear a loud voice, and when he reached the outer rim of the square, he recognized General Lex standing atop a newly constructed platform. The soldier who had passed Devlyn on the road stood at the general's side. No less than twenty additional Perrien soldiers stood behind and around the platform, all fully armed and clad in their grey cloaks.

From the back of the crowd, Devlyn couldn't catch all the general's words but did hear him speak about the superiority of the humans of Perrien over their enemies to the south. He also caught a reference to foul-souled wielders. Devlyn had only heard rumors of wielders but had never met one. Once, when he was young, he asked Abbot Entiel whether they really existed and in response, the abbot hit Devlyn full across the face and forbade him from ever mentioning the witches. After that, Devlyn never again spoke of wielders, although he kept his ears open for any mention whenever he walked about in the village.

Prone to gossip, Cor'lerans often spoke in hushed tones, but also often mentioned wielders. Devlyn overheard some speak hopefully of the Ei'ana returning, but others spoke critically about the southern witches.

Today was such an occasion. The general himself loudly proclaimed his denouncement of Lucillians and wielders alike.

"They are nothing more than corruptors of nature and destroyers of peoples!" Lex preached from his platform. "Never forget what happened in Yanil all those years ago! Their own wielders brought Nauto's Wrath on their capital, leaving the entire city drowned beneath the waves! The Yanilean outlawed wielding as a crime punishable by death in his country! Imagine, two thousand years without anything unnatural or devastating occurring."

Devlyn was unfamiliar with Yanil, but that was not the case for many in the gathered crowd, for they proudly cheered the general on.

Devlyn noticed that the only ones in the crowd not applauding were by and large the slouching Lucillians and noticed that he too had resumed slouching among the crowd.

Every Lucillian in Cor'lera slouched in an effort to diminish their height. They also covered their pointed ears with scarves or hoods and kept their grey eyes with hints of green downcast, to avoid being on the receiving end of spiteful looks. Lucillians were of an older folk, like many others whose ancestors had lived between the Bethyl and Illumined Wood, unlike this new folk who could only trace one to three generations in the village.

Tiring of his uncle's hateful ranting and aware of time passing, Devlyn guided the donkey and cart around the outskirts of the crowd and down the street, toward the main body of the shops.

Side street after side street, shop after shop, the lewts and angots decreased with every visit. Finally, the cart was nearly full and only one item remained on the list, his Aunt Vine's favorite candies, only found in an obscure shop filled with baubles of a foreign nature, a shop owned by Walei, or rather Waleisius, but usually called Walei.

Walei's shop was on the easternmost edge of Cor'lera, nearest the Illumined Wood where most of the Lucillian population lived. Devlyn had always wondered whether a connection existed between Lucillians and the Illumined Wood. He remembered hearing that those with elven blood had some sort of intimacy with nature. Never truly feeling sentimental about trees, Devlyn simply doubted it altogether. But if what they said about the elves and their intimacy with nature was true, then the elven blood in him and the other Lucillians must have run dry with their supposed immortality, leaving behind only angled features, long pointed ears, and a freakish height.

Aunt Vine was Alex's mother, and like her two living brothers, she had no love for Devlyn or any Lucillian tainted with elven blood. But she did love the candies Walei carried. Walei claimed to import the candies from a southern city; the precise location he refused to disclose. Walei was friendly enough to the villagers and most of them paid only as much mind to him as he paid to them—almost none.

The neighbors found him curious; after all, as far back as the villagers could remember, Walei and his grown daughter were the only people to have moved to Cor'lera from a kingdom outside of Perrien. The villagers' memories stretched back generations.

Walei refrained from sharing his own opinions on the broader world and never mentioned the Lucillian Alliance. He seemed to care only for his small shop, which served the village well, especially since many of them, like Aunt Vine, enjoyed the unique and exotic wares he collected from the south.

For reasons beyond Devlyn's understanding, Walei even managed to stay out of the debate surrounding the superiority of Perrien and full-blooded humans.

Devlyn walked through the shop door and saw Walei stocking and organizing the shelves, his usual occupation when no customers needed attention. "Hello, Master Waleisius. How's everything today?" asked Devlyn.

"Just Walei, Master Devlyn," replied Walei without turning from the shelves. The back of his head showed his thick greying hair. With Walei's round body and even rounder face, Devlyn doubted that anyone had ever considered Walei thin; no fewer than three chins supported his cheery face. Sometimes, Devlyn could swear he counted four.

"Are you here for another batch of candies for your aunt? She's my best patron, you know."

"And you know my visits are dependent on uncle Ents's supply of my aunt's favorite candies. Although, if he heard you refer to her as my aunt, you would get an earful of how it simply is not plausible for tainted elven blood to mix with a full-blooded human. I've also heard him say that once his brother married my mother, the relations between my father and him ceased to exist. Anyway, the order is quite large today." Devlyn really didn't want to discuss his uncle.

"Ah. It's not for that party the good ol' abbot is throwing tonight, is it?"

"Well, yeah, how'd you hear?"

"Call it a lucky guess. Although a talkative village helps." A smirking Walei turned away from the shelves. "Well, my young friend, how much do you need this time?"

Pulling the list out of his pack, Devlyn showed the amount to Walei.

"That's a bit more than usual, I wonder how much is intended for the party and how much for your aunt." Walei waddled to the storeroom, chuckling the entire way, his large belly rumbling with every chortle.

While Devlyn waited, he peered at the shelves holding items of all shapes and sizes and colors.

"By the way," hollered Walei from the back room, "it seems that I'm not the only foreigner in Cor'lera this week."

"What makes you say that?" asked Devlyn, paying more attention to a small glass figurine depicting a bird engulfed in flames than to his friend. The bird and the fire appeared to dance before his eyes; in fact, Devlyn thought they actually moved.

"You mean you haven't heard? A finely dressed woman strolling about town, looks like a noblewoman, I'd say Lucillian, but her hair's all wrong. Never known a Lucillian to have locks of red such as those."

Turning from the figurine, Devlyn shifted his attention back to Walei, realizing that he spoke of Velaria. "Do you think she's up to something? I mean, where do you think she's from?"

"Couldn't say. Haven't seen hair that red in any of my travels. Couldn't rightly place her. Although her stature and physical features do remind me of Lucillians, so perhaps she has some of that elven blood in her. Have you met?" Walei held a suspicious look in his eyes as he waddled back to Devlyn.

"I think I'd remember seeing a noblewoman." Devlyn's eyes were glued to his feet and he turned slightly away from his friend, figuring the fewer people who knew of his meeting with Velaria the better.

"Hmm. Perhaps you'd be a better liar if you didn't care about the person you lied to."

"What're you talking about?"

"You really shouldn't lie," said Walei, before continuing in a hushed tone, "but I suppose it a necessary precaution. It's all right; you don't have to explain yourself. Velaria and I go way back. She's a secretive woman, like as not, she probably asked that you not mention your meeting. Although she would never lie, she detests lies and liars. She finds her way around telling the truth without uttering a single deceptive word. Quite the art form, really. Anyway, I won't say too much here, it's not safe, you see. She's trustworthy though. You have no need to worry about her steering you astray."

"How…" Devlyn didn't know what question to follow with, leaving him mouth agape.

"How indeed. You'll know when we meet again. But that won't be for quite a while, I think. You should be on your way. May we merrily greet each other again one day."

With more questions roiling in his mind than when he'd started out, Devlyn was kindly sent out of the shop after handing over the last three lewts and ten angots. He placed the parcel of candies in the cart and as he untethered the donkey, the unkempt Cor Inn caught his eye. Overwhelmed by unanswered questions, he led the donkey and cart to the side of the abandoned inn and sought the back entrance to what had once been his home.

Cor Inn

The inn's neglected condition and its boarded windows and doors had become a familiar sight to the Cor'lerans over the past eleven years. Devlyn paid little mind to its exterior as he made his way around the back where he found an entrance to the kitchens with one of the original doors still on its hinges and not boarded over.

Giving the handle a turn and a nudge, he was surprised at how easily the door opened to what had been the working kitchen. The interior's state of destruction far surpassed the exterior's; chaos had claimed the room. Broken furniture lay scattered across the kitchen, with shattered glass strewn on the floor, and a heavy coat of dust and cobwebs lay on everything. The only light streaking through the dusty air came from the opened door behind him.

Walking deeper into the kitchen, Devlyn noticed a faint light emanating from the far side of the kitchen, just around the corner in what appeared to be a shallow hallway or vestibule. *Was that light there when I came in?* Devlyn thought.

The amount of debris littering the floor worsened the closer he drew to the soft light. Rounding the corner, Devlyn's heart skipped a beat when he caught sight of a bird in flames perched atop a pile of debris.

It looked like the bird from his dreams—the one he'd seen that very morning, above the Illumined Wood. The sight of it in person and so close was much more terrifying.

Devlyn's eyes connected with the bird of light, a connection that seemed to pull Devlyn closer as if he was in a trance. Taking a single step was all it took for the bird of light to open its wings and take flight.

"Wait," Devlyn gasped, his hand grabbing for it. Too late, he caught only empty air as the bird flew away faster than a bird of its size should be capable of. It flew through the doorway past the rubble and into the dark room beyond. Its glow diminished the deeper into the room it went.

Devlyn approached the shattered remains of what might have been a door, now scattered about in a disorderly pile of debris in the vacant doorway. Taking a closer look, Devlyn was shocked not to see any scorch marks.

Picking up a remnant, his arms strained at the weight. The shard of wood was no more than a foot in length, yet its weight equaled that of a bar of iron. As his mind and body struggled to make sense of the disparity in his hands, he noticed the golden shimmer of a coin buried under the remaining pile.

"Wood from the trees of Eldin," came Velaria's voice behind Devlyn.

Caught off guard, Devlyn dropped the shard onto the pile causing a loud thud attesting to its weight, but still managed to snatch the coin and conceal it in his palm before rising.

"A gift from the elves of Eldinare. The trees grow strong there; it was said that no power was known to harm them."

"I didn't know mythical elves of the past gave so generously." Devlyn's fingers clasped the coin, the unfamiliar material warming with his touch.

"A gift yes, but it came not from a myth; perhaps a forgotten legend in some parts. But that's a story for another time." Changing her tone, Velaria turned to Devlyn and asked, "Would you like to go beyond the threshold and visit your former home?"

Looking through the darkened doorway, Devlyn hesitated before replying. He had never entered the inn, at least not that he could remember. Abbot Entiel had forbidden him from going near the inn as a young child, but in recent years had stopped lecturing him to stay away, presuming the lesson entrenched in Devlyn's mind.

"Well, I suppose I didn't come here to just look at a ruined door."

Devlyn stretched one of his long legs over the pile of debris, careful to not tread on it. He crossed the threshold with ease and entered a few paces into a dark room whose only light came from the kitchen behind. Windows boarded from the outside prevented any light from entering. Not even a crack permitted the tiniest sliver of light.

Velaria followed, holding a lit candle whose source of flame Devlyn did not see, but which allowed him to take in his surroundings. Too young to remember the room as it once stood, he did see indications of a cozy living room. Nearly all the furniture was shattered and scattered around. A few dishes had miraculously escaped damage. Even the rare pieces of furniture still identifiable as furniture lay overturned this way or that. The comfortably sized living room looked as if it had been turned upside down and shaken, as if the shaking might result in something of value falling through the cracks.

Stepping carefully through the wreckage, he saw that Velaria had found a glass teapot, one of the few surviving dishes. She held the delicate piece carefully in her hands, cradling it as she would an infant.

"Is there a story behind it?" Devlyn couldn't understand what made it so special to Velaria.

"A memory of a tea party, long ago. I can still see your mother walking out of the kitchen with it, asking in her gentle way if we wanted sugar." A sad smile lined her face as she stood lost in a distant memory of Evellyn.

Deciding it best to leave Velaria to her thoughts, Devlyn walked from the living room toward what seemed to be a hallway. As he approached, the same faint light from the kitchen now flowed from a half-open door off the hallway. Following the soft light, Devlyn pushed the door wide open onto a simple room with a bed in the midst of the same chaotic disorder found in the other rooms, starkly awash in the golden light of the bird now perched on an overturned dresser.

Devlyn dared not approach again in case it flew off again, something all too common in his dreams. Instead, he looked into its golden eyes as it returned the gaze, and as they remained looking at each other, a faint, yet familiar song chimed through the room. Before he could identify the tune, the bird vanished.

It did not move, it simply disappeared.

"Incredible," he muttered to himself. Approaching the spot where the bird had been, he noticed a small object glimmering on the floor. He bent down and retrieved another translucent golden coin with the profile of a woman of exquisite beauty and pointed ears, beginning on the right edge of the coin and filling half of it. Turning the coin on its side, Devlyn observed a wing in flight stretching from where what had to be an elven queen's profile had begun, across much of the back of the coin. Devlyn couldn't imagine anyone but a monarch would be depicted on a coin, even though she bore no crown.

Devlyn took the first coin he'd found out of his pocket and examined it as well. One side boasted a single wing, just as the other coin did, but on the opposite side. Turning the coin over, the profile of what Devlyn took to be an elven king came into view, also stretching from the opposite side. He held both coins next to each other and observed that the two profiles faced each other, and the wings on the opposite side went together. The two figures were oddly familiar, but he could not identify them.

Devlyn had never seen a golden crown before, but he knew that these were not crowns. Perrien would never have an elf on their currency, let alone any other human kingdom. The abbey school refused to teach anything that involved the elves, leaving Devlyn unable to give either monarch a name. Devlyn had never seen an image of the Lucillian king and queen but doubted the profiles belonged to them. Something about the profiles made Devlyn think that they were not merely Lucillians with dried up elven blood but actual immortal elves.

Not able to make any sense out of the coins, he placed them in his pocket and took in the small yet somehow familiar room. A soothing voice that had once sung him to sleep filled his mind.

Returning to the corridor, Devlyn closed the door behind him, knowing that it had once been his room.

With his hand pressed against the door's wooden frame, Devlyn looked about and noticed portraits lining the walls of the small corridor. Portraits of every size and shape hung skewed on the walls. Some had fallen to the floor.

Toward the center of the wall that held the most portraits, Devlyn noticed a vacant discolored square. From that square, a faint silver line curled from its upper corner to the painting on the right showing a family. All the paintings on the walls of the hallway had family portraits. The faint silver line continued downward to the portrait below, then to the left, and the line continued to spiral around the central empty square. Stepping as far back as the narrow hallway allowed, Devlyn was amazed to discover a single line of silver connecting every portrait or discolored square. Fallen frames lay on the floor below the discolored squares.

Returning to the beginning of the line, Devlyn searched the ground for the frame that corresponded to the vacant square. Because the space was larger than the surrounding frames, it was easy to identify the missing portrait lying face down not far away.

Lifting it to eye level, he saw a strong, yet noble man in the center, strands of blond in his golden-brown hair, and with eyes of silver shifting to emerald. To his right sat an astonishingly beautiful woman, also with golden-brown hair and sparkling silver eyes. Devlyn assumed she was the man's wife. Children and young adults of various sizes and ages surrounded the couple.

In the end, Devlyn counted a total of eight children. The similarities between the children and their father and mother were unmistakable. Each child had more of their mother's features than their father's, but each child also had his two-toned hair and eyes. Their faces made Devlyn feel like he belonged to them, a feeling he had never experienced at the abbey school.

Taking a closer look, Devlyn saw that the woman looked not toward the artist capturing the scene, but rather in the direction of the youngest child resting on her husband's lap. And that child, a daughter, also gazed away from the artist and into her mother's gaze. Devlyn was lost in that connection between the mother and daughter, imagining himself as that child gazing into the comforting eyes of a father and mother.

"Impeccable resemblance, don't you think?" Velaria had approached without his noticing.

"Sorry," he replied, not paying attention to her words.

Velaria repeated herself without any hint of irritation at not being heard.

"I guess there's a small resemblance."

"More than slight in my judgment," said Velaria, crossing her arms in a knowing manner. "If I didn't know better, I would place them as your own father and mother rather than your ancestors, with no less than thirty generations separating you."

"Thirty generations, huh. Why so many?"

A small smile found its way to the corners of her mouth as she pointed to the silver line. She began to count each frame along the line, and by the time she slowly reached four, Devlyn got the point.

"Oh, very funny. But I don't see any other portrait here connecting us."

Velaria began to rummage through one of the pockets in her blue cloak. To Devlyn's astonishment, half her forearm disappeared into it before reappearing with a rolled-up portrait, the same size as the others but without a frame, in her hand. She turned to the opposite wall, where fewer portraits hung and placed the painting where the silver line ended. The portrait must not have hung from that spot long, for no aged square on the wall showed its proper place.

Quiet disbelief overcame him as he looked at a family of five smiling in his direction, no, not in his direction, but rather *at* him. The man was easily recognizable as his father, since Devlyn had seen a family portrait of the younger Entiel, Dolan, Vine, and Lex in the abbot's office. In this portrait, Dolan stood tall, gray eyes bright and pointed ears poking out amid strands of red in his midnight-black hair. The ears were not evident in Entiel's portrait. Velaria pointed at the woman standing next to him, but Devlyn had known he looked at his mother from the first moment he took in the portrait.

Boundless love flowed from her eyes. Devlyn knew those eyes. While he shared the same brilliant silver to emerald eyes with her, he remembered a time long past when those eyes gazed into his own, her long golden-brown hair wrapped about her shoulders and a quiet song on her lips. For the first time in eleven years, Devlyn saw those loving eyes again and just seeing them, the song she had once sung sprung from his heart, the same tune he'd heard when he stared at the bird of light just moments before, but now, Devlyn could hear words rising and falling with the tune.

Doing his best to prevent a tear from falling, he pulled his gaze away from his mother's image to a young man, not yet seventeen, slightly to her right, his half-brother Liam. On Evellyn's left, stood Leilyn, his sister, aged six. And in the center, a toddler. The younger children shared the golden-brown hair, and the brilliant silver-green eyes of their mother; even their facial features resembled their mother more than their father. But their hair had hints of their father's black and red amid the brown-blond of their mother. Liam had his father's features, black hair with hints of red and sharp grey eyes.

Devlyn gazed on his family, sure that the portrait validated Velaria's conviction that his mother was no murderer. Everything he had been told about his family was a lie.

And the bigger lie that Devlyn now struggled with was the one that called Lex a hero. Suddenly struck by the potential danger of Velaria's presence while Lex was also in Cor'lera, the happy thoughts of his family fled as he considered what might happen when the general recognized Velaria.

"Do you remember the head of the village guard in Cor'lera all those years ago?" Devlyn asked.

"A ruthless man by the name of Lex perhaps? He's a general now, is he not?"

"That's him. He's in Cor'lera and his brother and sister are throwing him a party this evening. My father was also their brother. The general wasn't expected to arrive until later this afternoon, but I saw him in the town square giving a speech. He talked about Lucillians and wielders. He made them sound like criminals."

"I thought he might be close behind me. He's been giving the same impassioned speech for the past twenty years, even when he was a lowly village guard. No man in Perrien despises wielders and elves more than he. If he's tracked me from southern Perrien, then there's no doubt he'll be taking this opportunity to check up on you as well."

"Why would he want to check up on me? Hasn't he caused enough damage?"

"It's not so much the trouble he can cause, although he can be quite disruptive, but rather the trouble *you* are capable of. The enemy is dedicated to zero opposition. Besides, they still think a powerful weapon is concealed somewhere in Cor'lera that could undo them if given the chance. It's fortunate they've forgotten Aelish."

Devlyn looked questioningly at Velaria, having never heard of Aelish before.

"It's the language once spoken by elves, now limited to academic circles." Velaria looked once more to the portrait of Devlyn's family on the wall.

Is she going to ask me what I've decided?

Devlyn's palms grew sweaty, his gaze shifting between the image of his family and Velaria.

"Walei said I should trust you."

"He and his daughter are thoughtful people. I'm happy you connected with them; I imagine it was difficult growing up in a village where most view you critically."

"You really think he's right? About my mother?"

"It matters little whether I believe it. What matters is what you believe."

Devlyn looked again to the image of Evellyn. He held little doubt now about her supposed criminality, but the residue of the other lies left him uneasy.

"If I may be honest," said Velaria, her gaze fixed on the image, "I do not believe Lex is here by accident, nor do I believe he came for me alone. There's more I would tell you, and your cousin, but speaking of such is not safe in the village, not yet at least."

"What do you mean?"

"I think, as does another, that you will not be safe if you remain in

Cor'lera."

"Forgive me, but how am I to trust you?"

"The other who thinks so about your safety is just there." Velaria's hand extended toward another portrait, connected by a single silver line to the portrait of his family. The oldest of those children wore white robes and had a peaceful smile. Despite the age difference, Devlyn recognized his mother as the youngest of the children.

"I thought her siblings were all in Gneal's dungeons."

"He's an ei'ceuril steward and has spent the majority of his life at the Temple of Ceur in Ceurenyl."

Devlyn looked between the two pictures, and the silver line connecting them.

"Forgive me for saying, but matters become urgent, Devlyn. I had not anticipated Lex arriving so soon. I'm afraid you must make your decision now, because tonight will be our only chance to leave Cor'lera."

"The abbot's party would make it easy to slip out unnoticed."

"Your uncle Arlyn thought the same. Nevertheless, we must stick to our plan." Velaria overlooked Devlyn's confusion and continued. "I'm already known in town, which means Lex undoubtedly knows that he's finally caught up with me. You should return to the abbey school at once before anyone makes a connection between us. Lex being here might work to our advantage. He's a suspicious man and will concoct some intricate plot. He'll surely chase me to my own country. Unfortunately for him, we're not taking that path. Not yet, at least. By the time he figures it out, we will have quite the lead. Wait until the night is quiet. You'll find me where we spoke this morning."

Devlyn was perplexed, but before he could ask any questions, Velaria continued talking.

"I'm sorry, but we do not have the time. You must leave at once."

Annoyed at not having his questions answered, Devlyn walked swiftly back through the living room, out the kitchen, and into the back alley. He slowed as he walked around the corner of the Cor Inn and felt his heart freeze when he saw the last person he hoped to encounter digging through the parcels in the cart.

UNEXPECTED VISITOR

Once, Devlyn would have been merely annoyed to witness Lex's curious rummaging through the cart, but since seeing the portrait of his family, seeing his whole family for the first time, a family devasted by Lex's duplicity, something different happened. His skin crawled, and his teeth began to ache. When he realized that they clenched tightly in anger, he understood that he now thirsted for justice for his family.

Now, he saw the general in a different light.

Masking his emotions with effort, Devlyn managed to speak quite civilly in spite of his feelings. It helped that he unclenched his fists before he spoke.

"Can I help you with something, sir?"

"Ah, nephew," said Lex, still poking through the contents of the cart. "It looks like there's enough in this cart for all Cor'lera to feast on. That brother and sister of mine don't intend to invite the lot of them, do they?"

"That would require them to open the abbey school's doors to those they consider beneath them." Devlyn hoped he didn't sound sarcastic; there was no need to bring on Lex's ire.

"Too true. I know my brother is just as uncomfortable with allowing their children through the doors for a proper education. But that might not stand for long." Lex cleared his throat. "Anyway, I was surprised to see the abbey school's donkey and cart in this part of Cor'lera. I asked myself, what purpose is there for a full cart in front of the old inn? Surely none from the abbey school would want to be in this part of town. I ask myself again…" Lex stopped and took a breath as if to add authority to his statement. His voice grew stronger, escalating with each passing word.

"Why would anyone abandon a cart full of supplies? Next thing I know, I see you walk around that corner there, and if my memory serves me right, a back door is also just around that corner. Is there not? Now, would you be so kind as to enlighten your dear uncle about what one might preoccupy themselves with in an abandoned inn?"

The general's voice rose to a frightening volume.

Devlyn's righteous anger leaked from his body and he felt his shoulders hunch, shrinking as panic overtook him. "Well, I don't ever remember going inside before, and I just wanted a quick peek. I probably wouldn't have thought of it before, but it's where I was born and today is my birthday."

The general seemed to mull over the fabricated story, even as he held Devlyn's gaze. Devlyn hoped that the veracity of the slightly altered story was written in his eyes.

At last, the general spoke, sounding convinced. "Well, that certainly sounds authentic. After all, I also relish in returning to the place of my birth, not that it could ever be compared with this dreary inn. I would hate to limit such a visit to a quick peek. How about we extend that visit and take another look? Surely you didn't have the chance to tour the entirety of it. Memory lane can be quite *revealing*, I find."

Unable to speak, Devlyn nodded in agreement; fear that the general would find Velaria paralyzed his vocal cords. *It's not like I can refuse; I'd end up in a greater mess than I'm already in.*

"Excellent, very wise choice on your part."

Lex led the way to the back door with Devlyn close behind. Once they stood in the kitchen, Lex slammed the door shut and roughly shoved one of the few chairs still whole beneath its handle. "We wouldn't want anyone to disturb your memories, now would we."

Devlyn was convinced that the general was more concerned about someone leaving without his knowledge.

Lex chose a door opposite the innkeeper's quarters, still hanging on its hinges. Devlyn assumed that it led to the inn proper. No stranger to the layout of the Cor Inn, Lex strode through and took a look into possible hiding places as he moved along. Except for the dust and cobwebs, this part remained in reasonable condition. A thorough cleaning would return it to working order.

Devlyn followed Lex through the inn, beginning with the common room and going through every bedroom and even the closets on the floors above. After searching through its entirety, they returned to the kitchen with only the innkeeper's quarters left unsearched. He did not understand why Lex had insisted on searching through the entire inn because clearly, based on the footprints left in the dust, they were the first in many years to walk through the common room. When they returned to the kitchen, Devlyn saw the fresh tracks they had left in the newly disturbed dust and kept his observation to himself, especially since part of him had wanted to see the rest of the building. It was also more enjoyable to walk behind the general in silence than to state the obvious and possibly suffer the general's ire.

Lex threw a quick glance toward the exit, grimacing in disappointment as the chair blocking the door remained undisturbed. Without speaking, he stepped on and over the debris of the broken door and moved on into the innkeeper's quarters. He had struggled a bit over the debris in contrast to when Devlyn had easily stretched his longer legs over it in a single stride not an hour past.

Disgusted by Lex's demeanor and unwilling to follow, Devlyn stayed in the kitchen, listening to Lex shuffle through the rooms beyond.

Several minutes had passed when, to Devlyn's astonishment, Velaria stepped over the ruined remnants of the door from the hallway into the kitchen, she too, in one long stride. She pressed a single finger to her lips for silence, leaving him gawking at the woman before him, whom by all accounts should have been discovered by the general.

The noise in the innkeeper's quarters grew louder and at last, Lex returned to the kitchen. The still-barred door and the unmoved chair caught his attention. His eyes flickered in Velaria's direction, but it was such a quick glance that Devlyn was not sure whether he'd really looked. Velaria stood there in plain sight! Instead, his gaze fell on Devlyn as he dug into his pocket and drew out a rolled-up parchment, slowly unrolling it to examine it.

"Odd," he said at last, "I don't recall finding this in there before. Which is truly odd, since I gave the place a thorough inspection all those years ago."

Devlyn's heart dropped. He knew what Lex held.

"Do you recognize this?" Turning the paper, Lex revealed the portrait of his family and Devlyn could only nod as Lex held it between his fingers.

"By law, this ought to be destroyed." A flame sprung from Lex's opposite hand, shocking Devlyn.

"You're a wielder? I thought you wanted to abolish the Ei'ana!"

"Well, you see, boy, wielding is a powerful weapon, and the fewer who hold it, the fewer there are to use it against us. The peasants easily latch to anything you tell them. We might have had a more difficult time to sway them against wielding, but Lankor's ancient error serves our needs quite nicely. It's easy to make people hate the witches for something they didn't do."

The flame still aloft in his hand flickered in and out, unstable. Devlyn had difficulty reconciling what he saw.

Shifting his gaze back to the portrait, Lex said, "I forgot about the red strands in your father's hair, and those grey eyes, not to mention his ears. Perhaps my pious brother is correct in saying that you're no relative of ours. But seeing as the only ones who would know have perished, we'll have to rely on those wiser than ourselves." The flame above Lex's hand disappeared, Lex's jaw muscles contorting as he struggled to keep it alive. Devlyn knew little of wielding, only that it was incredibly dangerous for men. And the man who denounced wielders could, and did, do so himself.

"Consider yourself lucky that we don't have an image of the whole criminal family together in our records. This will do nicely. I'm not sure how or when this came here, but when you see her again you can give her my gratitude, personally. And yes, I know she was here, I don't know how she's managed to remain concealed, but I know that you and I are not the only people to enter this inn today!"

Still unable to speak, and not daring to shift his gaze toward Velaria still standing in plain sight, Devlyn remained frozen.

Content with this reaction, Lex made his way to the door and with a swift swipe, pulled the chair from its place and hurled it.

The chair crashed against the wall behind Devlyn and shattered into several pieces. "I believe that you're late for your morning lessons. Get back to the abbey school before you cause any more mischief. The abbot will receive a full report on your behavior today. I expect you'll be punished," Lex's smile said he hoped so. He strode away out the door and out of sight.

Devlyn and Velaria allowed several long breaths to pass before speaking. When Lex's heavy footsteps had faded into silence, Devlyn at last asked, "How could he not see you? You stood right before the both of us and I could see you clear as day, standing where you are. He saw nothing, just the wall and debris behind." Another thing that Devlyn could not reconcile in a day that was still morning, yet full of incredible events.

"Perhaps, he could have. But some eyes are so clouded in shadows that nothing in the Light can be seen."

The riddle did nothing to explain things to Devlyn, although he did understand that Velaria referred to Anaweh's Light. It sounded like something Brother Bernard might say, but he had never heard the old ei'ceuril speak in riddles. Little of it made sense to him, and as he mulled it over, it became clear.

"He wielded." Devlyn was still too shocked to say more. What else was there to say? Devlyn had seen the unstable flame dance above Lex's opened palm. Part of him wanted to know how Lex managed to wield. Every story Devlyn had ever heard about male wielders resulted in catastrophe. What made him furious was that the general now had a portrait of his family and had casually threatened to burn it.

"He did, and I don't understand how he didn't burn the entire building down. Men are incapable of wielding with control. Now, it really is getting late and you're going to be in enough trouble with the abbot as it is. I doubt the general will be pleased to discover that you lingered here. When all is quiet, we'll meet again. Wait for the stillness."

Without quite understanding what the stillness meant, Devlyn left the inn and returned to the donkey and cart. He led them both through Cor'lera, retracing the way he had taken earlier. It had begun to snow, and the villagers sought warm fires within, leaving the streets deserted.

The fear that had taken root in him over the last couple of hours lifted once he passed through the gate and went on his way to the abbey school. It was as if he left it within the walls of the small village of Cor'lera. In its stead came a growing resentment toward Lex, heightened as he recalled the general's actions over the portrait. For the first time since Devlyn could recall, he had seen his entire family, and that image had been taken from him, the message all too clear in Devlyn's mind.

PREPARATIONS

The parchment before Devlyn was pristine, free of any notes on the old kingdom of Thellion that Magister Elias lectured about. He stood behind the podium, entirely still with only his mouth moving, droning on monotonously as he spat out facts and dates. *Does he want us to fall asleep in his class?* Devlyn thought as he shifted in his seat.

It was impossible to take his mind from the events earlier in the day. His pointed ears still burned from the scolding he had received from Abbot Entiel, not only for returning so late from his errands and the side trips into the Cor Inn that he missed the entirety of the morning class and lunch as well, but also for his rudeness toward the general. General Lex had sent a report to the abbey school via one of his soldiers on a swift grey courser. Devlyn's trip with the donkey and laden cart had necessarily been slower. Fortunately, he had arrived back at the school in time for Elias's class, for which he was grateful given the magister's earlier threat in the kitchen.

Aunt Vine, Alex's mother, had arrived while Devlyn was in Cor'lera. Not a thin woman, but not large either, Aunt Vine had the blue eyes typical of Perriens, and short blond hair. Her solid stature did not resemble the abbot's though, since the abbot's gaunt and crooked form always made Devlyn think of a vulture waiting to devour a weaker prey.

She personally inspected the cart all the while muttering racist curses about Lucillians and their vile elven blood. She kept at it, blue eyes sharply scrutinizing all the packages until she recovered the candies at the bottom of the cart following Lex's poke-through, all the time pretending to be checking that Devlyn had purchased everything on the list. He'd had to stand by while she did so, which was why he'd not been able to even grab a sandwich before the afternoon class.

Now, despite his best effort to pay attention to Magister Elias's drone, every word fell on deaf ears. The one bit of information he did retain was that the king of Thellion had managed to reign over all the lands east of the Vespien and Shadow Mountains. Considering the world in its current divided state, such a feat simply did not seem plausible, let alone repeatable, especially with the deterioration of the Lucillian Alliance. Somehow, no one ever mentioned that.

"Does anyone know who the last king of Thellion was?" Elias asked the uninterested students. "Hmm. No one knows, eh? Well, it's something you should put to memory. Just because Lerenaen's the last day of classes this week does not mean that the week is over! Saraen and Karaen won't begin until today ends!"

A single hand shot up.

Elias peered down at the boy toward the front of the classroom. "Yes, Master Tyler, would you like to try your luck?"

"Evellion, last king of Thellion retreated from the capital in the midst of civil war and led the entire population of the city to safety in the Vespien Mountains, where they settled and grew into a great kingdom."

"Even the so-called brightest of this class reads history incorrectly. What Master Tyler is unaware of is that Evellion certainly became a king, and he certainly fled in retreat, but he was no king of Thellion. His father was the last of that ancient reign. Evellion's younger siblings saw that he was unfit to wear the crown in their father's stead, so rather than watch their eldest sibling deliver ruin to the entire kingdom, they divided it to lessen the harm to the greater population." With that, Tyler's confident posture slouched, his pride wounded.

"Poor Tyler," whispered Alex, covering his mouth so Elias would not see him. "You'd think he would've learned to not respond to Elias's questions, especially when he's in a particularly foul mood."

"I hope he doesn't try to argue with him again. Remember how that ended last week?"

"The owner of the voice I hear will report to my office after class." Elias did not turn his attention from Tyler. "Is that understood, Devlyn?"

"Yes, magister."

"Now, as I was saying," Elias went on, but Devlyn again stopped paying attention and shifted his focus to the window at the front of the class overlooking the Bethyl River. He watched as a light snow fell from the sky, adding to the already snow-covered ground. Devlyn had difficulty locating the still-frozen river beyond the classroom windows. Who could believe that today was the first of spring?

The class came to an end, but as the bells tolled loudly throughout the abbey school to mark the hour, a girl walked in carrying a note for Elias. He read it with a disapproving air and glared at Devlyn.

"It seems you already have a list of chores and Magister Bernard requests your immediate presence. Don't fret, dear boy, you and I will meet next week. Now, off with you. We wouldn't want to keep Magister Bernard waiting, now would we?"

"Is Brother Bernard in his office or in the library?" asked Devlyn in an improved mood at the summons.

"You will refer to him as Magister Bernard, and you will find him in his office," sneered Elias.

"Thank you, magister," Devlyn responded, and quickly left the class-room.

Although the abbey school was not a large structure, it was very old and the layout oddly segmented. To get to Brother Bernard's office, he had to go down the corridor, through several turns, and up two different flights of stairs and down another corridor. Devlyn had a hunch that the building originally had been two separate buildings now connected by an addition between them.

As Devlyn started toward *Magister*, no, Brother, always Brother, Bernard's office, he had to shuffle through the oncoming rush of students headed in the opposite direction through the narrow corridors. Every student was expected to assist with last minute preparations before the evening's party, so they headed to their dormitories at the other end of the school to drop off their books and other school supplies before returning to assist with party preparations.

The crowd began to thin out as he drew closer to Brother Bernard's office and when he finally arrived, he knocked softly on the closed door.

"Yes, yes, just a moment. Just going through some old manuscripts," came a startled voice.

"It's me, Brother Bernard, Devlyn."

"Oh Devlyn, well, why didn't you say so? Come in, come in. I could use your help if you don't mind." Not a single hair remained on Brother Bernard's shiny head, but he always wore an infectious smile.

"Well, considering you got me out of detention, I'm very happy to help you with whatever you need."

"Detention again? Well, that's a shame. I'm sure Steward Elias has his reasons."

"It's pretty clear that it's related to his feelings about pointed ears in general, although mine especially, since he said…"

"That's quite enough," interrupted Brother Bernard. "You'll never see him in the Light if you keep talking of him in such a manner. Besides, he's your teacher, and an ei'ceuril steward no less!"

"All right, I'll stop. Well, I'll try, at least." Brother Bernard was one of the few ei'ceuril at the abbey school that Devlyn liked.

"Good. Now come along and give an old brother some help. Those boxes there need to go back to the library. They're filled to the brim with books, so, do be careful to not hurt yourself. Don't try to carry them all at once either, that's how fools hurt themselves. And you, just at the age where you think you can! When you've finished, head down to the stables, we need to make room for all the extra horses we're expecting tonight. Don't forget, be like a leaf…"

"…upon the wind," finished Devlyn. "Seems a foolish prayer, if you ask me."

"Above any other! It's what brought me here, and who knows where else it'll take me."

"Will there be time for a bite to eat? I was in Cor'lera and missed lunch."

"Oh, of course, of course; go grab something once you're done with these. It won't take long."

Devlyn lifted the first box and headed out the door into the corridor and toward the library. Fortunately, the halls had finally cleared and Devlyn had an easy stroll through the school in spite of the weight of the box. The thought of exiled witches raced through his mind as he struggled with it to the library.

He knew that the Ei'ana had been recently exiled from the abbey school of Cor'lera, although that was still before Devlyn's birth and before he came to the school. Brother Bernard always seemed sympathetic to them; he had even corrected Devlyn on several occasions saying they were called ei'ana, not witches.

With thoughts of ei'ana in his mind, it came as a surprise when the doors to the library appeared before him. It usually seemed to take longer to get there, and it had always seemed strange that, as librarian, Brother Bernard's office was not closer. The library itself was empty; the students typically found there were off preparing for the party and Brother Bernard was in his office.

Devlyn left the first box on a table and made his way back for the second. Brother Bernard had left his office and Devlyn hadn't the slightest idea of where the old ei'ceuril had gone. Not wasting any time, he took the box to the library and hurried to the dining hall for a snack.

The school's dining hall was large enough to hold all the ei'ceuril and students. Devlyn had never counted the number of students enrolled at the abbey school but imagined at least 150 from Cor'lera and the nearby villages attended. Even so, most of the ei'ceuril ate among themselves in the private dining room next to the dining hall and ignored the students. Brother Bernard was the exception. Unless he'd lost track of time and unintentionally missed a meal, he always ate with students.

The school cook refused to leave hot food out beyond set mealtime and instead left cold sandwiches on a tray for the unfortunate student who missed lunch or dinner. Devlyn quickly grabbed one so that he could get started in the stables and finish in time to attend the party.

He made his way outside and crossed the snow-covered yard to the stables, eating the sandwich in big bites. The amount of work before him was overwhelming. The stables might not currently house horses, but the stalls were anything but empty. Besides the one where the donkey stood quietly munching hay, the other stalls had pushcarts and tools scattered throughout, and chickens scurried about everywhere. The clutter in the stalls seemed to have been there for years, and it seemed that the honor of cleaning out the muck and mess left behind by long-gone horses had been left for years, waiting for Devlyn. He'd only been attending to the occupied stalls so far, and no matter how frequently he shoveled them out, it always accumulated at an alarming rate.

The chickens went first. He ushered them to their coop near the barn. Next, he pushed and pulled the carts, large and small, from the stable and into the yard, lined up to make a wall of sorts beside the entrance. Devlyn collected the various scattered tools and placed them neatly in the drawers built into one of the stalls where they belonged. He shook his head at the neglected tools, some of which now showed signs of rust from their mistreatment.

The process was long and arduous and by the time Devlyn finished, several inches of fresh snow had already accumulated on top of the old. A wave of warmth hit his chilled body when he reentered the school; he had not realized how cold it was outside, having kept relatively warm by his hard work. Even his fingers and toes had lost some feeling, so the indoor warmth was quite welcome. A few students hurried about with last minute adjustments in the dining hall where everything was set for the general's welcome. Most had completed their tasks and now relaxed in the common rooms, idly chatting among themselves. Too exhausted to join in, Devlyn went straight to his tower dormitory.

In their room, he found Alex lying on his bed, eyes closed and breathing heavily, an opened book on his chest. Treading lightly to avoid waking Alex, he walked over to the dresser to get the clothing he thought he would need for his trip with Velaria.

The dresser drawer squealed as he opened it.

"I'm not done reading yet." Alex's groggy voice suggested a snooze no longer than just a few brief moments.

"Sorry about that." Devlyn started pulling clothing from the top drawer.

"Packing, are we?"

"Yeah, I ran into both Velaria and Lex in the village. I know he's our uncle, but he lied about what happened to my family. I don't know how, but he's involved somehow."

"What happened?" Alex pushed himself upright, his forgotten book thumping to the floor.

"He threatened me."

"Ents does that five time a day."

"Yeah, they're definitely brothers." Devlyn replied, too tired to force any merriment in his tone.

"Did anything else happen? You look exhausted, Dev, and over-whelmed."

"Lex is a wielder—fire sprung out of thin air right before my face; I felt the heat and saw the flames. He threatened to burn a portrait of my family in front of me."

"You can't be serious! We've known him our entire lives, and not once did he have anything good to say about wielders." Alex's brain caught up to the other thing Devlyn had said. "Hold on, where'd he get a portrait of your family? I didn't think you had any family paintings."

"I didn't, I bumped into Velaria in the Cor Inn…"

"You went inside?" Alex's eyes widened.

"Long story, but I was curious, and I was already at Walei's shop next door. Anyway, she had a painting of us, a small one, my parents, my broth-er, and my sister and me. I was still a toddler."

"So, does this mean we're leaving?"

Grimacing in apology, Devlyn shrugged his shoulders. "You don't have to come if you don't want to."

"What, and let you have all the fun? You know I've always wanted to see Gneal. Besides, I already packed for us both. A blanket, an extra pair of pants, some shirts, I even remembered your small clothes. I left our jackets and cloaks unpacked because I figured we'd need them tonight."

"Thanks, although neither one of us had decided yet."

"Yeah, well, even though I do not trust this Velaria, I know how much you want to learn about what really happened to your family. And after hearing what you just said about Lex, I hate to say it, but we're better off trusting Velaria than our dear uncle."

As Alex spoke, an image of the flame in Lex's palm popped into Devlyn's mind. "Definitely."

"I almost forgot, we're on stable duty tonight; greeting the guests and stabling their mounts. We're expected at the stables just before dusk and we're to stay there until the last guest has left."

"So, we're to miss the entire party?" Devlyn couldn't decide whether to be angry with the abbot for making him stay in the stables all night or to thank him for making it easy to sneak away in the stillness of the night. "How did you get roped into stable duty? Not that I'm upset about it, but you've never been assigned to the stables, Ents always sees to it that you're given less, ugh, smelly jobs."

"Well, after this morning's stunt, he told me that if I was so eager to do your chores, I might as well join you tonight as well."

"Never saw Ents as the considerate type." Devlyn tried to laugh, but only managed an extended yawn.

"You should lie down while you can, it'll be a long night."

"Not a bad idea." Devlyn made his way to his bed and flopped down with a loud squeak from the bedframe. "Make sure I'm awake when we're needed in the stables," he mumbled and drifted off to sleep.

Dusk approached the dark of night. A thick layer of clouds hovered above Cor'lera and as far as Devlyn's eyes could see. A lantern already burned brightly in the stables and the donkey brayed at their arrival.

The first guests arrived shortly after Devlyn and Alex did. Alex greeted and directed them to the abbey school's main entrance where other students would guide them to the dining hall. Devlyn unsaddled their horses and led them to an empty stall, where he unbridled them and then hung the tack on the partitions separating the horses. For the guests who arrived in carriages, the boys also unhitched the horses and pushed the carriages into a tidy row between the barn and the stables

Aunt Vine had spoken briefly with Devlyn and Alex before they'd gone to their assigned duty. She made it explicitly clear that their job was to welcome the guests as they arrived, and that they must keep the horses company in the stables. If they got hungry during the party, only one of them could go inside to retrieve food, this last said while looking directly at her son.

The first hour saw a steady flow of guests, most walking, a few riding a horse and even fewer with a carriage, representing the wealthiest villagers of Cor'lera, and Aunt Vine's closest acquaintances. None of the guests lived within the walls of the village, confirming Devlyn's suspicion that no Lucillians counted among them. Abbot Entiel and Aunt Vine's bias was clearly represented by those in attendance, a bias extending to the wealthy Lucillians. None had been extended an invitation, nor to those friendly with Lucillians.

Most of the party guests had arrived before the general and the other soldiers rode through the gate on a combination of the grand grey coursers and more mundane chestnuts. The rowdiness of the bunch suggested a prior celebration, and perhaps explained the two latecomers who walked in while Devlyn and Alex stabled the horses.

The general and his soldiers ignored Devlyn and barely paid attention to Alex's directions to the door. When Alex came to help Devlyn with the horses, he was shaking his head.

"And those are the soldiers protecting our people! They're nothing but thugs, I tell you," he said, then added more quietly, "It's a good thing we're leaving, because I don't trust them. Just meeting them makes me feel better about Velaria."

"They do seem pretty rough. Some seem odd too. I can't say why, but I don't think they're all Perrien," Devlyn replied. Several of the soldiers had much darker skin than Devlyn was accustomed to seeing in Cor'lera. Their skin was leathery and a mixture of brown and burnt red.

"They did look different. They're most likely from Gneal. I hear cities attract all sorts of foreigners. Anyway, I'm starving. Want me to get you something?"

"You read my mind. Do you think your mother would mind if I went in to get it?"

"Ha! She'd be more likely to throw it at you than allow you near her guests. Don't worry about it, Dev, you won't have her, the abbot, the general, or any other racist snob to worry about once we get away from here."

"We'll see. Now stop stalling and get us some food." Devlyn pushed his cousin out the stable, his stomach growling as a reminder of the insufficient sandwich he'd grabbed earlier. Having missed both breakfast and lunch due to the trip into Cor'lera, he was starving.

Thirty minutes passed before Alex returned with their dinner. "My mother's in her glory, you should see her. She's juggling several conversations at once and keeps turning from one guest to another and won't stop boasting about her two brothers."

"I think I can manage without seeing that."

"I did hear quite a commotion about the Lucillian Alliance and the witches. It sounds like Perrien's preparing for war or something. They're even talking of boosting Perrien's presence along the Cyrillean Pass." Alex handed Devlyn a plate filled with roasted chicken, potatoes, and broccoli. "And they're not just talking of the Lucillians, but full-blooded elves, along with other races. You remember the stories the older Lucillians told in town when we were young, during their annual spring festival, the one my mother forbade me from going to, but I went with you anyway? I don't remember what they call it, it had a funny name, something like the name of the month."

"Aurephaen?"

"That's it; you remember those stories, right?"

"The ones about elves, centaurs, and dwarves? Wait, are you saying that they're actually speaking openly about other races?"

"Not openly, I only overheard it while I waited in the buffet line. One of the strange-looking men said it. He wasn't all too thrilled when he saw that I'd heard him."

"Did they mention goblins, merpeople, and giants as well?"

"What? No idea. I thought such creatures were only myths to entertain children. And you and I both know that the elves died off over a thousand years ago."

"I'm not so sure what to believe anymore, let alone from whom. Was anything said about the Lucillians here in Cor'lera?" Devlyn absentmindedly rubbed a pointed ear.

"The usual crimes. Corrupting values, hoarding the ice grape vineyards, giving Cor'lera a bad reputation. They brought up your mother and the rest of your family as examples. It's getting bad in there. They seem ready to start burning down the Lucillian houses and shops, then either send them on their way or throw them in chains."

"I guess that's expected. You should have heard the way Lex went on in town this morning, ranting on against elven blood and ei'ana."

"I still can't believe Uncle Lex can wield. I bet Velaria's an ei'ana. What other reason would Lex have for hunting her down? After all, she did that invisibility thing." Alex shoved a piece of chicken into his mouth. "I still think this all sounds suspicious. Do you think they're working together? Setting a trap or something? Don't get me wrong, I'm still coming, but don't think I'm letting my guard down around her."

The two continued to eat while quietly discussing what they might encounter along the trip with Velaria and by the time they had finished, some of the guests were leaving. It had been dark for several hours, and the walkers commented on the late hour and the long walk before them. The general cheeriness of the group suggested that they'd had their fair share of Cor'leran Blue.

LEAVING

From the slightly opened door of the darkened stable where he and Alex waited for the right moment, Devlyn watched as the lights in the abbey school went out. One by one, every candle was snuffed and before long, not a single window glowed from within. Even so, they waited another hour.

"All is quiet. I doubt we'll get a better opportunity," he said as he shouldered his packs and headed out. Alex quickly gathered his own and quietly closing the stable door to avoid raising suspicions too soon, followed Devlyn toward the opened gate.

They walked to the hill where they'd had their lengthy conversation with Velaria, just above the frozen River Bethyl. There, Velaria stood elegantly holding her horse's reins in one hand and the reins of two chestnuts in the other. Devlyn gaped and Alex made a soft whoosh sound.

"How'd you get those?" asked Alex.

"I was enjoying a leisurely evening on a hill some ways off, just over there." Velaria waved in the direction of the road. "A group of soldiers rode by; the sun had already gone down, so I was not concerned about them catching sight of me. Well, two of them sat rather unsteadily in their saddles and when their horses took a fright, they couldn't control their mounts. While the rest of their company traveled on, they hit the ground with only the padding they were born with to soften the landing.

"Their horses galloped away leaving their masters to walk the remainder of the way to their destination, which I assume was the abbey school. About an hour later, these two came up to investigate my lovely

Penny," Velaria's voice held a note of satisfaction as she patted the patient horse's neck.

"That sounds a bit farfetched," said Alex. "But I reckon you couldn't take on an entire company of mounted soldiers. And we did see those soldiers; you're right, they didn't seem to be in full control of themselves let alone their horses."

"Are they safe for us to ride?" Devlyn asked, more to keep Alex from showing his ongoing distrust of Velaria than because he had a concern about the horses. As military horses, they were likely too well-trained to be anything but safe to ride, although they might not appreciate inexperienced riders.

"They allowed their previous masters to ride them, and those were cruel men. Perhaps if you treat them kindly, they won't run off at the first opportunity." Velaria patted both horses with her palm as she spoke in a consoling manner. "I assume you do know how to ride. But if you don't, I find experience is always the best teacher."

Devlyn and Alex shared a look, understanding that this was their last opportunity to turn back and preserve their accustomed lifestyle. Nodding at each other, they then approached the closest horse. Brushing his hand along the horse's cheek, Devlyn wondered what his name might be. A powerful creature such as this deserved a dignified name.

Well I doubt I'm going to learn that from staring into his eyes, he thought, and putting his left foot into the stirrup pulled himself atop with relative ease. Not surprisingly, the stirrups were a bit short, and Velaria adjusted them before getting on her own mount. No need to adjust Alex's stirrups though. *That's what happens when you're a more normal height*, Devlyn thought.

Velaria turned Penny west, moving down the hill at a moderate but steady pace in the dark and quiet night, with Devlyn and Alex close behind.

They slowed to cross the frozen Bethyl, each horse stepping carefully in a single stretched-out line. Once across the river and with a mile between themselves and the abbey school, Velaria quickened their pace to a trot, quickly increasing the distance between themselves and Cor'lera.

Of the three, Alex looked the most natural on his steed, while Velaria and Devlyn seemed to be better suited to a different mount. Devlyn thought he rode well enough but felt that his body did not complement the horse as well as Alex's did, and neither did Velaria's.

Velaria kept the pace steady, and two whole days passed with only brief breaks to allow the horses and themselves to rest. Even when they needed to sleep, it was for no more than three or four hours before they pressed on. The landscape became hillier, blocking the view of what lay beyond. Velaria finally called for a respite as the sun set on a second day that found them far to the west. They stopped in a shallow valley, shielded somewhat from the harsh wind that had besieged them all day. Grateful to finally pause and rest for the night, Devlyn allowed some of the tension in his body to relax, a tension that spoke of both the chill and the unaccustomed jarring of the horse's movements.

Once they'd seen to the horses, they began to set up for the night. Since this was the first real camp, Alex volunteered to start the fire, Devlyn sorted through the packs to find everyone's bedding, and Velaria located the sack with the provisions she'd brought.

Devlyn lay the bedrolls out near Alex and the fire, or in this case the absence of fire. Although Alex had easily found smaller bits of kindling and a few larger pieces of wood, he had yet to manage to light it. Devlyn watched with amusement, soon joined by Velaria who took pity on Alex's struggle and offered assistance. Tired and stubborn, Alex refused and insisted on kindling it himself.

"It's frozen through." He furiously struck the flint again. A few minutes passed with Alex no closer to igniting a flame, despite repeated strikes on the flint, with not even a puff of smoke to encourage him.

To Devlyn's amazement, smoke began to rise from the twigs but to the left of where Alex directed the flint. Before long, a fire sprung forth from that wisp of smoke, although from Devlyn's viewpoint, it was no where near Alex's ongoing effort. As the flames grew to an agreeable size, Alex strutted over to Devlyn and Velaria.

"See, I told you I didn't need your help," he smirked.

"Yes, so I see." Rather than push the issue, Devlyn simply stood there scratching his head.

Velaria did not say anything as she brought the food closer to the fire, although she did show that curious small smile Devlyn had seen before. She also set a small pot full of snow near the fire. Devlyn thought it might be tomorrow's drinking water.

Devlyn hesitated about saying anything about the fire lighting process. He knew that his cousin's efforts had nothing to do with the start of that flame, but he also hadn't seen Velaria move a muscle. Surely, if she could wield, it was difficult to believe that it could be done without moving at all.

Stories of the Ei'ana floated in his mind as he ate; most of the tales spoke poorly of the witches and always ended in disaster. Some of the Lucillians in Cor'lera spoke well of them, but only in guarded situations. A piece of him yearned to know whether Velaria had indeed wielded before his eyes, not just now with the flame, but back at the Cor Inn. The rest of him wanted to accept that nothing unnatural had occurred. After all, Alex had not noticed anything odd, and he had started plenty of fires with that very flint in the past.

"I have something to confess. I had a second mission to tend to in Cor'lera, which I kept concealed from you both. And I did not travel alone," Velaria began when little remained of the food. Until now, there had been little conversation among the three, given what seemed to be Velaria's natural reluctance to part with any more information than necessary. It seemed that now was the time.

"What kind of mission?" Alex crossed his arms which clearly indicated his overall skepticism about Velaria's credentials. "And who is this other person?"

"Devlyn's uncle Arlyn and I were sent to rally the elves living there. They know better than most how things stand in Perrien. What is spoken secretly in pubs and common rooms is spoken openly by the humans who dwell along the fringes of civilizations; their pride blinds them." Velaria addressed them both. "What the elves in Cor'lera are not aware of, is that those soldiers did not travel across the entirety of Parendior simply to inspect the village's security; they came with the sole intent of enslaving them. Arlyn and I informed the elves that every elf in Cor'lera has a cell awaiting him or her in Gneal. We told them that their only chance for freedom is to stand against Perrien's soldiers. As you might imagine, they were apprehensive.

"Their sense of defeat is so great that they willingly submitted to the Council of Perrien, and in so doing, submitted to Emperor Erynor Meriden. We reminded them that Cor'lera is a strong village, with walls woven from the trees of the Illumined Wood. With the exception of Lucillia, there is no safer place than within those walls for an elf of Luminare to mount a resistance.

"So long as they remain within the village walls, they will remain protected. Only if Perrien brings its entire military against them will those walls fail. By now, the elves will have safely secured Cor'lera from harm. The general's arrival and the party provided the perfect opportunity. All the anti-elven supporters were invited to the abbey school and drawn out of the village proper. By coming to join me, you missed hearing that by the time they tried to enter the walled portion of the village, they found the gates secured against them, and only elves and humans sympathetic to their cause behind those enchanted walls."

Stunned by the revelation that the Lucillians had secured the town, Devlyn could only share a bewildered look with Alex.

"Will the Lucillians pick up swords and attack the humans?" asked Alex. "And who's this Arlyn? Devlyn has another uncle?"

"An attack is unlikely. The elves that settled here are a peaceful people who migrated away from the politics of Lucillia. And Arlyn is Evellyn's oldest brother. He returned to Cor'lera with hopes of teaching wielding to anyone capable of it, and eventually seeing that they travel to Gwilnor to become ei'ana. Arlyn's wielding ability diminished many years ago, so even if he does lose control of the erendinth, he won't cause any harm, but that does not prevent him from teaching the little he knows about wielding—mostly theory. And he's an incredible teacher, the kind the abbey schools were once accustomed to."

"A man wielding? I thought men couldn't control it, resulting in catastrophe," Devlyn latched on to the mention of wielding with concern.

The small flame in Lex's hand still haunted his thoughts.

"Arlyn will not be teaching the men, only the women in Cor'lera. And again, his ability to wield is too diminished to be dangerous."

"He's actually in Cor'lera?" asked Devlyn, finally getting to the other surprising bit of information. Velaria nodded. She had mentioned Arlyn to Devlyn when they were at the Cor Inn, but evidently, Devlyn had not picked up on it. Not surprising given the many surprises there for Devlyn.

"Why didn't he come to see me?"

"He desperately wants to see you again, but the risk was too great. The ei'ceuril at the abbey school would have recognized him. Lex has no authority over an ei'ceuril, especially a steward, but if he found out Arlyn was in Cor'lera, he would never have permitted his soldiers to attend the party. They would have patrolled the village the entire night, ensuring their plans would not be spoiled."

Still distressed, Devlyn's mind shifted.

"Elves? You said elves several times. They died out; they lost their immortality and their descendants dwindled until only the children they shared with humans remained."

"Devlyn, that is a lie. Ask yourself, what makes an elf? Is it their immortality or their essence? Look within yourself. Look into your heart and you will see it shining there, fogged over by ignorance. Don't you find it odd that you have pointed ears, while Alexander does not? Is it not odd how all the Lucillians have angled features and look markedly different from the humans in Cor'lera? Not to mention the height difference. If you stopped slouching, you would stand nearly a head taller than Alexander.

"You are an elf, a full-blooded elf, descendant of the elves of Luminare. Your ancestors migrated from that great Skyland of Luminare and settled in the lands that became known as Krysenthiel, so named by a human trying to speak Aelish, calling it a land of golden flowers. The Luminari built their capital, Arenthyl, on a mountain island surrounded by Lake Saeryndol. It shimmered like crystal in the sun. When they lost their immortality, they were forced to migrate once again, this time as slaves, and settled in what would grow and flourish into Lucillia."

Unable to accept the revelation, Devlyn persisted. "But, that's not possible."

"I understand that it's difficult to grasp, especially in this age when even the elves believe themselves a myth. Our immediate concern is Gneal though, and to rescue as many of Devlyn's family as possible, particularly his mother and brother. It won't be for several weeks until a road is available to us, not until after we cross the Arvil, and I hope to stay clear of them even after we cross."

"Exactly how are we supposed to cross the Arvil without a road leading to a bridge?" Alex asked with a gleam in his eye. "I've never seen it, but my father said the river is so wide that Cor'lera could float along its waters without getting stuck on the banks."

Devlyn knew his cousin well enough to know that Alex believed he'd found the unravelling flaw in Velaria's plan. Granted, Devlyn found himself sharing that same opinion; only one bridge crossed the Arvil River and that was far to the south in Selma.

"The bridge at Selma is the easiest route across the Arvil; however, it is heavily guarded. No one enters the town and crosses the bridge without an interview. I wish I could say that I wasn't responsible for that, but Lex is very anxious to hold me for questioning, so before he pursued me east, he boosted the town's guard with his own soldiers and gave them explicit instructions to not let anyone pass without papers from the Perrien Council."

"So how are we expected to cross?" asked Devlyn.

"There is a second bridge to the north; it was used by the old kingdom of Thellion. The bridge lies just south of the Wooded Hills of Thellion, but far enough north that the Perriens have long forgotten its existence. One of the advantages of this route is that we will avoid many towns and villages, and more importantly, the people who live there. If we are seen, it won't take long for Lex to receive word about three strangers heading for Gneal. Unfortunately, there won't be any way to conceal ourselves once we attach ourselves to a road close to the capital. By the time word of our location reaches him, Lex will most likely be in the Cyrillean Pass, hoping to cut us off."

The remainder of the evening was spent mostly in silence, especially in Alex's case, as he felt the sting of the several counts of being proven wrong. Although it seemed as if he might speak several times, he reclined with his mouth closed. They divided into watches for the night, Velaria first, followed by Devlyn, and lastly Alex.

UNTOUCHED

The following weeks passed in much the same way as the first two days, although eventually, they spent longer spans walking, allowing the horses to maintain their strength through the hills' increasing ascents and descents. It was hard on everyone, although the horses could more easily step through the deep snow; the slipperiness made it prudent to tread carefully. The snow had yet to begin melting, leaving Devlyn to wonder whether the entire country lay blanketed in snow six weeks into spring.

The month of Marenth had ended and Aurenth was halfway along as an almost full moon had shone down on them the night before. Devlyn wondered whether Cor'lera was celebrating the spring festival of Aurephaen. From atop Dart, the name he'd chosen for his horse, Devlyn watched the sun rise. Soft pink shifted to pale blue as the dawning sun filled the sky with a clear and crisp light. Keeping his eyes on the sun, Devlyn remembered to say a quiet prayer to Anaweh the Creating Light through Auriel. He had not learned that ritual from the ei'ceuril at the school, but rather from the older elves in Cor'lera. It was one of the few occasions where he felt comfortable around people like himself. Whether or not actual elves still existed was a different story.

Finishing his prayer, he thought of Cor'lera and the people secured behind its walls. If they were safe, as Velaria had said, from Perrien's soldiers and the prejudice of the Perriens who migrated to Cor'lera, then they could celebrate Aurephaen out in the open without ridicule.

"Why the good mood?" Alex asked.

"What do you mean?"

"You're smiling pointy ear to pointy ear!"

Alex was right, Devlyn was grinning. He tried to stop, but his lip muscles refused to bend downward.

"I never knew a Luminari to frown on Aurephaen," said Velaria. "I trust the elves in Cor'lera celebrate in the same manner as those in Lucillia, if not on such a grand scale."

"Is it really Aurephaen already?" Alex asked.

"Didn't you notice the almost full moon last night? It'll be full tonight, marking the middle of the month."

"It was pretty full, wasn't it?" Alex turned to Devlyn. "How's that prayer go? The one that decrepit Lucillian taught you last year."

"I don't remember the words, only the intent behind them."

"The words would have been a poor translation from the original Aelish. They were never meant to be spoken but sung. And as I understand it, the chant has a fluid nature," said Velaria.

"I bet the Lucillians are celebrating like they never have in Cor'lera today." Alex had lost interest in a chant in a different language.

"Why do you say that?" Devlyn asked.

"Well, just think about it. It's the first time in a hundred years since the Perriens took over Parendior and moved into Cor'lera. You and I both know Cor'lera was a very different place back then! Just imagine how they'll act without being constantly surrounded by prejudice."

"I hope they've stopped slouching," added Velaria.

Devlyn laughed unexpectedly. Velaria's constant reminder to stand up straight left Devlyn pleased by the shift of focus for her criticism to someone other than himself.

The day stretched on as the sun reached its peak and fell to the west. A chilled breeze brushed against Devlyn's neck. Pulling his hood over his head, a degree of warmth returned.

Reaching the apex of a large hill after weeks of relentless travel, Devlyn looked down on a wide river rushing northward. *At least it's not frozen*, thought Devlyn, hopeful for feeling a spring sun on his skin again.

The River Arvil curved its way around the hills stretching as far north and south as Devlyn could see. Five times the Bethyl's width, the Arvil had once served as a barrier between Perrien and Parendior.

Animosity had always existed between the two. Perrien on the western side, with Gneal and other large cities, looked on the rural east as slow and suspect, while Parendior to the east of the Arvil was large and sparsely populated with farming villages, and even they were far and few in between. Parendians thought of the folk in Perrien as aggressive and irreverent. Now one kingdom, the two sides still viewed each other with disfavor. Devlyn recalled Elias' lecture on how only in the past century, Perrien had crossed the mighty Arvil and supported by her military strength, gave the scattered small towns and villages two options: surrender or be slaughtered. Since Parendior had no central leadership and consisted of a collection of small towns filled with farming folk and no soldiers, they offered little resistance against the might of their western neighbors. One by one, the eastern towns and villages fell to Perrien, and before long every town flew a flag with the grey courser of Perrien above its gates. Devlyn did not know if Parendior ever had its own flag flying over her villages' gates.

Relieved to be on his feet, Devlyn carefully walked down the snowy slopes to the Arvil's shores. Once out of the shadow of the hills, they could see an intricate stone bridge arching high above the river, with no visible supports between the eastern and western shore. The bridge soared over the river and somehow managed to support its own weight. Devlyn had never seen such a bridge, let alone heard of such a thing.

As they drew closer to it, they could see that the bridge was anchored on a hill on each side of the Arvil, which gave the bridge additional height.

Velaria paused at the base of the bridge. "We'll set up camp here for the night and cross in the morning."

Devlyn continued to gaze at the bridge before relieving Dart of the bridle, saddle, and saddle bags. His eyes lingered on the river. He had grown tired of eating Velaria's provisions of dried meats and dried fruits, small portions reserved to twice a day. The food served at the abbey school was certainly not exquisite, but neither was it dried out in salt. While the river might have provided a fresh option for tonight's meal, Devlyn abandoned any notion of catching a fish from the river, since they carried no fishing poles and nets on their westward trip on horseback.

The rays of the setting sun struck the silver-colored bridge making it glow vividly, shifting from a soft orange to a deep red before fading to a subtle purple.

Devlyn unrolled everyone's bedding and saw Alex yet again struggling with the flint. Sparks flew from it onto the cold branches and tinder, landing without resulting in a single puff of smoke.

"Have you noticed anything odd about the tracks we've been leaving behind?" Alex whispered, another series of sparks following the crisp sound of the flint.

"I haven't paid attention."

"Well, there aren't any. I thought it was just the wind at first, but our tracks are completely gone—as if we never passed. Horses leave deep prints in the snow; the wind can't make them disappear so easily." Alex looked over his shoulder.

"What are you suggesting?"

"That Velaria is an ei…"

Before Alex could finish the word, the fireless tinder set before him combusted into a roaring fire. Alex yelped and fell backward, scooching away on his hands.

"Your suspicions are correct, Alexander," said Velaria as she walked over to the warm fire. Alex gaped at the blaze before him.

"You've lit every fire, haven't you?" Devlyn asked.

Velaria's small smile revealed itself.

"No, I did!" Alex pushed himself up from the ground but kept his distance from the fire.

"I'm afraid the tinder found along our journey has been too frozen for a flint to be effective."

"So, you're telling me that I've wasted half an hour every night for something you could have done in two seconds!"

"You came close on several occasions; the tinder only needed another ten minutes before it would have thawed and caught flame. But I was cold and hungry," Velaria admitted.

"Anything else you want to tell us, *Ei'ana?*" Alex asked, crossing his arms.

"That's hardly necessary. I imagine there's quite a bit of information you'd benefit from. I doubt Cor'lera's abbey school gave an honest historical account."

"Fine, then who was the last king of Thellion?"

"Evellion of course. He ceased being king of Thellion when he and the refugees of Elothkar reached their mountain refuge and birthplace of their new kingdom. The royal family belongs to House Thellion, maintaining their heritage through all these years."

"So, Tyler was right," said Devlyn thinking of his last class with Magister Elias. "Lex mentioned a good deal about some southern kingdom, I can't remember its name but I think it started with a Y."

"The general does enjoy lifting Yanil as a banner in his crusade against the Ei'ana and Lucillia. What would you like to know about them?"

"Lex spoke about them making a mistake and paying a severe price, resulting in the outlawing of wielding."

"I can't go into every detail; courses at Gwilnor Academy involve entire months of lectures on the events in Yanil that resulted in the Yanilean outlawing wielding. The simple answer is the Ei'ana of that time carried the blame for flooding the entire city of Lankor, an event called Nauto's Wrath. Erynor swooped in and promised to help the submerged people and constructed them a new city that floats on the water, so they would never have to worry about their city flooding again. In exchange, they had to submit to the Erynien Empire, which they readily agreed to."

"Does Lex admire them because wielding is a crime there or because they joined this Erynor figure?" Alex asked.

"Those are not the only reasons he advocates them, but they are two of the reasons."

Devlyn's stomach rumbled and he looked once more to the river, thinking of the fish swimming beneath the northern current.

"Tired of dried meats and dried fruits?" Velaria asked.

Devlyn nodded with a guilty smile.

"Me too." Velaria turned and walked to the River Arvil. She held her arms loosely in front of her, before swinging them downward and then upward, followed by a splash of water and a flopping fish at Devlyn's feet. His stomach rumbled louder as his mouth salivated.

Alex's eyes widened. "Does this mean we've been eating salty food the entire time when we could've had fresh meals?"

"I suppose I could catch small game in a similar manner," Velaria replied dryly.

Alex grumbled under his breath but readily picked up the fish and started to filet it.

"Now that you know who I am, I might as well ask if you have any clothing you would like cleaned. I don't know how most travelers manage going without washing their clothes for so long in the wilderness, but I can manage it with a simple wield."

"I wondered why your clothes always looked so clean," said Alex, focused on the fish.

"Again, your suspicions were well placed; I've been washing my clothing while on watch."

"You could have told us earlier that you're an ei'ana," grumbled Alex. "My clothes have never smelled so bad! If it wasn't for the cold temperature, it would've been unbearable."

"Want me to grab your dirty clothes, Alex?" Devlyn asked, eager to have clean clothes but uninterested in having Alex handle his soiled garments while preparing their dinner.

"Sure, just get them out of my bag."

Devlyn quickly retrieved their bags and took them over to where Velaria had hollowed out a basin in the snow and wielded water into it. "Just dump them in," she said.

Emptying both bags, Devlyn watched as the water began to bubble and swirl. Velaria barely moved her hands and before he knew it, each piece of clothing, small clothes included, dangled in the air dripping water. Droplets sprung from each garment too quickly to turn into ice and each item returned on its own to the correct bag.

Devlyn's mouth dropped as he watched the quick procedure. "That's all it takes?"

"That's it."

"Thanks." Quite impressed, Devlyn replaced the bags next to their bedding.

"It benefits us both." Velaria smiled.

———

Devlyn woke the following morning before the sun rose and tidied up his belongings and returned them to his saddle bags. It had been so long since he'd worn clean clothing, since they'd left Cor'lera in fact, that he had forgotten how uncomfortable soiled clothing could be.

Now that Velaria no longer concealed her ability to wield, evidence of the camp disappeared before Devlyn's eyes. It was as if they had never stopped for the night.

Devlyn, walking Dart to the edge of the bridge, was shortly joined there by Velaria and Alex. Still on foot and leading their horses, they moved onto the stone surface where the horses' hooves clopped for the first time in their westward journey. Devlyn looked on in awe, running his fingers across the glassy railing, marveling at its pristine condition; he would place its age at no more than a hundred, not several millennia.

"How is this bridge still standing as it is? No stone quarried here can weather this climate so well. It looks as though it was cut and fitted yesterday."

"You're right, Alexander, no stone of this country *is* capable of withstanding the ice and snow of Parendior and Perrien. This stone, however, was not quarried from this land. In fact, it was not quarried at all. The elves of Aldinare were great friends with the people of Thellion. When one of the kings of that old kingdom fell in love with an elven maid, the elves honored that union and as a marriage gift, they wielded the stone of the Skyland of Aldinare. The silvery stone flowed through the sky, as would a breeze, and fell on this place, crafting a bridge for all to cross from one shore to the other. In those days, this river went by a different name, long forgotten now, just as many have long since forgotten this structure, the Aewen Bridge," Velaria explained.

As was his custom with Velaria, Alex appeared doubtful. However, Devlyn had never seen stone so finely crafted, and the closer he looked at the silvery stone, the more apparent its translucent quality. Assuming that the surface was slick with ice, he was relieved that no snow covered the bridge.

Elaborate designs adorned every surface, some portraying an elf on the back of a winged unicorn in flight in looping thin scrollwork. The sides of the bridge had half walls with interlacing designs of the same silvery translucent stone, allowing those crossing the bridge to look down on the river below. Not once could Devlyn find a break in the stone, not even along the half walls—the entirety melded, as if it was cut from a single stone. Like Alex, he found Velaria's story difficult to swallow, but he could not imagine this bridge coming about using human tools.

Devlyn had known that the Arvil was a large river, but as they crossed high above, he realized just how very wide the span was and dared not think of its depth. At long last, they reached the western shorebank, much the same as the other; for some reason, he had expected it to be better.

They pressed on, and it was another three weeks before they came to the first road since leaving Cor'lera. Before that, all they'd seen were trees that grew smaller and the snow melting substantially under the warming effects of spring as they traveled south. Velaria stayed clear of the road, still cautious lest they meet other travelers who might identify them.

Their slow journey passed without much notice but Devlyn was still shocked as the moon of Aurenth faded and the new moon of Delenth began. Spring was now entering its last month and still they came across the odd patch of snow, although thankfully only in shaded areas and fast disappearing.

The following days involved crossing roads under the cover of night-fall. Familiar with the land, Velaria managed to pace their journey so that they crossed the roads just after night had fallen and the moon and stars became visible. Every road they came across had a well-traveled look and once they had crossed it, Velaria pushed them on an additional hour away before setting up camp for the night. Well before first light, they broke camp, Velaria performed the wield that made all traces of their stay disappear and they rode on toward Gneal.

Their pace slowed as the rolling nature of the hills soon gave way to a series of hills steeper than those east of the Arvil. Rarely did they see anyone and only caught the sounds of civilization when they drew close to a town or farm, but Velaria saw to it that they maintained a safe distance. The only other sign of people were horse and cart tracks on the roads they crossed.

Soon, Velaria allowed them to travel entirely by road, since it was doubtful whether they would have been able to guide their horses up the steep slopes, which at some points fell off sharply into cliffs. The sight of them gave Devlyn pause, for neither he nor Alex had seen such a thing before. He grew excited, now that they traveled on the road, because it meant that they would soon reach their destination.

GNEAL

Midmorning on the fourteenth of Delenth, the group first caught sight of Gneal part way up on a large hill that towered over the other smaller hills in the area. The northwest side fell in a sheer drop, while the other sides sloped gently into the city and beyond. Nestled at the cliff edge and overlooking the city stood a stout castle, supported on and surrounded by strong walls with the occasional tower jutting above. Ramparts on the sides not backed by the cliff provided security.

Once home to the royal family of Perrien, the castle was now divided into apartments housing the members of the Perrien Council. The Council had ousted the monarchy nearly a century ago. The reasons behind the ousting had not been part of the history lessons at the abbey school. Somehow, Devlyn doubted that there had been innocent intentions; more likely it had been the result of resentment over the power of the monarchy.

They approached the northern side of the city and, from this perspective, could only see a small portion of the city. A newer and larger section lay to the south, so the section they could see was Old Gneal which, along with the castle, had been built during the time of Thellion. The section referred to as New Gneal was at most a century old; in fact, Devlyn remembered Elias saying that it had been completed just within the past twenty years.

The closer they drew to the city, the more crowded the road became. Devlyn wondered how Velaria had managed to avoid such large crowds until now. And even though they could see the city, it took the better part of Thenaen to reach Gneal.

They arrived on foot late that day at the old north gate, leading their mounts, Devlyn back to his usual slouch and Alex nearly skipping with excitement about finally reaching their destination.

Velaria led them beneath the large portcullis. The looming castle overhead seemed oppressing and unwelcoming.

Despite the intimidating entrance, the guards took no particular notice and they passed beneath the solid stone walls, walls thicker than Devlyn thought necessary. People of all sorts traveled in both directions through the deep gateway. Devlyn wondered how welcoming the city would prove.

The snow finally a distant memory, the air seemed a bit warmer, but with rain replacing the snow, they still felt chilled to the bone.

"Good thing it's raining, our hoods help conceal our identities," Velaria commented quietly. "It's easier to pass unnoticed." Alex raised a skeptical brow but said nothing.

To a degree, it made sense to Devlyn. Everyone in the crowded streets had their head down and wore a cloak with its hood pulled tightly shut.

Unlike in Cor'lera, the people of Gneal rarely saw anyone who looked slightly different; differences drew significant attention, especially toward those with pointed ears and angled features.

Velaria's claim about him being an elf still seemed doubtful and unrealistic. The stories said that elves were immortal, and neither he nor any of the elves in Cor'lera were immortal. They all died, just like every human. It was certainly possible that some of their ancestors were elves, but as far as he was concerned, they had died.

The number of people braving the rain amazed Devlyn. The people of Gneal showed little concern, more preoccupied with reaching their various destinations than having to deal with inclement weather. They simply went about their business as though the sun shone. If it wasn't for the cloaks and shawls wrapped about their faces, Devlyn doubted they would have even noticed the rain.

Velaria guided them through Old Gneal on foot, still leading their horses and sticking to the main and crowded roads. Devlyn had never seen roads so broad; he doubted Cor'lera had enough cobblestones to complete even one of the expansive roadways in Gneal.

Another gate appeared before them, much like the first, but not as heavily guarded.

"We just crossed into New Gneal," Velaria explained once they'd passed the guards.

The roads here were not as impressive and the buildings lacked the grandeur of the original portion of the city. Stone was the preferred building material in Old Gneal, with many carvings and ornamentations, while New Gneal favored largely unadorned wooden structures which paled in comparison.

"These look rickety," Alex commented quietly, reflecting Devlyn's thoughts. Could they withstand a strong wind, let alone the combined weight of the people and furnishings within?

It was clear that this was home to Gneal's impoverished, making Devlyn wonder as they walked along the narrow streets crammed with people how one of the great cities of Eklean could have just as many poor folks as wealthy ones.

Velaria took them down a side road, which they stayed on until a slightly larger building came into view. The wooden sign above the door had a gate painted on it. Just to the side was the stable, similar in appearance but much smaller.

"Do your horses need stabling?" asked a boy, clad in rags. He seemed tired and listless. Devlyn wondered whether he ever just played with other children.

"That would be much appreciated," said Velaria, with a small smile for the boy.

With no further words, the boy led their horses to stalls, while Devlyn, Velaria, and Alex carried their saddlebags and packs inside, where Velaria tipped the young boy three shiny silver jents. In response, Velaria received a wide grin featuring a missing front tooth.

Devlyn appreciated the meaning behind the smile, remembering his own elation early on in their journey when Velaria had entrusted Alex and himself with ten silver jents and fifteen copper lewts each. He had never carried that amount of wealth in his own purse before. He still had the two unfamiliar golden coins he'd found in the Cor Inn, but he had no way of knowing their worth and he intended to keep them secret.

The inn's interior was just as depressing as the rest of New Gneal. Fortunately, a fire burned in the hearth, and as small as it was, Devlyn was eager for the warmth and the change of atmosphere it offered.

Behind a counter, its surface cluttered with disorganized piles of books, papers, and keys, a gaunt old man stood. He looked toward the newcomers with a forced smile displaying crooked yellowing teeth, with gaping spots indicating an ingrained lack of care. Clear deceit lurked behind the ugly smile as his eyes lingered on Velaria's purse.

"Travelers," the innkeeper began, eyes narrowing as he took in details about his new patrons. "And Lucillian if I'm not mistaken."

"It would be generous of you to not remember." Velaria slid a gold crown across the counter.

Devlyn had never seen one before, not even when he went to Cor'lera on errands. Abbot Entiel would never have trusted him with such an amount. He thought of the strange coins hidden in his purse and again wondered what they might be worth.

"After all, does not generosity better respond to generosity?" Velaria held one finger on the coin as she held the innkeeper's gaze.

The innkeeper held the gaze a moment longer before nodding once and dropping his eyes. The single crown could easily pay for every room the inn had to offer. "As you wish, *travelers*."

"It'll be doubled on our leave," Velaria added, causing the innkeeper's mouth to gape.

"We require two rooms, if it's not too much trouble."

"No trouble at all. Please, let me show you to them," he offered, grinning more genuinely as he led them through the inn to a pair of rooms adjacent one another. "A key for you, ma'am." He pulled a single key from his coat pocket. "And a key for the young masters." He retrieved a similar key from the same pocket and handed it to Alex before leaving them. Devlyn wondered how he'd known which key belonged to which room.

Alex unlocked their door, and Devlyn followed him in, quickly going over to sit on one of the beds. He was pleased with the soft mattress and lack of squeaking but would also have gladly slept in his old bed in his tower dormitory at the abbey school. Sleeping on the ground held much less allure and comfort than any bed, no matter how much that bed squeaked.

"Don't get too comfortable, I smelled dinner wafting from the kitchens, and judging by the time, they're probably already serving it," said Velaria from their doorway before going to her own room.

"Now that's what I wanted to hear!" Alex wasted little time in dropping his pack and saddlebags with a thump on the wooden floor and headed straight out the door, into the hallway, and down the stairs with Devlyn soon behind, delayed only by taking the time to place his own belongings under his bed, hang up their still-dripping cloaks and shut and lock the door.

Reaching the common room himself, Devlyn found Alex already drooling over a hot dish of stew, wasting little time as he spooned it into his mouth.

"It's not the best I've ever had, but it's hot!" Alex's spoon continued its rhythmic motion between his mouth and the bowl. Even as he ate, he raised a hand toward the young woman balancing a tray on one hip, trying to get her attention. "Can we get another two bowls?"

"Only if you have the coin," she replied saucily.

Fishing through his coat pocket, Alex pulled out four angots and handed them over to the server.

"I don't think Velaria's coming down just yet," said Devlyn.

"Who said the second bowl was for her? This rain sucked away every bit of energy I had. I need food!"

Devlyn cracked a quick smile at the server now approaching with two bowls and tackled his own as soon as she set it down before him. His insides thawed as the hot stew flowed though, reaching the bottom of his cold and wet toes. Despite his inability to identify what was in the watery mush before him, whatever it was, he gladly ate it.

They did not stay long in the common room, even with Alex finishing two bowls of the stew. The innkeeper had wisely sat them at a poorly-lit table away from the other patrons who would find it difficult to make out any details about their appearance. With Devlyn's appetite satisfied, he longed to sleep in a real bed.

The following morning came quickly and Devlyn found himself exploring the city with Alex after a much-needed rest and a hearty meal of oatmeal. Velaria had something that needed doing on her own and had asked that he and Alex stay clear of Old Gneal, explaining that the inhabitants there would more likely recognize Devlyn's ancestry by his appearance. Old Gneal also had the tendency of having more guards, not that New Gneal was without its own share patrolling the streets. Devlyn could not believe how many he counted; in Cor'lera, guards only stood at the two village gates.

Constantly aware of his height, Devlyn made a conscious effort to remain slouched to blend in whenever a guard crossed their path. Over the past couple of months, he had tried and mostly succeeded to stand tall, both on foot and in the saddle, but here, it seemed wiser to maintain his usual slouch.

Despite their height, the buildings of New Gneal were unimpressive compared to those in Cor'lera. Devlyn doubted that they would endure over many decades let alone centuries.

"It looks like they were thrown up overnight," he commented to Alex as they paused before a particularly uninspired building. "Did you notice that some of them don't even have a stone foundation, only lumber jutting up from the dirt?" Alex merely grunted in reply and continued moving through the crowded streets. Devlyn followed, making sure he kept his pointed ears concealed beneath his hood.

Before long, they arrived at an intersection with a grand view of one of the original gates leading into Old Gneal. Devlyn had not intended to draw close to the gate, but now that they found themselves here, he admired the magnificent structure built within the wall itself. He imagined what it might have been like for a foreigner to approach those walls, awaiting to be deemed worthy to gain entrance. How many had been turned away from these gates? How many foreign armies had demanded access to what once had been a fair city built on the premise of justice?

Deciding it best to change their course, Devlyn led Alex down the intersection to the road leading away from the gate. They weren't more than half a block away when they heard a brash horn, its call reverberating through the crowded streets. Some paid little mind to it and kept about their business, but most paused and turned toward Old Gneal, curious about its source, which irritated those who had to maneuver around them.

As they waited in anticipation, another horn reverberated and soldiers from every direction marched for the gates.

Uneasy, Devlyn backed as far off as possible from the middle of the street, pulling Alex beside him. With their backs pressed against a building, Devlyn noticed that people on all sides also hugged the walls and kept their heads downcast. Apparently, others shared his wariness, trying to avoid standing out in the crowd. Once the guards passed, the boys decided it best to return to the inn and remain out of general sight.

Musty air filled Velaria's lungs as she walked through the dark subterranean corridor under Gneal's castle. She had no sense of the walls breathing here, no sense of fresh air flowing through to cleanse the atmosphere and doubted whether much had changed since the completion so very long ago of the substantial structure above her head. This portion was sealed away, not only from the rest of the castle, but also from the rest of civilization, and although there had to be some air coming in somewhere, it wasn't enough to keep it fresh. Cold and dimly lit, the passages had none of the decorations featured through the rooms above, a clear and unvarnished message to those who passed into the pit of the castle under the menacing guidance of the guards. Twisting corridors and iron-clad doors allowed no opportunity of escape. No hope lived here, only doubt and despair.

Velaria was one of the very few who moved of her own accord in this desolate place, willingly entering the forsaken depths of the castle of Gneal. She had hoped to wait another day or two, time spent gathering more intelligence on the state of the city and its organization before developing a plan based on what she learned.

But when she'd received an anonymous note from a Vyoletryn observant, a note slipped under the door of her room at the inn while she slept, a note that said a formal brunch was being held today at the castle with guests coming and going all morning, she decided to seize the opportunity.

Subtle hints pointed to the note's origin. She had nearly missed the simple image of the purple eagle of Vyoletryn hidden in one of the finely scrawled letters, although the purple ink was specific to the reports from the Vyoletryns. Few received them and fewer still knew from whom they originated.

There was a saying among the Ei'ana: Only the snake heeds not the eagle. Velaria had always found it an odd saying, since she had always understood serpents to be clever creatures, but she figured that perhaps their cleverness was also their downfall when it came to their wisdom, often degenerating to pride.

Stepping quietly along, Velaria soon came up to a solid iron door. Assuming the castle's gaolers sat on the other side, she placed her hand on the door hoping to get a sense of how many occupied the next room. Embracing the erendinth, she sensed three warm bodies, vaguely touching on their consciousness. Not overly concerned with what she sensed, she gave a knock on the door. Shuffling sounds came from the other side, followed by the grinding and clacking of metal against metal as a key turned in the complicated lock. When it swung open, a frowning middle-aged man greeted Velaria. Two others sat at a little table inside the small anteroom that led to the cells, a deck of cards between them.

"Another one, eh? I don't see why two of your kind are needed for the likes of them," grumbled the gaoler who'd opened the door. "Well, get on with it. I don't have all day to watch you stand in a doorway. Especially when we'll have to clean up after you."

As she grasped the meaning behind his words, her heart skipped with a suggestion of panic. She knew Perrien was no longer loyal to the Lucillian Alliance, but she had not expected the presence of other elves in Gneal. And the only elves who would have allied themselves with Perrien were Cyndinari, operating from their imperial capital, Broid. Thinking fast, she figured it was probably best if these three didn't tell anyone that a second Cyndinari had come into the dungeons. Luckily, they couldn't tell one elf from another. Embracing the erendinth, she shot a quick flash of light that threw all three of them sprawling unconscious on the stone floor. Although they would only remain unconscious for an hour, when they did wake up, they would have full recollection of what happened; by that time, she hoped to be away from Gneal.

Stepping over them, she quickly made her way to the dimly lit passage which led deeper into the dungeons. Peering around a corner, she noted that the passage was brighter due to light coming from a cell further along. Even as she noted a sound of soft weeping, she also noticed, to her horror, a figure veiled in shadow standing in the doorway to the cell.

A shadow elf! Now why would the gaolers think she was one of them? Risking another peek around the corner, she noticed at least a dozen recently dead Luminari strewn across the floor of the open cell. Velaria recognized some of them as Evellyn's relatives from their golden-brown hair with hints of blond. Her heart ached at the loss.

One was still alive although breathing with difficulty. *Liam?* she thought, catching sight of black hair although he remained partially hidden from her view. She dared not draw closer to get a better look, lest the shadow elf notice her.

"I'll ask you again," the shadow elf said aggressively, "where is the weapon entrusted to your family? You have kept it hidden for all these years, and apparently so successfully that you have yourself to blame for these deaths." The shadow elf gestured to the corpses on the floor. "You'll join them soon. Your spirit will be mine and you'll join them in spending eternity extending my life. But not until you tell me where the weapon is."

"I don't kn…know of any weapon. I've told you all I…I could, just as th…they did. But you di…didn't listen."

I know that voice, Velaria thought, straining her ears. No longer capable of staying upright, the elf fell to the floor, weeping softly from the pain.

Unmoved, the shadow elf pointed a finger at the prisoner and a thin dark line streaked across the room, sucking all the light from it. It connected to the elf's chest and a horrifying ear-splitting scream escaped, piercing

Velaria's heart. *Liam, it's Liam!* Velaria couldn't believe that he still lived.

"Don't worry, that's not enough to kill you. Granted, a few years of your life are gone, but you won't live long enough to miss them. I know you don't know the location of the weapon, but it's been a pleasure trying to get you to tell me. You see, these Perrien imbeciles did not think it important to mention that you are no child of hers. That's why we're having your brother brought here; he's a true child of Evellyn."

"H…He was only a b…baby when you had us taken away," Liam managed.

"Don't bother groveling, he'll join you soon enough. He'll have the privilege of watching you die, just as I gave you the privilege of watching these miserable slaves die. Your death will serve your brother well. We might even bring Evellyn to witness it. Perhaps Devlyn's torture will open her tightly pursed lips."

Time was running short for Velaria. She needed to act now, while she could still surprise the shadow elf. She jumped out from behind the corner, arms outstretched and fire springing from her hands as she ran toward the shadow elf.

It responded to Velaria's attack by shooting shadowy bolts at her, leaving the room in a constant shift of light and darkness.

As they battled, Velaria found her opponent rather clumsy, but the unstable erendinth he wielded far surpassed her own. *He's too strong.* Uncertain of her ability to maintain her attack long enough to tip it in her favor, Velaria felt Darkness fill the room. Just as she felt herself approach her last reserves, a scream pierced her ears. The black lightning faded, a burst of lighted figures escaped, and the dim light returned to the room. The shadow elf lay in a puddle of his own blood; Liam, barely able to stand and heavily panting, clutched a knife and stared at Velaria.

"I'm going to assume you weren't friends, but if you were, just finish it. I just watched what was left of my family have their life sucked from them."

"We were not friends. But he did not kill all your family, Liam."

"Tell me what you mean, witch. Tell me or I swear I'll use this knife on you too." Liam wobbled on his thin legs, hunched over but still managing to wave the knife threateningly at her.

"I traveled from Cor'lera with Devlyn. He's well. Although he scarcely remembers his brother, he wishes to see you freed. As do I."

Liam stared at Velaria in disbelief before responding. "What of Leilyn? And Evellyn?"

"Leilyn is known to live freely in the Illumined Wood. Though blind and mute, she still lives. As for Evellyn, there are only rumors. I had hoped to find her here. But if she is not here, then she is most likely in Broid, center of the old Erynien Empire, now rising from its grave."

"That's where he said we were going." Liam glanced at the corpse of the shadow elf. "It's good to hear that Leilyn and Devlyn are safe."

"It's been a long time."

"It has. I remember you. I thought you were involved with them. That red hair of yours is unforgettable. A lot of them have that red hair."

"We can't stay. Let's leave this cursed place."

"Gladly. But I can barely walk. I'm not sure if I have the strength." Even as he spoke, he visibly weakened, shaking as the anger that had temporarily supported him faded.

"Let me help so we can get out of here then. Your absence won't remain unnoticed long." Velaria drew close to Liam and placed her hand softly against his chest. "Light save us. A shadow dwells over your heart. My wielding is not strong enough to remove it, but I know where we can go to take care of that. In the meantime, I can slow its progress, and perhaps weaken it."

Without waiting for Liam to respond, she wielded kiara. She surrendered herself to the erendinth as they filled her, moving the energy through her and into Liam. The erendinth interlaced themselves into the shadow covering his heart. Her training in healing wields was limited—she was an Azurelle, not a Crimsyn—but she hoped that even her limited knowledge would slow the shadow covering Liam's heart.

Velaria removed her palm from Liam and asked, "How do you feel?" She no longer held the erendinth and the world appeared dimmer; she felt less. But the memory remained. If only she could wield lumenys or any of the transcendental erendinth, perhaps she could have removed the entirety of the shadow. But, no one living was capable of that.

"Better. What did you do?"

"A healing of sorts. I can't correct it, but that should slow the process. If you're well enough, we need to leave."

BENEATH A TREE

In their room at the inn, Devlyn and Alex waited for Velaria's return from wherever she'd had to go. Alex sat at the writing desk in the corner of the room while Devlyn lay on his bed, thinking about all the things that had so recently come to pass.

From just outside the door to their room came a hushed shuffling, the noise of someone trying hard not to be heard. Alex grabbed the knife he had strapped to his calf, and Devlyn sat up to listen hard. The inn was a loud, boisterous place, making it peculiar that someone would attempt to go unnoticed down the hallway. Usually, the other guests tramped loudly past.

A barely audible tap came at last. With a quick glance at Alex who was standing now, knife concealed under his tunic but still held in his grip, Devlyn went to unlatch the door.

A stocky man in a faded brown jacket over a dirty shirt waited outside the door. There was nothing particularly noticeable about him. He had blond hair and blue eyes, very similar to Alex's, but that's where the resemblance stopped. Just as Devlyn opened his mouth, a quick gesture of the man's fingers hushed him. The man pushed his way into the room and softly closed the door behind. Even as he moved, he held out a coin to Devlyn, a motion that had Alex stepping forward, knife showing. In his other hand, he held a purse he'd taken out of his pocket, and with a hasty glance at Alex and the knife he held, the man stood quietly waiting while Devlyn examined the coin.

Devlyn stared at its curious features. The coin was gold, with a rich purple background effect that outlined golden figures, two of which looked like elves, although Devlyn remained skeptical. They stood naked, male and female, each holding a staff. An eagle in flight, also in gold, flew above them.

When it became clear that Devlyn had had a good look, the stranger held out his hand, and while he didn't get the coin's significance, Devlyn returned it to its owner. Once he had it back, the man produced a neatly folded piece of paper which he handed over to Devlyn. Devlyn took it and looked over at Alex who had relaxed a bit, but still held the knife. Devlyn unfolded the paper, which turned out to be a letter.

> *I have fled the city with your brother. There is much you and your cousin need to hear, but I cannot risk writing it. Trust the man who presents both the letter and coin. He will lead you to my location. If all goes well, I'll see you tomorrow. Do not delay.*

The letter was unsigned, but there was only one person who could have written it. Devlyn handed it to Alex and started to gather his belongings.

"She's in my head now! I could actually hear her voice and tone as I read it!" Alex grumbled as he also moved to pack his things.

When they were ready, the man, who still had not introduced himself—in fact, he hadn't even spoken—stopped in Velaria's room to retrieve her pack. *Now, how did he get the door unlocked?* Devlyn thought. They made their way down the stairs to find the common room just as crowded as on the previous night.

The innkeeper stood behind his counter keeping a close eye on his patrons. From his coin purse, the strange man they now followed produced an amount that Devlyn could not see. The innkeeper smiled gleefully at it and bowed at the man before turning and going about his business. They hurried out of the inn and toward the stables where they retrieved their horses, quickly saddling them, and loading their packs.

In almost no time, they had walked through the still-crowded streets leading their horses—the still-nameless man had taken charge of Velaria's—past the guards at the gate then mounted their horses before riding away on the road heading west into the hills.

As soon as they were far enough from the gate, the man turned to them as they rode alongside, and finally spoke.

"My name is Karl; I'm an observant of Vyoletryn and a son of Gneal. It's not often we work with an Azurelle; observants tend to stick to their own School. But I received explicit instruction from the Chair of Vyoletryn, herself."

"What in the Light's name are you talking about?" asked Alex.

"Did she not tell you that she's an ei'ana of the Azurelle School?"

"She must have conveniently forgotten to mention the Azurelle part."

"Be that as it is. We'd better quicken our pace; it won't be long before they find a dead shadow elf and their prisoner gone from the castle dungeons."

Devlyn and Alex looked at each other before Alex inquired, "What do you mean by a dead shadow elf?"

Before Karl had the chance to respond, a loud blast of horns in a series of three pierced the air from behind. It seemed that the discovery had been made.

"Shades!" cursed Karl, "Move!" They kicked their horses to a full gallop.

Karl kept them at a swift pace most of the afternoon until the light began to fade. They had left the road, and now found themselves riding through the muddy valleys well away from other travelers.

Karl had said nothing about their destination since they'd heard the horns; in fact, Karl hadn't said a word in hours and all Devlyn knew was that they headed west. When it was nearly dark, Karl eased their pace to a trot. Alex was clearly losing his patience with Karl, and it was no surprise when he rode past to ride abreast with him.

"Would you mind telling us where you're taking us?"

Karl glanced quickly at Alex before shifting his gaze back to the landscape, apparently searching for something. "At the moment, I hope to find us a safe camp for the night. We need to find some sort of shelter to protect us from the elements; a cave would be nice. As you can see, the sky is thick with heavy clouds and it won't be long before rain begins to fall again."

In no mood for a discussion on the matter, Alex didn't respond.

Karl brought them to a halt to get a better feel of their surroundings. Devlyn inspected the countryside to no avail. He really wasn't experienced enough in such things to locate a suitable shelter, since they'd just followed along to wherever Velaria had chosen from the time they'd left the abbey school. It now looked as if they would sleep in the open without protection. Soft sounds came from a short distance ahead; the sound of something or someone walking through the mud.

"Do you hear that?" asked Devlyn, his ears straining. He wished his hearing was as good as his eyesight.

"It's just the wind playing tricks on you," said Alex.

"The wind plays no such trick. Step back, and be quiet," whispered Karl, dismounting and drawing his sword. They waited in anticipation as the shuffling grew louder.

"Who's there?" came a voice from somewhere, leaving Karl disturbed that he could not see the speaker. "State who you are before my knife finds your gut!"

"Simple travelers. My name is Karl."

"And the other two?"

"I'm Devlyn, and this is my cousin, Alex."

"Simple travelers you say. You don't look like simple travelers; two humans and an elf before my very eyes. I don't know about you other two, but I've never come across a distrustful Son of Luminare, especially one of so noble a lineage. My name is Arbol."

When he spoke his name, his body became visible, forming from the tree behind him. As Arbol walked away from the tree and into the grey evening light, Devlyn was shocked to see a short stubby creature with a horn on each side of his brow and fur-covered legs. The creature's knees bent in the wrong direction, like the hind legs of a goat. The boys looked perplexedly at the creature standing before them.

"This, my friends, is a faun, and you should count yourselves fortunate to meet one," Karl said. "Few are granted such a privilege. As you saw, they are quite capable of remaining unseen."

"A faun? What's a faun? I've never heard of such a thing," said Alex.

"Aye, and you also think the elves dead, don't you?" replied Karl. Shifting his gaze to Arbol, he asked, "I'm curious, what business has a faun this far north? Surely, your kind don't cross the Cyrillean Pass frequently. As I recall, you tend to avoid the northern chill."

"It's not that we avoid the north. Although why anyone would want to live here is beyond me. But you're right; we rarely venture this far north. It just so happens that a settling was rumored to have traveled this way. There're enough poachers down in the south, it would be terrible indeed if some nasty human got their hands on him and tried to farm his vitality!"

"A...did you say settling?" asked Alex, bewildered. Devlyn tried not to be too obvious about staring at the creature.

"Well o'course I did. You haven't seen one, have you?" Arbol asked rather excitedly.

"No, well at least I don't think so. What is it?"

"You don't know about them? Oh, good. That means the northerners remain ignorant. Settlings are tree-like creatures. You could call them baby trees, but that wouldn't be right. Some of them are very old indeed, much older than us. They wander about until they find a comfortable place to settle, and once they do, they grow into a magnificent tree, a miervae. As a faun, it's become my responsibility to track down settlings roaming across unfriendly lands and guide them to a safe location to settle. But this one has been quite obstinate and continues to travel north. I've been tracking him for the better part of the month. Never has it taken me so long to catch up to one."

"Do settlings like to be around other trees?" asked Devlyn, quite interested.

"Well o'course they do. What kind of a question is that?"

"Have you thought about going to the Wooded Hills of Thellion?" Devlyn was somewhat taken aback by the faun's bluntness.

"Where do you think I'm heading? O'course I'm headed for those trees. Some of the sleepiest trees I've ever met! And to think, the Aldinari planted that wood!" Arbol began muttering, clearly done with the travelers.

"I hate to interrupt, but you wouldn't happen to know of some sort of shelter around here, would you? It's getting late, and we need to find something suitable," said Karl.

"There is a shelter, you'll have to squeeze through though; you're a bit bigger than myself. No place for the horses though; will they be all right outside?"

"They'll manage."

"Well, tie them up and come inside." Without saying another word, Arbol turned toward one of the trees and made his way through a hole between two of the roots that had grown above the soil.

"You two get inside. I'll take care of the horses," Karl didn't give them a chance to argue.

Devlyn dismounted, and approaching the roots, saw the hole that the faun had crawled through. Getting on his hands and knees, Devlyn easily crawled through the small opening into a tunnel that angled downward rather than straight across, and into a hollowed-out room at the end of the tunnel.

"Wow, how did you do this?" asked Devlyn as he stood and looked around.

"Me? It was the tree, o'course. It's not so old and sleepy as it seems."

"How could a tree do such a thing?"

"Well you certainly won't find out if you only ask me and not the trees!" said Arbol, just as Alex crawled through the entrance to the room beside him.

"Asking trees? Are all fauns this crazy?" Alex stood and walked around to inspect the small space.

Devlyn also took the opportunity to do likewise. The roots of the tree above formed a ceiling. The dirt walls showed many scrapes, some large, some smaller, and thinner.

"It looks like someone dug this place out. It must have been here for a long time. I didn't see any dirt outside."

Arbol ignored Alex's comment; instead he looked attentively at Devlyn. "You have curious eyes. How did you come across them?"

"Sorry? I don't understand."

"You know; how did you acquire such a green within your eyes? I don't recall any other elves with such a color. The stories I heard said they usually had silver eyes, although some were even gold! Magnificent eyes! But what I want to know is why do your eyes have the emerald color? Aside from us fauns and the centaurs, the only others who have the emerald eyes are the druids of Kweil Aitch. You don't seem intimate with the Wood."

"I was born with these eyes."

"Centaurs? Still roaming the woods, are they? I guess I could believe that, especially after everything that's already happened. But druids? What, tell me, are they?" Alex asked. Evidently, he'd been listening even as he checked out the room.

"Curious eyes indeed. They're changing. Did you know?" Arbol ignored Alex. "To what I can't say. But they're changing."

A sound from the hole indicated that Karl was joining them. As he entered, he instinctively looked about for dangers and finding none, he relaxed.

"Our thanks, Arbol, for inviting us into your sanctuary. I don't know of any Perriens who have been admitted. You truly honor us."

"You do *me* the honor. Could I offer you a meal?"

"Now you're talking," blurted out Alex. "What'd you make?"

Arbol had prepared a pot filled with cold water and herbs. To Devlyn, it looked and tasted like liquid bark and didn't seem like it could be filling. Alex slurped it quietly and Karl sipped it without commenting on the taste. Arbol, on the other hand, eagerly consumed every last drop. He seemed invigorated by it and ready for action.

"What will you do this evening?" he asked.

"Do?" asked Alex. "I plan on sleeping."

"Oh, that's right. Neither of your races are nocturnal, such a curious thing, if you ask me. Why anyone would want to waste the night away is beyond me. But such as it is, I must be on my way. There's a settling begging to be found, and I mean to do just that. I'll probably have to follow it all the way to the Wooded Hills of Thellion."

"You're leaving?" Alex asked, surprised.

"Well, o'course. I can't waste an entire night. Anyway, it was very nice to meet you. Stay as long as you wish, but the tree above might grow sleepy again and close its roots without my presence. But who's to say. You can try speaking with it, if you want." Arbol climbed up the hole and out of sight.

"What a weird creature. Are all fauns like that?" asked Alex.

"He's the first I've met. But, I imagine so," Karl replied. He took another look around the small space. "We should probably take the opportunity to rest and get a good night's sleep. I'll take the first watch. I'll wake one of you in a couple hours for the second." Karl crawled up through the hole, leaving Alex and Devlyn alone in the small underground clearing.

"I don't know about you, but I'm exhausted," Devlyn said and yawned deeply.

"I could sleep," Alex replied.

Removing his boots, Devlyn spread his blanket out on the ground and lay down. "Do you think Velaria's all right? Do you think she really has Liam with her?"

"That's what her note said." Alex yawned too. Before long, his eyes closed and his breathing steadied.

It took Devlyn a bit longer to doze off; recent events tumbled about in his mind, but mostly he thought about the brother he could not remember. It had been so long, and he had been only a toddler when Liam had been taken. Since Velaria had not mentioned his mother in the note, Devlyn feared the worst. Despite his thoughts and fears, he eventually drifted off to sleep.

They left early the following morning after Devlyn woke Karl and Alex just as the sun rose at the end of his shift. When they exited the tree cavern, Devlyn was certain that it had shrunk overnight. Maybe Arbol was right and the tree had also fallen asleep.

Karl led them west through the valleys, carefully avoiding the crest of the hills where they'd be easier to spot. It was midafternoon when they came to an abandoned farmhouse. Karl dismounted from Velaria's horse in front of the house and threw the reins over a limb on a nearby tree. Devlyn and Alex followed suit, and soon found themselves inside.

The place looked like it had been abandoned decades ago. There wasn't any furniture left, only a thick layer of dust and cobwebs.

Karl disappeared through a doorway, returning almost immediately. "It doesn't look like they've arrived yet. I hope they didn't run into any trouble. But, just in case they are being followed, we should ready ourselves. I have some extra swords lying around somewhere."

Neither Devlyn nor Alex had ever held a sword before since they were prohibited in the abbey school, swordsmanship not being a requirement.

"This is your place?" asked Alex, looking up at the cobwebs in the corners. Karl glared at him, and for a moment Devlyn wondered whether he intended to answer.

"It was my family's farm, but while I was a student at Gwilnor, Perrien soldiers arrived and took my family captive as traitors. I returned, too late, the Council had already charged them with treason for being sympathizers of the crown. Granted, that's exactly what they were, and in a different era, they would have been honored. Anyway, it didn't feel right to return, so I moved to Gneal, and kept vigil. Velaria and I decided this would be the best location to meet. It's far enough away from Gneal to not draw attention, but close enough to serve as a hideout if necessary."

"Do you really think they ran into trouble?"

"Hard to say. Velaria's pretty good at avoiding it, but that was no small feat she managed in Gneal. It won't go unnoticed. In any case, let me take you to the storeroom and find you some proper arms." With that,

Karl led Devlyn and Alex toward the rear of the house.

FROM THE SKY

Too anxious to sleep, Devlyn kept watch as Alex and Karl slept inside. They had only spent an hour or so learning the finer points of swordsmanship with no significant improvement. The other two had decided to take a rest, while Devlyn offered to keep watch until night fell, when they would eat dinner and take turns watching through the rest of the night. All remained calm, until about two hours into his shift, he spotted a figure soaring through the darkening sky.

Hoping that he might be again seeing the phoenix he'd last seen months back on his birthday, somehow, he knew otherwise. Even from this distance and with the fading light, Devlyn could see that whatever it was, it had a bluish quality about it. It also flew through the sky much more powerfully, not rising and falling as the phoenix had done as it danced through the sky. This figure remained steady on a level plane. The closer it drew, the larger it grew, much larger than any bird Devlyn had ever seen. Panic flared, and he rapped loudly on the door to signal Karl and Alex.

Karl shook off his grogginess as he came out followed by a bleary-eyed Alex holding a sword in a limp hand. Karl's quick assessment of the surrounding area didn't reveal the cause for Devlyn's alarm, but then he noticed that Devlyn stared at the sky, not the landscape. Now, he too saw the beast soaring toward them, and then descending. Catching sight of it too, Alex finally took a more aggressive stance with the sword he held.

It knows we're here. Devlyn's thoughts scrambled as he watched the flying figure grow larger the closer it neared.

"Quick, bring the spears; leave the bows, they won't do this beast any harm," said Karl.

"It's not what I think it is? Is it?" Devlyn was not at all eager for the answer.

"Depends; do you both think they too are only a myth? If you have any tricks up your sleeve, boy, now would be the time."

What does he mean by that? Devlyn stared blankly before picking up one of the spears Karl had propped against the farmhouse exterior wall earlier that night, the bows and swords left unattended.

"All right then, stand at the ready, both of you." Even as Karl barked out the order, Devlyn thought, *just what are we supposed to do?*

A few brief moments passed before the beast came lower and closer, then circled about the farmhouse before landing in front of them, shaking the ground beneath them. Devlyn's heart raced; he couldn't see straight, and his fatigue had finally caught up with him despite the added adrenaline.

The dark blue beast's sinuous neck stretched to its full length above them and its fiery eyes looked down on them. It folded its outstretched wings against its side, hardly diminishing its overall size.

Clutching his spear tightly, Devlyn could not believe his eyes; a dragon, that ferocious terrible beast from stories, stood before them. Karl and Alex stood on either side of him, and Devlyn wondered if their palms were as sweaty as his own. He waited for Karl's command to attack.

No command came, but behind the dragon's head a small dim light appeared. Devlyn tried to peer around the massive head and was overcome with relief at the familiar sight of Velaria. She slid down along the side of the great beast, and then she held a hand out toward the back of the dragon. Another body came into view and slid down although not as elegantly and regally as Velaria had done. The second rider faltered on landing and had to support himself against the dragon to stand. Velaria helped him shift his weight onto her and they turned toward the farmhouse.

As they approached, Devlyn recognized the man. Liam, older and gaunter than the young man in the portrait, stood before him. Devlyn's spear fell through his fingers to the ground with a thud and he moved toward his brother.

Liam pulled himself away from Velaria's support and walked a few slow difficult steps toward Devlyn before the brothers embraced, clinging to each other.

Liam's grip was surprisingly strong even as his emaciated ribs pushed against Devlyn's own.

"He said they had you." Liam managed as tears streamed from his eyes.

"Who?" Devlyn wiped a tear from his own eye.

"A shadow elf. He said they were bringing you to Gneal, to torture and kill you. Velaria came and the two fought." Liam spoke with difficulty. "I...I stabbed and killed him."

"They never had me." Devlyn realized only now that Lex had had a second purpose when visiting Cor'lera. "I'm here now and that shadow elf is dead and you're free."

"I am." They loosened their hold on one another, finally aware of the others who watched them, including the dragon, whose eyes clearly showed intelligence. It stood proudly above all present, as if awaiting an introduction.

"This, my friends, is one of the free blue dragons. She has long evaded the Erynien Empire, cut off from her kind. She and I have known each other for ten years. We have an uncanny way of showing up for each other when in need. When Liam and I fled Gneal, our pursuers quickly caught up. They surrounded us on all sides, led by General Lex; he somehow knew we'd be in Gneal. You can imagine their shock and my relief when Yelaris swooped out of the sky, breathing fire and forcing the soldiers back before flying us to safety. I have no doubt that Lex and his soldiers are still pursuing us; he won't stop until he has us in his grasp."

"How can we keep running from him? He has all the resources of Perrien behind him. What do we have?" asked Alex, clearly discouraged, a feeling shared by everyone present. "He's our uncle; perhaps if I talked with him I could convince him to leave us alone."

"Talking with Lex would achieve nothing." Velaria dismissed that possibility. "I can assure you, we have much support and more than Perrien does. We need to get away from here, to go to friendlier lands. The Cyrillean Pass is surely under heavy watch, so we will have to take another route, one that lies due west in the mountain city of Belin's Watch. It's not the capital of Evellion, but it's a strong city, and it's our gateway to allies. We can rest tonight, but tomorrow we'll have to continue our journey west, as quickly as we can."

Still in various states of relief, wonder, and apprehension, the company agreed it best to take the evening to relax. Alex started a small campfire so they'd all have room to sit nearby and stay warm. Devlyn was convinced that the dragon watched Alex with his flint. Karl and Velaria prepared a simple stew for dinner. Devlyn and Liam stayed close to each other, neither wanting to be far apart again. Liam's haggard face scared Devlyn; he had never seen a young man who looked like he was fifty and dying. Despite Liam's appearance, Devlyn was overjoyed that his brother was safe.

Devlyn ate his meal anxiously; he had many questions for his brother, the story he had been waiting to hear for eleven years, a desire stirred up by Velaria. When everyone finished eating and sat quietly lost in their thoughts, Devlyn finally found the courage to question Liam.

"Liam, what happened all those years ago at the Cor Inn?"

Liam stared into his lap, lost to his thoughts and nightmares. A moment passed before he looked up and said, "I expected you would ask about that night. But, no matter how much I prepare myself, it's still difficult to bring those memories back to the surface."

Devlyn thought it best to not press Liam. The group sat quietly around the fire, watching the flames dance toward the sky. Liam looked intently into the flames, his lips parting occasionally as if to speak.

"They came on a cold evening; it was still winter, but toward the end, during Lierenth, I think," he finally began. "We all sat in the living room. Da was reading while Evellyn sang to Leilyn and you. She was doing her best to cheer you up; you had been upset the entire evening. Leilyn was so good to you. She kept rubbing your back, telling you to not worry. Evellyn wasn't singing any words, just a tune; a lovely simple tune. She sang it to you frequently, especially when you were upset. But her singing had no effect that night. If I didn't know better, I'd swear you knew what was about to happen." Liam swallowed, his eyes intent on the ground between his feet, pausing before going on.

"A hard knock came from the door. I got up to answer it, but Evellyn urged me to step away. The knock came again. Da looked worried, with eyes only for Evellyn. They both knew who stood outside the door. How, I can't say, not even after all these years. Neither dared say. A third knock never came. A loud sound came from the other side of the door, and the wood bent and twisted before exploding inward. Shards shot everywhere; I still have a scar on my leg. Da met the soldiers first as they pushed in. He'd picked up one of the larger shards, and skillfully wielded it against the intruders. I picked up a shard myself and joined in the fight, but I was nowhere near as skilled as Da. He was caught in a heated fight with one of Cor'lera's town guards. Da had the advantage, and even managed to badly injure the guard, but once the guard was stabbed, he tore off his helm.

"Da was shocked; it was Lex, his own brother. Da stumbled back and dropped his weapon. Lex took advantage of that and somehow managed a frenzied attack. Next thing I saw, Da lay on the ground in a pool of his own blood. He just couldn't fight back once he saw his younger brother's face.

"You and Leilyn cried the entire time. When Da was killed, you let out such a wail that Lex had to cover his ears. I lost it at that point; I rushed in against our uncle. He was much stronger and easily pushed me out of the way. It was only then that I noticed what Evellyn was doing. The air itself seemed to flex around her. Beams of light appeared from her hands, fire ate up some of the soldiers. Her attention shifted to Lex when she saw that he and I were fighting. Her hands waved in the air and it looked as if she might bring the entire inn down, but then a high-pitched scream stopped everybody. Leilyn was on her knees, blood flowing from her eyes, and behind her stood a figure cloaked in shadow, his hands squeezing her temples.

"I had no idea at the time, but I later learned that it was a shadow elf. Evellyn quickly understood what that meant and stopped wielding. Once she did, the shadow elf shot a dark beam, pulsing with varying shadows, at Leilyn. Evellyn darted for her when Leilyn screamed again and the shadow elf told Evellyn that she'd live, so long as Evellyn cooperated. Lex came from behind and knocked her unconscious.

"One of the other soldiers hoisted her over his shoulders like a sack. Another bound me in iron and dragged me from the room. Leilyn managed to run out, and the last thing I saw there was you crying on top of Da's body. I pleaded to be left behind, to take care of you, but they hit me on the head and I passed out. I woke outside the walls of Cor'lera, in the middle of Evellyn's family, all of us in chains. They herded us like animals, forcing us into covered wagons, and from Cor'lera they took us to Gneal, mostly in the dark so we wouldn't be seen. I doubt anyone in Gneal knew of our arrival. We reached the castle in the dead of night and were taken directly to the dungeons. But then they took Evellyn away shortly after, perhaps a month later.

"For eleven years they left us down there, in despair and with no hope of getting out. They began to kill us off, oldest first, looking for something we supposedly knew. Shadow elves feed off the spirits of the living, and they fed off us, stealing our lives to prolong their own. The day that Velaria arrived, those of us still holding on were told that we were going to die that day. I watched as a shadow elf murdered the rest. It was awful. He described to me what he was doing, stealing their spirits to extend his own life." As Liam's story unfolded, Devlyn was appalled, but dared not interrupt with the questions that boiled within.

"He wasn't the first," Liam continued. "A series of shadow elves came through those dungeons over the years, leeching the life off us. I killed that last one. I would've killed the other one too, but Velaria stopped me." At that, Liam glared at Velaria. "Why did you stop me?"

Velaria smoothed her clothing and looked intently at Liam. "I know you don't want to hear this, but his ability to see us as we fled indicates that he was not a shadow elf. I'm not sure who he is, but the Shadow has not claimed him, nor has he claimed it."

"You didn't see what he did to us! He tortured us all. He was always in the castle. He was with those who had us cornered before Yelaris arrived. They probably wouldn't have caught up to us as fast if you had just let me kill him!"

"I'm not saying he's innocent. I have no doubt that he's a Cyndinari, but not a shadow elf, and it's obvious that his masters trust him enough to send him as an emissary to Gneal," Velaria said calmly. Devlyn noticed that Liam, lips pursed and eyes unblinking, had the same reaction to this explanation as Alex and himself. "That's now in the past; we should plan for tomorrow. It will be a long day, and we have to find a way to shake Lex and his soldiers off our trail."

"How do you intend to do that? It's not like we're in the best condition to outrun the Perrien Army."

"To start off, you're not strong enough to travel on horseback, Liam. That shadow elf did you quite a lot of harm. Yelaris has agreed to fly you to Ceurenyl. You'll be able to receive proper healing once you're there. The ei'ceuril at the Temple of Ceur should have no trouble with the shadow over your heart." It seemed that Liam wasn't pleased about being sent off.

"Don't worry, Yelaris will remain hidden in the clouds. No one will be the wiser about your flying off on a dragon."

"Hold on, why don't we let Lex and that lot see Yelaris?" Alex interrupted. Until then the others had sat quietly back, listening as the story unfolded.

Now, they all looked at Alex, trying to understand what he meant.

"Hear me out. We want to create a diversion to get them off our trail, right? Well, what better diversion than a dragon? She'll have the entire lot of them on her tail heading straight for the Laudien Mountains to the south."

"Alex, Yelaris has remained hidden her entire life. The blue dragons have only remained free by keeping themselves away from the general population. If one blue dragon is seen, it won't be long until the enemy realizes they still live and they will begin to hunt them down again."

"But they've already seen her," Alex persisted. No one had anything to say to that.

While they all sat pondering their options, a melodious call came from the sky, its maker hidden in the dark clouds. Yelaris responded instantly to the call and leapt from the ground, her wings extended to their full width, bearing her upward. A moment later, the thick clouds concealed her too.

Two lights shone dimly in the clouds, one constant, but the other flared and faded. Instinctively, Devlyn knew what flew above their heads. He strained his eyes, trying to see into the clouds themselves, and almost without noticing, his gaze shifted, and he found himself looking through another pair of eyes. The clouds surrounding him glowed in reds, purples, oranges, and golds. Yelaris soared beside him, sporadically breathing fire toward the heavens. The dragon circled about, before locking her gaze with Devlyn's.

They looked into each other, and he was aware of a language of sorts, terribly unfamiliar to him, but somehow understandable. The language from the dragon held power and an incredible wealth of wisdom, while the language emanating from the phoenix, from him, was musical, intricate beyond knowing, but above all, authoritative and ancient and impossible to ignore.

The connection ended as Yelaris broke away and swooped from the clouds, returning to the ground. Devlyn watched as the dragon descended beneath him and then his view shifted, and the dragon now rushed toward him on the ground. The lighted sky faded once again to night and a deep sense of loss filled him.

When he looked around at the others, Velaria stared back at him but it seemed as if she did not recognize him. Everyone else watched the dragon's descent.

Yelaris landed before Devlyn with a thud; she inclined her head to him, then tossed her big head back, roaring and breathing fire into the night sky. Velaria looked in astonishment at the dragon who looked back at her; somehow, Devlyn knew that they communicated with each other. A few moments passed in silence. Yelaris stood unmoving when Velaria spoke at last.

"She has agreed to allow herself to be seen; in fact, she insists. Yelaris will take Liam at daybreak to Ceurenyl. Once there, they'll go directly to the Temple of Ceur because once the knights see a dragon, they'll assume it is an attack from Erynor. Yelaris will grudgingly present herself as submissive to avoid conflict. Ideally, Yelaris would leave Liam at a location outside the city, avoiding any potential conflict, but Liam's condition requires immediate attention. The dragons were thought to have all gone over to the service of the Erynien Empire. Few of the ei'ana and ei'ceuril know about the free blue dragons. Present the letter I gave you to the first person you come across; it will explain everything and place you under my protection. My sister Azurelles know of the blue dragons, since we were once common companions before Erynor and his empire brought chaos to all the lands. Make sure you ask for Therril, he'll know how to communicate with Yelaris."

"So, it's decided? Will the rest ride west for Belin's Watch as planned?" asked Karl.

"Yes, we'll never break through the Cyrillean Pass unhindered. So, we must make our way through the mountains. The cities of Evellion are strong. We'll have safe passage there."

"Well, if that's the plan, we should get some sleep; tomorrow will be a long day for us all. You three have a fortnight's worth of travel ahead of you, and I can't imagine that a dragon ride is restful, especially if you are unwell. I need to get back to Gneal. I feel blind without my informants."

"You're not coming with us?" asked Devlyn.

"Absolutely not. My place is in Gneal, not some city hidden in the mountains surrounded by a bunch of Evellions. How many times must I remind you that I'm a son of Gneal? And besides, you're not the only lot requiring my attention. And I certainly can't stay here. Look at the ground, dragon tracks all over the place." Karl stood as he spoke and walked into the house. The rest soon rose to follow, leaving Yelaris to stand guard.

"Shouldn't we wait for the fire to go out?" Alex asked, watching the flames lick the air.

Without warning, Yelaris planted a single paw into the embers leaving nothing but wisps of smoke seeping from under her paw. Devlyn thought she was smirking.

The Watch

Devlyn stood apart from the others with Liam as the first lights of dawn peeped over the eastern horizon. They watched the sky shift, deep purple giving way to a light red with orange streaks.

"It won't be long now," said Devlyn, still surprised at how clear the morning sky was. The thick clouds from the previous days had finally dissolved, and soon the sun would warm the chilled land. Even the muddy ground somehow seemed less wet.

A speck of light peeked from behind a hill. Soon, the sun was wholly visible as it lifted into the sky, rich gold and casting its light onto everything below. The hills themselves seemed to bow before the rising sun, and the damp ground gleamed happily in its presence.

"Stay out of trouble. I only just found out that you are alive, safe, and well; I don't want that changing."

"We've managed to stay out of trouble so far."

"Still, be careful with these shadow elves. They're strong. If you're able, avoid them and don't confront them unless there's no other option."

Devlyn only nodded. They embraced once again, and when they released each other, Liam ruffled Devlyn's hair, to which Devlyn quickly responded by patting it down with both hands. The two laughed and walked back toward the others. "All set. Is Yelaris ready?"

"She is quite insistent on allowing herself to be seen for some reason," said Velaria sourly, while looking sharply at Devlyn. A low rolling sound came from Yelaris, smoke billowing from her nostrils.

"All right! If we're going to do this, we'd better get on with it. Don't forget to hand that note to the first person you meet in Ceurenyl."

Liam lifted his pack and walked toward Yelaris as she bent her front legs so he could climb up onto her back. Once he sat securely, Yelaris stood at her full, and imposing, height.

"We'll see each other soon. Stay away from those shadow elves, they mean business and they don't intend to talk it over," Liam called just as Yelaris sprang into the air.

The sight was incredible; she leapt with such velocity that it seemed unnatural for a creature of her size and weight to accomplish, but her wings pulled her ever upward, her deep blue scales gleaming in the sun. Yelaris and Liam soared high above their heads in a matter of seconds.

Devlyn, Alex, and Velaria stood gazing into the sky and watched the dragon become a speck that quickly disappeared.

In short order, the dilapidated farmhouse was behind them as they traveled west across Perrien, leaving Karl to return to Gneal.

Over a week had passed since Devlyn watched his brother fly away on a dragon. The weather remained moderate although rainy and the sun appeared on several more occasions, but never lasted long. A thick cover of clouds clutched Perrien and continued to threaten the northern country with more rain, growing ever thicker the closer they drew to the mountains. Luckily, even the rain could not prevent summer from beginning in a few weeks.

Only two days ago, the already dangerous terrain had become more severe; the hilly country gave way to rocks and crags; hills ended abruptly or started anew in cliffs. In the distance, the clouds touched the earth for much of the day, and when they finally cleared, Devlyn gaped in awe at the gargantuan size of the mountains in the distance. He'd always imagined that mountains rose twice as tall as the hills he was accustomed to, perhaps three times as high for some. But, the further west he traveled, the taller those peaks grew, on a scale that Devlyn had difficulty fathoming.

Devlyn had never seen a mountain before he left Cor'lera. Although he was aware of the Laudien Mountains in southern Parendior, there had never been a reason for him to venture beyond Cor'lera before, and Cor'lera was located in an area that boasted nothing higher than rolling hills. Even if he'd wanted to go look at a mountain, he doubted Abbot En-tiel would have permitted such an expedition, let alone have approved of this current one.

After another few days of travel, the enormous scale of the moun-tains became evident. The peaks disappeared into the clouds as the range stretched as far north and south as his eyes could see. Devlyn vaguely recalled one of the magisters speaking of Thellion's Wall, but he could not remember whether the magister referred to an actual wall, or to the western mountains that formed the border of that ancient kingdom. Either way, Devlyn could not imagine any wall more impregnable than the Vespi-en Mountains rising before his very eyes.

"We're only a few days from Belin's Watch. We should arrive by the beginning of the week, on Gwynthaen," Velaria said as they walked their horses through a craggy ravine.

There was no saying what day of the week it was. Devlyn knew they had left Gneal in the middle of the week on Ramaen but had no recol-lection of how many days had passed since they fled the city. Every day was much the same since Liam had disappeared into the sky with Yelaris. Wasn't Gwynthaen, the first of Dynenth, the official start of summer? Just the thought of the summer sun's warm rays falling on his skin excited him.

"It would be prudent if we talked about what occurred at the farm-house, before hungry ears listen to our every word." Velaria caught Devlyn unprepared at her approach. She had hardly spoken since they'd left the farmhouse behind shortly after Yelaris took flight.

"Wh…what do you mean?" Devlyn stuttered, having an idea that Velaria knew more about the phoenix than she was letting on.

"The others might not have noticed what flew above our heads and summoned Yelaris to the sky, but such a one is not unknown to me. I was reassured by the few who knew of its existence that it was indeed safe and near to you, but never have I been in its presence." For the first time since Devlyn met her, she truly looked concerned, motherly almost. "Do you understand what is happening to you? What will continue to happen?"

Devlyn's gaze fell to his hands, clenching the horse's reins, as if an answer might be there, although he doubted it. *There's no way she could know what happened that night and the time before we first met.* Although he did not understand it, he did feel something changing inside him. He did not want to admit it, let alone acknowledge it openly, and wished Alex would distract Velaria from asking questions better left unanswered.

"Nothing's happening to me," he said as he continued looking straight down the path ahead, hoping it would grow narrow so they could not ride beside each other and have a conversation. Concerned by what had occurred with the phoenix, Devlyn had secretly hoped that the first time had been no more than part of a dream, but since the night Yelaris had flown up to the light in the clouds, he could no longer deny it. He had been wide-awake when it had started, and he remained so as it ended.

"Light emanated from your eyes, dimly, mind you. No one else noticed. They were looking up and missed what took place beside them. The more this happens the more natural it will be and the more will your eyes take on the qualities of the phoenix's. You will not be able to hide it."

"Hide *what* exactly?" asked Devlyn, suddenly interested in what Velaria had to say; obviously, she understood what was happening to him and could explain.

"Few remember the golden eyes of Luminare, but there was a time when those eyes featured commonly among your ancestors, and they did not pass on through genes. Those bound to a phoenix were gifted with many blessings, but particularly their eyes, both the color and the acuity, the sharpness of vision. Those eyes have never belonged to any but the Luminari. If Erynor learns that those eyes have returned to the waking world, you will be in great danger, as he will be most eager to shut them indefinitely, as he did before." She stressed the words about danger, but Devlyn had stopped listening. He did not want to hear any more, and Velaria did not press.

"My eyes feel fine," he lied. He knew something was changing, but not its cause or what exactly was changing. He did think it odd that he had been the first to see the mountains, hours before the others had noticed.

His sight had always been sharper than Alex's, so that was no surprise, but Velaria knew the real reason behind his increasingly sharp vision.

"I'm just warning you to be careful when you allow it to happen. For anyone who cares to look, it will be obvious. The more often it happens, the more your eyes will change. It's unclear how long the process will take, since no one has observed it in over a thousand years, not since before Krysenthiel fell at the hands of the Erynien Empire." Still unwilling to hear more about his eyes, Devlyn dared not ask for details about Krysenthiel and its fall. He already had too much to think about, although he remembered Velaria mentioning something about the name being linked to golden flowers.

Finally, the path narrowed, the ascent steepened, and they had to dismount and lead their horses single file along the edge of the mountain's incline. The light from the sun did not linger along the eastern slopes of the Vespien Mountains. Long shadows crawled about their feet and soon hid much from their view.

Suddenly, Velaria stopped stiffly next to her horse, and motioned for Devlyn and Alex to remain silent with a flick of her hand. A moment passed, and she relaxed.

"Your eyes might be keener now, but your ears certainly are not." Devlyn thought she meant it as an insult.

"Tell me, have either of you met a dwarf before?"

"A dwarf? Aren't they those grouchy half-sized men that live underground while greedily hoarding gold and jewels? And don't they…" Alex trailed off as thick voices grew distinct and heavy footsteps came from the path ahead of them.

"I wouldn't go so far as grouchy and greedy; that's quite insulting coming from a human. And little? I could squash you with a single hand if I wanted. Look at you, nothing but skin and bones!" said one of the two heavily muscled dwarves who now stood squarely before them. They both wore leather jerkins and a leather helm.

"You're lucky that you travel with an ei'ana, and not just any, but Velaria Treyven of Azurelle; a blue dragon indeed! I'm not sure what you've done to deserve such company, boy, but it must be noble," the other dwarf added before he shifted his position toward Velaria. "We received word from a Vyoletryn observant, never mentioned his name. A pigeon brought the message just yesterday. Said things are hectic in Gneal, and to keep an eye out for you. Said you were coming this way, but not why." Devlyn picked up a shift in in the dwarf's tone as he mentioned the pigeon, as if for some reason the dwarf disliked such birds.

"Thank you, Gluhn. You are very kind indeed. May I introduce Devlyn and Alexander. We're heading with all haste for Everin. I fear we bear grim tidings."

"Well, you've never been held as a bearer of fortune. If you're in absolute haste, we'd better get to Belin's Watch tonight then," said Gluhn.

"I thought we were still a few days off," said Devlyn.

"On your own, you might be. Perhaps more. But the thing with dwarves is that these mountains are ours. We know them, and we've tunneled high and low. To any other eye, our tunnels go unnoticed, but through dwarven eyes, now that's something different. You see, elf, we dwarves, we don't just see the mountains with our eyes; our entire being sees them. Apparently, it's some kind of wielding that we do, minor, mind you, not enough to cause any harm, but inherent to our very essence; a gift from Mundi, the Dwarf Father. We learn from an early age to know the mountains."

"Hold on," said Alex. "I thought humans lived in Belin's Watch."

"That, they certainly do, but Belin's Watch belongs not only to those living above the mountain. From its very founding, it's belonged to both, human and dwarf alike." Devlyn thought he saw Gluhn push his chest out some as he spoke.

"Not to mention, Belin of Oern Schtam. Evellion himself named the new settlement after him in thanks for the help he offered in their time of need," said Velaria. Gluhn beamed at the mention of the famous dwarf and seemed quite pleased that an elf knew dwarven lore.

"Few can claim such nobility as he." Gluhn spoke reverently. "Belin actually went against the counsel of his own matriarch, who forbade him from opening his tunnels to any travelers. But Belin, he saw the need and sincerity of that people. Forgive me, I could speak all day and well into the night of Belin. Let's be on our way, the tunnel is just ahead."

Gluhn and the other dwarf, still silent and unnamed, led them through the narrow, rocky pass that grew narrower the further they walked. Several minutes passed before Gluhn approached the wall of a cliff to their side. Rubbing his hand against the coarse rock, he commented, "Isn't she grand?"

Devlyn and Alex looked at each other perplexedly; either they were losing it now, or this dwarf had lost it long ago.

"Why are you both looking at me like that? A shame you can't see as dwarves do."

"Is that the entrance to one of the tunnels?" asked Alex, slightly confused.

"Does this look like a blasted tunnel to you?" Gluhn banged roughly on the side of the rock with the head of his axe. The sound echoed off the rock walls reverberating along the narrow pass. "Nothing but solid stone behind this one!" The dwarf chuckled a bit before gesturing Devlyn and Alex to come close. Once they approached, he pointed down along the rock wall toward a split between two rocks.

Devlyn walked toward the split and was shocked to discover the depth behind. "It looks natural!"

"Of course, its natural! Why bother carving something that's already there? The inside however, now that's something entirely different. Go on, have a look." Gluhn urged them inside.

The rough edges of the weathered stone yielded to smooth surfaces. The roof of the tunnel was just as exact as the walls, yet it sloped upward, and the two sides came together in an arch. Devlyn focused his eyes into the depths of the tunnel and found that he could not see the end. He noticed that the tunnel curved on an incline, but he could not discern any transition within the stone itself.

They made their way slowly through the dim dwarven tunnel, always upward, but the straight lines of the tunnel were disorienting. After an hour of walking Alex blurted out, "Are we just walking through the mountains or will this tunnel ever intersect with another and take us to where we need to go!"

"You must forgive us, Master Alexander, but you see, these tunnels were designed for dwarves, not other races. As a result, they tend to put others on edge. As a matter of fact, they're supposed to, but we have not ceased changing direction since we first entered, ever so slightly mind you, but constantly. Our tunnels flow along the veins of the mountains and we simply follow those veins, deeper and deeper as we mine. Halls like this are nothing when compared to our schtams, but you won't be seeing the likes of those. They're sacred to us dwarves, and it is written in our laws that only a dwarf may enter a schtam." Gluhn continued to speak of the glories of the schtams and how they were restricted from the other races until the dim tunnel soon began to grow brighter. The tunnel broadened to a large gate carved from the very rock.

Devlyn stared at what appeared to be the world's strongest gate; both dwarves and humans stood guard, some on the ground level and others in archways above the open gate. The four guards on the ground level were fully armed. The dwarven guards wore no common color, unlike the human guards who wore colors of dark and light blue with a white eagle emblazoned on the left breast. Both dwarves and humans wore a pin on their right breast bearing a tower with a horizontal straight line cutting through the middle. "My lads and lady, I introduce you to the Watch of Belin. They have protected this city since its founding and have remained vigilant ever since."

The Watch looked sternly at the new arrivals coming from the depths of the tunnels. If not for their dwarven guide, Devlyn doubted they would appear half as friendly as they did, not that any of them smiled at their arrival. A dwarf, clearly in command of this gate, stepped forth to speak with Gluhn. They spoke in a language unfamiliar to Devlyn. Gluhn's face grew long as he spoke with his fellow dwarf, Velaria looking intently toward them. Clearly, she understood their foreign tongue.

"Your haste is no longer a mystery here," Gluhn said when he returned to the small company. "Perrien has massed its forces and marches for the Cyrillean Pass. You will be safe here, but you will meet only peril if you travel south to Everin. The crowned city of Evellion is strong and well protected, but there will be little hope of you leaving there. Surely by the time you reach the city it will be under siege, if you even manage to arrive."

"It's not Everin I fear for now, but that's not of consequence. We're fortunate you found us during your patrol; it appears we do not have the luxury of time. Is there a place that would welcome us for a night or two, to relax and regain our strength?" Velaria asked, her voice slightly heightened.

"If you intend on resting, there are plenty of inns, both below and above, whichever you prefer," said a human of the Watch.

"Above would be preferable, it will be nice to see the sky and breathe the fresh air."

"Beg your pardon, Ei'ana, but you'll be getting plenty of that if you intend on traveling to Everin. The mountain passes leading there have nothing but sky above," said a dwarf of the Watch.

"A shame. Gluhn, would you be willing to lead us to one of the inns?"

"Certainly." Gluhn turned his attention to the Watch of Belin. "We'll be on our way then. Thank you, Gorund, for the update on Perrien. You have our gratitude."

"Of course, Gluhn. Be well."

TUMBLE ALONG

Gluhn led them through the gate and down a few streets, but several blocks from the gate, Velaria took the lead, apparently quite familiar with the interweaving tunnels.

"Beg your pardon, Ei'ana, but where are you leading us? The main tunnel to the surface with the most inns is that way." Gluhn gestured in the opposite direction.

Belin's Watch was an impressive city. Every building stood no less than six stories, varying only because of the height of the tunnels. Carved directly from the mountain, no blocks were used to construct the impressive structures. The dwarves only hauled unneeded stone out of the excavated city. Despite the shorter height of the dwarves, each level rose twice as high as Devlyn was accustomed to; even their doors were wider.

"I just remembered that I have need to stop in on Oma. She insisted that I visit her the next time I found myself in Belin's Watch; I had almost forgotten." Velaria's embarrassment was evident.

"Oma? The old stone seer? Is this what you ei'ana call charity, visiting batty old women who press their ears to rocks all day?" asked Gluhn.

"Perhaps. But nonetheless, I did promise." Velaria did not slow her pace. They walked swiftly through the tunnels, their horses trailing behind. Unlike the tunnel outside the city, these tunnels had dozens of intersections and buildings carved into the mountain lined the walls.

Devlyn wondered whether the entire area was excavated, with only walls separating one room or tunnel from another. They passed both dwarves and humans alike as they went, but mostly dwarves. They all smiled and greeted them cheerfully. Devlyn was shocked to find that the dwarves had such a friendly temperament; he had heard the cruelest stories about them at the abbey school, among others, that they greedily hoarded their gold beneath their mountains.

After passing through several intersections, Velaria halted before a small entryway with a simple bronze door. As the group halted beside her, a grey-haired dwarf poked her head from an opened slit. She looked both ways cautiously with wide and penetrating eyes before quickly motioning them inside, including the horses, showing them where they could tether them in the entryway.

"Were you followed?" asked the dwarf. Velaria shook her head.

"Hmpf. I doubt that. These tunnels have seen strange characters lately; too many strangers in my opinion. But no one cares about that! We should have locked our gates to the outside years ago. But you know how humans are; always carelessly placing themselves in danger and worse, inviting it in!" The dwarf took them through the entryway to a corridor with a slight downward slope.

The corridor was dark and damp; it made Devlyn wonder when the last time fresh air blew through. The heavy moisture pressed against his skin.

"Strange company you travel with, Ei'ana. Where might I ask, did you pick these two up?"

"You should ask them yourself," Velaria replied.

"Hmph. Well, where are you two boys from? You look to be from Parendior, but it's difficult to place," said the dwarf. She stopped her descent to turn on them. "The stones would have me believe that you're both from eastern Parendior. Not that I doubt you've lived there, perhaps your whole brief life even, but I know you come from other lands. But where exactly might that be?" she inquired, poking Alex and Devlyn in their chests as she spoke.

"How could we be from somewhere other than where we were born?" asked Alex, his eyes drawn to where the finger the dwarf poked at his chest.

"How indeed? Let me ask you, how is marble found among granite? Hmm? Or limestone among obsidian?" The dwarf paused for a moment staring intently at Alex and Devlyn. "You don't know, do you. Well, I'll tell you. Someone puts it there. Did you expect it to move there on its own? That the granite would form the marble itself? Hmph. Not the brightest of companions. Have the Azurelles lowered their standards?"

"Sorry, but who are you?" asked Devlyn.

"Ah, what a question. I suppose my name will suffice your curiosity; Oma. The last of a dying breed. Dwarves are no longer interested in listening to the stones, hmph. You see, stones are very observant, they see everything, and most importantly, they endure. Can you not feel them pressing in on you? Entering your skin, your very bones? That is not moisture you feel in the air boy, it's the stones pressing against you; they feel you. These stones tell me more about you than you could imagine, Devlyn. Before you so much as knocked on my door, I knew you had arrived in Belin's Watch, making your way for my home. I know you traveled across all of Perrien. I even know about the bridge you crossed. I ask, did that stone seem familiar to you? Well, Devlyn, son of Evellyn? Hmm? What of you, Alexander? I ask, have you crossed that bridge before? Was the stone warm beneath your feet?"

Not waiting for their answers, Oma quickly turned and continued her descent through the tunnel. Devlyn stood still, both surprised by what Oma already knew and had shared and curious about what more she knew but had left unsaid.

"Come on, Dev." Alex placed his hand on Devlyn's back, urging him forward. "She's just a crazy old bat, she probably just guessed all of that or had someone tell her before we got here. That bridge was oddly warm. You noticed it, right?"

Devlyn didn't answer; he couldn't recall whether he'd noticed the temperature of the stone.

The curving corridor opened at last to a cavern far below the entryway and unlike the rest of the city above. There, smooth tunnels had been carved out with precise cuts; this cavern looked natural, completely unrefined, its rocky walls sloping upward to meet at the center of the cavern above their heads. A young dwarf sat below the center point of the cavern facing a large stone floating before his eyes. The sight disturbed Velaria; she looked at the dwarf and then to Oma, frowning.

"Calm down, Ei'ana, he's weak. Even if he does reach his potential, he won't be able to do more than what he's doing now." Oma was unconcerned. "Besides, he actually shows an interest in stones."

"And how long do you expect yourself capable of controlling him? Even if he is weak, your strength will not be enough to confine him. You know the risks with kien wielders."

"Yes, yes, yes. Now if you want to scold me over him, have your fun, but that won't get you any closer to Everin, will it now? As I hear, you intend to race an army and raise the alarm. Or…" Oma paused. "Is there another reason you wish to reach Everin in all haste? Something you're not letting Oma know. Is that not your destination? You can only hide it for so long, my dear Azurelle."

"You are not the only one still capable of listening to the stones. Need I remind you of the schtams to the south."

"Do not speak of those abominations. They are lost to us dwarves. There is no schtam south of the Gap!" cried Oma. Devlyn had not noticed the passion that stirred in her before, and he did not know why she felt so strongly now. "Hmph. As it is, they have no power in this cavern."

"So long as you remain here, they have no power here. Forgive me, but I cannot risk speaking about it aloud. Only within the Temple of Ceur would I dare speak what I cannot here."

Oma glared at Velaria suspiciously and gave a quick nod. "Very well. If it's Everin you must get to, you might as well arrive as fast as possible. How much rest do you require?"

Except for the glowing veins shining from the walls, darkness sheathed the cavern. Devlyn hadn't noticed the veins earlier, but now that he saw them, he couldn't understand how he had overlooked them before. They covered the entire cavern, interlacing at various points and in varying thicknesses. Nearby, the others began to stir, and soon everyone had gathered their belongings and stuffed their blankets in their packs.

"Is there a reason why we have to do this so early? Or is it late still?" asked Alex between yawns. It was impossible to tell the time of day in here.

"Quiet, boy!" snapped Oma. "If you intend on gabbing all the way to Everin, don't think I won't leave you here."

"All right, all right."

"I said quiet!"

Alex kept his mouth closed and hoisted his pack onto his back.

"Now, the fastest route to Everin is through the Great Dwarven Tunnel. You know, the one that doesn't exist, the one that doesn't connect every schtam in the Vespien and Laudien Mountains. However, under no circumstances are any allowed to pass through it unless they be a dwarf."

While Devlyn and Alex looked at Oma with curiosity, Velaria remained unconcerned.

"How do you expect to get them all the way to Everin undetected?" asked Gluhn who clearly disapproved of Oma's willingness to allow others into the Great Dwarven Tunnel, let alone speak of it.

"Hmph. If you could be patient, I would tell you. As it turns out, stone seers have a way of traveling swiftly through the tunnels; my mother passed it on to me, and her mother to her and so on and so forth. Now, follow me and be quiet." Oma led the way from the cavern into a small tunnel with a steep decline. "Curious Gluhn, you will have the honor of going first." Oma was barcly audible, yet no less stern. Previously, Devlyn hadn't thought her capable of speaking softly; she sounded almost pleasant.

With a long-suffering look, Gluhn walked toward her, and then shock took over when the stone he stood on began to climb up his feet.

"Don't scream."

The stone stretched up his small stout body, engulfing him entirely. The shape of the stone shifted, transforming into a round form resembling a large rock.

"Well, one's done. You're next, Alex."

Before he could reply, small rocks crawled up his legs. A look of horror crossed his face, disappearing with him into the stone, just another boulder. Oma smirked mischievously.

Without warning, Devlyn felt small rocks crawl up his own legs, the sensation taking him by surprise as they moved up his legs, then up his midsection to his chest before covering all but his head. He just had time to take a deep breath before the rocks covered his mouth, but to his surprise, he could still breathe easily. He was forced to a fetal position and imagined he too took on the shape of a boulder like the others.

Just as he began to feel restless, he began to roll, slowly at first and just as dizziness took over, the pace quickened, and he soon lost all track of direction. He could not guess the speed at which he rolled, nor did he want to know.

Minutes turned into hours and the hours soon became days. All sense of time had vanished. He passed into an unsettled slumber. He could not say whether he ever truly slept or whether he just lost consciousness. The incessant spinning finally began to slow, and as it did, he understood the extent of his disorientation. He grew nauseous, but just when he thought he might be sick, the rocks released their grasp and he found himself in a fetal position on the ground, clutching his knees to his chest and shaking violently.

It still felt as though he was spinning. His body might have stopped, but his mind certainly had not.

"It's jolting, but please refrain from making noise; silence is still necessary," whispered Oma, as she glanced to Alex. "Rest for a moment, but we must move quickly. Anyone can see us here. I assume, Velaria, that you don't want anyone to know you've entered the city."

Velaria managed a weak nod. Still, she looked in better condition than Alex. His face had turned a shade of green that Devlyn had never seen before, and his eyes, set deep into their sockets, stared at nothing. Since Devlyn felt just as Alex looked, he imagined his own appearance was no better.

Oma did let them rest briefly, but all too soon, she gestured them to stand. As she led the company through a small tunnel leading from the larger one, Devlyn took a brief dizzying glance back and was astounded.

Yelaris would easily fly through the tunnel they were leaving behind! Only at the base did the wall form an angle with the floor. From there, the walls stretched up and joined in an arch high overhead. The walls were laced with thick gold and silver veins, pulsing with light, and flowing through the mountain like a river. The veins stretched from the polished floor, seeming to have roots even thicker than what was visible beneath their feet. He stood frozen in awe at what must be one of the wonders of the world.

But Oma had no intention of being discovered by another dwarf and had pressed on with the others. Devlyn had fallen behind and although he walked quickly to catch up, he soon found himself lost. With intersections at every fifty paces, the choice of which tunnel to take was confusing. Before long, doors cut into either side of the walls appeared.

Soon after coming across the doors, Devlyn heard voices ahead. Hopeful that he'd managed to catch up, he drew closer only to discover that the voices did not belong to his friends. These voices spoke quickly and again in an unfamiliar language, similar to the language spoken by Gluhn back in Belin's Watch. He listened to the strange guttural sounds.

Rather than approach the unknown dwarves, he turned down another tunnel and was pleased to find it was on an incline. Slowly walking up, Devlyn was caught unprepared when someone tugged his cloak from behind.

"Are you lost, elf?" The voice was gruff yet gentler than other dwarven voices he'd heard so far. Devlyn turned to find a dwarf standing behind him, arms crossed and not at all pleased.

"Sorry, I've never been down here before. I thought I would be able to find my way out, but one turn led to another," stammered Devlyn, speaking honestly. "Do you know the way out?"

"Course I do. I'm Uon of Glyol Schtam. What's your name? I've never seen you in Everin before; granted, I don't go up to the surface very often."

"Devlyn."

"I'm not one to ask an elf his business, but you're a long way from Lucillia. Anyway, follow me. You were on the right path; I'll give you that much. Close to the castle we are, I suspect that's where you're coming from. I hear the king has been in an off mood lately, anxious for at least the last month and worse this past week. Word came that Perrien is marching its army south for the Cyrillean Pass."

"Do you think they intend war?"

"Never knew an army that marched just for the fun of it. Soldiers cost coin. The longer they march, the more coin owed. King Amry might be on the younger side, but he's definitely able. He's his father's son, that's for certain. He will meet Perrien in battle if they so choose."

Devlyn followed Uon upward through the tunnel and was soon greeted by a blinding light, forcing him to rub the spots dancing before his eyes. Devlyn looked over his shoulder with a fleeting hope of seeing Alex and the others appear behind him, knowing he could not ask Uon about them. A single elf was suspicious enough.

EVERIN

Devlyn's eyes adjusted to the light and as they did, mountains filled his sight stretching toward the heavens in every direction, cradling the city he had emerged in. A grand castle clung along the edge of the mountain closest to him. White stone rushed high above, forming strong walls as buttresses and spires tested their limits in piercing the sky. Slender towers loomed high over the city.

This must be the mighty castle of Everin and Devlyn could not imagine any surpassing it in strength or grandeur. He started toward the road leading to it with Uon following closely behind and stopped just a few paces from the tunnel when an affectionate voice called out.

"Uon! So wonderful to see you. What brings you from the Dwarven Hall?" A beautiful blue-eyed woman with flowing blond hair, accompanied by two guards stood nearby. Her blue lace and silk gown complemented her eyes, and a heavy shawl of white fur kept her warm. Struck by her appearance, Devlyn missed the golden diadem crested with diamonds and sapphires resting on her brow.

"Your Majesty." Uon bowed with a flourish in greeting. "Devlyn, here, wandered into the Hall and found himself lost in the tunnels below." The queen looked at Devlyn with interest.

"We've been expecting a Devlyn for quite some time now," she said, drawing closer and briefly placing her hand on his cheek. "You certainly have a way of bumping into people, Uon. Would you care to join Devlyn and myself for a cup of tea?"

"Your Majesty is too polite; however, my presence is required in the

Hall. You'll have to forgive me. The Matriarch of Glyol Schtam is visiting."

"Then I will accept your apologies, dear Uon. You'll have to invite me to the Hall on your leisure."

"Of course, Your Majesty. Good day." Uon again bowed with a flourish. "I enjoyed meeting you, Devlyn; I hope our paths cross again." Uon turned and descended into the tunnels beneath the ground.

The queen turned from the tunnel entrance and beckoned Devlyn to follow. "We have not met before, and from the look on your face when Uon addressed me, I doubt you knew that I am Queen Lara. You have come from Cor'lera?"

"Well, yes. But, how did you know?"

"We can discuss that over tea; there are too many ears out here in the cold." Queen Lara led the way toward the castle, saying no more. At the castle gates, the guards parted to allow them entrance.

Devlyn was awed by his first sight of the castle's interior. A soft blue rug lay beneath their feet. White marble walls stretched high, their windows paned with colored glass depicting beautiful blue flowers. Queen Lara led him toward massive wooden doors on the far side of the entrance where two more guards stood at attention, opening the doors when they drew near.

The soft blue rug and the same white marble walls streaked with blue veins continued. Here, beautiful clear windows overlooked a courtyard of lovely flowers on the left; to the right hung portraits of men and women that Devlyn assumed were previous monarchs of Evellion.

The queen ignored them as she strolled through with her chin held high. She led him through several other corridors, some not as ornate as the first, but still impressive. They reached a broad stair and climbed four flights before continuing down another corridor.

Devlyn was beginning to think they would never reach their destination when she at last paused before a wooden door to their right.

The two guards that had accompanied them through the castle now remained posted by the door as he followed the queen into a room filled with blues of every shade; even the light blue marble walls had darker blue veins laced through. Devlyn noticed a familiar severe curve in the walls. "Are we in one of the towers?"

The queen chuckled lightly. "We are. Have you been in one before?"

"My bedroom back in Cor'lera was in the upper room of the tower at the abbey school, more of an attic, really."

"It must have been cold in that room. If you ignore the elevation of Everin, we're comparatively low in this tower. The higher you go, the cooler it is. Would you like to look out on the city? The window is just over there, and it's a spectacular view." The queen gestured to the far side of the circular room.

Devlyn made his way across, walking between blue cushioned couches and other finely made furniture. The window stood just behind the writing desk. From there, he gazed out onto the city of Everin, surprised by both how high above the city he was and the vast size of the city sprawling below. Buildings of white marble or limestone filled the valley, their roofs still showing signs of snow on top of the grey slate shingles.

"Oh my…" was all he could manage.

Despite their altitude, he still could not see past the mountains surrounding the city. After getting his fill, he turned and stubbed his toe on the writing desk as he walked toward the couch where Queen Lara sat. Gasping and biting off a curse, he hopped on one foot, waiting for the shock to subside. "Is that eldin wood or something?" he asked through gritted teeth and quick breaths.

"It is, but the proper name is stellendi wood; it's from the Eldin Wood. I did not expect you to be familiar with it."

"I had no idea what it was until Velaria told me about it," said Devlyn, suddenly regretting mentioning Velaria. The queen noticed the slip and smiled softly.

"No reason to regret speaking of Velaria. I know her well. She is how I knew of you and from where you came. She asked me to anticipate her arrival, but I must say, I did not expect to find you without her."

"Yeah, I got sidetracked and fell behind them. Before I knew it, the whole lot of them had disappeared." Devlyn was still embarrassed about that, although it seemed to have turned out well.

"I have no idea how she manages to always get her way. To have the dwarves allow her admittance to that tunnel of theirs is quite the feat." The queen smiled at his obvious shock. "What else would you be doing down in those tunnels? Besides, if you had entered the city through any of our tunnels I would have known before you walked more than two blocks. I suppose I'll have to post some guards to watch for Velaria. Now tell me, have you really seen the phoenix? Velaria set her letter in riddle, so I had difficulty deciphering it." Queen Lara seemed excited and stared directly into his eyes.

Remembering Velaria's words about his eyes, he shifted his attention to the light blue carpet. "I saw something very bright fly in the sky."

"Anaweh save us! You connected with it!"

Confused, Devlyn said faintly, "I had no control over it—it just happened."

"The evidence is in your eyes as I'm sure Velaria has told you. Have you witnessed the night as day? The legends of the Phaedryn all speak of the brightness seen through the phoenix's eyes."

Devlyn nodded.

"Can you wield kien? Legend says that most who bound with a phoenix were elya."

"Hold on, wielding? Wielding is dangerous for men. The stories about them wielding all end in catastrophe. It's bad enough that women wielders can do what they can. Besides, I've never wielded." Devlyn felt more and more anxious by the second. He shifted his gaze to the carpet and away from the queen who seemed amused. An awkward moment passed and Devlyn returned his gaze to her.

"Out of curiosity, what's a Phaedryn and…did you say elya?"

Before she could answer, a knock came at the door and it opened. A guard handed a parchment to the queen who took a quick glance at it.

"Thank you, Sir Vorin," she responded before turning again to Devlyn, "You'll have to excuse me. It seems that your disappearance has been noted. This is from Velaria requesting my aid in searching for you. Please wait here while I go to her. I should not be long." The queen followed the guard out leaving Devlyn alone in the circular room.

Rather than sit and ponder everything he'd just heard, he returned to the window, his heart racing from another discussion about wielding and his supposed ability. The room felt stuffy, so he eased the window open and allowed the cool wind to wash across his face. He felt the air press against him and spiral around his entire body. *What is this queen talking about? Not only is she claiming I can wield, but that I'm an elya, whatever that is. If that's true, why would Velaria hide something like that? And what in the Light's name is a Phaedryn?* Devlyn fretted, and the more he thought, the angrier he grew. He felt that he'd been duped into some ei'ana scheme, and frustration grew over how much he still did not know. *Alex was right all along!*

The wind grew stronger; Devlyn felt it. More than felt it, oddly enough, he sensed it. An impulse from within beckoned him to force himself on the air. From the core of his being he pressed himself against it, gently at first, and then more and more firmly, his emotions fueling the push. The wind no longer blew *against* him. Now, it moved over him, responded to his intention, and although his feet never left the ground, he was in the air, directing it, changing its course, and sending it out into the open sky; he felt it flow up high, sensed a bird fly through it. Now he directed it downward toward the city and blew through a crowd of people making them clutch their cloaks in the unexpected rush of wind.

Suddenly, the door on the other side of the room opened. Startled, his attention shifted behind him and the wind shot through the window and crashed against the door slamming it with a loud thud.

Devlyn quickly turned away from the window and stared in disbelief. The neat and orderly room he had turned his back on now lay in complete disarray. Only the writing desk of stellendi wood stood untouched. Everything else, furniture, the parchment that had been on the desktop, even heavy decorative pieces, lay piled up across the far side of the room.

The door was again pushed open, this time with more effort and by one of the guards.

"What is wrong with you? First you run off and now you're slamming doors in my face!" yelled an irate Alex, head tilted back, blood streaming from both nostrils. "My nose is crushed thanks to you. And what have you done to this room?"

Behind Alex stood Velaria and Queen Lara, both focused on Devlyn across the room, and apparently unconcerned about Alex and the blood on his face.

"Lara, what have you told him?" Velaria asked.

"Honestly, nothing I thought you hadn't already," she replied.

"Devlyn, how do you feel? Do you know what happened?" asked Velaria.

"I…I don't know. One moment the wind was blowing against my face…the next I was moving it about…I was in it," stuttered Devlyn. "What happened to me?"

"It's not a matter of what happened to you, but rather what you did. Devlyn, has this ever happened before? Have you ever noticed the air in that way?" asked Velaria, concern thick in her voice as she sidestepped the overturned furniture toward him.

"Never like that. Sure, I've noticed it before, but I've never controlled it. Somehow, I became part of it, and I could make it go where I wanted it to. I didn't mean for it to turn inside; I didn't even mean to control it. It's just…I heard the door and was startled. And before I knew it, the air came back into the room and slammed against the door," he explained, a little panicked, backing away from Velaria.

"It's all right, please calm down." Queen Lara came up beside Velaria.

"All right!" said Alex rather nasally, pointing to his bloody nose. "Does this look all right?"

Velaria went over to him and placed her hand on his brow. Devlyn saw a faint glow around her hand as she held it there for a few seconds. When she removed her hand, Alex touched his nose. He massaged it gently, a look of suspicion changing swiftly to surprise.

"What did you do?" Alex spoke normally again.

"I healed it. A simple thing really, considering," Velaria replied, then shifted her attention back to Devlyn. "Did you see the glow?"

"Yes. It came from your palm. Does that always happen?" Adrenaline flowed through his veins and he could feel the energy as it rushed through him, building.

"Kien and kiara wielders can see the erendinth, especially when they're wielding or have just wielded, as in your case. Some have a keener sight than others. When any erendinth is wielded, it becomes visible and is easily seen by those who can also wield. You'll learn more about this later, but here is not the place."

Between the energy flowing inside, and the shock of hearing that he was a wielder since he had not only seen the glow, he had also controlled the wind, Devlyn was scared. All the stories he had heard about wielders, especially men wielding, said that it was dangerous. All this time, everyone in the abbey school and in Cor'lera had been in danger from him. He could have unintentionally burned the village to the ground!

"Let's relocate to another room. I'll have this one cleaned and put back in order in the meantime. I wager you could all use a meal as well. It's almost midday after all." The queen led them out of the disordered room.

The private dining room was paneled in light wood with blue window hangings draped from floor to ceiling. They sat at a large oval dining table in the center of the room laden with food of every sort. Grapes spilled over their bowls onto the table cloth while roasted chicken and diced potatoes sat neatly piled on their platters.

Shortly following their arrival, and after Alex filled his plate, the king entered, accompanied by four knights, bringing everyone to their feet. Like Queen Lara, the king was clad in blues, although his clothing tended to have a darker hue. The left breast of his tunic had an embroidered white eagle in flight.

"When I requested a private dining room, everyone thought it clever and admirable," he said, intense blue eyes taking in everyone in the room. "Little did I know then of the definition of a king's privacy." A smile appeared in the middle of his short-cropped beard, directed mostly toward his wife. The knights standing behind shared a hushed chuckle. "Would you care to introduce your guests, my queen?" The king took his seat at the head of the table and began to fill his plate, signaling the others to return to their seats.

"Certainly, Amry, my love. You have met Velaria before, since she has been our guest on several occasions, never long enough in my opinion. These young men are from Cor'lera, Alexander Vaerin and Devlyn Telvin."

Devlyn thought she lingered a bit on Alex's family name, and also noticed that the king raised an eyebrow at it.

"Cor'lera? I've never met anyone from there before. Nor have I heard of someone traveling from there. Devlyn you say? Peculiar name if you ask me. The suffix is common I'm told among the Luminari, but I'm also told it hasn't been used since Arenthyl fell." The king looked intently at Devlyn.

"As I understand it, everyone in my mother's family shared that suffix. It's not uncommon in Cor'lera," Devlyn said, even as he puzzled over what Arenthyl was or how it fell. *Perhaps it's some famous statue that toppled*, he thought, not wanting to reveal his ignorance on the topic.

King Amry nodded, then returned his focus to his queen.

"We've received troubling news from Cyril. It looks like Perrien wasn't heading immediately for the pass; their target was Cyril. Several scouts have not returned to the city, but those who did return reported siege engines in the distance. The ones who have not yet returned are feared either dead or captured. Eagles have been flying nonstop between here and there with messages; other birds attacked the pigeons midflight."

The room fell quiet; no one knew how to respond.

"Oh, Amry," Queen Lara walked to her husband and placed her arms around his neck. "Cyril is strong, it can withstand any siege and there's enough provisions to last them an entire year if necessary. Your uncle won't allow harm to fall on his city. After all, the Duke has been expecting Perrien's aggression and has taken proper preparations."

"What does that base Council think it's doing? Never have they dared attack us, why so bold all of a sudden. Wasn't Parendior enough to quench their greed?" The king's voice rose with every word.

"They do not move on their own accord. Perrien has always been a cowardly country, jealous of their stronger neighbors, and even more so with this Council. It was long ago that Perrien first desired to see Evellion fall at their hands. However, they have also known that they could not act alone. They require an ally, a strong one to bring the White Eagle to his knees," said Velaria.

"Are you suggesting that Parendior provided the required strength?" the king asked.

"Parendians will not fight for Perrien. They have strength enough, but they are a farming folk, and they are still unaware that their combined numbers are powerful. The Council is content to let it be so, as long as they continue to produce their wares, especially the Cor'leran Blue." Velaria paused to allow King Amry to ponder other possibilities before continuing. "An ancient foe has been sleeping, regaining his strength unseen all the while. Where he has been hiding is unclear, but what is clear, is that he no longer sleeps, nor will he continue to hide. He stirs, testing his strength, and biding his time as he forges anew his empire."

The king did not doubt her. "You refer to Erynor. I understood that he died over a thousand years ago. Do we know when or how he returned?"

"That is uncertain, but we can assume that he was involved with deposing the Perrien monarchy a century ago followed by Perrien's bold assertion over Parendior shortly after. But no, he did not die all those years ago, and he is rebuilding his empire from Broid. I assure you, Perrien moves only at his behest. We can also assume that shadow elves move with his forces."

"What of the Deathless?"

"There's been no sightings of the Deurghol."

"Very well. Do you intend to remain in Everin?"

"We are needed elsewhere."

"Of course. Thank you for your counsel. You must excuse me,

Ei'ana, I must inform my generals." King Amry rose from the table and strode out taking his knights with him.

The room remained quiet. Alex was the only one still eating. Queen Lara turned to Velaria.

"When do you intend to leave?"

"The sooner the better. The road between here and Ceurenyl is dangerous enough. The longer we wait, the more likely will we run into trouble. Besides, Devlyn must begin his studies at Gwilnor; it's the safest place for him. If he truly is an elya, we'll have no need to worry about him harming anyone or himself."

Alex's head shot up and he glared at Velaria, then quickly stared at Devlyn with a look that clearly expressed how right he had been about her from the beginning. She had never mentioned she was taking them to another school.

"Can I offer any aid; provisions perhaps?" asked the queen.

"They would be most welcome; as you know, we left the horses at Belin's Watch. It would be safest to remain west of the Eindol River for as long as possible, perhaps as far south as Wexly. Once we cross the Eindol, we must be well-rested since we will need to push our mounts as hard as possible. It's not a short journey."

"You do have a talent for saying what you need without ever asking for it," Queen Lara said with an admiring smile. "Three swift horses should be easy enough to spare. And as it happens, a trader from Wexly is taking a barge south at the end of this week, on Saraen. I will have someone look into passage for you with him. In the meantime, I will have someone show you to the guest quarters. I believe you will find them adequate. I will also inform the castle guard, so that you can come and go from the grounds as you wish." She rose, bade them farewell, and went out to deliver orders to the staff.

"And she says I'm talented at getting what I want. You two might as well take in the city; it truly is magnificent. It was mostly built at the same time, all the buildings constructed in the same style with the same materials. But, before you go exploring, it would be best if Devlyn and I talked about what happened earlier. I'll tell you what I can but know that it won't entirely satisfy you."

"What am I supposed to do in the meantime?" Alex asked around a mouth full of food.

"You're more than welcome to remain here and continue eating, or you can rest for a while in your room. Just ask any of the guards where to go." Nodding, Alex stuffed another forkload into his mouth.

"Devlyn, Queen Lara mentioned an adequate space not far from here, where we can speak privately." Without another word, she stood and headed for the door.

Devlyn shared a quick look with his cousin before following Velaria out the door and down the corridor.

DISCOVERIES

Velaria led Devlyn to a spacious room that opened onto a quaint garden. A fire roared in the hearth to keep the chill from passing through the three arched doors, open and allowing a frosty breeze entrance. Devlyn had just become used to the warm summer sun on the lower elevation, but here in the Vespien Mountains, it was far too cold for Dynenth. Not even Cor'lera held onto winter's grasp this far past Delenth. But here, despite the month, powdery snow still covered the mountain peaks, and frigid air filled his lungs.

"Why are the doors open if they're trying to warm the room with a fire?" asked Devlyn, looking to the doors. *Waste of firewood.* He could hear a soft trickle of water and assumed there was a fountain in the garden.

"Don't pay too much mind to it. That should be the least of your concerns at present." Velaria paused to spare a look out the doors before turning her gaze to the fireplace. Closing her eyes, she held her arms out before her, palms up, and waved them toward the fire in the hearth. Not a second later, the flame divided in two; one remained in the hearth, while the other dashed through the air toward Velaria. It spun and twirled about her before resting above the open palm of her hand.

"When the elves first settled in their respective Skylands, for reasons now forgotten, they became Guardians of the Four Winds. Our people went to four separate Skylands, and as the lands became our home, they defined us from each other, no longer one people. Legend claims that the North Wind is protected by the elves of Eldinare, the East Wind by the elves of Luminare, the South Wind by the elves of Cyndinare, and the

West Wind by the elves of Aldinare.

"Each group has a certain kinship with the wind they are guardians over and the Greater Anadel it is entrusted to. You might not have guessed, but I am a Cyndinari, a fact very few know, despite my red hair. The same blood that once coursed through the shadow elves flows through me. My ancestors witnessed Lucillia's kindness and remarkable character before they disavowed their brethren. While none have doubted my intentions, there are few who would dare place their trust with an elf of Cyndinare. I trust you with this knowledge because I hope to gain your confidence. You, Devlyn, are an elf of Luminare."

In those seven words, Devlyn learned more about himself and the elves than he had ever heard before. Something indiscernible in his mind aligned. Velaria had been telling him he was an elf for three months but hearing her say it again, with those six words, made him now believe it. Seeing a dragon in person also had something to do with his newfound belief; he felt as though anything was possible now. He was vaguely aware of distinctions between the elves, mostly that the elves of Cyndinare were evil, while the others were not. With Velaria identifying herself as a Cyndinari, he did not know how he should react. Still unable to reconcile the tale with the fact that elves truly still lived and thrived in the modern world, least of all that he himself belonged among that number, and despite his confliction, he believed Velaria.

"Is it dangerous for me to wield?" he asked, less concerned about his heritage than whether he might endanger others.

"In ordinary circumstances, a boy wielding for the first time would have caused catastrophic consequences, especially one with your potential, becoming more dangerous every time he presses into the erendinth. It is important that you know that what you did in Queen Lara's sitting room is called *kien*. It is the form in which men wield. To say 'male wielders' is simply incorrect; they are *kien* wielders. *Kiara* is the form used by women; we are *kiara* wielders.

"In ordinary circumstances, the moment your aptitude to wield was discovered, you would have been knocked unconscious, most likely by an ei'ana, and would have remained so until safely within the Temple of

Ceur, where you would be incapable of wielding. There are several unique circumstances surrounding you which have not occurred since before the fall of Krysenthiel, one thousand four hundred seventy years ago."

Over fourteen hundred years? Surprised that he had a connection to an event that had happened so long ago, Devlyn looked at Velaria quizzically and then another thought occurred as he glanced at the flame still resting above her palm.

"Queen Lara mentioned that I'm something called an elya, and a Phaedryn." He did not want to sound accusatory, but he did feel betrayed by Velaria's omission. "I've never heard of them before, not even in hushed whispers. Are they wielders, some kind of ei'ana?"

"The short answer is yes, they're both wielders. One is an innate gift and the other acquired. Such wielders have not lived since Krysenthiel fell. A person is born an elya. In Aelish, it means the Called, and it refers to wielders of incredible power, their limits never definable. An elya begins to wield without any instruction, and the limitations placed on wielders today do not apply to them. For example, for a male to wield safely, a kiara wielder must teach him control. And only a wielder who has reached their full potential is able to instruct another.

"The reason kien wielders are so dangerous is because no kiara wielder has reached her potential; they require a kien wielder to aid them, just as the kien require a kiara wielder. The Balance broke when Krysenthiel fell and the Erynien Empire enslaved the Luminari. The city of Septyl, home to the ei'ana, was lost entirely during the war. After the Phaedryn, Erynor saw the Ei'ana of Septyl as his next greatest threat, so he attacked them in their home city, starting the Ceurendol War. Wielders could no longer instruct pupils. The new generation of kien wielders never learned control, wreaking havoc on the world as they tried, flattening cities, crumbling palaces, and worse. But as you saw, you caused minimal damage in the queen's sitting room."

"So, you're saying it's safe for me to wield," said Devlyn curiously.

"Wielding is always dangerous, Devlyn, to you and to others. I would ask that you do it sparingly, especially since you are not fully trained. Even though you are an elya, we ei'ana must observe you carefully. We have not permitted a man to wield since the Councils of Ceurtriarch Telerius in 6714 of the Third Era."

"Don't you mean the Third Age?"

"No," Velaria replied. "Actually, it was the thirty-sixth year of the Fourth Age. The First Age was believed a beginning of human recognition, so they marked the start of Thellion's kingdom as the First Age. However, the elves also marked that date as an end and a beginning, but by their reckoning, it was the Third Era. After a couple of thousand years, a new Age begins for the humans, but an Era endures. There is talk that the Third Era is ending. It's difficult to presume what that might resemble. Only those who live through the change of an Era can say for certain."

None of the magisters at the abbey school ever mentioned an Era. Whether it was willful ignorance, or they simply disapproved of the time table, Devlyn never learned. He wanted to believe that he had received an adequate education from the ei'ceuril at the abbey school, but with every day he spent beyond its walls, the more aware he grew of how much he did not know.

"I believe you can wield safely." Velaria returned to the subject. "However, by not placing you in the Temple of Ceur, we take a substantial risk. Besides, there is another reason we are taking a chance with you. You are becoming a Phaedryn; one who bonds with a phoenix. The Luminari once joined with the phoenix, bonding for life. In the days before the fall of Krysenthiel, the Phaedryn were a common sight across all Teraeniel, their magnanimous deeds known to all.

"When Erynor began his conquest, he feared the Phaedryn the most. He made it his mission to exterminate all of them; the elves he killed mercilessly, while Erynor's dragon consumed the phoenix, trapping them in its fiery stomach, preventing their rebirth.

"A single phoenix remained in its egg, left under the protection of the Guardian Knights, also known as the Eklean Knights. That phoenix hatched at the moment of your birth in 7861 of the Third Era or 1183 of the Fourth Age. The two of you have already begun to bond. You must tell no one of this; if the enemy learns that a phoenix soars the skies again, he will bend the entirety of his strength toward its destruction."

Devlyn was confused. "What does that have to do with me wielding safely? It's good to know, but I don't understand how my bonding with a phoenix prevented the destruction of Everin, let alone why a phoenix is bonding with me in the first place."

"Only the elf chosen by the phoenix can say for certain why he or she was chosen. It has never been common knowledge, especially among those who do not hail from Luminare. It's speculated that the phoenix originally taught the Luminari how to wield the erendinth. The experience you have when you and the phoenix join, is it not akin to when you wielded aerys?"

"Aerys?"

"It's the proper name of the erendinth associated with air."

Devlyn recalled both events before responding. He found himself sensing the air about him and beginning to press into it, just as he had unexpectedly done with the phoenix.

"They are kind of similar," he said at last. "But how could a bird teach a person to wield?" The very notion was ridiculous.

"They are much more than birds. We know that they are intelligent creatures, just as dragons are. However, there is much more that we can only presume. Erynor killed the only ones who had a profound understanding of the phoenix."

"So, you're saying that every time we join, the phoenix is teaching me to wield?"

"Yes, and for that reason I want to test you with the other elemental erendinth. Now that you've begun to wield, you will continue; it cannot be stopped, especially since you're an elya. For that reason, I want to be with you when you wield the other elemental erendinth for the first time. Although the damage in the queen's sitting room was minimal, that does not mean we shouldn't try to avoid it. You will begin by wielding kien with the erendinth aquaeys, using the water out in the garden."

Withdrawing into himself as he instinctually had done before, Devlyn focused his attention on the source of water he could hear out in the garden, gently pressing his being against the water in the pond, much as he had done with the air but this time, with an intent to manipulate the water. It felt just as one would expect, cool and refreshing. The initial shock of its chill faded, and a sense of breathtaking purity pervaded. It wanted nothing more than to wash over filth and cleanse it of its stains, to nourish living bodies.

He eased himself further within; the water was vibrant, but curiously still at the same time. It seemed wedded to the ground, always longing to join with it, to seep further in. Nearly weightless, it lifted easily into the air when guided. A stream of water flew from the small pond as Devlyn guided it, swirling about the room, precious and pure. He brought it close to himself so that he could run his fingers through the floating stream as it passed.

It felt different on his hand. In the short span since he'd begun wielding, he had grown accustomed to its feeling. When it touched his body, he became aware that he was touching the water in two very distinct ways. He guided it back to the pond before withdrawing from it and letting it splash clumsily back into the rest of the water.

"Well done, Devlyn. You should be proud of yourself." Velaria sounded very much like a teacher.

"How is it that it feels different when I wield it?"

The phenomenon truly surprised him, he'd expected aquaeys to feel just as it should against his skin; with the wielding, it had a character to it that Devlyn had never experienced before. It made him think of one of Brother Bernard's stories, one that had different elements in it; each with unique characteristics, as if they were people. Brother Bernard often told stories, entertaining the students when he sat with them in the dining hall at the abbey school in Cor'lera.

Velaria smiled. Devlyn could not tell whether she was proud that he'd thought to ask the question or whether she thought it foolish.

"You have to remember that you do not wield water, you wield the elemental erendinth, aquaeys; it is not incorrect to identify it as the essence of water. Let's give terys a try, shall we?

"When you begin, you will become very aware of the great weight of the stone in this very castle. Stone longs to fall to the ground. Do not give into that temptation, ignore the walls of the castle and focus your attention on a single boulder in the garden," Velaria instructed.

As Devlyn closed his eyes and opened his awareness to terys, he was instantly aware of the groaning of the castle walls. They wanted nothing more than to crash to the ground. He felt an incredible tension in them yet, their compressive strength overshadowed the tension. They would easily continue standing strong for thousands of years. Diverting his attention from the castle, Devlyn found a small boulder in the garden, about the size of a small barrel. As he pressed himself into it, he felt the ground beneath it as he entered its sustaining vastness. Much weighed down on it; Devlyn could not believe that anything could support the ponderous weight that the ground did. Despite the weight, he also felt the richness of the garden's soil and the life sprouting from it, along with all the trees and plants rooted in the dirt, standing on a firm foundation.

Exerting his will, he pressed deep into the ground, and dug deeper, and further. He could sense the entire city of Everin resting atop the stone of the mountains and even the Dwarven Hall beneath. He felt hundreds of footsteps atop it, trampling without concern. Devlyn grew sorrowful for the stone and withdrew. As he came back into himself, Velaria spoke.

"It's all too easy to get lost in the vastness of terys. Did you notice how it's all connected? The dwarves have an incredible sense of it. They boast that if they desired, they could know what happens on the other side of Teraeniel."

Extending her palm out to Devlyn, the flame still dancing above it, she said, "Lastly, I want you take this flame from my hand. Remember, ignys and aerys are very different; it will react differently."

Devlyn again withdrew into the quiet within and focused his attention on the flame before him. He felt its heat permeating the surrounding air, craving to expand. As he pressed his consciousness against the flame, he felt himself ease in. The heat was incredible; it wanted to spread throughout the entire room in a playfully robust manner.

"Do not lose control of it," came Velaria's voice as though through a haze. Her voice flickered, almost pulsing with the flame. He felt it grow as its heat increased. A fleeting thought crossed his mind: *stop*. It was so beautiful though, and he soon found himself roiling the flame through the room, expanding and desiring to multiply.

"Go to the hearth," Velaria's voice flickered in.

It seemed logical; wood lay in the hearth. He aimed for it and the flame engulfed the wood and stretched upward through the chimney. He eased himself from the fire and returned more fully to his own body.

"That was great! I didn't expect it to be *that* different from aerys. It reminded me of a passion, hungering to grow!"

"You did well Devlyn, but just as with your passions, you must also control ignys. You began to lose control just before I asked you to go toward the hearth."

"They're all so similar, yet distinct. Each one explains the previous. It's as if they form a whole." Devlyn's appreciation of the erendinth deepened.

"You begin to understand. But there is much more for you to learn. These four are not the whole, but you might learn the whole in time." Velaria looked proudly at Devlyn as he looked toward the fire in the hearth, seeking a deeper explanation.

"I wanted to make sure that you became familiar with their touch. I am very pleased with your response. Ignys might be a challenge for you, but you will grow to understand it. As you said, it appears similar to aerys, but it is very different. I believe you will learn much from the phoenix. That will conclude today's tests. I think Alexander will be waiting for you in the guest quarters. In the meantime, there are a few people in the city that I must speak with. I'll see you both tonight." She stood and walked out to the corridor.

Devlyn fell into a cushioned chair. Although he no longer wielded, he was still aware of the erendinth. Taking a deep breath, Devlyn closed his eyes, relieved he had not made the castle collapse. After a moment, he pushed himself up from the chair and went to find a guard to ask for directions to the guest quarters. It took some time before he finally reached the room he was to share with Alex after having to stop for more directions as he lost his way in the winding castle. No one was there, although he saw his pack on one of the exquisitely carved wooden beds. Devlyn's eyes lingered on the bed, its noticeably soft mattress beckoning him to lie down. Drawn to it, Devlyn found a note in Alex's untidy script on the pillow.

Dev,

Exploring the city. One of the knights told me about a pub called the Splintered Keg. You'll find me there.

Alex

Devlyn gave the bed a final lingering look before he left the room closing the door behind him. He was eager to find Alex and tell him about what happened with Velaria. This time, he only had to ask twice before finding the exit.

The streets beyond the castle grounds bustled with activity. Soldiers marched regularly in twos or threes, and vendors cried out their wares in hopes of attracting customers. As he walked through the streets, Devlyn noticed that not a single building stood shorter than four stories. The white stone buildings sprawled artfully through the city in every direction. If it wasn't for the castle resting above on the mountain slope and in clear sight, Devlyn would have easily mistaken any of these buildings for a palace.

A small crowd blocked one of the roads, gathered around three street performers. The one breathing fire might have impressed Devlyn at one time, but following his recent experience with ignys, Devlyn just pushed his way through.

He passed several shops and inns, all the while asking for directions to the Splintered Keg. Limestone appeared to be the favored construction material for the shops and houses he passed while marble was reserved for civic buildings and the palatial homes of the wealthy. Most of the marble buildings stood in key places: at a street's terminus or arranged to form a broad plaza. While the marble buildings clearly had a heightened significance, every structure was built with the same craftsmanship, as fluted columns rose to ornately carved capitals, supporting heavy entablatures, and pediments. Even the windows and doors were adorned with intricate molding.

He soon spotted a sign with a leaking wooden barrel painted just above the name THE SPINTERED KEG hung above a door.

A young woman smiled at him as he entered, but before he could say anything, Alex hollered from one of the tables to one side.

"Joining your friend, sweetie?" she giggled as she led Devlyn to Alex and asked them both, "Can I get you anything?"

"If it wouldn't be too much trouble, I would like another. My friend here will have the same." Alex spoke in an annoying voice, noticeably flirting with the server, a buxom blonde.

"Certainly. I'll be back shortly," she turned away as Alex gawked, his eyes following her swishing hips.

"Why are you acting stupid?"

"Isn't this place great? The environment, the people," exclaimed Alex to no one in particular, seeming to have not heard Devlyn. "It's great, Dev. I walk in, and how does she greet me? Go on, guess." Alex waited for his cousin to respond but answered his question quickly after asking. "A kiss! A big fat wet one right on the lips! They sure do hospitality right around here."

"You're ridiculous and you're acting stupid."

"What was that?" asked Alex, again not paying attention to Devlyn's words.

"Never mind." Devlyn wondered whether Alex intentionally ignored him or perhaps the buxom server had rendered Alex incapable of listening to anyone but herself. Either way, it was annoying.

She quickly returned with their drinks making Alex both happier and more obnoxious as he thanked her profusely.

"So, Velaria had me wield again." Devlyn was curious about Alex's ability to listen.

"Is she crazy? You'll kill us all!" It seemed Alex's ears still worked.

"Apparently, I can wield kien safely. I'm something called an elya."

"Sounds made up. I knew we shouldn't have trusted her; what's next, is she going to teach you to fly or better yet, level cities with a swipe of your hand? She's not telling us the whole story and you know it!"

Devlyn kept quiet and stared into his drink. Alex was right, it felt like every single day they learned something new that Velaria had conveniently omitted.

"Anyway, what do you suppose people do to earn money here? All I saw as I walked around were pubs, shops, and street performances. I can't imagine how they would manage a farm up here in the mountains." Alex's eyes stayed glued on the server's hips as she waited on other patrons.

"Don't forget about innkeepers and soldiers."

"Won't find me in an army. Quick way into a grave, if you ask me." Alex clanked the coins in his coat pockets together. "It sure was nice of the queen to give us five jents each. Couldn't think of a better way to spend it. I've always wondered what pubs were like. And besides, my mother's not here to keep me from getting an ale for once."

Devlyn watched the condensation drip along the side of his mug. Since Alex was more interested in chatting to the server and took every opportunity to do so with great cheer whenever she neared their table, it left Devlyn to his own thoughts, some of which were that it might be better if his aunt was present.

Minums and Seguians

Devlyn had grown weary of Alex's behavior and was about to leave the pub when two women entered, took a quick look around the room, then walked to a corner table that offered some privacy. Devlyn changed his mind about leaving when he overheard one of them say as she passed, "Does she really think us so ignorant? An elya hasn't been born since Ceurendol was lost."

"Quiet, you fool!" the other hissed.

Their conversation diminished to hushed whispers, preventing Devlyn from hearing more. He knew they referred to him, so he strained his ears to hear the rest of their conversation.

"How about another?" asked Alex, slapping Devlyn on the back, distracting him.

"Huh? No, I'm fine, thanks." Devlyn waited until Alex shifted his attention back to the server before straining his ears again, but the more he tried, the less he heard. "Actually, I think I will get something. I'm going to see what they have at the bar." Devlyn walked the long way around to the bar which conveniently placed him near the two women. The bartender took his order, and Devlyn sat on a wobbly stool waiting for his tea.

"She clearly means to manipulate us. I'm not sure what she intends, but why else would she make such an outlandish claim?" It was the first woman again. The other woman did not reply.

Devlyn wished they would not whisper; even from his new vantage point, it was hard to hear them. He knew they discussed him, and he needed to know exactly what they said. Even as he strained his attention toward the two women, his back to them, he felt a familiar sensation, a sensation that was akin to those he'd had when Velaria had him wielding.

He could sense the air in the room and could feel vibrations through it; intelligible vibrations. Everything present and in contact with the air was now accessible to him. Loud murmuring filled his ears; he was aware of every chair scraping the floor, every slurp from a mug, and every voice. With surprising ease, Devlyn narrowed his focus on the small table behind him, turning slightly so that he could see them out of the corner of his eye.

"Clever." The quieter woman cast her eyes around the room, peering in every direction, before settling on a spot just beyond him, not looking directly at him, but clearly addressing him, causing Devlyn's heart to pump fiercely. *How'd she do that?* he wondered, turning his head away so that he could no longer see her.

"Clumsy, though. I'm not sure who you are, boy. Consider yourself fortunate that this is our first meeting. Otherwise I would see you hung by your toes and dragged all the way to Ceurenyl. If it happens again, you will be punished. Stop being doltish, withdraw from aerys, and join our table—*now!*" The woman's tone gave him little choice, even as it continued at a level that no one else in the room could hear.

Devlyn now turned his head fully toward the women and saw them both staring directly at him. The one he'd previously thought of as the quieter one was clearly the one who had identified him. He did as she commanded, withdrew from aerys, and walked to their table.

"Sit. You are the boy from Cor'lera, yes?" asked the woman. Devlyn nodded apprehensively. "Don't fret, boy. We're ei'ana; Queen Lara spoke with us not an hour past. Truthfully, I thought it a hoax; granted, I did notice the clumsy wielding of aerys as it passed through the streets earlier. The queen did not deceive us. Now, tell me, what is your name, boy?"

"Devlyn. Might I ask for yours?"

"We're Vyoletryn ei'ana and we'll be asking the questions. When did you learn to wield? What you just managed with the air is not particularly easy. An ei'ana requires years of study before she can enter an erendinth so subtly."

"Only this morning. I didn't intend to; it just sort of happened. I made a bit of a mess in the queen's sitting room," Devlyn admitted.

"Most kien wielders would cause the castle to crumble when they wield for the first time. Consider yourself fortunate." said the first ei'ana, eyeing Devlyn. "I'm not certain what the birth of an elya signifies; we'll have to ask an Albien. I'm sure they'll have several theories regarding such an event. I doubt we'll find any Albiens here though. Those women concern themselves too much with what's written in books and scrolls, in my opinion."

Devlyn scrunched his eyebrows. He had never heard of an Albien before—granted the list of terms he was unfamiliar with grew by the hour—let alone that he was an elf, something he was growing more comfortable with and had even started to believe. He had also noticed that he was sitting and standing straighter as well.

"Are Albiens ei'ana as well?"

"Of course, they are. Didn't they teach you anything at that abbey school up there? The Ei'ana of Septyl have seven Schools, each founded by one of the original Chairs. When a young woman is studying at Gwilnor Academy, she chooses from among the seven; every ei'ana belongs to one of them," the second ei'ana replied before the other signaled her to a pause.

"He'll receive a proper education once he reaches Ceurenyl; no need to lecture him now. If I didn't know better, I might mistake you for an Albien; a white owl disguised as a purple eagle before my very eyes." The ei'ana stared daggers at each other, the first all too clearly pleased with herself.

Her gaze returned to Devlyn, a question on her lips just as the door to the Splintered Keg opened, allowing a rush of brisk air through, along with a new patron. Since Devlyn's back was to the entrance, he did not see who it was; however, the ei'ana were clearly acquainted with the patron who was now the recipient of their steady gazes. Devlyn decided it best not to seem too interested. He did itch to turn around though to see for himself.

"I must have missed the proclamation stating the Azurelles had begun to accept kien wielders again." The first ei'ana addressed the new-comer mildly. "Nor that they had the authority to do so. Would you like a refresher on the Counsels of Telerius?"

"It's nice to see you Dian, and you as well, Orella. Has Queen Lara informed you of recent events?" Velaria's familiar voice delighted Devlyn.

"She has. Are you aware that she has asked Orella and me to accompany a small party to Ceurenyl?"

"Yes; I fear we require all available aid to reach Ceurenyl safely. Devlyn must begin his studies."

Dian appeared uninterested. "I don't know what you're bothering yourself about, going through the trouble of traveling by horse. I for one certainly have not that kind of time to waste; *my* affairs in Everin are of prime importance."

Devlyn watched as the two subtly parried and wondered what the outcome might be.

"You must know this holds high priority; the request is from Mother Paurel and the other Chairs," Velaria skillfully concealed her growing frustration with the unyielding ei'ana before her.

"Certainly." Dian continued in a lower voice. "A minum arrived in Everin today, one of the time wardens. He would not share his name, as they tend to do, but requested your presence, and the presence of anyone accompanying you. You will find him in the Dwarven Hall with Uon. If I'm correct, you might not have to concern yourself over acquiring new horses after all."

Velaria appeared appeased, even grateful, at Dian's revelation. "Thank you, Dian. We must leave at once then. Until we meet again." Velaria stood, and Devlyn followed suit. They walked to Alex who was yet again cooing in the server's ear.

"I'm sorry, dear, but you will likely never see him again," Velaria addressed the server in a kind voice and added, "Come, Alexander."

Alex's beginning argument sputtered, then stopped when he caught her look. He dug into his pocket, kissed the server's cheek as he put some coins in her hand and followed the other two out of the Splinted Keg and into the brisk air.

Velaria strode away at a pace that the boys were hard-pressed to match. Devlyn caught sight of the greenery he'd seen once before—it seemed so long ago now—falling from the sleeves of her cloak. Even Alex noticed it this time and elbowed Devlyn and pointed. Before either could say anything, Velaria tucked the greenery back into her sleeves.

"I'll explain later, but, now, we must hurry."

They wove rapidly through the crowded streets, the inhabitants of Everin not pleased as they were pushed aside but refraining from confrontation when they took note of Velaria. The way she held herself demanded respect, ei'ana or not. In no time, the castle gates rose before them on the far side of a broad plaza, up a curved street. The guards nodded to them as they passed through the gates, but rather than continue toward the castle, Velaria led them to the Dwarven Hall. They passed through the castle gardens and entered an arched portal, the same one that Devlyn had come through earlier that same day. Just inside the tunnel waited Queen Lara.

"It appears that you get your way once again, my dear Velaria. Your belongings are with Uon and the minum. He does not seem eager to linger long and his urgency troubles me, Velaria." The queen stood tall and poised, regal despite her unease, and began to walk as soon as the others reached her.

"I'm not eager to remain here either, Lara. The Shadow is growing, and Darkness once again threatens our world. It is clear that it intends to strike the kingdom of Evellion first to display its reclaimed strength. It pains me that you must remain here as the Shadow encompasses you on all sides."

"My place is here with my people, protecting them in any way I can." Queen Lara replied firmly.

The small party proceeded quickly through the tunnel, turning at odd angles until they reached a moderately sized, nondescript chamber where three dwarves and a smaller creature stood by Devlyn's and Alex's packs. *Is that supposed to be a minum?* thought Devlyn as he looked at the strange, oddly small creature. He also recognized Oma, Gluhn, and Uon, and was surprised that he was happy to see all the dwarves again. He had begun to wonder where Oma and Gluhn had gone. The last time Devlyn had seen the two, still dizzy from the rolling trip through the tunnels, he hadn't been able to see straight and his face must have been greener than his eyes. Whatever Oma had done to get them to Everin so quickly, he hoped the minum offered a different means of travel.

Before any of the dwarves could greet the newcomers, the small creature approached. "My service is yours, Devlyn, youngest of Gwendolyn and Feolyn."

Devlyn had no idea why the minum referred to people he did not know.

The minum was cloaked, his face hidden beneath a hood until he lowered it, revealing larger than expected eyes and a pointed nose on a somber face.

"I am Skimp of the free town of Freiton. The time wardens sent me to bring you safely to Ceurenyl."

Alex's half smirk made his left eye squint slightly and manifested his skepticism, which Skimp clearly did not appreciate.

"Thank you, Skimp, but Ceurenyl is leagues away and an army occupies the Cyrillean Pass. Surely, they'll track us down once we leave the city," said Devlyn, thinking of convenient tunnels. It would be impossible for a creature as small as the one standing before him, barely reaching his waist, to lead them unscathed through an enemy force.

The minum smiled and before Devlyn could wonder why, Skimp held his hands together, cupped around an empty but rounded space, as if he held an invisible ball. He expanded his hands, and to Devlyn's amazement, he felt the air around them shift into the center where a light grew larger. The edges of the sphere where hazy, blending into their surroundings. The closer Devlyn looked toward the center, the better he saw what seemed to be a small room draped in blue. The minum said nothing.

"Farewell, dear friend." Velaria embraced Queen Lara who then bade her guests farewell. Velaria embraced her again and said softly, "May you be a light in the Shadow, sister." The queen nodded and smiled at her friend.

Velaria moved toward the sphere and walked through without bumping into Skimp. Devlyn could see her move farther into the room in the sphere. Oma and Gluhn followed, and again, Devlyn saw them safely in the room.

As Alex hesitated to follow the others through the sphere, an Evellion knight rushed into the chamber.

"Your Majesty, your presence is required at once. Cyril has fallen." Devlyn and Alex shared a look of horror but the queen did not so much as quiver.

"Your time in Everin has sadly come to an end," she said. "Quick, through the seguian. Tell Velaria what has happened, and that I expect servants of Shadow likely infiltrated Cyril months ago, perhaps even years ago. Shadow elves are also a distinctly possible influence. Those walls are impenetrable; they would not have fallen to an external force so swiftly, if at all. Study well, Devlyn, much depends on you."

Without waiting for an additional farewell, the Evellion queen turned and walked back through the tunnel, accompanied by the knight. Alex and Devlyn quickly passed through the seguian.

Once through, Devlyn immediately looked back and saw the small hall in Everin, now on the other side of the seguian which quickly closed leaving Skimp standing in its place.

Devlyn quickly told Velaria about the fall of Cyril and passed on the queen's message.

"I feared so." She was not surprised. "Skimp, is it possible to get news to the Aryl of Lucillia?"

"At once, Ei'ana."

GWILNOR ACADEMY

Devlyn sat in a straight-backed chair of finely carved dark wood. An entire week had passed since he had arrived in Ceurenyl with the others, and not once had he been permitted to leave Gwilnor Academy. The castle was larger than anything he was accustomed to and he imagined that the entire village of Cor'lera would easily fit within it several times. Not that he had explored the premises; he was confined to a single wing.

Since arriving, Devlyn and Alex had each been given a temporary room in the Azurelle wing of the castle. Devlyn supposed that it was because Velaria belonged to the Azurelles. Alex had permission to roam about freely since he was not a wielder, which meant that he often abandoned Devlyn. Devlyn had managed to discover that the Azurelles occupied one of the southern towers, the largest of all the towers in the castle and commonly known as the Dragon Tower.

The corridors of the wing were draped in vibrant blues of varying intensities; tapestries of magnificent landscapes and sculptures of blue dragons featured throughout, along with portraits and busts of prominent Azurelle ei'ana. The depictions of the dragons all held an incredible likeness to Yelaris. Devlyn had been told that she was somewhere in the city. He had also been told that Liam was with the ei'ceuril in the Temple of Ceur and although Devlyn did not know what went on in the temple, he was anxious to see his brother again.

Today was the first day he was allowed to leave the Azurelle wing, which was why he now sat in this uncomfortable straight-backed chair.

Early that morning, he had received a formal letter of summons from the Seven Chairs of Septyl, with instructions on where and when he was to present himself. Devlyn had not the slightest idea what the Seven Chairs meant and wondered whether they might be similar to the Perrien Council.

He had hoped he would have a chance to speak with Velaria before attending the summons, but he had rarely seen her since leaving Everin. During their brief, almost accidental meetings, she had asked how he was and whether his room was comfortable before disappearing again for a day or two. Every time Devlyn asked her a question, she simply told him she was busy. He could not imagine what kept her so occupied.

Just when he noticed how uncomfortable the chair he sat in was, a tall woman walked through the large oak doors. "The Seven Chairs will see you now."

Relieved, Devlyn rose from the hard seat and followed the woman through the doors into a dimly lit corridor where she pointed him to an open doorway at the end. As soon as he was through it, the doors closed behind him with an intimidating thump.

He walked into a seven-sided chamber that could hold a much larger number than what currently occupied it. Seven women waited there. He felt it was a safe assumption that the women were also ei'ana. Each sat in a large chair on a balcony midway up each of the seven sides of the room, looking down on the newcomer. Every chair was different, some large, others small; all exquisitely carved, yet no two the same.

A heavy panel of distinctly colored fabric hung from the ceiling behind the chairs, purple, blue, green, orange, brown, red, and white. In front of each hanging drapery, a large golden emblem depicted elven figures and an animal within a circle. At least, he thought the emblems were gold.

As he walked to the center of the room, where a vacant platform waited, Devlyn was surprised to see Velaria in the chair draped with blues. The large emblem behind her had a naked male and female elf, their arms held aloft with a dragon set behind them. Like all the other emblems, the emblem of Azurelle was cast in maybe gold, with a thick rim of the same material encasing the figures, but without a field behind them so that the blue drapery provided the background for the space not filled by the figures. Devlyn had grown accustomed to seeing it through the halls of his current residence.

Velaria was noticeably the youngest of the seven women present. The others all had grey or white hair; none bore the color of their youth, making Velaria's vibrant red hair more striking than usual. The older women held a beauty about them; none reminded him of a gentle, elderly grandmother.

The woman who appeared the eldest among the seven spoke formally in a strong voice, "I, Mother Paurel Roendryn, Chair of Vyoletryn, call account of those present." She rose from her seat on the purple balcony and continued, "I, Mother Paurel Roendryn, Chair of Vyoletryn, am duly present."

"I, Mother Selenya Waeyn, Chair of Albien, am duly present." This woman, who appeared almost as old as Mother Paurel, had entirely white hair in a tight bun. The white balcony she stood on suited her.

"I, Mother Agnelle Phanstienne, Chair of Auburnis, am duly present," said the woman on the brown balcony. Of the women present, Mother Agnelle looked the closest to the kind grandmother that he expected of women at their age.

"I, Mother Loretta Javie, Chair of Crimsyn, am duly present." She stood at the red balcony.

"I, Mother Tiera Weldon, Chair of Emradiel, am duly present," said the woman from the green balcony.

"I, Mother Lenora Hanaryld, Chair of Arantiulyn, am duly present." Lenora spoke from the orange balcony. Something about Mother Lenora's tone made Devlyn feel like he should be cautious with her.

"I, Mother Velaria Treyven, Chair of Azurelle, am duly present." Velaria concluded the ritual.

"Devlyn, son of Evellyn and Dolan Telvin, you are summoned before the Seven Chairs of Septyl." Mother Paurel's eyes pierced Devlyn and not once did she blink. Wrinkles etched the skin of her face, yet they did nothing to detract from her authoritative stance. The emblem behind her depicted a naked male and female elf, each holding a staff to oppose any threats and an eagle soared above the pair. The forms stood out in clear relief against the purple drapery. "Do you know the reason for your summons?" Mother Paurel asked.

Devlyn faced the Chair of Vyoletryn from where he stood in the center of the room. He wondered whether his voice would hold, aware of not just her steely gaze, but of the gazes of the others in the chamber.

"Mother Paurel, truthfully, I'm not sure why I was summoned here; I'm not sure why I'm called an elya or even what that is; I'm not sure why I was confined to a single wing of Gwilnor; in fact, there's much I'm not sure of, and that list has only grown since leaving Cor'lera." Devlyn was rather proud that he was able to speak loudly enough. He assumed the Seven Chairs were the seven women who sat on the sides of this seven-sided room although he remained unenlightened as to what the Seven Chairs represented.

"Mother Velaria has informed us that you have wielded. Is this true? Are you able to wield, and more importantly, wield with control?" asked Mother Selenya, sitting in the simple white chair. "Is it true, are you an elya?" As he opened his mouth to reply, another voice broke in.

"Mother Velaria has also mentioned that you destroyed the queen of Evellion's sitting room by *accident*. That doesn't sound like control to me." Mother Lenora seemed the fiercest of the seven, and the second youngest next to Velaria. Her hair was mostly grey, and only beginning to shift to white. "He should be placed in the temple. The city must be protected. Who knows what destruction he will cause if given the freedom to wield kien."

"I tested him with the other elemental erendinth that same day. He retained control throughout the testing. I propose we admit him into Gwilnor Academy. He will be able to learn to wield in a safe environment, surrounded by hundreds of ei'ana." Velaria's voice held a hint of exhaustion. "Besides, he was born an elya, as was his sister. Steward Arlyn and I confirmed that eleven years ago."

"You cannot seriously contemplate admitting a kien wielder to the school," said Mother Lenora.

"Not to mention, admissions ended five months ago, and this year's lessons began four months ago," added Mother Selenya. "And how would he cover the cost of tuition? We cannot create an undue precedent."

The Seven Chairs debated among themselves, never asking for Devlyn's input. The women argued for well over an hour as Devlyn tried not to shift too much from his standing pose, or slump as he was used to. Finally, Mother Lenora rose from her orange chair.

"This debate is fruitless and will continue so. I demand a demonstration. I won't allow a kien wielder to roam Gwilnor's halls freely unless I know with certainty that he is capable of controlling the erendinth."

A simple vote followed, and agreement was unanimous. Mother Paurel invited Devlyn to display his wielding of the elemental erendinth.

Thinking that it would be acceptable to ease his muscles as he prepared himself, Devlyn closed his eyes, rolled his shoulders slightly, and sensed his surroundings, locating the elements throughout the seven-sided chamber. He felt the stone beneath his feet, the air about the room, even the moisture it held, and the fire emanating from the braziers. In Everin, Velaria had instructed him to wield one erendinth at a time. But that now seemed like a waste of time, and these women wanted a demonstration displaying his control. In Everin, he had felt as if he could do more; now, he was sure he could.

At once, he pressed into all four elemental erendinth at once. The air spun about the room, water separated from the air and hung suspended around his body, and the pebbles lying on the tidy floor rose to eye level. The fire concerned him; he recalled his previous encounter with it and how it had wanted to consume and expand recklessly. Nonetheless, he pressed into it and the fire leapt from the braziers and flew into a single, stable flame before him. He had a passing thought that perhaps wielding the elemental erendinth simultaneously held ignys balanced. There must be someone he could ask about that.

As he withdrew from the erendinth, and the air, moisture, pebbles, and flame returned to usual, the fullness he had just experienced was replaced with emptiness, leaving him feeling dim, feeling hollow.

"This boy is reckless!" bellowed Mother Lenora. "Tell me, boy! Do you intend to strut about with your chest out during your entire stay at Gwilnor? You should not have been able to wield all four of the elemental erendinth at the same time!"

"Temper yourself, Mother Lenora." Mother Paurel sat calmly in her purple chair. "Devlyn, was this intentional?"

Yes, it was.

He looked up to the elderly woman. "It felt right, like an instinct. I did not plan to do so, when you asked for a demonstration, but once I began, I could feel all four elemental erendinth, and simply pressed into them all at once. It was familiar, as if I had done it before. It was like when…" Devlyn stopped himself, not wanting to tell these women about the phoenix, remembering what Velaria had told him.

"So, it's true," gasped Mother Selenya amid murmurs from the other women. "The phoenix has hatched and has chosen you. A Phaedryn will walk this land again."

"We must allow him to study among us," said Mother Agnelle, sitting in the simplest of all the chairs. "If Mother Selenya is correct, and he is to become a Phaedryn, we must admit him. There is much he will learn from Gwilnor. Mothers, allow the peace of the Light of Anaweh to enter your hearts. You will see it to be the right decision." As she spoke, Devlyn eyed the emblem behind her. It showed two naked elves, male and female, kneeling on the ground, raising a garland into the air; above them flew small birds that reminded him of larks; on this wall, the drapery was brown.

"You are right, Mother Agnelle." Mother Paurel looked down from her dais to Devlyn in the center of the room, then up toward the other Chairs. "We shall decide. Do we, the Seven Chairs of Septyl, admit Devlyn of Cor'lera, son of Evellyn and Dolan Telvin, to Gwilnor Academy?"

The Seven Chairs remained silent.

Devlyn felt the air thicken and begin to stir, and an incredible sensation rushed through the room. Every woman held her head high with arms outstretched at their sides, palms open. Behind each woman, the emblems glowed. The room flooded with the seven colors, as beams leapt from the various emblems to collide in the center of the room, above Devlyn's head. They joined and bathed the room in a brilliant light.

The light faded and Devlyn stood quietly waiting, somewhat awed by the display.

Mother Paurel stood from her chair. "Devlyn, son of Evellyn and Dolan Telvin, you are the first kien wielder admitted to Gwilnor Academy since before the Balance of kien and kiara was broken. You will be instructed in the ways of wielding, along with the study of histories, languages, theoreticals, physics, arithmetic, politics, and philosophies. You will be expected to maintain your studies. If you appear to lose control of the erendinth, you will be sent to the Temple of Ceur with the rest of the kien wielders. Chancellor Oranna will keep vigilance over your studies and abilities. She is the ei'ana entrusted with the oversight of Gwilnor Academy. You will meet with her following this session; your tuition will be discussed with her."

Once Mother Paurel pronounced the decision to admit Devlyn into Gwilnor, all Seven Chairs rose from their seats, and retreated behind the large fabric panels, leaving him alone in the heptagonal room. *There must be passages concealed behind.*

He had hoped to speak with Velaria, but as he watched her exit, he doubted he would have the chance. He turned and headed for the door he had come through and just as he remembered its earlier closing with force, it opened smoothly and silently, and he saw the young woman who had informed him that the Chairs were ready for him.

"Admissions closed on the twentieth of Lierenth and lessons began on the first of Marenth; this is quite irregular. Winter is well behind us, you've missed the entire spring term, and we've even begun the summer term," she said without telling him her name, nor how she knew what had happened in the chamber, and without making any move toward leading him to the chancellor.

"Is that an issue?" Devlyn figured he might as well get information from whoever was willing to answer his questions, and this woman was upset enough by the events to loosen her tongue.

"Only if you intend on receiving exceptional marks on your exams."

"When are exams?"

"Do you know nothing of Gwilnor?"

Devlyn shook his head.

"They're seasonal. You have missed the first round which concluded at the end of Delenth. You'll never be able to finish the year's study with more than common marks, and that's only if you receive exceptional or foremost marks on the remaining exams."

"Is that difficult?"

"Few receive exceptional marks and only one student per class receives foremost marks, *obviously*. Now please, follow me. I was asked to show you to the boys' dormitory in the North Tower."

"What part of the castle are we in now?" Devlyn asked, noting the lack of windows.

"This is the securest location the castle offers, the foundation of one of her seven towers, and not by accident, the chancellor's office is directly above. The Chamber of the Seven Chairs is near the center of the castle, beneath the entrance hall, deep in the bedrock of the mountain. These walls are the original stone of the mountain, the thickest walls of the entire castle. The ei'ana who built Gwilnor wielded the stone itself to create rooms and chambers in these lower sections."

"Sounds sturdy. I'm sorry, but we haven't been properly introduced yet. I'm Devlyn."

The woman eyed him before responding. "Saendre of Lucillia. I recently returned from my novitiate in the Illumined Wood and will soon choose a School and declare my intention to profess the counsels with that School and be raised to ei'ana. Before the Choosing ceremony, I'm to perform menial tasks to prepare myself, tasks such as escorting newly admitted student wielders. Now, if you'll follow me, Chancellor Oranna is expecting you, and first, we must retrieve your school robes from your dormitory."

"Why are the robes necessary?"

"You can't meet with the chancellor of Gwilnor in…" Saendre eyed

Devlyn's clothing with evident disdain.

"What's wrong with my clothes? I just met the Seven Chairs in these clothes." Devlyn pushed his hands into his pockets.

"And you're fortunate they didn't ask you to leave on sight!"

Chastened, Devlyn followed Saendre through the lower reaches of the castle, twisting and turning through the corridors. They ascended several staircases, none similar to the last. Tapestries and paintings, exquisite masterpieces the likes he had never seen before, hung throughout; they were complemented by the finely carved molding and balustrades that wove upward or downward. Devlyn looked through the pointed arched windows onto a large courtyard on their left as they walked through a long corridor with doors on their right, presumably opening to classrooms or offices. The corridor was paced with pilasters on either side, forming a square as they rose to the groin-vaulted ceiling above. Dozens of students passed in both directions. Devlyn noted the young men who practiced with swords and shields in the courtyard, older knights instructing them in the finer points of combat.

The corridor ended with a wide enclosed stair hall, but rather than taking it, Saendre walked around it and along a short corridor much like the rest they'd walked through. A massive pair of wooden doors sat closed at the end.

Saendre effortlessly pushed one of the doors open, revealing a hall crowded with evenly placed square tables and expansive windows framing either side of the room, with the largest window he had ever seen at the far end. It followed the curious roofline, which started to curve into an arch before rising to a high point. The central aisle was free of tables, but not of students brushing past each other. Devlyn found the structure of this room impossible. Easily three stories high on its own, its large windows appeared to support the roof above them, a roof turned in on a low angle before a clerestory section rose in a vertical wall. Above the clerestory, the roof rose to an impossible height at a pointed arch, doubling the height of the entire space. The upper roof had two levels of dormers. Throughout the entire space was a forest of columns and larger pillars, their lines stretching upward, abandoning the structural members to form the vaulted ceiling. Two large crossings split the long hall, large windows at either end.

"This is the dining hall," said Saendre, remaining at the entrance doors. Devlyn thought that was obvious, given the tables and the lingering smell from the previous meal. "There are several smaller dining rooms throughout the castle, but most of the students eat here, while ei'ana prefer the smaller halls, particularly the ones in their own School's wings."

Saendre turned around and left the dining hall. Devlyn followed her back to the stair hall they had passed, which Devlyn now noticed was another heptagonal space. It was much used; servants, knights, students, and ei'ana ascended and descended the stairs. Devlyn followed Saendre up the winding set of stairs, stairs that appeared to have no end as they went on up and up, passing one landing after another, constantly climbing.

The higher they went, the more disoriented Devlyn became. He no longer knew which floor they were on, having lost count when they passed the sixth floor. Despite the height, he imagined they were still below the roofline of the dining hall.

At last, another eight or so floors later, Saendre paused on a landing and turned into the corridor, leaving Devlyn to trail behind. "This part of the North Tower, and the floors above are the boys' dormitory. The interior rooms are for communal use, such as common rooms and lavatories, while the exterior are bedrooms." Saendre didn't pause or even turn to see whether Devlyn kept up.

She stopped before a simple door, identical to the others in the tower corridor. "Consider yourself fortunate; most newly admitted students share rooms, but since you're the only kien wielder, you get your own, a privilege reserved for senior students. You will find your robes hanging in the wardrobe. Students of Gwilnor Academy are required to wear their robes at all times. The clothes you wear now can either be stored or disposed of." Saendre's tone implied that tossing them was the better of the two options.

"What about in the city? Am I still required to wear them?"

"If you are given permission to leave the castle, you are required to maintain your appearance as a student of Gwilnor Academy. Your lessons will begin tomorrow morning; they will consist of both communal and private lessons. Today, you have a meeting with Chancellor Oranna to discuss your schedule. You'll also be given the option to train with the Septyl knights and their pupils, if you desire. Customarily, Gwilnor does not train male students in wielding, it's forbidden of course; however, Gwilnor has offered the young men who study here the opportunity to train with the Septyl knights while receiving an exemplary education. You will find that they are the finest swordsmen in all Eklean. Or that's what I'm told."

"Thank you, Saendre."

"Naturally. Take a quick look inside and change into your robes. I have to escort you to Chancellor Oranna." She turned away from the door impatiently.

Devlyn turned the doorknob and pushed open the simple door to find a modest room, now his room, behind. A bed rested against the wall, with a small table beside it. On the opposite wall, a plain wooden chair sat before a desk. A wardrobe stood near the desk and Devlyn opened it to find two identical grey robes with straight clean lines. Even with his height, he could tell that the robes would reach the floor once he put them on. A long hood in the same color fell down the back. As Devlyn examined the robes, he could not find a single stitch in all the fabric. A crest on the left breast had seven animals, each a different color. A purple eagle, a blue dragon, a green stag, an orange lion, a brown lark, a red dog, and a white owl—the same animals he had seen on the emblems behind the Seven Chairs.

Set in the far wall was a small, single window that came to a pointed arch at the top. Devlyn drew near the window and was greeted by an incredible view of the city; beyond it, along the side of the mountain to the north was what Devlyn assumed to be the Temple of Ceur. A series of half and quarter domes escalated upward, growing larger with every level before rising to a vast dome that covered most of the building. None of the domes were a full half circle, just the top third of a proper dome, with a shallowness that prevented them from extending higher. *Perhaps the size prevented the builders from constructing the domes more fully.*

In the sunlight, it was difficult to place the type of stone used. It had a cloudy character. A river flowed in front of the temple, splitting into two arms that cascaded down the side of the mountain. One flowed east out of the city while the other flowed south, twisting in front of Gwilnor and through the city before splitting again to exit on either side of the only city gate.

Returning to the wardrobe, Devlyn exchanged his clothes for one of the grey robes, pulling it over his head, buttoning up the front and tying the sash at the middle. The grey fabric was surprisingly comfortable. Quite fond of his Cor'leran clothing, Devlyn folded them neatly and placed them on a shelf in the wardrobe before returning to Saendre.

"I was under the impression your gender was supposed to dress more quickly." Saendre turned away to return to the winding staircase of the North Tower.

"You said to take a look, so I did," Devlyn replied to her back. Saendre did not acknowledge him but led him through what felt like the entire castle, through many of the same corridors until she paused in a great hall. A single large door with a colossal rose window above framed what Devlyn could only assume was the main entrance. The massive door opened and closed irregularly as students and ei'ana passed through and into the sunshine. Colored rays of light flowed from the rose window, and when Devlyn looked more closely, he saw seven circles surrounding a larger circle. The outer seven each displayed one of the sigils of the Seven Schools, while the central circle featured the same crest as the one on his robe.

This hall was constructed similarly to the dining hall, with the two separate rooflines separated by a clerestory level, only this hall lacked the windows on either side, and the multiple levels of dormers. Opposite the rose window, seven pillars surrounded a twin set of winding staircases. The stair and pillars disappeared above.

Saendre began the ascent, taking Devlyn up through another tower. The twin stairs stopped on the fourth level, and a single curved stair wound its way to the uppermost floor. At least, Devlyn assumed it was the highest level, since the staircase stopped at a beautiful wooden door. His legs ached.

"This is the chancellor's office. I trust you can find your way back to your dormitory?"

"I should be able to manage it."

"Splendid, then I'll leave you to your meeting." Saendre didn't wait for Devlyn to thank her or say goodbye before she started down the stairs.

Alone before the closed door, Devlyn rapped three times on the wooden surface, inhaling deeply before it opened. Peering around the door so he could greet whoever had opened it, he found himself in a heptagonal office lined with shelves crowded with books. The only wall space not dominated by shelving were the seven circular windows. Each wall arched to a steep point, with an even more severe angle forming a pointed roof above, piercing the crisp mountain air in a sharp steeple.

"May I be one of the first to welcome you to Gwilnor Academy, Devlyn of Cor'lera," said a woman sitting behind a large desk at the far end of the room, her head bowed over a piece of parchment and a quill ready in her right hand.

"Thank you, Chancellor Oranna."

"You realize this is quite irregular, yes? On numerous accounts."

"So I'm told."

Oranna chuckled. "I'm sure you have been." She lifted the parchment that had held her attention and handed it to Devlyn. "This is your schedule."

Looking at the slender lettering in the blocks of the chart, he saw that on the first five days of the week, from Gwynthaen to Lerenaen, classes began at the third hour of the day, and ended around the eleventh hour. Toward the middle of the week, on Thenaen and Ramaen, the tenth hour was free. The schedule rotated daily, two or three classes after lunch, each an hour long, but the morning lessons lasted a full three hours.

Just looking at the schedule was tiring.

"Are you prepared to pay for your tuition?" asked Oranna.

"Um, how much is it?" asked Devlyn, well aware of the lightness of his coin purse.

"One crown per term, totaling four crowns a year; however, in your circumstance, it will only be three crowns this year, since you've missed the spring term entirely."

Devlyn fished through his coin purse. Velaria had given him and Alex several jents and lewts each. Counting the silver jents, he was short two to equal a crown. Sparing a guilty look at Chancellor Oranna, "I only have eleven jents."

Oranna held him in an unmoving gaze.

"Oh, wait," Devlyn remembered the unfamiliar coins he had found at the Cor Inn. "I'm not sure what they're worth though." He reluctantly pulled them from the purse, not entirely willing to reveal the two gold-like coins.

Chancellor Oranna looked down at the elven profiles, covering her mouth as she took them in. "Where did you get these?"

"I found them at the Cor Inn, where my family used to live." Devlyn tried not to sound guilty about the discovery, as if he had stolen them.

"Do you know what these are?"

Devlyn shook his head.

"They're called lumols; they were part of Krysenthiel's currency, before Erynor started his wretched war. Each lumol was equivalent to three crowns, but that was before the coins disappeared entirely. We have heard reports of them popping up again, with features becoming more visible."

"So, will one cover this year's tuition?"

"You don't understand; they *were* worth three crowns. I know ei'ana who would offer ten times as much today for a single lumol."

Devlyn's heart dropped at the fortune he held in his hand, suddenly feeling much heavier.

"I cannot accept them from you for your tuition. Here, give me the jents that you have, and any lewts. We'll worry about the tuition for the subsequent terms when they start. This term began several weeks ago, so I'll accept this payment for this term's tuition."

With that, Delyn left the chancellor's office and returned to his dormitory where he collapsed on his bed, uncertain whether he was more exhausted from the various meetings or whether it was simply due to traversing the castle, ascending and descending three of her towers in a matter of not much more than an hour. His eyes closed, and his thoughts wafted along the events of the day. He still did not really understand what the Seven Chairs represented, but he did know that they were ei'ana who appeared to be very powerful.

ROBES

D evlyn was uncertain how long he had been sleeping when a soft knock at his door woke him. The knock at first sounded distant, yet it persisted. He managed to roll off the bed to answer the door.

"Good afternoon, Devlyn. Did you have a nice nap?" Velaria asked with a small smile.

Devlyn scratched his head. "How did you know I was napping?"

The smile broadened as Velaria pointed to the mirror next to the wardrobe. He walked over and saw his light brown hair standing every which way and made an eager attempt to flatten it with his hands before turning around.

"I must apologize for my absence," Velaria said, making her way to the window. "You must have a hundred questions about what has happened to you so far. I should have known that once the Azurelles discovered that Yelaris had bonded with me, they would elevate me to the Chair of Azurelle. It's an ancient custom that the Chair of Azurelle ought to be bound to one of the blue dragons. That custom faded when the dragons went into hiding, to save themselves from either serving Erynor or being killed. After Yelaris' astounding appearance with Liam, I was summoned before the entirety of the Azurelles and named Chair almost immediately after we arrived here."

"The question I've wanted to ask all day is, what are the Seven Chairs? Do you manage Gwilnor Academy?"

"No, we do not have that responsibility. We are heads of our respective Schools, and by extension, the seven of us are the elected superiors of the Ei'ana. The first Chairs founded what came to be known as Septyl, and in return, the Seven Schools were named after them. All the original Chairs were Luminari, and after many years, they decided that they wanted to share their prowess in wielding with others. They came here and built this castle, naming the school Gwilnor Academy. It's still a mystery why they chose that name; there isn't any mention of the word in any book or scroll. We don't even know what it translates to: it is possibly an homage to a great educator." Throughout her explanation, Velaria maintained her gaze out the window, only glancing over every now and then at Devlyn who was sitting on his bed, leaving the chair for Velaria's use.

"To answer your second question, the Seven Chairs do not manage Gwilnor; that's the responsibility of the chancellor. However, we are responsible for designating the chancellor and for granting admittance to students. It's not required for a wielder to become an ei'ana; however, Septyl is charged with overseeing the proper use or misuse of wielding. You'll learn more of this in your studies. It might be worthwhile getting a book from the library about Septyl's history." Velaria paused a moment before continuing, her gaze still on what lay beyond the window. "Would you like to join me for a walk? I always enjoyed leaving the castle grounds when I was a student."

"Uh, sure," Devlyn replied, hoping that his nap had enabled him to take on more of the endless corridors and stairs.

Velaria walked past him out the door and led the way through the castle, descending hundreds of stairs until finally reaching the ground floor.

Devlyn paid attention to every stair they walked down, careful not to trip over the hem of his robes. They took some getting used to; he'd had a few near-accidents going to and from the chancellor's office. The entry hall of the castle was a good walk from the North Tower, as they retraced the path he'd taken with Saendre earlier that day. Bright colors danced about the hall, playing against the pale grey stone.

Velaria effortlessly pushed the oversized door open and walked into the bright, late afternoon sun.

Shielding his eyes while they adjusted to the sunlight, Devlyn accompanied Velaria on the semicircular plaza surrounded by an arcade of slender pointed arches that formed a barrier of sorts around the plaza to the entry hall. The arcade had a golden appearance and reminded him of the lumols in his coin purse. As they walked along, Devlyn noticed the architectural features he had missed before. The tall portals had two layers, the inner twice the height of the outer, yet they all connected through pointed arches of the same mysterious translucent stone transformed by the afternoon sun. An arched bridge stretched beyond the plaza to the other side of the narrow river he had seen from his dormitory window. In the distance, the landscape was dominated by the vast white dome that was the Temple of Ceur.

Several Septyl knights stood guard outside the large doors; each bowed to Velaria reverently and addressed her as Mother Velaria.

This was the first time that Devlyn found himself outside the castle since arriving through the seguian, and he was unable to resist craning his neck to get a look at its exterior when he reached the zenith of the bridge. Towers flew into the sky from every direction and intricate flying buttresses supported the vast halls with their large stained-glass windows. Dormers poked through every roofline. The stone of the castle looked like a grey granite with a lighter grey for the pillars and molding. He counted seven tall towers, none shaped like the cylindrical drums he had seen elsewhere; instead, each had seven sides, just like the Chamber of the Seven Chairs and the chancellor's office. Thick pillars rose from the ground up the edges of the towers. The walls of each side arched in a peak with a grand window, repeating twice more, but rotated just slightly, before a steep spire rose from the uppermost level. He grew a bit dizzy as his eyes followed the vertical lines up the slate roof to an unimaginable height. As incredible as the castle was, especially when looking at it from its foundations, such a structure should not be able to stand.

"Will I be able to see Liam anytime soon?" Devlyn asked, turning from Gwilnor to focus on the road ahead of them. He began to count the days that had passed since he had seen his brother.

"There's something I need to tell you about Liam." Velaria's steady pace continued across the bridge, but her tone sounded careful and calculated. "When the ei'ceuril took him into the Chamber of Light to lift the shadow covering his heart, they discovered that your brother also has the ability to wield. Since he is not an elya, the castle is not a fit place for him to live; he has agreed to take up quarters in the Temple of Ceur where he will be kept under surveillance. He has not begun to wield yet, so he is free to come and go at will. However, we suspect that it's only a matter of time. He is rather old to not have started doing so before. When that happens, he will be confined to the temple with the other kien wielders. Truthfully, the shadow covering his heart probably prevented him from doing so while a prisoner. Most begin to wield accidentally by late adolescence."

Devlyn looked down at the street recalling how he had wielded for the first time only a week ago. He felt sorry for Liam but knew that nothing could be done to prevent him from accidentally wielding. Devlyn was still unresolved about his own ability, especially after hearing how dangerous it was for men to wield, and the destruction they were capable of, the destruction *he* was capable of.

"Right now, though, he's with Yelaris in one of Ceurenyl's parks. The two of them have grown quite fond of each other since they left us. He's even managed to keep the many curious people in the city at a distance." Velaria led Devlyn through the crowded streets.

"Will people in the city know that I'm a wielder, since I'm wearing these robes?" Devlyn gestured toward them, loose fabric billowing in the gentle breeze created by their pace.

"All of Gwilnor's students wear those robes, even those who cannot wield. However, word leaked from the castle that a kien wielder capable of controlling his wielding has been admitted. It won't take long until the people in the city know your face. Your presence here was of top secrecy; only the Chairs were informed."

"So then, how did everyone find out?"

"As I said, it was of highest secrecy. Nothing at that level remains unknown for long, especially when it involves one such as yourself."

Now it seemed to Devlyn that the people they passed eyed him suspiciously. He felt a strong urge to slouch and become inconspicuous, even though most of the people he passed shared his height and pointed ears.

"Try not to pay too much attention to that. No one has seen a kien wielder walk freely in living memory. Remember, they all think you're going to obliterate the city and probably all of Teraeniel while you're at it." Devlyn's thoughts turned to what he could do to avoid being seen as a potential world destroyer as they continued to walk.

Eventually, Velaria brought Devlyn to a park on the edge of the city proper. The park sloped up the side of a mountain toward the Temple of Ceur, with the mountain looming behind it. They continued through the tree-covered park, Velaria walking without hesitation, as though she knew exactly where Yelaris and Liam waited. A clearing soon opened before them, and there Devlyn saw a blue mass sprawled on the green grass. He blinked to readjust his eyes before he recognized the magnificent Yelaris soaking in the sun, her blue scales shimmering in the afternoon sunlight.

Liam lounged against the side of the dragon but quickly pushed himself from the grass and leapt toward Devlyn to embrace him. Velaria greeted Yelaris with just a small pat on the nearest leg and settled herself in Liam's place.

"I hear there's a dangerous kien wielder in the city," chided Liam as he ruffled Devlyn's light brown hair before moving away from the dragon to allow the bonded pair to be together. "How long until you bring the city down? I've heard men wager not a month will pass until you're tossed into the temple. Which, might I add, is quite accommodating."

It was impossible to miss Liam's improved disposition. The time spent away from Gneal had brought color back to his skin; his hair was no longer greasy and a natural sheen highlighted his dark locks. He wore black slacks and a green shirt, topped by a finely made jacket of a deeper green.

"I take it they've been treating you well?" Devlyn asked. "And by the looks of it, they've been feeding you too."

Liam chuckled as he patted his not-as-lean stomach. He had gained some healthy weight and had lost his previously emaciated appearance.

"Those ei'ceuril certainly know how to eat. The meals are simple, nothing extravagant, but what's lacking in quality is fully supplied in quantity. Ever since I've arrived, they've done nothing but insist that I eat more.

They've placed me on a soldier's ration! I've even been training with them, the temple knights that is. They took me on shortly after I recovered; I'm also taking some classes with the ei'ceuril students; they talked about sending me to Gwilnor for classes but feared that the overexposure to wielding would only trigger my own aptitude, or something like that. They are letting me train with the Septyl knights on occasion. I've sparred with Alex a few times already; he too has started training with the Septyl knights."

"If you're a student, why aren't you wearing robes?" asked Devlyn, jealous of his brother's normal clothing.

"They did mention a requirement regarding them, but our robes are different in the temple," Liam explained. "I've been wearing them to class, but we wear training clothes when practicing with the knights. It's a bit difficult to use a sword wearing a robe."

Devlyn was happy to share his own news about his recent move into the boys' dormitory, and how he had been restricted to another part of the castle until this very morning. Devlyn even told Liam about the Seven Chairs, and how Velaria was now one of them. When Liam did not show the slightest bit of surprise at that news, Devlyn realized that Liam had already known.

"You knew?" he asked.

Liam chuckled. "The whole city knows, Dev. It happened the very night after you all arrived, with public proclamations in every city square. They had even made bright blue banners showing Velaria and Yelaris. I'm surprised you didn't notice them when you walked through the city." Bells began to toll sonorously, ringing eight times.

"Is it already the eighth hour?" Liam had to speak up. "I'll have to start heading over to the castle soon. I have training with the Septyl knights during the ninth hour. As you can imagine, they don't tolerate tardiness well. Would you like to join? I'm sure Alex will be there, and besides, you can use some muscle on those scrawny arms of yours!"

At that last comment, Devlyn punched Liam in the arm.

"That's it?" Liam feigned surprise. "In that case, you need to spend some time with the knights!" Liam again ruffled Devlyn's hair and waved to Velaria still leaning against Yelaris before the two made their way to the castle. The city streets still teemed with people, just as crowded as they had been not so long ago when Devlyn walked through them with Velaria, if not more. Not a single face did he recognize from earlier. *Can there really be so many people living in one place where you never see the same person twice?* he thought as he walked beside Liam, who did not seem bothered by the many unfamiliar faces. Liam led the way, preferring the smaller side streets, rather than the broad boulevards and their spacious plazas.

The sound of water lapping in the river or in a fountain in the distance reached Devlyn's ears. He searched for the water with his senses, seeking its source and location. There! A serene and precious rise and fall came from a fountain a few streets over. He pressed himself gently into the water from where he walked. The water was continually propelled up into the air from a spout at the center of the fountain before falling into a large pool. What amazed Devlyn was that the fountain never reused the same water; in fact, after the water fell into the fountain, he felt it wash into a drain at the bottom and flow through a pipe beneath the street to the river. The water came from another part of the river, fed through a small pipe with an extreme amount of pressure that allowed the water to splash high into the air when it reached the fountain.

"You really should not be doing that outside the castle," came a soft voice that startled him. He quickly removed himself from aquaeys and turned to the source of the voice: a girl so beautiful that he thought she belonged to the fabric of dreams. The girl's eyes struck him first; a vibrant green encircled the pupil and flowed to a clear, light-filled silver to the iris' edge, just like his own. Her flawless face was framed by brown hair lighter than his; hers could easily be mistaken for blond. The sun reflected off it in such a way that it looked like a silvery gold. She stood just beneath his height and Devlyn could tell from the way she held herself that she had never slouched. She wore the same grey robes of Gwilnor that he wore, but not even the uniform could diminish her figure.

He wanted to respond, but he seemed to have forgotten how to talk, his vocabulary diminished to single syllable words.

Liam was also aware of her, but unlike Devlyn, still had use of his words. "We have every right to walk beyond those walls, thank you," said

Liam, unaware of Devlyn's wielding.

"My apologies, but I was not referring to your walking." The girl smiled at the brothers. It was only then that Devlyn noticed that she was not alone. Four other students stood with her, all wearing Gwilnor's robes; one of them held the girl's hand in his. He looked strong and a few years Devlyn's senior. His expression was similar to Liam's, a slight puzzlement about what the girl meant. The other three girls present giggled in their own way, much like the girls at the abbey school, but here, Devlyn assumed that they too knew about his wielding.

"It's incredible that you're able to control it on your own," said one of the girls. "I heard a rumor but didn't dare believe it to be true."

"I guess so." Devlyn finally remembered how to talk.

Liam looked down at his brother, displaying his disapproval, but chose not to say anything further in front of the others.

"I was only just admitted today, and no one mentioned that I wasn't allowed to do it outside of the castle." Devlyn chose his words carefully to avoid drawing attention from anyone else on the street. "I'm Devlyn, and this is my brother, Liam."

"Pleased to meet you. I'm Ellendren, and this is Trethien," said the girl with hair spun of silver gold who had spoken first.

"Princess Ellendren of the Royal House Roendryn," clarified Trethien in a deep voice. Amazed, Devlyn swallowed his tongue. "And it's Lord Trethien of House Narielle."

"*And*, this is Myranda Lariviere, princess of Sorenthyl, Danielle of House Aerquin, and Fyona Orendi," Ellendren released Trethien's hand and gestured to each of the three girls as she named them. Myranda had long blond hair and bright blue eyes, the only one in the group without elven features. Danielle and Fyona had features similar to Ellendren's however their hair lacked the same luster and was more of a light brown than blond. They appeared older than Ellendren, except for Fyona; Devlyn assumed she was the same age. "We were just walking back to the castle as well; would you care to join us?"

"Don't see why not, although I do need to get back in time for practice." Liam was by far the eldest in this group.

"I haven't been late yet," Trethien replied, not quite boastfully.

Once they started walking, Trethien grabbed Ellendren's hand and held it once again in his own. Ellendren had a curious smile on her face as she glanced down at their joined hands.

"Tell me, Devlyn, are you enjoying Ceurenyl? It's such a lovely city, isn't it? And ancient as well. The exact date of the temple's construction has been long forgotten. We assume the builders were elves, but there's no documentation, only mention of it by scribes before the time of Thellion," said Fyona.

"It's more than I'm used to, that's for sure." Devlyn tried to imagine how many times Cor'lera could fit in Ceurenyl but stopped counting once he reached ten.

"You're nothing like what my classmate described." Myranda gave Devlyn a quizzical look. "She said you wouldn't stop pestering her with the most pointless of questions."

"Do you mean Saendre?" Since Saendre was the only other student he had met at Gwilnor, he thought that must be who Myranda meant. He did not think he had asked her that many questions, and in his opinion, none of them had been pointless.

"Of course. She and I both returned from the Illumined Wood within a week of each other. We're still novices, but we'll soon choose one of the Seven Schools and make known our intention to profess the counsels. She has never been one for long conversations though. I think she intends to choose the Albiens. She's always preferred her scrolls and books to people." Myranda continued to talk casually about her classmate during the rest of the journey and even talked a bit about her time in the Illumined Wood, which meant that no one else did much talking.

The bridge to the castle stretched before them, arching over the river beneath, and from this direction, Devlyn could see that the castle stood on a series of hills with precipices falling between the different structures composing the castle. Two knights stood guard at the castle gates in the plaza with the double colonnade of pointed arches. Devlyn noticed that all the knights wore a similarly styled armor, bright burnished steel covering only parts of their body. Their dark grey tabards had a secondary color outlining the edges and one of the seven emblems of the various Schools emblazoned on the breast.

One of the knights standing guard wore the Vyoletryn emblem and his tunic had a purple outline and emblem. The other wore the Aranti-ulyn emblem with an orange outline and emblem on his. Although Devlyn didn't know whether these were the same knights he and Velaria had passed when they left the castle earlier, he was surprised when both knights ignored all the students as they passed by.

"They are expected to treat all students equally, whether highborn or not. We are to learn to become ei'ana, and as such, we are all equal. Once we profess the counsels, no ei'ana is greater than another, even if she does one day become queen," Ellendren explained when she noted the look on Devlyn's face.

Devlyn could not believe it; surely, they did not expect such person-ages to be on the same level as everyone else. Before he could respond or even think too much on it, Ellendren continued, "Well, we must be off to our lessons, and I assume you are all off to your own. If I'm not mistaken, you'll be joining us in some of our classes, Devlyn. It was nice meeting you both."

Devlyn and Liam responded in like manner. Trethien kissed Ellendren's hand and bade her farewell, somewhat ignoring the rest of them. Devlyn, Liam, and Trethien went to the training grounds, a courtyard on the north side of the castle, the one Devlyn had seen from the window earlier. When they reached the knight's courtyard, Devlyn once again looked up, but from here, he could only see three towers stretch above the castle. Gwilnor Academy was certainly a very large school.

FIRST LESSON

Devlyn woke to the first toll of the bell. It rung only once, signaling the first hour of the day. He found himself glued to his bed and assumed that the sun was beginning to rise, but his eyelids refused to replicate the process. His entire body was sore from the previous day's training. He had not expected to train as long as he had with the knights and their pupils and was certainly not at all eager to repeat the training any time soon. His body ached in places he never knew could ache, and his arms felt as if they would fall from his shoulders.

Too sore to move from bed, he did manage to roll over.

When he heard the bell ring again, this time tolling three times, his heart leapt in his chest at the third toll as he realized that he had slept in on his first day of lessons. Aware of the late morning hour, Devlyn jumped out of his bed, regretting it instantly as his body complained. His first class at Gwilnor would begin in fifteen minutes, whether he was present or not. He splashed freezing water onto his face in the washbowl and hurried into his grey robes, tried to flatten his disheveled hair, and grabbed his pack.

He stole a quick look at his schedule, paying close attention to the script beneath the day, Lerenaen, before tucking it into his pocket and rushing out the room and through the boys' dormitory. He lunged down the first flight of stairs, taking two or even three steps at a time, careful to not trip over his robe. He darted through the corridor lining the knights' courtyard and rushed through the subsequent corridors, paying little attention to whatever or whoever he passed. His class at Gwilnor was on the opposite side of the castle, requiring him to cross both bridges, before running through the final third of the castle.

The door leading to the theoreticals class finally appeared before him. His first class at Gwilnor and he was late. When he opened the door, he saw every eye in the room turn to look at the latecomer.

"Huh, huh, huh," the magister bellowed throatily from the front of the room. He was an elderly elf, with only a few strands of wispy white hair left atop his scalp. His piercing silver eyes penetrated Devlyn to the core.

"Well, if it isn't my newest victim! Might I assume this to be Devlyn?" His broad but mischievous grin did not bode well.

"Yes, magister," said Devlyn before apologizing for his tardiness.

"No need for apologies. You see, one of the *privileges* of tardiness, is that your fellow students kindly left the seat closest to the front just for you. You really ought to thank them."

Devlyn nervously scanned the room for another seat but soon found that he had no choice but to take the proffered seat, dead center of the front row.

"I'm Brother Therril, magister of theoreticals. Now, as I was about to ask, does anyone know the principles of theories?" Therril looked across the room, looking at each student with piercing eyes. "What about you, Devlyn, can you tell us anything about theories?"

Swallowing, Devlyn looked up nervously. "Does it have something to do with a personal theory?" He tried to remember what he'd learned at the abbey school in Cor'lera. There, the study of theoreticals was condensed into another class and given little attention.

"Oh, that's certainly part of it, indeed. But the question is, how does one take all the personal theories and turn them into a theoretical? For this we need principles." Another moment passed before Therril shifted his view to another student. "Yes, yes, please enlighten us, Ellendren."

The entire class turned toward Ellendren. "They are the Communal Principle, the Authentic Principle, and the Absurd Principle." As dozens of quills began scratching against parchment, Devlyn took the opportunity of not being directly in the eye of the magister to rummage through his own bag for a quill to do the same before forgetting the principles.

"Wonderful!" exclaimed Therril and went on to discuss the three principles in detail.

Devlyn did his best to take proper notes on the subject, but he knew he did not capture every word, let alone every point.

When the class came to an end, Therril asked Devlyn to stay behind. Once the class emptied, Therril came close to him and looked intently at his face. "You look so much like your father," he said at last.

"Really? I was always told I looked like my mother."

"I'm sure she does too." Evidently, Therril's thoughts had moved on. "Tell me, has a guide been assigned to you yet?"

"A guide? What's that?"

"They're advisors of sorts. They oversee your studies and mentor you in wielding. If there is no one already assigned, as an ei'ceuril I would like to take you on as your guide. Others will without a doubt soon be fighting over you, if they haven't started arguing among themselves already. Especially the ei'ana! They simply don't trust a man who can wield, particularly one with a claim to wield with control! A poor bloke a few years back claimed to have control. Anyway, we can meet at the end of the day on Uraen, after your lessons, of course. You'll meet with several ei'ana and ei'ceuril throughout your studies for private lessons, but only your guide chooses who are to instruct you in those. So, what do you say?"

"I thought any man capable of wielding was restricted to the temple," said Devlyn in confusion, since from Therril's words, he thought the magister had every intention of instructing him in wielding.

Therril let out his throaty laugh, which Devlyn was growing accustomed to, especially after three hours of class with him. "I won't be instructing you in that sense. I deal purely with theoreticals. It's proper and fitting that an ei'ceuril carry out the private lessons for lumenys. We do live in the Temple of Ceur after all. Besides, the ability to wield lumenys has been all but lost, even among us ei'ceuril. There have been rare occurrences when one of our order managed it; as I hear, your own uncle, Arlyn, had managed it before his ability to wield dwindled to nothing. Something has been lost to our knowledge concerning lumenys, as well as the other transcendental erendinth, umbrys, and animys."

Devlyn tried to understand what Therril was saying. "The other transcendental erendinth?"

"The ability left to the ei'ana is minuscule, while the ei'ceuril capable of wielding are forbidden from doing so. We simply do not have the control nor knowledge to wield them as we once did," explained Therril. "It's for that reason the ei'ceuril will conduct your private lessons with the transcendental erendinth. While we aren't able to wield them or instruct you on how they are to be wielded, we will be able to provide you with our theories and traditions behind them, and what we have that survived the fall of Krysenthiel."

It was a lot to take in and without Devlyn intending to, a few quiet moments passed as he considered all that Therril had said. Finally, the magister pressed for a reply.

"Well, what do you say? Will you have me as your guide?"

"Um, sure. You seem to be, um…experienced." Devlyn certainly admired the old ei'ceuril before him, even if he seemed a bit eccentric.

"Huh, huh, huh, that I certainly am. In that case," Therril pulled a slip of paper with several names scribbled on it from a pocket concealed in his white robes, "these are the ei'ana and ei'ceuril that you are to meet with for private lessons; they are your tutors. There are seven, myself included, of course. These lessons will refine your wielding; a large classroom can only provide so much. I have also placed Ellendren on that list as your fellow. It's vital that the two of you meet and practice together. I want you to meet with her following each of your private lessons. Is that clear?"

Suddenly feeling overwhelmed, Devlyn looked down at the list with all the names scribbled on it. Devlyn was relieved to discover Velaria listed, but doubted she had the time for private lessons; he had rarely seen her since her elevation to the Chair of Azurelle. After a quick glance at the list, he returned his attention to Therril. "How often will I have private lessons?"

"Let's see, there are no lessons on Saraen and Karaen, so that leaves five days a week. You'll have to take double lessons on two of those days, to fit all seven of them in. On those days, you only need to meet with Ellendren once; I would suggest in the evening after supper. She really is a busy girl."

"Will she be all right with meeting so frequently? After all, won't she have to do the same?" asked Devlyn, not wanting to dominate Ellendren's schedule, even if he did want to spend time with her after only meeting her twice, and one of those times was only sitting in the same classroom.

"She's a bright girl. Besides, she'll need a new fellow soon enough. Her current fellow will be off to the Illumined Wood to start her novitiate soon. Now, I would like you to track down the ei'ana and ei'ceuril on this list and ask them if they will take you on for private lessons, and to arrange a time to meet with them. Your private lesson with me will always start at the twelfth hour on Uraen, after your other classes are finished for the day. I suggest you don't schedule any other that day," Therril said in a curious tone before continuing. "You might not have the energy. Now let's get to my office; today's the exception. I'll not have someone else give you a proper lesson before I get to you!"

Devlyn grabbed his things and followed the magister to his office. It had a large, west-facing window that flooded the office with sunlight. Devlyn squinted to look into the bright light beyond the window but even so, he could see no further than the edge of the city walls. "Why can't I can't see further past the city?" he asked Magister Therril. No one had explained why a dense fog constantly surrounded the city. Every morning, he saw the fog, and every morning he expected it to disperse by midday, but not once had it lessened.

Therril frowned out his window. "That, I'm afraid, is a story for another day. What you look on is Krysenthiel, the fallen kingdom of the elves of Luminare, frozen and forgotten within the Shroud. I insisted that my office and classroom face west, to serve as a reminder so that I might never lose hope."

Therril's explanation did nothing to clarify things for Devlyn, and his confusion was clearly written across his face. Therril told him to not worry himself over it and went on to the lesson.

"Now, please, take a seat on the ground, with your legs crossed like this." Therril sat and crossed his legs, surprisingly agile for someone his age. "No, no, no, face me and come closer."

Once they sat on the ground, too close for Devlyn's comfort, Therril began to recite a story from memory. "There once, and still are, seven siblings who are brothers and sisters to all. Created by Anaweh, the Living One, the Creating Light, as gifts to any who asked for them, these are the irythil, the seven anadel who brought the erendinth and thus created Teraeniel, the World-Below. Their names are Uriel, whose gift is lumenys; Gwynthiel, whose gift is animys; Ramiel the betrayer, whose gift was umbrys; Theniel, whose gift is aquaeys; Sariel, whose gift is terys; Lereniel, whose gift is aerys; and Kariel, whose gift is ignys. These gifts are the seven erendinth. Four are known as elemental erendinth, and three as transcendental erendinth. From what I have heard, you have already wielded the four elemental erendinth together. I want you to demonstrate it now, for me. I must know where you are presently."

Therril's piercing gaze held him. Devlyn nodded under the pressure from that look before closing his eyes. The process began much as it had the previous day; he first noticed the air, then the water, next was the stone of the office floor and walls, followed by fire from the hearth. He pressed himself into each, aware of their unique and various strengths and qualities, and maintained a balance between them all. He did not see the four rings of the elemental erendinth swirling about him and Therril with his eyes, but Devlyn did *see* the erendinth, even with his eyes closed. The elements themselves did not swirl about the room, only the erendinth; the elements' essence.

"Very good. Now, tell me, is there anything discernible about them?" Therril asked.

Devlyn tried to focus on the various erendinth. At one moment, they were similar, the next unidentifiable.

"Now, I want you to focus within; continue to hold on to the erendinth, but place your focus within, inside yourself," came Therril's voice, making Devlyn think that he was not doing it correctly.

His focus shifted away from the erendinth, even as he remained aware of them, to within himself. He could now feel a pull from inside, from his very core, begging almost to be noticed.

That's your heart. Go deeper—deeper. He could hear Therril's request, except it didn't come through his ears. He wanted to pull away from himself, but he followed the request, somewhat timidly, and allowed the interior pull to draw his awareness deeper within, even though he wanted nothing more than to withdraw.

Now, he felt the familiar presence of the erendinth. He recognized their characteristics in himself, mirroring his exterior motions. Slowly, he pulled out of himself, and just as slowly, he withdrew from the erendinth.

"How is it that the erendinth are in me? And how is it that they mirror what I do with the erendinth externally?" asked Devlyn, noticing his exhaustion for the first time. An onslaught of questions begged answers. *Was Therril inside my head?*

A broad smile spread across Therril's face. "Actually, you have it backward. But, to start off, what you just did, by today's standards, is impossible. What you did just now is proof that you are able to control your own strength, which might I add is without limit. You know that you are an elya, I trust?"

Devlyn nodded, the term still fresh and unfamiliar, only a week old.

"Internal awareness is the key to control. All it takes is to know yourself. Women learn to do by natural instinct what you have just done. We men have difficulty in delving deep within ourselves and seeing what is at our very core. I want you to practice that excrcise frequently. Get to know yourself better! Secondly, what you do externally reflects what you do internally. The reason kien wielders lose control is because their interior is in chaos. They need a kiara wielder to teach them control, a control that women seem to instinctively understand. Unfortunately, there has not been a kiara wielder strong enough to teach a kien wielder control since the Balance between them was broken."

Before Devlyn could ask further questions, Therril continued speaking, anticipating Devlyn. "The genders need one another to reach their full potential; the different wielders cannot exist in a vacuum. Just as a kiara wielder brings the kien wielder to his full potential, so too, does a kien wielder bring a kiara wielder to her full potential. This Balance has been lost to us since the massacre of Septyl. The reason that kiara wielders have not been strong enough is because they have not been able to reach their potential strength. In this case, kiara wielders require kien wielders to tap that potential strength. The two depend on each other and nurture each other. Since the Balance between the two was lost, neither can aid the other."

"You make them sound as if they're intended to be complementary."

Therril smiled proudly at Devlyn but did not say anything.

"Is that why I was brought here? Do the ei'ana hope to have me aid them in reaching their potential again?"

"Huh, huh, huh. They would very much like that. But it's not as general as they think, especially coming from one so young. Perhaps in time, when you mature in your wielding, you will be able to instruct kiara wielders on reaching their potential strength, but only they can tap the incredible strength lying within. A certain bond must take place. You, for example, will only find a handful here who will be able to learn from you. I have a hunch that Ellendren is among that limited number. Do not think yourself exempt. Simply because you are an elya and can wield with control does not mean that you do not need to learn from kiara wielders. It is vital that kiara guide kien and vice versa."

The thought of being alone with Ellendren for extended periods of time as they practiced together was making Devlyn nervous. It was not long before the bell began to toll once again; to Devlyn's amazement, it tolled a total of eight times. "There's no way that can be right. It can't be the eighth hour of the day already!" Devlyn did not quite believe the bells.

"They work just fine. I told you, our private lessons would be exhausting." Therril wore a curious smile.

"But I didn't even notice the time pass; a whole two hours," said Devlyn.

"Time is a funny thing, especially when you enter your heart; it's as if it doesn't exist there." Therril had the same curious, yet oddly mischievous grin. "I guess I've kept you long enough. You'd better hurry off to your next class; and don't forget to find your tutors afterward."

SCHEDULES

Dim lighting filled the classroom. Thick grey draperies covered the lone window. A few candles, scattered around the room, cast obscure shadows due to their peculiar placement. Twenty or so students sat in desks facing the elderly magister at the front of the room. Devlyn had been a little surprised and also pleased to discover that Alex was also in this class. He and Alex were identifiably the oldest students in the classroom by at least two years.

At dinner the previous night, Devlyn had learned that the magister, an Albien ei'ana named Ethyl, had been teaching history for over fifty years. More astounding than her tenure was how little her lessons had changed over those fifty years. The knight's pupils he'd sat with had gleefully told him that notes and tests had been passed down from year to year since she was a young magister, when a group of clever students first discovered that her lessons and exams never changed. In fact, some ei'ana now well into their fifties and sixties who had studied under Ethyl claimed that her dry monotone voice remained as unchanged as the lessons she taught.

Devlyn could look past the droning voice, and possibly even the dim lighting in the classroom, but the combination was more than he could manage so he was surprised as he heard Ethyl say in a slightly louder voice, "…due by our next lesson."

Turning toward the student sitting next to him, Devlyn saw a young girl jotting down the assignment on her parchment, a parchment that had little other writing covering it.

"The Yanilean's mask; seventy-five lines," the girl whispered as she caught Devlyn craning his neck to catch a glimpse of her notes.

Devlyn never managed to learn her name that day, nor anyone else's in his history class. Therril had kept him so long that not only was there no time for lunch, he had also arrived late for his second class at Gwilnor.

Leaving the dimly lit classroom with the other students, Devlyn and Alex made their way through the crowded corridors toward their next lesson. Devlyn was determined to reach at least one class on time today. Rather than walk around the central courtyard through the corridors, they took the nearest door and walked straight across the main courtyard toward their politics class. Devlyn vaguely understood and respected the reasoning that placed Alex and him in a low-level history course. The abbey school they had attended at Cor'lera was notorious for teaching history from a certain perspective. Unfortunately, that particular lens was not entirely accurate and managed to omit anything that shed a positive light on elves, ei'ana, and the Lucillian Alliance.

They walked through the heavy door into their politics class to find it empty. "So, this is what it's like to show up early."

"We could have walked slower," grumbled Alex. "I still can't believe they're making me take classes here and pay a tuition! My parents will be livid when they receive the bill."

"You didn't pay your tuition?"

"'Course not, I wasn't handing over my only coin for school. It's silly they're making me take classes in the first place. I don't know why they won't let the knight's pupils just train."

"Probably because they don't want mindless drones like Trethien." Devlyn looked over his shoulder to make sure the class was still empty.

"I take it you've found that noblewoman from your dreams?" Alex asked, suddenly interested.

"They look nothing alike, but she's certainly the stuff dreams are made of." Devlyn's mind glazed over.

"Well, your goofy smile says you're enjoying that dream. I'll be back, I need to use the lavatory."

Devlyn took a seat near the rear of the classroom, not wanting to be the center of attention again and tried to stop smiling. He pulled his schedule out to look up the name of the magister for this class. Kai—could it be the same Kai that Therril wanted him to have private lessons with?

Not a moment later, a woman with silky black hair shot through with strands of white in a tight bun atop her head entered from a door along the front wall. Her facial features angled slightly, similar to an elf's, but nowhere near as extreme and her ears were rounded. Icy blue eyes looked to the only student in her classroom.

"Are you Magister Kai?" he asked, rising from his seat and going toward her.

Her eyes narrowed, becoming thin slits. "Typically, a student knows their magister." Uncertain whether to take that as an answer, Devlyn considered rephrasing his question. "But, yes, that is my name. You're Devlyn, correct?"

He nodded a friendly smile. He pulled out the hastily scrawled list of names and erendinth Therril had given him. "Magister Therril assigned me to learn terys from you, um…privately."

"Typically," Kai said flatly, "a magister requests such of the student, not the other way around."

Devlyn felt the blood in his veins pulse. Had he breached some sort of ancient protocol?

"Clever old man." Kai seemed to consider her possibilities. "Very well, we shall meet mid-week, every Ramaen at the sixth hour."

Devlyn returned to his seat as other students began to pour through from the corridor, Alex among them. Instantly, he was relieved to note that they seemed to be nearer his own age.

"Is it true? Can you really wield without losing control?" asked a boy in wrinkled robes who took the seat next to him. He had the common Lucillian features, light brown hair with silver and green eyes and pointed ears. He dropped the stack of books tucked under his arm onto the desktop.

Caught off guard by the unexpected question, Devlyn assured him that he could, and introduced himself.

"Sorry; I'm Kevn Weyvien. I saw you come late to Therril's class. I make sure to never be late for that one. He gets some weird enjoyment out of making students sit front and center. And he makes sure to have just enough seats; that way, someone always has to."

"I thought that was odd," Devlyn replied just before Kai called for the class to quiet down.

Kai spent most of the hour speaking of the strained relations between the kingdoms of Yanil and Tiel, even though they were closer allies with one another than any other kingdom to the north.

The sound of quills scratching against parchment filled the room. Devlyn wrote everything he could but noticed that Kevn did not so much as pull out a single piece of parchment.

Ellendren sat near the front of the classroom, her quill moving rapidly. Several other girls surrounded her. Devlyn recognized Fyona and Danielle, but that was it. He knew that he had to ask Ellendren about being fellows, but the thought of asking her in front of the other girls was nerve-wracking. He decided to concentrate on the magister's lecture instead of worrying about it, but not before Alex caught him staring and kicked Devlyn's leg. Devlyn turned back to his parchment, ignoring Alex, and before he realized it, he was out in the corridor again walking next to Kevn.

"Do you have algorithms with Jayna?" Kevn asked.

"Let me check." Devlyn pulled his schedule out of his pocket and stole a glance toward the bottom. "Yeah, how do we get there?"

"This way," said Kevn, walking through the crowded corridor.

"I'll see you later, Dev, I have class with the knights," Alex called out as he walked in the opposite direction.

"Ok, see you later." Devlyn waved to Alex and turned back to Kevn. "I also need to find Velaria, to ask her if she'll be one of my tutors, along with some other ei'ana and ei'ceuril."

"Shouldn't be too much trouble; I overheard someone mention she had meetings in the temple today. We can go over after Jayna's class."

"How long have you been in Ceurenyl?"

"Over three years now. Ten is the earliest anyone can enter Gwilnor Academy. They don't want irresponsible children running about after all." Kevn deepened his voice for the last part. "You weren't here yet, but you should've seen it when that dragon of Velaria's showed up. The whole city was up in arms when it flew directly toward us, and not just that, but toward the temple! Ei'ana and Septyl knights alike rushed to the temple to defend it. They ordered all the students to their dormitories, not like that would have kept us safe from a dragon if it turned on us, but the boys' dormitory has a spectacular view of the temple. Crazy times we're living in.

"Anyway, the abbey school I attended back in Lucillia sent me here to study and become an ei'ceuril. I was all for it, until I decided that I didn't want to do it anymore. Did you know, they can't have a wife and children? I suppose I knew that before I left Lucillia, but never put one and two together or I was too young to care. It only hit me after my second year. I asked the ei'ana if I could study at Gwilnor instead of the temple. Since I'm not a wielder, I only had to meet with the chancellor."

"Are you studying with the knights as well?" asked Devlyn.

"Absolutely not. Don't get me wrong, I practice with them when required, but no matter how much I try, I simply can't gain any muscle." Kevn squeezed his skinny bicep in demonstration. "Besides, those pupils sure know how to give you a bruising. I can't say whether it's the same for you, but I certainly don't intend to live with bruises all my life."

"Yeah, and the worst is waking the morning after. I was so sore this morning that I couldn't get out of bed! That's why I was late for theoreticals."

"I'm one of those normal students you don't hear much about. I take the regular class load, but since I'm not studying to be an ei'ana or a knight, my private lessons are devoted to research. I work a lot with the Albiens; they run the library here. They've been collecting scrolls and manuscripts for centuries. They would love to get to the actual city of Septyl, west of Lake Saeryndol up in the mountains, but apparently, to pass through the Shroud is to die, or something like that. I'm all for recovering forgotten knowledge, especially the books and manuscripts the Ei'ana of

Septyl locked up, but I wouldn't call myself too eager to go there. Although some of the Albiens might actually kill to get their hands on the scrolls left there before the fall of Krysenthiel and the Shroud."

"Sorry, I've heard it mentioned before, but I'm still not sure what it is."

"You don't know about it, do you? Wow, you really are from the edge of Eklean!" Kevn stopped walking to look at Devlyn as if he had two heads. "Emperor Erynor Meriden devised the Shroud, you know, the evil Cyndinari emperor back then. It covers all Krysenthiel, what was once the kingdom of the Luminari. The Shroud not only encased it all, but also froze it. Lake Saeryndol is a huge block of ice because of it. They say that such bitter cold is known nowhere else in the world, not even in Glacien. Anyone who enters freezes, and that's if the Shroud doesn't poison you first. Ei'ana attempted to enter with their wielding, but only one returned, and the records mention that she barely escaped with her life. There's a record of her testimony in the library. I read it and was instantly convinced that I never want to get any closer to that Shroud than I am currently."

"Wait, I thought Ceurenyl was part of Krysenthiel," said Devlyn quite confused over how the Shroud functioned. "Does it ignore Ceurenyl?"

"Now that's a fun mystery you're poking at, Dev." Kevn's knowing smile showed his excitement. "It's the Temple of Ceur. For some reason, the temple prevents it from encasing Ceurenyl. The ei'ceuril say it's only by the grace of Anaweh that the city is protected. Others say it has something to do with how the temple was constructed, and whatever wielding was used on it. You'll see it soon, the Chamber of Light; for one, it's larger than you could ever imagine, second you can't see the top of the dome, all you can see is that light flooding through."

Devlyn tried to imagine what Kevn described but could not imagine a light so bright that it prevented someone from seeing the ceiling. *Isn't light supposed to make it easier to see something?*

"Next you're going to tell me you've never heard of the Erendinth Games."

Devlyn just stared blankly.

"Truly? It's a great spectator sport, well, for guys at least. Since only girls can wield safely, the game's limited to them. Perhaps they'll let you play, since you can wield safely after all."

Algorithms began and ended in a rush. Jayna appeared nice enough, but she did not stop talking the entire class, showing examples and problems. By the time the bells tolled, Devlyn was surprised that an entire hour had passed as he and Kevn made their way out of the castle. Kevn had said he'd show Devlyn the temple.

The streets were just as crowded today as the day before. Devlyn wondered whether they were ever empty. By the time they reached the main road leading up to the Temple of Ceur, Devlyn was amazed as he looked at it from the street. No buildings lined the road to the temple, because even if the people of Ceurenyl had decided to build along the road, they would have had to do so along the precipitous slope of the mountain. As it was, the street to the temple swerved up the side of the mountain in a series of switchbacks.

Most of the gradient was terraced with gardens where trees hung over the street at almost every step. From every level they climbed, they could look down on the trees of the level below, which, until a few moments prior as they walked along, had been above. *It can't be that much further to the temple.* Because of the terracing and trees, it was impossible to see what lay beyond them.

They finally arrived at the slender arched bridge before the magnificent Temple of Ceur, the curves of its cascading domes filling Devlyn's vision. The trickling sound of water rushed beneath them. Devlyn couldn't identify the stone the temple was made of. It had a cloudy, semi-opaque appearance, white, but not white, just very different from anything in his previous experience. He knew it was a large building; that much was obvious from looking out his dormitory window, but that did not compare with standing in front of its entrance, where the sheer immensity created a formidable impression. When he had looked at the temple from his window, it had appeared as a single unified mass but as he walked in front of it, he noticed the various forms jutting out of the central mass with the largest dome. Each section cascaded toward the ground in an elegant slope, making the building feel approachable as the scale of each piece diminished until the smallest element welcomed people inside. The semi-circular form was crowned with a half dome. Nestled in its center sat a curved alcove sheltering the entrance. It looked like someone had taken a spoon and scooped the stone out of the larger form to create the alcove.

Every step Devlyn took toward the temple revealed another layer of the temple that he had missed earlier. From his dormitory window, Devlyn overlooked the incredible amount of ornamentation lining the building. From here, he could see the intricate openings for enormous windows wrapped around the walls and balconies ballooning away from the building.

Within the alcove stood massive wooden doors, guarded by a temple knight on either side. Carved panels lined both doors, depicting scenes Devlyn wasn't familiar with. He assumed they had something to do with Anaweh or the Ei'ceuril.

Many of the knights had been sent to the Temple of Ceur because of their ability to wield. They did not wish to become ei'ceuril, but neither did they desire to sit around and do nothing for the rest of their lives. With limited options, some of them chose to become temple knights.

Six knights stood guard, none of them capable of wielding. Kevn had described to him on their way over that no man capable of wielding was permitted to leave the temple. The knights stood at attention, but two did move from their place to open the doors. Devlyn thanked them and followed Kevn inside.

For a temple devoted to the Light, Devlyn had expected it to be brighter. Inside, however, a foreboding haze claimed the entryway. Lit braziers in sconces along the walls barely illuminated the space. The dark stone walls, another stone Devlyn did not recognize, held a surprise. When he approached the glassy surface on one side, Devlyn was shocked to see his own reflection staring back at him. Wide pillars lined either side of the corridor.

Kevn noticed that Devlyn looked at every pillar as they passed. "Each one is said to represent a different people. It was first thought that they represented the different races, but the ei'ceuril are fairly certain that there aren't that many races."

They continued their walk through the long corridor until they reached a set of doors just as large as the last, with an additional six temple knights standing guard. "Who wishes to enter the Light?" they asked in unison.

"Kevn. I am not worthy to enter into such splendor, but by the will of Anaweh, the Creating Light." Earlier, Kevn had explained the required words which allowed entrance to the temple, so Devlyn repeated them.

Without responding, two knights opened the colossal doors and the others moved away. Light flooded into the dark pillar-lined corridor, illuminating the entire space, and lighting the dark walls. Devlyn could not believe how the once-dark corridor now gleamed in the light. It was almost blinding and the dark stone now resembled the cloudy exterior stone.

Kevn passed through the doors, Devlyn right behind him into a space that took Devlyn by surprise. The room was square, but it looked as though a lighted sphere filled the center, descending from the vast dome above. Devlyn followed Kevn around the edges of the walls, looking up in awe as the walls simply faded into the light above. It was as if he stared into the heavens themselves. The source of the light came from the upper reaches of the dome and flooded the entirety of it. The light was so strong that he could not even see clear across the room; in fact, he doubted that he could see beyond a quarter of the distance from where he stood.

The further from the doors he walked, the lighter he felt, as if his body wanted to rise to the uppermost reaches. "Am I supposed to feel like I'm about to float?" asked Devlyn, becoming increasingly aware of the sensation of his body drifting.

"Whoa!" exclaimed Kevn as he grabbed for Devlyn's arm to pull him back down. "That happens sometimes. Never to me, but it's not all uncommon to see an ei'ceuril bobbing about in here. Come on, let's find Mother Velaria."

The Temple of Ceur

Velaria sat attentively in her straight-backed chair, waiting as the men around her argued vociferously. All had something to say about the newest arrival at Gwilnor and since she was in session with a group of ei'ceuril wise ones, none of an eminence lower than a steward, she waited patiently as they expressed their views. The patient waiting did not preclude her mind from wandering to thoughts of just how many wise ones the Ei'ceuril might have. The inter-workings of their order were reasonably well-known; however, their politics made no sense, and Velaria, along with other ei'ana, had never found any logic in the inner-temple politics. So, for now, she listened.

They all sat at a large round table with dozens of chairs of the same style surrounding it. One chair did not match the others, though. If there was a head to this round table, it was where *that* chair was placed. Finely carved, it was made of wood from a particular tree, a tree not unlike the stellendi trees of the Eldin Wood; however, this species hailed from the Skyland of Aldinare, not Eldinare.

At the top of the chair back, a sun had been carved into it, its beams of light cascading down to the rest of the chair. Ceurtriarch Ealyndol Roendryn, the High Archsteward, definitive leader of the Ei'ceuril, and Arbiter of the Light, sat in *that* chair. When the room had been designed and furnished, the intention had been to create the impression that all who sat at the table held equal status. However, the chair clearly indicated that one was above the rest.

Nearly three hours had passed since Velaria had taken her seat at the table. It always stunned her that ei'ceuril, an order of peaceful and prayerful folk, argued so fiercely. As a child, she had had the impression that ei'ceuril could do no wrong, especially the stewards, let alone the stewards deemed wise ones, some of them archstewards. However, today, the seats around the table held no peaceful or prayerful folk. She half expected them to start cursing. Velaria had sat through more than a few shouting matches among the ei'ana, particularly when the different Schools had to work together, but ei'ana were not ei'ceuril. They did not consecrate themselves to the Light. Becoming an ei'ana certainly had its fair share of sacrifices, but the life of an ei'ceuril was based on self-denial, the ei'ceuril a beacon of peace in a world torn by violence and discord, a witness that peace in the Light was possible.

Ealyndol slouched in his chair, as most old men do. Velaria couldn't tell whether he was sad or tired. A long thin beard that ended on his lap prevented her from making out the pattern of the intricate gold and silver scrollwork on the front of his white robe.

"The boy should be brought here immediately!" yelled one of the ei'ceuril. He looked to be in his fifties and although he was bearded like all the other men in the room, his beard was not as long, nor did it have as much grey and white. "All of us here understand the risk we are placing him and everyone else in."

The discussion was a bitter one and the more they argued, the more logical it sounded, since they all agreed that Devlyn should be in the temple. The argument instead centered on which reason was the strongest for bringing Devlyn to them. Velaria had the challenging task of preventing that from happening. However, each of the ei'ceuril was convinced that his reasoning was the best one to support the move.

"Please, stewards." Velaria glanced across the large table and waited for the wise ones to quiet down. "Devlyn has passed the tests. He's capable of wielding the elemental erendinth with control. I've tested him myself, and he was again tested before the Seven Chairs. He places no one in danger. Who knows, one day he might wield the transcendental erendinth. Surely, you all see the good in that—Balance restored at long last."

Several of the wise ones seemed intent on resuming their arguments but paused as Ealyndol cleared his throat. He had not spoken thus far, and his soft voice required the others to remain quiet to hear him.

"My daughter, we do not doubt his strength nor his control. He will become a fine wielder if he remains at Gwilnor Academy. However, we must not forget the prophecy spoken from the lips of Lucillia herself and validated by the time wardens." He cleared his throat again before reciting the prophecy she knew all too well. "Lucillia herself prophesied, 'Two sons of Light I shall birth. Alone, one shall rule. When the Age of Shadow returns and the Darkness all but engulfs the Light, the last bird of Light shall hatch as a new sun rises. The lesser brother shall give his life untarnished and the glory of the Light shall shine from Arenthyl to reach every crevice darkened by Shadow.'"

Ealyndol looked carefully at Velaria before continuing. "You know its meaning, as do we. All will be lost if he does not become an ei'ceuril. Only death awaits him and us all if he does not. Surely you do not want him to meet that end."

Velaria remained unmoved in her chair, debating whether to speak against the prophecy. She knew it and its accompanying interpretations well, but she had never quite settled with them after she left the Illumined Wood as a novice.

"My daughter, think of what is at stake here should he not himself become an ei'ceuril."

"You have my word that I will consider it. But this must be brought before the Seven Chairs. The decision is not ours alone, but ultimately belongs to Devlyn." Velaria stood and formally bade farewell to the Ceurtriarch and his wise ones.

Kevn turned into yet another corridor in the temple, leading them to a pair of doors at the far end. Devlyn had no idea where they now stood in the temple, only that they now walked far beneath where they had originally entered. They had descended a beautifully carved staircase, before Kevn led the way along several corridors. Thoroughly lost, Devlyn marveled at the size of the temple.

As they approached, the doors opened. Kevn grabbed Devlyn and pulled him behind one of the wide columns lining the corridor, easily concealing them both.

"Abhorrent woman!" came a voice, clearly disturbed over whatever had taken place in the room. Kevn pressed a finger to his lips. Devlyn did not feel right about hiding behind a column like a common thief.

"Quite right," came another voice. Both voices sounded like elderly men. "She has no reverence for prophecy. Who knows what will happen if she and the other ei'ana continue in their stubbornness. It's been verified, Erynor has returned. If that boy she brought doesn't become an ei'ceuril, either he will die, or all the living will fall back into Shadow! Under what authority does she presume to prevent him from fulfilling his destiny?" the voice held irritation bordering on anger.

Too concerned about remaining hidden, Devlyn did not see them as they passed by, but his mind raced at what he overheard. *Prophecy? Did they refer to me? Why did Velaria say nothing? I'm going to die?* He grappled with it as they stayed hidden while several others exited the room; the ei'ceuril did not speak much, just moved away with feet scraping against the floor. Devlyn and Kevn emerged from behind the pillar when the sound of the last pair faded into silence. Kevn shot his new friend a quick glance of concern.

"You look like you've seen a ghost," said Kevn as he patted him on the back. "Are you all right, Dev?"

Without answering, Devlyn walked toward the doors. He wanted answers. He had gone through so much in the past months, and to now discover that he had been led blindly by Velaria was more than he could handle. He hoped she was behind the doors; an onslaught of questions demanded answering. Blood rushed through his veins; he felt angry and betrayed. Devlyn pushed the doors open to a circular room with a round table in the center surrounded by chairs.

The room was empty.

Kevn patted Devlyn on the back again. "Why didn't she tell me?" Devlyn finally asked, struggling to hold back tears. "We traveled for four months together. Not once did she mention any prophecy!" He'd refused to follow Alex's better judgment; he'd trusted her.

"This room is off limits," a woman's voice came from the doorway behind them. "Kevn, is that you? What in heavens are you doing back in the temple? Here of all places!"

"Sorry, Sister Lillianna, we were, um…" began Kevn as he attempted to concoct a story.

"Do not allow deceit to touch your lips, Kevn. I overheard some of what he said." She took one look at Devlyn, noted his expression, and rushed to him. "Oh, dearie, not to worry. What's troubling you? You can tell Sister Lillianna what's on your mind." Devlyn looked at her and saw a youthful looking woman. She had dark-brown, almost black, hair peeping out from under the shawl covering her head, brown eyes, and freckled cheeks. Her simple white robe, tied at the waist by a green sash, covered her entire body. "Might I ask who has hurt you so?"

Uncomfortable with opening up to a stranger, he asked instead, "Who are you?"

"As I said, I am Sister Lillianna. I was once an ei'ana of the Emradiel School, but now I'm an ei'ceuril, consecrated to the Light."

"There are female ei'ceuril?" asked Devlyn. "I thought only men can be ei'ceuril and ei'ana are only women."

Sister Lillianna smiled. "It might appear that way. So few women have joined the Ei'ceuril in recent years. But there was a time when only female ei'ceuril filled the abbey schools. In fact, it was the Ei'ceuril sisters who restarted them. It was a time of chaos; it was near the end of Erynor's rule all those years ago. If he had not been overthrown, the abbey schools would have surely been destroyed again. Unfortunately, he had already seen to exterminating the female stewards during his early reign."

Hearing the name Erynor reminded Devlyn of the prophecy. It must have been written on his face, for Lillianna asked yet again if he was all right.

"I'm fine. We should get going." Devlyn truly did not want to talk about what troubled him.

"All right, dearie, but if you ever want to talk, don't be afraid to come find me," said Lillianna in what was possibly the politest voice Devlyn had ever heard. It made him feel a little guilty for not telling her what bothered him, but he decided it was best to keep it to himself and moved back to the door of the room.

"Exactly where in the temple are we?" Devlyn asked Kevn a few minutes later as they walked along yet another corridor.

"Beneath the Chamber of Light—almost everything in the temple is. Between the Chamber of Light and where we are now, are offices and living quarters. The archstewards and the wise ones live closest to the Chamber of Light. Beneath us are even more living quarters. At the bottommost level are the quarters of the men capable of wielding but who chose not to become ei'ceuril or temple knights. There're quite a few of them down there. I was told that the chambers have never been so full as they are at present. It's rumored that they outnumber the ei'ceuril in the temple. Ei'ana speak highly of it, as if it's an accomplishment, while ei'ceuril speak of it as a disturbing nuisance. I hear they live like nobles down there though. The Ei'ceuril provide everything they need to remain happy and placated."

Kevn continued with more rumors and gossip surrounding the Temple of Ceur. Some of them seemed outrageous, while others seemed quite plausible.

KIEN AND KIARA

The sword swung toward Devlyn's midsection. He lowered his own just in time to parry the attack. The powerful strike came again, but this time Devlyn was not quick enough and it landed on his outer thigh with a thwack, promising a purple bruise.

"If this was a real sword, you would be on the ground in a pool of blood." Andrew, a fifth-year student, stood back to let Devlyn sort himself out. Although shorter than Devlyn and most of the other elves, Andrew was quite strong and his ability to wield a sword was impressive.

"Where did you learn to fight so well?" Devlyn asked as he fought back the pain from his thigh and pushed himself upright.

"Born and raised in Sudern. Kids learn to use a knife when they start walking there. Only those in the grave don't have a knife in their hand in Sudern." Andrew's smirk went well with the gleam in his deep brown eyes. "Either you get stabbed in the gut by your fellow Sudernese or allow those awful Tieli to take away our independence. Again."

He and Devlyn raised their swords and prepared to duel yet again. This session was devoted to learning to parry, learning how to defend himself without making an offensive move. In the early stages of learning the finer points of using a sword, the knights had the pupils practice one form at a time, working with more advanced students. Knights only dueled with the pupils toward the end of their studies when they prepared to become a knight themselves, and the knights did not use wooden swords then either.

Devlyn's sword rose and fell as Andrew pressed the offensive. *Man, he's strong.* Devlyn's wooden sword reverberated from a heavy hit. Andrew's footwork was impressive and constant, and although Devlyn tried to keep up with the swift pace, he kept tripping over his own feet. Andrew landed another blow on Devlyn's other leg followed almost immediately by a blow to his midsection, blows that seemed to be incessant over the full hour that passed before Andrew finally lowered his sword.

"Good duel. You have to fight with your whole body, not just your arms. Your legs and footing are just as important, as is your core." Andrew took Devlyn's wooden sword and returned the two to the practice shed.

Despite the many bruises he had just received, Devlyn enjoyed the time spent training with Andrew, especially since Andrew was kind enough to practice with him before their lessons. Dueling allowed him to focus only on the present moment. Self-preservation took control and he scrambled for the best response to the coming attack. There was no time to think of Velaria or of some old prophecy while a sword aimed for his head, even if that sword was only blunt wood. He had spent most of the weekend with the pupils training to become Septyl knights, knowing he was avoiding Velaria and his problems but not caring.

"Surely, you're not giving up this early in the day?" came a girl's voice. She strode toward Andrew and Devlyn as her lips curved in a smirk amid a face full of freckles. Her emerald eyes focused on Andrew. Devlyn had never seen eyes so green before. They even smiled. "Well? Are the little boys tired and ready to toss in the towel so soon?" She pulled her curly red hair back from her face and knotted it in the back, out of her eyes. Unlike Velaria's smooth and silky hair, the hair on this girl was a darker red and Devlyn doubted the curls could ever be straightened.

"Morning, Abbie," said Andrew.

"That's Abbie Wintyr to the likes of you. And who might this be? I haven't seen you before." Abbie drew close to Devlyn and looked straight into his eyes. "Ah, you must be the elya everyone has been talking about. The green in your eyes is almost as green as mine." The last part involved fluttering her eye lashes.

"I didn't know people are talking about me."

Coming even closer to Devlyn, she whispered into his ear, "And what kind of dreams does one such as you have?" She turned away quickly just in time to catch Andrew's jealous look.

"Now what are you whispering into his ear like that for?" Andrew demanded, clearly annoyed with her. "Do you do that to all the boys you meet?"

"Oh, the jealous type over here," she placed her hand on Andrew's chest. "Do you want me to whisper into your ear as well? Will that make you feel better? Has anyone ever told you, you're cute when you get angry?" She smirked, and her eyes smiled more than ever. "Well?"

"Well, what?" asked Andrew, forcing himself to calm down but looking confused.

"What do you mean, well what? I didn't come down to the yard to watch you get jealous! Go grab us some practice swords, I have a good hour before class begins, and I don't intend on wasting it on a cup of tea and toast!"

Andrew went to retrieve the wooden swords he had just returned to the shed. Devlyn thought about staying to watch their duel, but he knew that if he did he would not have time to wash up and retrieve his school robe from the dormitory.

"Thank you, Andrew, for the practice. I'll see you tomorrow," Devlyn called out to Andrew over by the storage shed. "It was nice to meet you, Abbie," he said with a little bow before making his way back inside.

At his back, Abbie yelled, "Don't stop dreaming!"

It was still early in the day, not yet the second hour, and Devlyn only passed a few students moving through the corridors leading to the dormitory, so he would be able to have a quick wash and ready himself for his lessons.

Every muscle in Devlyn's body throbbed as he left the courtyard and climbed the stairs of the North Tower. He had spent Saraen and Karaen trying not to think about anything and had therefore spent too much time over the weekend practicing with the sword. Despite his exhaustion, Devlyn looked forward to his first lesson in the art of wielding; a full three-hour morning block. Since his first classes at Gwilnor had started midway into the week, he had missed both the art of wielding and languages classes earlier in the week.

Getting ready took less time than expected and rather than stay in his room, he left the boys' dormitory and wandered through the increasingly familiar corridors, crossing one of the two bridges connecting the three separate structures which composed the castle. He found himself in the library and figured he might search for the book about Septyl's history that Velaria had mentioned, although he was more interested in familiarizing himself with the library and other parts of the castle he had not yet visited than checking out a book.

Pushing one of the large wooden doors open, Devlyn entered into a large rectangular space that reminded him of the dining hall with its massive pillars and vaulted ceiling. Sunlight flooded into the expansive space through large arched windows that came to a point on either side of the rectangular room. The larger windows had the familiar circular stained-glass panels with the sigil of the Seven Schools. Several floors of shelving crisscrossed the library, providing nooks for studying. Colorful mosaics lined the arched space between the groin vaulting on the ceiling. Mesmerized by the architecture of the library and not daring to consider the number of books and scrolls it contained, Devlyn walked past Ellendren without realizing she sat with her head buried in a book.

"Hello, Devlyn," she called from her writing desk, offering a polite smile. Devlyn nervously smiled back and walked toward her, embarrassed that he had not noticed her.

"Hello, Ellendren. What's that you're reading?" he asked and immediately regretted it. *Should have asked how she was, stupid.*

She smiled and lifted her book to reveal the cover, *The Origins of Erithel*, it read. It was a small book, and from where he stood, Devlyn could not make out the words of the minuscule script. "It's for my private lessons with Mother Loretta. After I expressed interest in joining her School, she was kind enough to take me on as my guide. She says that this book holds valuable information, not only of Erithel, but regarding the history of Crimsyn. It's rumored that Caelyn Crimsyn herself made Erithel her home for a time. Granted, that was a long time ago. There's a statue of her in a fountain there in front of the hospital; she is holding hands with a little girl who looks like an elf, but I couldn't say for sure if she is an elf. I visited it once, on my way from Lucillia to Ceurenyl, before I began my studies here." Ellendren looked back down to her book at the mention of Lucillia, and although it was obvious that something bothered her about the mention, she did not explain.

Devlyn wanted to ask Ellendren about becoming fellows, but wasn't sure how to shift the conversation, so he stood next to the writing desk, feeling awkward.

"You sounded quite brilliant in class the other day, knowing the principles," he ventured.

"Oh, it wasn't all that impressive. They're listed quite clearly in *The Studies of Theoreticals*. It's the reading that Magister Therril assigned for the class. It's an ancient manuscript, which was put into book form. We don't even know the name of the author."

"Right, anyway, uh, I was wondering if…I mean," Devlyn trailed off, trying to rephrase what he wanted to say properly. "Would you be willing to be my fellow?" Devlyn blurted out, surprised that he finally managed it. When Ellendren just looked at him, he added, "Magister Therril suggested it."

"Did he really? All right, that should be fine. I'm fairly certain that my current fellow will be off to the Illumined Wood soon. She's practically ready as it is. Truth be told, I'm not sure why she hasn't been sent yet." Ellendren paused before continuing. "I'm not sure how this is going to work though, Devlyn. I've never practiced wielding with a kien wielder before. Granted, no one has. Are you sure you shouldn't ask one of the more advanced students?"

Devlyn grew nervous again, thinking that she regretted agreeing and was now trying to get out of it. "Well, it was Therril who suggested we pair up. And I think he has good judgment, even if he does seem a bit, um… unfocused sometimes." Devlyn let out a soft breath of relief at his quick thinking, then hoped Ellendren had not noticed.

"All right, let's do it. I currently meet with my fellow twice a week. Did Magister Therril say how often we should meet?" asked Ellendren.

Devlyn took a big gulp before responding. "Um, he wants us to meet every day I have a private lesson." Devlyn hoped Ellendren wasn't about to call him crazy.

"Oh! I wasn't expecting that, although I always thought my current fellow and I met too infrequently. How about we meet at the fourteenth hour? That way we can have an hour to relax after dinner." Devlyn quickly agreed to the suggestion.

"Do you have art of wielding this morning? I have to start making my way over now." Ellendren gathered her things.

"With Magister Hannah?" Devlyn checked his crumpled schedule.

"That's her. You'll absolutely love her, she's wonderful." They left the library together and passed through the base of the White Tower in the Albien wing to cross the long bridge connecting the White Tower and the Dragon Tower. A hazy morning sun warmed them slightly; the sunbeams fell through a reluctant morning mist, reminiscent of the Shroud. Once again, the towers above the castle drew Devlyn's eyes. The vertical lines of the towers rose to arched points. From this perspective, Devlyn noted the strong pillars at the corners stretching in support of the heptagonal tower. The upper portion of the tower looked as though someone had made a smaller version of the bulk of the tower, twisted it just a bit before setting it down on the base, then repeated the process at a third level before topping it all with a steep roof. All the towers of Gwilnor had the same form; only their windows and sizes differed.

When they reached the classroom, Devlyn noticed that he was the only boy present. Considering the broken Balance, he concluded that things were not going to change any time soon.

Magister Hannah entered from the door to her office at the front of the room. Her dark blue dress brought out the blue of her eyes, and thick blond hair, showing the first hints of grey, curled past her ears. Magister Hannah was not a young woman—the wrinkles crinkling the corners of her eyes indicated that—but her face was kind and Devlyn decided she looked like a grandmother, not thin, not heavy, and not much like an ei'ana.

"Oh my, a new student," she greeted him warmly. "I am Magister

Hannah, and you must be Devlyn; I heard you would be joining us soon. Is it not marvelous how after so many years a boy is capable of wielding again? An elya in our very midst! I am so looking forward to your contributions to our class. I fear you will be teaching us more than we can teach you. What a historical day this is. Attention, ladies, do take note of this day and your involvement as the first stage as Balance returns. How exciting this is for us all! Since this is your first lesson with us, Devlyn, let's review the basics. How does that sound, class?"

The entire class agreed happily, without hesitation. The girls clearly respected their magister, an admiration which was taking root in Devlyn as well.

"Now ladies, will one of you please refresh our memories about Kiara." Several hands rose to the air, and Magister Hannah acknowledged one of the students with a nod.

"Legend says that Kiara was the first woman to ever wield. In her honor, the women that followed named the art after her, just as the men did who followed Kien."

"Very good. And since you mentioned Kien, can someone else tell us more of him?" the magister asked. Devlyn appreciated the kindness in her voice.

"His story is much the same as Kiara's. Legend also says that the two learned much and more from each other after they found one another," Ellendren explained in her quiet voice.

"Oh, very good indeed. Now, the real question: did these two elves actually exist? Was Kiara a real woman, or does she signify all women? And likewise, was Kien a real man, or does he also signify all men? Or do they simply represent feminine and masculine wielding?"

The class remained quiet, until the student who spoke first raised her hand again.

"There's no evidence of them truly existing. Reason tells us that it is no more than a story to tell children." The girl spoke proudly, pleased with her answer.

Ellendren, clearly not caring for the girl's opinion, raised her hand as well. "Sorry, Magister, but there's one thing about them that I have always been curious about. All the scrolls mention kien giving to receive and kiara receiving to give. Could you explain that in more detail?" When Ellendren first raised her hand, Devlyn had thought she was going to argue with the other student, or at least object, but was surprised that Ellendren had instead changed the topic completely.

"No need to apologize. It's quite the paradox. Receiving to give and giving to receive. The ancient elves translated their names in that way. In fact, in Aelish, the word for woman is receiver who gives, and for man, giver who receives. They did not have our modern conception of the words. It is also thought that such is not only the nature of the different genders, but it is also how the different genders wield. As you all know from your own experience, kiara wielders submit their very being to the erendinth, submitting almost completely, allowing the erendinth to enter. If you take that ancient riddle, it is only after we receive the erendinth do we wield them or *give* them, if you will. Tell us, Devlyn, what is it like for a kien wielder? All we know of masculine wielding comes from scrolls and historical accounts."

The entire class turned toward Devlyn, including Ellendren who still made Devlyn nervous. "The riddle only half makes sense. When I wield, I have to press myself into the erendinth. It doesn't follow that I receive them."

"Interesting; very interesting indeed. I think you have much to show us," said Hannah, looking directly into Devlyn's eyes.

He lowered his gaze, remembering what Velaria had said about his eyes and their transformation. Just thinking about Velaria angered him.

"Now, I would like us all to perform a simple exercise. Nothing difficult, mind you; we won't be holding the Erendinth Games in my classroom." A brief chuckle spread through the room; everyone but Devlyn found it funny. "I want you to join in groups of four and wield aquaeys with one another, passing it between each other in a circle. Remember, this exercise requires you to wield the erendinth and release it as you pass it on."

The girls quickly chose their groups, leaving Devlyn feeling a little out of place.

"We should probably be in the same group," said Ellendren from behind Devlyn. "We are fellows after all."

Swallowing before agreeing, Devlyn joined Ellendren, Fyona, and Danielle. Ever since Devlyn first met Ellendren, the other two were never far away. He half expected to find them studying with Ellendren in the library that very morning.

Magister Hannah watched them carefully from her desk. They stood in a circle and Fyona began. A globe of water floated between her hands, then she shifted it to Danielle, who then shifted it to Ellendren. Open to the erendinth, Devlyn sensed the globe, prepared to press into aquaeys when it came his way.

When Ellendren passed the globe of water to him, he pressed himself further into aquaeys, feeling the wondrous erendinth, again amazed by its purity and its incredible strength.

He was aware that every eye in the classroom was on him as he held the globe of water between his hands. He guided the water away from himself, and as he felt another touch the water, he removed himself from it. The globe returned to Fyona and again went around the circle. Once the other students in the class had satisfied their curiosity about Devlyn's ability and control, they too began wielding. *I bet they expected me to flood the entire room*. He smiled, pleased with his performance as he prepared to receive the globe from Ellendren again.

The rest of the class was devoted to that exercise. Magister Hannah urged the groups to increase their speed periodically. By the end, Devlyn felt satisfied with himself and his first official class in wielding; he had done quite well, refining his ability to take and pass on the erendinth.

"What private lesson do you have today?" asked Ellendren from behind as he left the room.

"Umbrys with Emdian," he replied, slowing so that she could walk beside him.

"I never enjoyed those lessons. Others say Steward Emdian is great, but there's just something about studying umbrys. They should forbid it.

Especially if it's true that the shadow elves are returning. We should be devoting our time to learning more about lumenys, so that we can properly overcome them." Ellendren expressed her opinions confidently.

"I suppose. Truthfully, I don't know much about it, so it should be interesting to hear what Emdian has to say."

Ellendren continued walking with Devlyn, which he found quite odd, especially since none of her friends followed. Devlyn did not mind them, but he always felt self-conscious around them, especially when he said something to Ellendren.

It was obvious that something was on her mind. "Are we still meeting after dinner?" she asked at last. It was not what Devlyn expected.

"Um, yeah." Devlyn felt more confused than ever.

"Terrific, I'll see you tonight." Ellendren ran off in the opposite direction, back toward the classroom. *That was weird.*

ELLE

Devlyn had not expected that the small room in the temple would be so cold. A single candle on the table in the center of the room cast a feeble light. The old ei'ceuril sat across from him on the floor, legs crossed with eyes closed and bearded chin down, his bald head gleaming slightly in the candlelight. Devlyn was in the same posture, but the ei'ceuril had not spoken in a while, so he took a quick peek to make sure Steward Emdian had not fallen asleep. To his relief, the steward spoke, albeit quietly. His dark-brown eyes opened a sliver and he looked at Devlyn.

"Look about the room, Devlyn. One candle casts all these shadows. I ask, what is a shadow?"

Devlyn wracked his brain for an answer. "Well, these are caused by the candle," he finally replied, a little mortified. *Brilliant! I just repeated what he said!*

"What else can you tell me about it?" the steward asked patiently.

"It's not the light," Devlyn thought out loud. "Is it a lack of the light?"

"Why do you say that?"

"Well, a shadow is where the light is not."

"Shadow is not evil, Devlyn, nor is it contrary to the Light. Umbrys was just as essential in Teraeniel's creation as were the other erendinth. Let me ask this: if the light creates the shadow, does that make the light evil? It is what people do in the shadow that is evil. This is especially true for wielders; umbrys is not a corrupted erendinth, Devlyn."

"But what about the shadow elves?" Devlyn blurted out. "They name themselves after the Shadow, how can they be anything but evil?"

"As for that, I cannot say. I have never met one. However, just because they identify themselves with shadow, does not mean it is itself evil." Steward Emdian paused for a moment, before continuing. "Further, if shadow is not the deprivation of Light, what, I ask, is?"

Truly lost this time, since he didn't know whether the steward was now talking about shadow and light from the candlelight, or the Shadow and the Light, Devlyn thought hard about the possible answers. He remembered when he had been younger, a few years after the events at the Cor Inn, when nightmares began to disturb his sleep. No light was present; his only thought when he woke, usually screaming, was Darkness. A cold shiver ran through his body. He remembered how he had felt back then, waking up screaming in the dark that was not the Darkness.

"Darkness," he whispered and the candle seemed to waver at the word.

He did not expect a response from the old ei'ceuril, nor did one come. Instead, despair fell like a shroud over his mind, filling every crevice with doubt. He felt it flood though his body.

"Do not dwell on it," said Steward Emdian soothingly. "I think that will conclude our lesson for today. I want you to spend some time in the Chamber of Light before leaving the temple; it will do you some good. Be sure to eat some dessert after dinner as well."

Did he feel what I felt?

Devlyn shook himself and thanked Steward Emdian before leaving. What had happened there? He had never been aware of such a feeling, such evil before. *Darkness*, he thought. Again, the thought of the word filled his bones with despair and his head bowed under the weight of it. He quickened his pace through the temple until he reached the Chamber of Light.

The same brilliant light shone from the dome, its source still indiscernible. The brightness of the light made it impossible to see much more than a few paces around him, and only if he kept his eyes downcast. Devlyn walked around the edge of the large chamber, and as he walked, he felt the heaviness of his heart begin to lift. Finally, he could look up, and he looked toward the ceiling he could not see.

Without realizing that he had left the edge of the chamber, he soon found himself closer to the center where, to his amazement, an old man floated right before his eyes. The man wore the white robes of a steward, and he bobbed up and down as he floated past Devlyn. Blinking a few times, Devlyn looked about to see whether there was anyone else in the room to notice the floating man. It was only then that Devlyn realized just how far into the room he had come. His heart skipped when he looked down to his feet and saw that they too floated several feet above the floor! With a growing sense of panic, Devlyn moved his legs to walk back to the edge of the room, but to no avail.

He remained exactly where he floated, no nearer to the edge.

His legs pedaled and his arms flailed as he tried to propel himself back to the perimeter, but he stayed just where he was, floating. The harder he struggled to move, the more his body remained in place. Devlyn gave up trying to move. As he floated there, he held a small prayer in his mind, concentrating on the thought of the edge of the room where he might be able to leave the temple.

Abbot Entiel and the other ei'ceuril at the abbey school had never taught the students how to pray. Hundreds of tomes with different prayers and chants filled the library shelves of the abbey school, but only the ei'ceuril had permission to read them, and not just because of their age and delicate condition, more likely to disintegrate at a touch than teach one how to pray. Devlyn had never heard Brother Bernard pray, but knew he was a prayerful man, so he tried to think of what Brother Bernard might say in his prayers.

It was easier to think of prayers when he couldn't see just how far away the floor beneath him was. Abandoning thoughts of when he might manage to leave the temple, he closed his eyes. In almost no time, he once again felt the solid ground beneath his feet, and he found himself along the edge of the Chamber of Light. Startled by the turn of events, he made sure to stay near the wall and made his way toward the exit.

Devlyn headed to the dining hall when he returned to the castle. Laughing and talking students crowded the tables, filling the space with a raucous volume. Devlyn went to one of the buffet lines, near where his friends typically ate, and filled a bowl with vegetable stew, since he was not all that hungry. Turning from the buffet, balancing the liquid in his bowl with the heavy pack on his shoulder, Devlyn spotted the back of Alex's head. His blond hair tended to be easily noticed amid the majority of Luminari with light brown hair. Andrew's black-haired head was similarly easy to find, and Devlyn noticed they sat together.

Devlyn pushed himself in the gap between Alex and Andrew, already finished eating but with their empty plates still before them, chatting with Kevn and Phil, another of the knights' pupils, sitting on the opposite side. Kevn had an open book next to his plate.

"Whoa, what happened to you?" Alex asked.

"Sorry?" Devlyn grabbed his still-unused spoon to use it as a mirror to see whether he could figure out what caused the comment. His hair was disheveled and pointed in every direction, as if he had repeatedly run his hands through it in the wrong direction, which is exactly what he had done in Emdian's office. The episode in the Chamber of Light hadn't helped. "I look ridiculous." Devlyn chuckled as he patted his hair down.

"Are you going to tell us why you look ridiculous? Aside from the obvious answers," pried Alex, smirking.

Devlyn shoved Alex with his shoulder. They sat too close for Devlyn to take a swing at him. "I'd rather not talk about it, just past it, really."

"Girl troubles," Alex supplied.

"Not even close. Although Ellendren and I are meeting tonight." Devlyn took a spoonful of the hot stew.

"You do know she's betrothed to Trethien, a Luminari lord, right?" Kevn asked.

"Calm down, we're just fellows. Therril assigned us." Devlyn's smile broadened.

"That goofy smile says something different. Don't think I don't know that look. Andrew has it whenever Abbie walks by." Alex smirked around

Devlyn toward Andrew.

"You're lucky Devlyn's sitting between us." Andrew leaned forward, clutching his table knife.

Devlyn finished his stew amid their ongoing teasing and chatter, and followed Alex, Andrew, and Phil up the stairs of the North Tower, while Kevn stayed on the ground level, headed to the library. Reaching their floor, they turned off the stair hall and walked around the heptagonal corridor toward their rooms. Devlyn's mouth dropped open when he saw Ellendren waiting beside his door.

"Are you sure you're just fellows?" Alex whispered. Devlyn punched Alex's arm, making Alex's grin broaden.

"Is everything all right?" Ellendren asked.

"Oh yeah, of course," stuttered Devlyn. "Alex made a rude comment about an ei'ana."

"I did not…" Andrew's large hand clamped Alex's mouth, preventing him from finishing.

"It was very rude of you," Andrew supplied. "You two go practice your wielding, and we'll see you later." Alex snorted a laugh through Andrew's fingers.

Once alone in the corridor with Ellendren, Devlyn smiled awkwardly. "You really didn't have to come all the way over here."

They stood uneasily outside Devlyn's room, until Ellendren finally broke the silence.

"Please, you can call me Elle. May we go in? I saw you in the dining hall at dinner and since I was done with mine, I decided to just walk up here."

"Of course, come in, Ellendr… uh, Elle. Sorry for the mess, I haven't been in my room since this morning and I forgot to make my bed." Devlyn quickly straightened the blankets. Calling her Elle sounded weird as he spoke it for the first time. He had heard some of her friends refer to her as Elle, but the list of those who did was not long and did not include Trethien. At least, Devlyn had never heard him call her Elle.

"That's quite all right, I just wanted to ask if we could wield with each other again," Ellendren said, a rosy blush tinting her cheeks. "Would that be all right?"

"I thought that was the intention of these sessions." Devlyn scratched his head.

"Oh, of course." Ellendren looked about the room before continuing. "It's just that, when we wielded together in class today, I felt…something. I felt strong, not that I'm weak in the erendinth, but I never felt the likes of it before. I tried wielding alone later in the day, but the sensation didn't return, it only happened when we wielded together."

"That's odd. Although, Therril did say something like that might happen. Want to give it another go?"

Ellendren nodded and they closed their eyes. Devlyn pressed himself into aerys and now felt the things the air felt, the scents in the room, the temperature, himself, Elle, the furniture, the glass of the window. He swirled it gently through the room before passing it to Ellendren, who received it and swirled it about the room just as Devlyn had done. They passed it back and forth between each other; neither spoke during their exercise.

Thirty minutes must have passed before they withdrew from the air.

"I have never felt so strong before," Ellendren said. "It was as though I could wield the air to bring the wall down, without even wielding terys. I could have shattered it. It was incredible; does every kien wielder really have that much strength naturally?" She did not wait for an answer but paced about the small room. There wasn't really much room to pace, but her excitement made her want to move. Her pace quickened, and Devlyn saw a hint of a smile. "Do you know what this could mean? If you help me reach my potential, then I might be able help the kien wielders in the temple and others throughout Eklean who haven't started to wield yet! It could be the dawn of a new age! Think of it, men and women wielding side by side again. No longer needing to imprison kien wielders born with a gift. Balance finally restored!"

Even as Ellendren continued to talk excitedly about the possibilities, Devlyn could not keep his mind from drifting back to his private lesson with Emdian. After Devlyn's fourth or fifth automatic response with the same affirmation, Ellendren frowned at him.

"What's on your mind?"

Devlyn did not respond at once; truthfully, he didn't know where to begin. It wasn't just the discussion in the cold, barely lit room of what shadow was, it was more than that. Most pressing was what had happened when he had thought of Darkness. Even now, thinking of talking about it brought the doubt and despair crawling through his limbs, dragging him down. The room felt cold and cramped, and he wanted to run, not from the room, but from what he was experiencing. Ellendren looked at him with concern, distress written across her face.

"Something happened today, Elle."

Ellendren did not press him, just waited patiently while he debated with himself. Devlyn trusted Ellendren but was not sure whether talking to her about such private and deep emotions crossed a boundary into inappropriate behavior; she was a princess, after all. But, he was on a first name basis with this princess, and not just that, she had offered her preferred name.

"Do you know the difference between Shadow and Darkness?" Devlyn asked, relieved to name it at last. The question weighed him down, and he felt better just asking it, but it caught Ellendren by surprise; at least, that's what he thought from her reaction.

"What do you mean by difference? Aren't they the same? I was always taught that Shadow was a servant of Darkness."

"That's what I thought, but Emdian spoke otherwise. He said that since shadow is caused by light, it can't belong to Darkness. And then he went into a lecture about how it depends on the wielder, since they can wield in the Light or in the Dark." Devlyn thought through the implications of it as he spoke.

"That might be true, but I've never heard of someone wielding umbrys for good. Granted, the transcendental erendinth haven't been wielded since before the reign of Roendryn. It was said that the shadow elves of that time wielded shadows through umbrys, hence their name, but their deeds certainly were not commendable." Ellendren spoke with confidence on the topic, but even so, the hint at Shadow and Darkness seemed to leave a flavor of distaste on her tongue.

Devlyn thought a moment before responding. *There has to be a way to wield umbrys in the Light; Emdian made it seem possible.* Unsure of how else to propose it to Ellendren, he simply blurted out, "What if I could learn to wield umbrys for good?"

Apparently, that was the wrong thing to say. Ellendren frowned, and she did not immediately respond, but she was clearly disturbed at the thought of anyone attempting to wield umbrys.

"I'm sure that's what Erynor thought at first, too. It's rumored that it was the Cyndinari's wielding of umbrys that mandated the elves to flee our ancient skyalnds. Because they dabbled in umbrys, Erynor and the other Cyndinari despised the Jewel of Life. His selfish desire to keep immortality reserved for the elves not only severed us from the effects of Ceurendol, but also every other race who was to benefit from it. Because the Ceurendol War began so soon after the Jewel of Life was created, pain and suffering were eliminated for only a short span for the mortal races before Erynor used umbrys to wrap the Jewel of Life and the entirety of Krysenthiel in that Shroud." Ellendren's voice carried both anger and sadness as she spoke of the reasons behind the past events. A tear fell from the corner of her eye.

Confused by her reaction, Devlyn wondered what the Jewel of Life was, and asked Ellendren to explain.

"Don't tell me you've never heard of it; the Jewel of Life, Diamond of Light, the Lieben Stone, the Heart of Hearts—Ceurendol! Do you know nothing of your own history?"

Taken slightly aback, Devlyn lowered his gaze and decided not to respond.

"When our ancestors, the Luminari, settled in Krysenthiel, they built a magnificent city of crystal stone, and named it Arenthyl in honor of Aren Lorenthien. Arenthyl became the nucleus of Eklean and all of Teraeniel. The Luminari fashioned Ceurendol after living among the mortal races for thirty-five hundred years. They saw the plight of mortals, how they suffered and died at a young age, mostly from disease. All the while, the elves never so much as caught a cold. They watched the other races die at an age younger than elven children. Against the wishes of the Cyndinari, the Luminari took it upon themselves to contrive a plan to relieve the other races of their suffering. They poured fourth their life essence, the gift of the elves, forming what was easily recognized as a jewel of magnificent beauty.

"By doing so, the Luminari sacrificed their immortal life into it. So long as they possessed Ceurendol, they had access to their immortality, but they knew that if they were cut off from it, they would surely die," Ellendren explained, no, lectured.

Devlyn listened intently to every word; he had never heard such a story before. He found it difficult to accept, although it did explain how the elves lost their immortality, shattering his previous theories.

"The day came when Erynor, a Cyndinari lord, declared himself Emperor of the Erynien Empire, claiming all of Eklean and beyond. It was not long before he wrought havoc on Eklean with his Shadow. He attacked Septyl first, murdering thousands of unsuspecting ei'ana, later severing the Luminari from the Jewel of Life with his Shroud, the same one which still covers Krysenthiel. Erynor brought nothing but death with umbrys. Survivors of what became known as the Ceurendol War were cast into chains. No longer immortal, the Luminari began to die. Because of Erynor's sin against the living, he and all the Cyndinari lost their gift of immortal life as well, giving birth to the shadow elves as they sought new and sinister ways to regain immortality."

The story sounded farfetched to Devlyn. *A jewel of life, how is such a thing possible?* he thought once Ellendren finished the tale.

"How do we know that the elves didn't simply intermarry with humans? It seems pretty convenient that both groups of elves lost their immortality at the same time." Devlyn wasn't ready to accept the story but Ellendren did not receive the criticism well and stared at the floor with her brow scrunched up in distress.

"Factions fall on both sides of the argument, even in Lucillia. Something seems very wrong about it though. I can't put my finger on it or even put words to it, but the idea does not sit well with me that we lost our immortality through intermarrying." She seemed to be struggling internally, trying to decide whether or not to reveal something else. "Believe me, the Jewel of Life exists, it's beneath that Shroud, and there's evidence of it all over. All you need is faith."

Devlyn had a feeling that she was leaving out an important detail, but he wasn't going to be able to figure it out any time soon, given that she did not provide any hints.

"May I ask you something?" she asked, changing the topic.

Devlyn quickly nodded, despite his uncertainty about where this was going.

"How do you wield all the elemental erendinth at the same time? Forgive me, I've only heard rumors that you could do such a thing, but no one doubts it."

"What's so spectacular about it; can't everyone here do it?"

Ellendren stared at him in shock. "No! To do so is incredibly difficult. Few ei'ana are capable of it and only after decades of experience; it requires a wielder of incredible strength to do so. All the Seven Chairs are able; it's required before one can be considered as a Chair," Ellendren continued with a list of different ei'ana who managed to wield all four of the elemental erendinth.

"That explains their surprise when I did it. I could teach you, if you want?"

"Would you? Could we try now?"

"Uh…sure. I don't see why not, we are fellows after all." Devlyn was growing accustomed to the word fellow. At first, he thought it an obscure term to use for two students studying together, but the more he heard it, the more it sounded suitable.

"All right, we should probably sit on the floor with our legs crossed. Therril made me do it when we met for our first private lesson. I'm not entirely certain how you can observe my wielding," said Devlyn before cutting himself short to close his eyes.

The feel of the elements surrounding him grew more familiar every time he wielded. He pressed himself into the elemental erendinth, now increasingly aware of each. He wove all four intricately about the room, sensing what each sensed.

"It's like there are four of you, each working separately," exclaimed Ellendren in awe.

"No, that's all wrong. You can't press yourself entirely into one. You have to be slightly within each, but not fully."

"I'm sorry, but your language is confusing. What do you mean by pressing? To wield, I have to bring the erendinth into myself. It's as if I open myself to them." She gestured with her arms, as if in an embrace. "There must really be a difference between kien and kiara. I never put much thought into it, but I don't see how it can be otherwise."

"Well, however you do it, give it a try. I'll continue wielding, and you can pick the erendinth from me when you're ready."

Ellendren closed her eyes; Devlyn thought she looked beautifully serene. She began with aerys, her hair tossing about as she wielded the air with little difficulty. Devlyn forced himself to remain focused on wielding and not how the air's movement made Ellendren even more beautiful. He felt ignys pulled from him; the unstable flame soared through the room. Her composure diminished as she concentrated and Devlyn could sense her struggle to wield two erendinth at the same time, eventually managing it.

The fire at last became stable, and not a moment too soon; Devlyn was just about to press himself back into ignys to stabilize her wielding.

Ignys and aerys soared about Ellendren. Her face and hair gleamed; the fire gave her hair a silvery golden glow. She contented herself with wielding just the two erendinth for a time before attempting a third. Devlyn felt a weak tug on aquaeys. There was not enough strength to pull it entirely. A second tug came, this time stronger, but as it was pulled from him, he was aware of ignys and aerys growing unstable.

He wasn't quick enough to help her. Ellendren no longer wielded ignys and aerys; they soared unguided through the room. The only chair in the room was closest, and before he had a chance to blink, it was thrown over and set aflame. Ellendren let out a small scream, before once again wrapping herself in the composure and serenity she possessed while wielding.

The water she had begun to wield was now in a puddle on the ground. Devlyn watched as she wielded it from the floor and doused the chair with it. Smoke and steam spread through the small room before Devlyn managed get up to open the window so it could escape into the night. Ellendren wielded aerys and guided the smoke and steam out the window.

The whole incident lasted no longer than a single breath before Ellendren had it under control. Devlyn's mind barely had a chance to register what happened. The charred chair was the only reminder that anything had gone amiss.

ANCESTRY

Devlyn followed Therril into his office after finishing a particularly difficult algorithms exam. Unlike Emdian's cold and dimly lit office, this room was comfortable, almost cozy in the fading evening light coming through the westward window. Therril gestured to one of two cushioned chairs. Once again, Devlyn sat front and center with Therril far too close for comfort. *At least we're not sitting on the floor again.*

"Have your private lessons been treating you well?" Therril's tone suggested that he already knew the answer.

"They've been all right. They keep me busy." How could he tell Therril that he had not yet met with Velaria? A full month had passed since he had hidden behind a pillar at the temple with Kevn and had overheard the ei'ceuril talking about Velaria's knowledge of a prophecy that said he would die if he didn't become an ei'ceuril. Feeling betrayed, he had avoided seeking her out after that. Did she think it was acceptable to conceal something so important? Was she simply playing with his emotions before tossing him into the temple?

"Do you like all your tutors?" Therril asked, narrowing the topic. Devlyn's stomach clenched. *How does he know?*

"And have you been meeting regularly with them all?"

Not believing his luck, Devlyn held his breath. Was it a good thing that the magister asked so that he would have to answer? Or was it bad luck that he now had to explain himself?

"Hmmmm?" Therril's eyebrows rose, head tilted slightly.

"All right! I haven't met with Velaria. There, I said it!" Devlyn's breath went out in a gasp as he spoke. It was over! He'd admitted his failure; so far, only Kevn had known that he wasn't seeing Velaria for private lessons.

"It always amazes me that students are convinced that the tutors don't discuss the students' progress with their guides." Therril smiled and then chuckled. Despite his current misery, Devlyn appreciated the throaty sound. "Now that I'm thinking about it, I do recall a time when a student avoided me. Avoiding me! Can you imagine? Anyway, I didn't see her for nearly two months, leaving me with the impression that she had left Gwilnor Academy altogether." A few moments passed, while Therril seemed to be thinking about something. Devlyn waited for the magister to continue, but finally decided to push the private session along.

"What happened?"

The lines on Therril's forehead deepened. "Well, as I said, I saw her after two months. Remarkable young lady."

Devlyn again expected to hear more on the subject, but uncharacteristically, the magister remained quiet. Was Therril always this absentminded? Odd that he had begun to tell a story about not seeing a student for a while, and then had not gone on to explain why.

"I should probably find Velaria, shouldn't I?" he prompted.

"Huh, huh, huh. You figured that out before coming to see me," Therril said. Devlyn liked the mischievous old magister who never answered anything directly, yet still managed to say exactly what he needed to hear. "Tell me, how are you and Ellendren managing as fellows? Isn't she wonderful? Absolutely wonderful!"

A little surprised by the shift in topics, Devlyn blushed slightly, telling Therril that he was quite fond of her and that their sessions were going well.

"I showed her how to wield the elemental erendinth together, and she managed to hold two of the erendinth quite well. Once she started wielding a third, she had difficulty grasping all three together before they fell through her fingertips."

"Oh good. Very good indeed. Keep at it, you two will learn quite a bit from each other, believe me." Therril stopped just as he seemed about to add something and looked intently out the window. At this time of day, the setting sun should be shining brightly into the room, but today it was hidden behind unusually thick clouds. An awkward amount of time passed in silence. There had to be other things to discuss during their scheduled private lessons. Waiting patiently, his thoughts wandered, and Velaria came to mind. Devlyn grew angry once again. *She should have told me!*

"Tell me Devlyn, on days such as this, how should we react? I can't see the light of the sun; it's actually been quite a gloomy day. But, because I can't see the sun, nor feel the warmth of its rays, should I be gloomy as well?"

Focused on his own emotions, Devlyn didn't quite grasp Therril's question. He had a feeling that the magister was not speaking about the weather or about his own emotions.

"I'm not sure. Sorry, I have something else on my mind."

"Oh, *really?*"

From Therril's tone and the twinkle in his eye, Devlyn thought the magister already knew what was on his mind. "Can you tell me about this prophecy? The one that says I will die if I don't become an ei'ceuril? It's driving me crazy, since it seems everyone knows about it but me."

"I don't think it's the prophecy that troubles you. But, do I know the prophecy? Better than most; however, you must hear it from another." While still said in Therril's kind tone, the reply left little room for further discussion. Therril led the rest of their time together with discussions of Devlyn's progress in his other lessons. It went well enough despite Devlyn's unfocused attention.

Aimless after his session with Therril, Devlyn walked about the castle, eventually finding himself at the base of the Dragon Tower. Most of the students were at dinner in the dining hall but Devlyn was not compelled to be around others, nor did he want to sit in his dormitory room. He knew he should find Velaria but could not bring himself to go searching; he supposed she too was here in the Dragon Tower somewhere.

The castle felt drearier than it had on previous days. *It's probably just the weather*, thought Devlyn, but it affected him nonetheless, and for no particular reason, he had an urge to see the phoenix. He had not seen the beautiful bird since the glimpse in the sky above Karl's farmhouse and wondered whether the phoenix had followed him to Ceurenyl. *Perhaps even that was a dream. But perhaps the phoenix knows I want to see him again.*

Trying to shake off his gloom, Devlyn decided to climb the various Dragon Tower stairs. There certainly were enough of them since it was the tallest of the towers in the castle. Stair after stair he climbed. Set on reaching the rooftop balcony, Devlyn was caught off guard when a very familiar voice called out his name. Intent on his upward climb, he had not paid attention to just where he was, so it was only when he stopped to look around did he notice that all the wall hangings on this level were blue.

Velaria stood just along the main corridor of this level. He immediately noticed that the greenery he had glimpsed on their first meeting was now quite evident without her ever-present cloak. In fact, Devlyn could not tell where Velaria's leafy dress actually began. With no obvious start or end, the greenery simply cascaded elegantly from every part of her body. The leaves and flowers seemed to connect one to the other, and not just as the dress, but also to her skin. Some parts of the dress showed skin beneath, and at first Devlyn thought it exposed too much, but as he approached, he thought that *revealing* was not the appropriate description. Her dress complemented her in such a way that it displayed Velaria's beauty marvelously without shocking. No hood or shawl covered her head, and Devlyn could see the flowers that wove into her long vibrant red hair.

He had not expected to run into her so soon, and he certainly was not prepared to see her in such an informal fashion. He still wanted to get to the roof, but he did not want to be rude to Velaria again, especially since he had so very recently promised Therril that he would try to patch things up with her.

"How are you today?" Devlyn asked politely, suddenly aware that his eyes were looking everywhere but directly at her.

"Aside from the weather, I'm well. Would you accompany me to my quarters?" asked Velaria. It still shocked Devlyn that even when she made a request, she left room for only one response. With no other option, he walked beside Velaria to her quarters, relieved that his eyes could simply look forward.

"Do you always wear that dress?" Devlyn asked awkwardly. How does one pose such a personal question to an ei'ana, let alone the Chair of Azurelle? But the sight of the dress was beyond anything he had expected when he first caught a glimpse of it all those months ago.

Velaria smiled as she caressed a flower along the arm of her leafy garment. "A gift from long ago, while I was still a novice in the Illumined Wood. When I donned it for the first time, the leaves and flowers wove themselves ever so delicately into my skin. They became a part of me. The need to separate myself from them has never arisen, nor do I believe it ever will. You should have seen the look on some of the Emradiels when I returned to Gwilnor. No other School in Septyl probed me so deeply with their wielding when they tried to figure out the mystery of the dress."

Velaria's quarters were not far from the stairwell, but they were surprising. Devlyn's jaw dropped at the incredible size, and Velaria chuckled at his reaction.

"One of the perks of sitting on the Chair of Azurelle. Have a look around."

Devlyn stared up at the ceiling, double the height of the corridor outside, and therefore ten times as tall as the ceiling in his dormitory. "This place is large enough to hold a dragon!"

"Well, actually," Velaria held a hand out toward the far side of the room.

A low growl came from beyond enormous blue silk draperies covering what Devlyn had assumed was a wall, but what was actually a large arched opening to another room. The draperies fluttered, and between two of the panels, Yelaris' head poked out.

"There's a reason that the Azurelle wing is in the largest tower of the castle."

Images of greeting floated in Devlyn's mind; he knew they came from Yelaris, but not how. He flashed a few images back, unsure whether that was how he was supposed to communicate, or whether he'd been successful. "Could you tell her I say hello?"

Velaria gave a small smile and assured him there was no need before sitting on one of the couches, inviting Devlyn to do likewise.

"I must say, Devlyn, you have me quite perplexed. I simply don't understand why you've been avoiding me."

A quick spit of anger flashed through him. He took a deep breath to try to calm himself before speaking.

"*You're* perplexed?" asked Devlyn, not managing his anger after all. His voice rose, flooded with hurt even as it cracked. "Why is it that I had to overhear two ei'ceuril mention a prophecy, saying that either I die, join the ei'ceuril, or doom the entire world to Shadow? When were you planning on telling me about this?"

The large room suddenly felt very small, although Velaria maintained her typical composure.

"Believe me, I wanted to tell you. But Ceurtriarch Ealyndol and the Seven Chairs forbade it; that was before I was elevated to the Chair of Azurelle and had a voice among them. They feared that you would refuse to follow me to Ceurenyl if you knew about the prophecy. Joining the Ei'ceuril is not exactly a boy's dream. The Seven Chairs understand that all too well; after all, we're accustomed to dragging kien wielders to the temple, unconscious and against their will."

Still unwilling to trust her, Devlyn sat stubbornly with his arms crossed, trying to spot a flaw in her story, eventually deciding not to argue with her about it.

"Could you at least tell me more now?"

Velaria sat with her back straight; she smoothed the leaves and flowers on her lap before speaking.

"I will, but there is something you must hear first." Velaria rose and walked to a cupboard along the wall where she retrieved a teapot. "Do you recall this?"

"Isn't that from the Cor Inn?"

"It is. I could not abandon it there; it is my only keepsake of your mother. When I visited your family years ago, your mother offered us all tea before sharing a story with us. I cannot say whether she did so intentionally, knowing that she would not be able to tell you the same story herself, but I believe she wanted others to know."

"I don't understand…are you saying that she knew something was going to happen to her?"

"I believe so. Arlyn and I tried to convince your parents to leave Cor'lera with us, but they refused." Velaria looked down at the small teapot, now a far sight from its original perfection. "Do you have time to listen to the story behind the song you are so familiar with?"

Devlyn nodded, his anger with Velaria dispelling at the mention of his mother and the song he often hummed quietly to himself, unaware that others had heard and taken note.

"In the days when Darkness covered all in Shadow," Velaria began slowly, "a time when no one was free, not even the children, all existed in fear. A time when it was said that even the Erynien emperor was a slave to the Darkness. But, the true slaves were the most deprived citizens of the empire, gathered from every corner of Eklean, from every race and class of people. Most prominent among the slaves were those who once called Krysenthiel their home—the elves of Luminare. Once enslaved, they were sent to a small settlement along the Illumined Wood's border, the least favored region of the Erynien Empire.

"Erynor reveled in the fear and despair of his new slaves as they journeyed to the eastern forest, a forest wrapped in mystery. In those days, nothing was more feared than those trees. Few expeditions attempted to uncover the mysteries there and even fewer returned. The emperor desired to control his slaves with the commonly held fear of the Illumined Wood.

"Centuries passed, and the slaves lived on in the settlement along the vast wood, under the charge of the imperial soldiers. Frequently, the inhabitants rotated through the settlement; rested slaves were transported to a different location to perform manual labor, while the exhausted ones would return to regain their strength. During a routine exchange, one woman was found to be pregnant and was returned to the settlement.

"Unlike most women in her condition who feared to bring a child into a world of slavery, she glowed with her desire to give birth. Fear had no hold over her. She declared that no child of hers would be cast into chains. For the many captives who had known only chains and forced labor, her manner, her faith in a positive future, was impressive and inspiring.

"Her spirit of freedom, her inspiration, began to spread, bringing the Light of Anaweh to a flicker in those dark days. As the flicker grew, so did the slaves' forgotten courage. A sense of purpose returned to the captive Luminari; they no longer avoided the soldiers' eyes. They held themselves proudly with their backs straight, once again caring for the sick and ailing, disobeying the soldiers' orders, willing to risk the lashings handed out in punishment for such insubordination. Their behavior became a great concern for their captors who feared that the spirit of the united slaves was transforming from a small flicker of light to an inferno. In a land covered by Shadow, the tiny flicker shone with incomparable brilliance. Afraid of this previously unknown phenomenon, the soldiers sent a request for orders on dealing with the situation to Broid, the imperial capital, far to the west and south on the Kinzdol Islands.

"Months passed with no word from the capital; influenced by the slaves' attitude, the soldiers in charge of the settlement themselves began to change, to become part of the movement stirring in their midst. Once, they had readily mocked the Luminari for their noble deeds of love and kindness, and whipped them for helping those too old, too young, and too sick to labor by taking on their workload, doubling their own. They willingly placed themselves in harm's way to help one another. Now, the noble deeds compelled all who witnessed them to lay down their weapons, to cease their dark deeds and instead, to pursue these nobler actions linked to the Light. The search for peace and goodness spread to all who dwelled in the settlement, slave and soldier alike.

"Having considered the request from the soldiers at the settlement of small importance, Erynor eventually sent a messenger with new orders to the commander in charge. However, when the messenger arrived, he found neither soldiers nor slaves, only a village of people living in harmony. Enraged at the defection of the soldiers, he drew his sword and demanded to know the reason for such heresy against Emperor Erynor Meriden. To his amazement, no one drew a sword in defense; instead, a pregnant woman with flowers in her hair walked up to him and spoke loving words. Regrettably, the messenger, heart consumed by hatred, was deaf to the message of love. He remained firm in his belief that the slaves and soldiers had set themselves against the empire.

"Considering himself in hostile territory, the messenger fled to Broid, relaying the seriousness of the events occurring along the empire's eastern fringe to the emperor. The news of rebellion enraged the emperor, a rage that had not been seen since the Ceurendol War. Erynor wasted no time in moving to squash the rebellion, ordering the army nearest the slave settlement to prepare for action. While the soldiers mobilized, he ordered a gathering of every slave in Broid to the great arena, a number so immense that slaves filled all the spectator seats surrounding the vast amphitheater. In the amphitheater itself, the palace slaves, all of them Luminari, were executed as an example of the consequences of opposing the Erynien Empire.

"Following the executions, the emperor himself, riding on his dragon, led a massive army to the slaves' settlement, stopping only to hold public executions in each of the cities and villages they passed through. When they arrived at the settlement, the emperor and his great army found that all the inhabitants had fled into the Illumined Wood. Further enraged, the emperor put aside his fear of that forest and charged in with his army.

"As they followed the tracks of the self-proclaimed free people, they came upon a woman who was falling behind the others due to her advanced pregnancy. Erynor understood that she would soon give birth and declaring that no slave would give birth to a free child, he sentenced her to death by his own sword.

"He closed the distance between them, prepared to deliver his mortal sentence, when something remarkable occurred. As the emperor unsheathed his sword, the woman cried out in Aelish, invoking a little-known prophecy. The surrounding trees shone with a brilliant light that engulfed the entire area yet centered on the woman. Unable to gaze on the light, the emperor and his horde retreated to the forest's border. Because they had pursued their targets far into the woods, they could not escape the brilliant light which seared them. No more than a tenth of the emperor's force managed to survive their flight from the Illumined Wood. Although he did escape the forest, Erynor disappeared that day, too wounded to resume his reign.

"The light reached every part of the Illumined Wood, blindingly bright nearest the pregnant woman. As it spread through the wood, the newly freed slaves' eyes became accustomed to its brilliance, almost as though they took it into their own eyes, mirroring the color of the surrounding trees. The eyes of those closest to the pregnant woman held a brighter emerald shade around the pupil than those further away. The brilliant light faded from their surroundings, wholly taken in by their eyes, and the freed people looked for the woman. To their astonishment, she was no longer there; instead, two infant boys lay calmly gazing about with the most captivating eyes: the silver irises of the elves, shifting to a brilliant emerald encircling the pupil.

"Mesmerized by the beautiful newborns, the elves did not at first notice the many individual lights approaching from the border of the woods. But as they drew nearer, the elves saw familiar forms within many of the lights, forms that soon became discernible as persons. The forms were so familiar in fact, that to some it was as if they looked into a mirror. Some of the brilliant forms emitted an incredible light, belonging to another world, while others sent out a softer, more natural light, one that evoked greenery, foliage, and plants, emulating trees. A song filled with wonder and beauty came from the many lights.

"The brilliant forms told the people present that Anaweh, the Creating Light, had brought the two boys forth from their mother's womb, a willing sacrifice by their mother who feared the death of her sons more than her own demise. The brilliant forms then encouraged the people to build a throne for the newborn twins, declaring that the twins and all their line to follow would sit on thrones. As the light began to fade, the more brilliant forms returned to where they belonged, but the forms that held the natural, tree-ish quality remained. They told the elves that they wished to give the free people a Pilgrim City to call their own, melded from the wood around them, if they consented.

"The people agreed and before they could blink, the massive trees began to twist and twirl in a dance; they swung and shifted, some bent low, some spreading up. The elves gathered there watched in awe as the trunks of the trees formed buildings. Magnificent mansions sprung from the trunks, and at the heart of the city, a majestic palace with a domed chamber melded from the tallest trees in the area. The palace looked over the entire city and the bare grasslands to the west.

"The boys grew into fine young men, each kingly in his own right. One was known for his exceptional fortitude and justice; the other excelled in temperance and prudence. As the boys grew, so did the city. The royal palace stood on the boys' birthplace, while the rest of the city stretched west, the furthest rim of it reaching the remains of the slave settlement. What was once their prison had become their home.

"To avoid fraternal strife between the two royal lines in future generations, the people of the growing city decided to allow only one of the twins to sit on the throne as their king. The people also agreed on an ancient Luminari statute, namely that no man or woman could occupy the throne alone; a marriage begotten of true love must precede any coronation.

"When the twins reached the age of twenty, they had to decide who would reign as king of the Pilgrim City under the Light. The love between the two brothers was strong, so they concluded without strife that the brother known for justice and fortitude would sit on the throne. His name was Roendryn. The prudent and temperate brother, whose name was Feolyn, was relieved to be able to live a quiet and simple life with his beloved. Roendryn was soon betrothed to his love; they were wed the following year, and both sat on a throne as the first Aryl of the Pilgrim City of Lucillia. The Aryl of Lucillia reigned for a great many years and brought forth the forgotten Light to places once covered by the shadow of Darkness.

"Feolyn and his wife remained in the Pilgrim City of Light for a short while following the Aryl's coronation, but they eventually traveled north in search of a quieter village away from the business and politics of the city. Before they left however, Roendryn and Feolyn sang to the trees, requesting that a likeness of their mother rest in the city at the place of her sacrifice. From the ground sprouted a tree that molded itself before all present into a beautiful statue of Lucillia.

"The Aryl visited Feolyn and his wife every third year. When the brothers began their own families, King Roendryn urged Feolyn to follow a practice of the Luminari of old, that of passing his line on to his youngest child, claiming they would remain friends with the throne for all ages, and Feolyn's house would never be forgotten by the people of Lucillia. Feolyn agreed and named his youngest child his heir.

"When he and his wife brought their last child into the world, he sang his royal lineage to the child. The same song of Feolyn has been sung to every child born least of Feolyn's line throughout the generations."

Devlyn sat quietly, held by the story. He felt as though there should be more.

"Does this story resound in you? Does it bring forth memories?" Velaria asked after a while.

"It does." Every word Velaria had spoken corresponded with an image hidden deep in Devlyn's heart, obscured as though he looked on it through a veil. He *knew* this story, he had heard it before, but only remembered the melody that was associated with it, but there was more to it. "That man, the one in the largest frame back at the Cor Inn, that was a portrait of Feolyn, wasn't it?"

"We have no reason to think otherwise. When we follow the descendants through the years, we come to you. You are the heir of the line of Feolyn in this generation. When Evellyn was young, the story was sung to her by her father. She told Arlyn and me that she had already passed it on to you. It's why that tune is constantly on your lips. She told us that the melody of Feolyn will reside in your heart all your days."

PROPHECY

Devlyn sat quietly on the couch across from Velaria. There was much to think about, and he needed to let the story take root. Accepting that his pointed ears and angled eyes were more than elven features passed down through mixed blood was still difficult to fully accept. Stunned by many of the details, Devlyn allowed the story, his mother's story as told by Velaria, swirl through his mind. Spoken in Velaria's measured tones, it rang true, and it settled many of his long-held feelings of abandonment and anger toward his family. Hearing the history that was his story made him realize just how different his life would have been if his mother had not been taken away and his father murdered.

Giving Devlyn time to absorb the momentous story, Velaria quietly replaced Evellyn's teapot in the cupboard and returned to her seat across from Devlyn.

Her movements pulled him from his internal ruminations, and Devlyn's eyes implored for forgiveness for his behavior over not just the past month, but since her arrival at the abbey school in Cor'lera. He had done nothing but accuse her and the other ei'ana of manipulating him to follow their own designs. He owed her an apology but had no idea where to begin.

"Earlier, I promised to explain the prophecy," Velaria said before he could find the appropriate words. "Knowing exactly what it says will, I hope, give you a better understanding of your station. It is the prophecy that Lucillia spoke just before giving birth to Roendryn and Feolyn." Devlyn held his breath as she paused and closed her eyes, recollecting the exact words.

"'Two sons of Light I shall birth. Alone, one shall rule. When the Age of Shadow returns and the Darkness engulfs the Light, the last bird of Light shall hatch as a new sun rises. The lesser brother shall give his life and the glory of the Light shall shine from Arenthyl to reach every crevice darkened by Shadow.'" Velaria paused to let the words sink in before going on.

"The lesser son refers to the heir of Feolyn; you. On the same day that you were born, two others also drew breath. One is Princess Ellendren. As I'm sure you are aware, she is heir to the Lucillian throne, a descendant of King Roendryn himself. The other is a phoenix, the last phoenix to hatch from its egg.

"The phoenix egg had been kept under the protection of the Guardian Knights. It is said that they had a fortress in the mountains surrounding Lake Saeryndol; none of those knights were thought to have survived the fall of Krysenthiel. I was only a student here when two of them came to Ceurenyl, surprising everyone. They walked directly to the Temple of Ceur in their unusual armor and sought an audience with Ceurtriarch Ealyndol. They explained that Ithendryl Lorenthien, High Queen of Krysenthiel, had entrusted them with the protection of a phoenix egg and had forbidden them from participating in the Ceurendol War that raged over the entire land. They told the Ceurtriarch that the phoenix had at last hatched on a specific day, your birthday."

It was a lot to take in. Not only had Devlyn been named in a prophecy, but the intricacies surrounding it stretched back centuries before the creation of the kingdom of Lucillia, and before Krysenthiel fell. Somehow, just now, the fact that he shared a birthday with Ellendren seemed almost a minor detail.

"What does this mean? That there are three choices: I become an ei'ceuril, I die, or I doom the world? And where in this prophecy does it mention anything about the ei'ceuril?" Doubt flooded his mind once again. It was becoming a common occurrence, and as far as he was concerned, all too frequent.

Velaria just held her small smile, and oddly enough, it was comforting.

"The meaning of the words 'lesser brother shall give his life' in the prophecy has been widely accepted as meaning that the one named will become an ei'ceuril; truly, the life of an ei'ceuril is the life of ultimate giving. While I agree with this, my grasp of prophecy in general shifted after my time in the Illumined Wood. My mind bloomed and the hard lines I grew up with faded. I would not say that the prophecy dictates your decisions; it's difficult to understand. If you *are* to become an ei'ceuril, you would have to do so of your own free will; no one can force it on you. There is a good chance that you will become an ei'ceuril, but it is not certain, nor is what this means for your future. What I am certain of, is that whatever you choose, the choice belongs to you alone."

Relief washed over Devlyn; hearing that he could not be forced into the Ei'ceuril meant the world to him. "What impact does the prophecy have on me now?" Devlyn asked.

Velaria's small smile was still present. "It is exactly what you have been doing. You live in it. Go to class, study, practice wielding, spend time with friends, and, of course, meet with *all* your tutors." Velaria's emphasis was supported by a low growl from Yelaris.

"There is another matter of importance I wish to share with you." Anxiety replaced the ever-present calm. "I received a bird, a white eagle, from Queen Lara."

Growing up, Devlyn had heard tales of birds carrying messages between cities, but no such exchange had been coordinated in Cor'lera, or even in all Parendior. The collection of villages had no need to communicate with one another. A rare bird occasionally flew in for Abbot Entiel, but few others received such messages. Velaria now handed him a small parchment bearing a fine script scrawled in orderly lines.

Dearest Velaria,

Daily, we hear tales about the horrors occurring in Cyril, and we have called our people to arms to protect their kingdom. We have asked the residents of villages in rural areas to go to Everin, Belin's Watch, or Hanil for better protection. We have no soldiers to spare. The brief messages from Cyril claim that shadow elves fill the streets; kien wielders are among their numbers. There is no explanation for how they control the powers without catastrophe, but you and our sister ei'ana should know of this. I am not certain we can withstand their wielding if they choose to mount a siege on Everin. All but one of our tunnels are sealed. Evellion has not the strength to meet this enemy alone; know that Perrien is only one fraction of many forces holding Cyril.

With sadness and much affection,

Lara

Devlyn skimmed over the letter a second time, his mind having difficulty registering the meaning of what he read. "Is it really that bad there? Who else but Perrien wishes to conquer Evellion?" Devlyn asked.

"It's difficult to tell, since only Perrien's flag has been raised, however my suspicion has always lain with Erynor, a feeling all the more solidified by the involvement of shadow elves. I believe he has reached out once again to his old supporters. I doubt the involvement of the southern kingdoms; he has other plans for them, I am certain. But there are others. The shadow elves for one, and probably the humans who once called Dwonia their home for another. They were banished from Dwonia after joining the Erynien Empire, abandoning their way of life and disgracing their people. They now live among the Shadow Mountains and the southern lands. They are numerous, and they are skilled fighters feared by any who cross them," Velaria explained.

"Will help be sent to Everin?" asked Devlyn. The queen had been so kind to him during his visit. Just thinking about her in danger was troubling, and he expected that Velaria might be feeling some strain, but she wore her usual calm expression.

"The kingdoms untouched by war so far are now preparing for what they know will cross their borders and cannot spare more than a few soldiers to help Everin. If the Dwarven Schtams can agree, they will help Evellion; a strong friendship exists between Evellion and the Schtamite. If Evellion were to fall, the dwarves would be left exposed beneath their mountains." There was no need for Velaria to explain. If Everin fell to a siege, the dwarven tunnel beneath the city would lie open to any intruder, jeopardizing the Schtamite.

It was growing late, and when both had sat quietly in their own thoughts for a few minutes, Devlyn had thanked Velaria and gone on his way to think further about all he had learned. They had scheduled their private lessons at the eleventh hour on Thenaen. The second day of the week was the only day where Devlyn still had available time.

Pausing just outside Velaria's door, Devlyn tried to remember why he had come to this part of the castle in the first place. Without deciding on a specific direction, he began to walk along the corridor, and when he came to a winding stair, he went up.

As he climbed, he thought of the sky, the view, and the thick roiling clouds preventing one from viewing much of the landscape, despite the high elevation. Thinking of the clouds jolted a memory of another day, a day when he had been at Karl's family's farmhouse on the outskirts of Gneal.

With that memory, he took the stairs two at a time until he reached the door at the top level. Devlyn unlatched the door and walked onto the covered balcony that wrapped around the heptagonal perimeter. Pointed archways were open to the elements with an intricate balustrade at the base of the openings. Each of Gwilnor's seven towers had a similar balcony but each had its own scale and some of the pointed arched openings were not arches at all but round openings. Above each balcony rose the steep slate roofs, transitioning from the exterior stone walls lining the balconies.

Devlyn overlooked the city below; everything beyond was blanketed in the darkness of night. Devlyn had never stood at such a height before. The thick clouds obscured the sky above; more clouds, clinging to the ground, covered all that lay west of Ceurenyl, what was once Krysenthiel. The low hanging clouds were sickly in appearance—green and grey laced with black. Realization struck. *The Shroud*. With the light of the sun faded hours past, the Shroud now revealed its true nature.

Looking away from the ominous, heavy mist below, Devlyn looked into the clouds above, searching for a link to what soared high over the city. He could not say how he knew, but there was no doubt that the phoenix soared somewhere above Ceurenyl. Devlyn focused hard, but to no avail;

the clouds were too thick to discern anything in or beyond them.

A melodious call came from on high, a melody that did not belong to the gloom beyond Ceurenyl. The whimsical song filled Devlyn, permeating his body, filling his heart. A familiar presence filled his consciousness as though Devlyn held the phoenix within; his soul sang and danced with the phoenix.

The world transformed; the clouds still hung in the sky, but they no longer prevented the subtle lights of night from streaming down on the land. Even though it was full night, Devlyn saw the world as if it was day, the sun at its peak, and the land bathed in light.

But the light did not touch all the land. The menacing mist that greedily clung to the ground remained, darker than Devlyn recalled from viewing it himself. The Shroud hungrily grasped at Ceurenyl, a city shaped like a peninsula jutting into the sinister mist, but its hostile tendrils withdrew more swiftly than they assaulted. No one had taken the time to explain to Devlyn how the Temple of Ceur protected the entire city from the Shroud. As he observed the Shroud's tendrils approach the city only to retreat, he wondered whether the temple pulsed with energy, emanating ever outward.

Devlyn wanted to call the Shroud black, but black did not describe it as well as dark did. The Darkness. A color could not carry the weight of that corruption.

A lake was known to lie at the foot of the mountains, but concealed beneath the Shroud, it was impossible to know whether it was frozen or not. Devlyn gazed west to a beam of light, not cascading from the sky, but emanating from below. Devlyn longed to look on this mysterious light, for surely no greater light could exist. As deeply as he desired to look on it, he knew the distance was great, much greater than he had time for.

The phoenix flew among the clouds, as Devlyn looked through his eyes, saddened by the Shroud beneath. Strengthened by the bond between them, melded into one, Devlyn began to wield, or maybe the phoenix began to wield.

Devlyn focused on the Shroud below, aware of an opening of sorts and a pull to submit to something greater.

The Shroud was dissolvable.

This new understanding struck him as he looked down on it. A burst of energy flowed through his connection with the phoenix, more intense than anything Devlyn alone had ever experienced with the elemental erendinth.

With their focus on the Shroud, the power sprung from them and pierced the darkness below. Devlyn felt the incredible strength of the Shroud as it fought the intrusion and the struggle between Light and Darkness began. Intensifying the strength of their focus, they wielded through, breaching the Shroud, the erendinth falling on the frozen ground beneath. Devlyn pressed on, determined to expand the small enclave, but the looming Shroud was too massive. It felt like trying to fill a sphere in the depths of an ocean, all the while the waters resisting, pushing back the sphere's attempt to expand.

Devlyn's strength was depleted; they had only managed to pierce a minuscule hole in the Shroud. Spent, he released the erendinth, and as he did, Devlyn wondered which erendinth they had wielded.

Lumenys. No words, no image, just somehow, an assurance from the phoenix that lumenys had been wielded through them.

Startled by the subtle communication, he tried to think of a way he could respond. He understood that with Yelaris, he had to communicate through images, yet he knew that was not appropriate with the phoenix. Even as he considered what might work, he suddenly *knew* that the opening they had made would not, *could not*, be reclaimed by the Shroud. It would remain, and the light of the sun would flow through it for the first time in over a thousand years. The sickness of the Shroud would withdraw, and the promise of life return.

The gloom of the clouded night sky filled his vision once more as the phoenix withdrew. A sense of loss filled Devlyn. *When will we be together again?* Devlyn thought, hoping the phoenix heard him, and then suddenly understood that not only were he and the phoenix always together, but they had been so since he was a toddler, curiously enough, because of Arlyn.

But what had his uncle done? Velaria had mentioned that she traveled to Cor'lera with Arlyn when Devlyn was a toddler but never said anything about what Arlyn might or might not have done to or for Devlyn.

Devlyn gazed out across the Shroud, searching for the puncture he and the phoenix had wielded. Far to the south he discerned a dip in the Shroud, noticeable even though it was far off, but Devlyn knew the dip was evidence that the Shroud was transitory. It was a small consolation, but a victory nonetheless. He lingered on the balcony of the Dragon Tower for a while longer, gazing across the Shroud and all that it covered. He now understood his purpose in life. The Shroud was his enemy, and he had the ability to remove it.

"And the glory of the Light shall shine from Arenthyl," Devlyn repeated the words of the prophecy.

26

WHISPERS IN THE NIGHT

Soft leaves scraped beneath Devlyn's feet. They weren't the usual brittle, dead, brown leaves that fell to the ground; these were still warm and saturated with green. Leaves fallen from the trees or ivy growing up out of the damp ground?

Where is she? She was just here, thought Devlyn. He was chasing a girl he knew, and she had just beckoned him to follow after her as she ran beneath the leaves of the tall trees and disappeared.

Light brown hair with hints of blond, black, and red flashed between two of the trees, so quickly that he almost missed it.

He made his way over to the trees and just as he got there, a warm wind blew and a branch with golden leaves swayed in the air. *Leaves, not hair*, thought Devlyn, disappointed.

"Over here, Devlyn!" a distant voice called.

I know that voice, he thought and yelled, "Wait, Leilyn!" He heard her giggle, and then leaves rustling as she ran off. Devlyn sprinted, wanting to reach his sister, dodging the trees that seemed to spring into his way. From above, he heard the melodious call that meant the phoenix flew with him high over his head. As Devlyn gained on Leilyn, she paused and turned to face him. Her eyes stopped him in his tracks. Leilyn's eyes were completely blue. There was no black pupil and no white encasing the iris. And as Devlyn looked into his sister's eyes, she began to fade, a cloud solidifying about her.

A faint knocking that grew stronger and persisted pulled him from sleep.

"Devlyn!" came a distant voice.

"Leilyn? Why are you knocking?" Devlyn asked dazedly, thinking he was still in a forest. Opening his eyes, he realized that he most certainly was not in a forest since cold stone walls surrounded him on every side. He was unable to see anything outside the darkened window.

"I'm coming in," came the distant voice. Squinting toward the door, Devlyn watched Alex enter in nothing but his small clothes.

"What are you yelling about? The whole floor is out in the corridor." Alex was obviously irritated. Devlyn came fully awake then, and he realized he was in his bed in Gwilnor. He heard Alex talking to others in the corridor, telling them they could go back to bed, he'd handle it.

"Bloody hell, you're soaked in sweat! Everything all right?" Concern replaced the irritation.

"Where's Leilyn? I just saw her," said Devlyn as he sat up in his bed. His entire body was wet, and his heart raced. Running his hand through his hair, he felt the greasy sweat.

"It's all right, just calm down, Dev." Alex soaked a cloth in the washbowl and pressed it against Devlyn's head. "It was just one of your dreams. Leilyn isn't here; Velaria said she's in the Illumined Wood. Remember?"

"What, no…I…I was just with her. Her eyes were completely blue. Alex, there wasn't any white or black, just blue." Devlyn felt a bit frantic.

"It was just one of your dreams; you haven't left this room. Look, you're still in your bed and practically naked."

"It felt so real; my legs feel as if I just ran hard." Devlyn massaged his thighs.

"That won't be the first time you woke from a dream you thought was real." Alex turned toward the door where a few of the more curious students still hung about.

"I told you, it's all right, just go back to bed, fellas," he called before turning back to Devlyn. "Don't worry about it. In a week, they'll have forgotten that you woke the whole dormitory with your dream fright. You should try to get some rest; dawn is still several hours off."

Devlyn agreed and lay down again as Alex walked out and shut the door behind him.

Closing his eyes, concentrating on slowing his still-rapid heartbeat and hoping to fade back to sleep, Devlyn saw Leilyn's face float before his own. Light brown hair with traces of blond, black, and red framed her face and her all-blue eyes stared into his own. He shot up and sat upright. *I'm losing it.* Getting out of bed, he crossed the small room to the washbowl. Disregarding the cloth hanging over the edge, he dunked his face into the cool water, holding it there until he was unquestionably awake. When he lifted his head out, the coldness remained, and goose bumps crawled across the rest of his skin, hair and face dripping beads of water.

Devlyn sat on the edge of the bed and looked out the window. The sky outside was clear, but still very dark. From the faint glow of the night sky, he could tell that a thin crescent moon hung somewhere above but hidden from his window. Stars speckled the sky, watching over Ceurenyl slumbering below.

A gentle wind blew across the city, and Devlyn wondered what the city was like as it slumbered, its usual busy streets without traffic. Students, he knew, were restricted from leaving the castle at night; in fact, they weren't even allowed to leave their dormitory. Then he realized that he did not have to leave his room to enter the city. He went to the window and opened it, allowing a breeze to flow into his room.

The wind gently caressed his face; Devlyn felt it, sensed it. The air seemed to invite him. Slowly, he pressed against it, pressing *into* aerys, entering it, and guiding it. He wielded the air across the North Tower and, from his body inside the tower, heard the wind howl. He guided the air, directing its flow down the tower walls, across the stream, and through the empty city streets. He felt the air's chill through wielding kien. Several minutes passed as he wielded through parts he had not yet visited, including the city's bell tower with twenty-four individual bells that signaled the hour of the day.

As he wielded aerys around the bells, sending them trembling slightly in the breeze, Devlyn discovered that each bell was different. There were four groups of six bells each, all the bells in varying sizes and each group made of a different material. Three of the groups were cast in what looked like gold, silver, and bronze, but wasn't, and the last one was made of a glassy material. Not a single bell was the same as another; each was unique.

As he flowed on with the air, he heard voices. Devlyn slowed the air and let it rest just near where the voices came; oddly enough, Devlyn could not feel the presence of the owners of the voices, only the voices themselves.

"You expect to go unnoticed in the castle. Even if you manage a disguise, they will know you as a wielder and will lock you in that temple," came a masculine voice.

"I've already entered," snickered the other voice. "And not one of those pathetic girls sees through my guise to question it. I walk in plain sight before them all. I am a resident." The voice sounded like that of a middle-aged man. Although Devlyn heard only two voices, he thought a third was present.

Neither spoke further. Devlyn withdrew from aerys beside the hidden figures. Back in his dormitory room, he found himself panting with anxiety, his heart racing. He grabbed his school robe and ran out to the corridor as he pulled it over his head. His instincts took over and he banged on Andrew's door, one of the few older students who didn't look at him oddly. Shuffling and muffled complaints sounded from inside just before the door swung open.

"You don't want to train this early now, do you?" Andrew asked, groggy and clearly just woken up after falling back to sleep. His roommates stared daggers at him from their beds.

"Can't, there's trouble. We need to rouse the Septyl knights. A shadow elf is living in the castle. I'm not sure how long he's been here. But he's out in the city now, and it won't be long until he returns. Don't ask how I know, you have to trust me. I have to warn Velaria," Devlyn's words tumbled out.

Andrew must have seen the truth behind the panic in Devlyn's eyes, for he nodded in understanding. "All right, but the knights won't be able to stop a shadow elf on their own." Andrew turned and began to shake his roommates out of their beds, kicking at one bed to rattle the slumbering boy.

Devlyn sprinted toward the stair hall, even as Andrew bellowed behind him, banging on other doors.

"To the armory! This is not a drill! To the armory!" Andrew's yells continued, bringing more and more students and knights rushing into the corridors as Devlyn raced down the many flights of the tower.

It dawned on him that he was unlikely to reach Velaria's quarters in time; they were on opposite sides of the castle. There was another way, he thought, and even as he sprinted onward, he frantically threw images out. Images of alert knights and trouble flashed from his mind; he even managed a crude image of a shadow elf inside the castle. He couldn't exactly direct the images, and he had no idea whether it would work, but he pushed them from his mind nonetheless.

He was near the entrance hall when he collided with Velaria. The impact almost took them both from their feet.

"Yelaris is not at all pleased with your intrusion. If it was not for the circumstances, I would quite agree that she is justified in her displeasure with you, but I appreciate your quick thinking. I've alerted the other Chairs; ei'ana are on their way as well, and the other entrances are sealed, as they are every night. I've sent ei'ana to ensure that the entrances remain sealed."

"I warned the knights; we'll find them gathering in the entrance hall by now," said Devlyn, as he went on with Velaria. Knights rushed past, making their way there with speed but with control as well. *Almost there,* thought Devlyn, just as an ear-splitting scream brought everyone to a near stop before they resumed at an even faster pace.

"Fool of a woman, she should've waited for us!"

Devlyn followed the others out of the massive entrance hall doors, crammed between knights and ei'ana. A woman hung suspended in the night sky above the bridge linking Gwilnor to the city. Something darker than the night, dark pulsing lances reminiscent of lightning but missing the light, pierced her body.

Velaria paused beside him, and Devlyn noticed that she was not looking at the woman suspended in the air, but at the two figures beneath the woman, on the far end of the bridge, not yet on Gwilnor's grounds. Stepping forward to meet the shadow elves, Velaria held an arm out in front of Devlyn, preventing him from advancing further. He shot her a look of frustration, but immediately understood as a figure of incredible girth flew from the near end of the bridge.

Whatever the figures had been up to, they stopped as soon as they caught sight of the dragon swooping toward them. The suspended woman immediately dropped to the ground, landing with a loud smashing thump as her body broke on the stone bridge. The sound was sickening and made Devlyn's stomach turn.

The shadow elves turned their attack to Yelaris. Desperate to help fight them off, Devlyn pressed himself into the erendinth, wielding all four elemental erendinth simultaneously. He felt the immense strength each possessed, strength that could be used for destruction.

Even as he pressed fully into the four elemental erendinth, he noticed a desire to submit to something foreign, yet familiar. It was similar to what had flowed through Devlyn and the phoenix to make a hole in the Shroud, but it was also unmistakably different.

He grew cognizant of the shadows surrounding him, shadows that held nothing sinister. He also felt a different presence, a life-force, two erendinth he had never been aware of before and recognized umbrys and animys. Devlyn instinctually embraced them within, made them part of himself.

As he prepared a wield he had not contrived before, he heard Velaria speak urgently.

"I need you to bond with me, just as we do during our lessons, when I observe your wielding. Quickly, give me your hand. I need your strength to overpower them."

Not daring to object, Devlyn grasped Velaria's hand and felt her shock as they bonded, allowing Velaria to sense what Devlyn already held in his wield. As he did, he felt another presence, Velaria's presence, take control of his wielding.

The air before them warped, aerys and ignys mixed with animys darting toward the shadow elves, piercing them both from behind as they faced and fought Yelaris. A globe of air and fire formed around the head of each shadow elf.

Velaria focused on the task at hand, standing solidly even as the wind whipped around her, sending her hair rippling wildly and the leaves and flowers of her dress rustling loudly. The wind's force was immense; Devlyn planted his feet and steadied himself to stay in place next to Velaria.

The wind lessened, and the globes of air and fire surrounding the heads of the shadow elves condensed. Both collapsed unconscious to the ground, and Yelaris pounced on their bodies, securing them in her powerful claws before bounding into the sky toward the Temple of Ceur.

Velaria released her bond with Devlyn and turned from the bridge. The sudden withdrawal of the erendinth left Devlyn with the sense of emptiness that was becoming familiar, although he also thought it intensified the more he wielded.

"Knights of Septyl, the Shadow has resumed its attack against Septyl. You are called upon to mount her turrets and walls and protect her, as you vowed." Velaria sounded every bit the commander as she ordered the knights to their posts. "No one is to enter or leave the castle without permission from the Seven Chairs. A quarter of you remain here, the rest are ordered to mount a defense of Ceurenyl. No one is to enter those gates or fly across our walls!" As he watched them move off to follow their orders, Devlyn shuddered, realizing that he shook from many emotions.

"The woman there," he stumbled over his words. "She was a Chair."

Sadness showed in Velaria's silver eyes. "Mother Lenora Hanaryld." She walked over to Mother Lenora, lying broken on the bridge. Devlyn trailed close behind and looked into the empty gaze of the Chair of Arantiulyn.

"I will come to you in a few hours, but first I must attend to our unwelcome visitors. Remain in a public area of the castle; I fear it is no longer safe to walk alone in Gwilnor." Velaria did not wait to explain herself; she strode across the expanse of the bridge and headed for the temple.

Devlyn wrapped his arms around his chest, trying to ease some of the shaking in his body. He was cold; even his legs were chilled.

Two orange-clad ei'ana arrived to take the body of the Chair of Arantiulyn. Between them, aerys gently lifted the corpse, and the ei'ana led it through the dazed crowds into the castle. Devlyn watched the small procession pass in silence. Knights bowed their heads as the body of Mother Lenora passed them. While the knights swore oaths to all Seven Chairs, dedicating their services to a particular school, it was the Arantiulyn Chair who functioned as their unified general.

The students who had come outside, all of them from the boys' dormitory, were ushered back into the castle. Female students still slumbered away in the girls' dormitory, wherever that was, unaware of the predawn events. No one opted to return to bed for an extra hour or two of sleep.

Devlyn knew there was no chance his eyes would close after the momentous events of the past hour. Stars glowed bright in the sky with sunrise still hours off.

27

SHADOW ELF

As he walked through the massive doors and into the entrance hall, Devlyn felt a pat on his back, followed by a grip on his shoulder. Still shocked and dazed, he barely reacted.

"I'm not sure how you knew, but we got 'em. Way to go," Andrew's hand remained clapped on Devlyn's shoulder. They joined the stream of students heading toward the dining hall; Devlyn was not hungry, but he also did not want to be alone, aware of the prudence of Velaria's advice about remaining in a group.

In short order, the entire student body from the boy's dormitory filed through the doors into the dining hall and gathered on the benches at the long tables.

All of them knew that Devlyn had uncovered the shadow elves, and they also knew that to do so, he had wielded. Men were skeptical enough about women wielding, but if there was anything they trusted less, it was a man wielding. After all, two male wielders had just murdered the Chair of Arantiulyn, and every student here was convinced that Devlyn was just as capable of doing the same.

Devlyn knew what they thought; only Andrew, Alex, and Kevn sat with him, and a large empty space surrounded them. The rest kept their distance, eyeing him suspiciously, Devlyn feeling the weight of their peering eyes.

From any perspective, it had been a strange night, but Devlyn had had more than one strange experience, most within the last couple of hours. First, he woke the entire floor because of a dream involving his sister. He still didn't really know what woke the others, since Alex had only mentioned yelling. *Probably didn't say more for my own good.* Not too long after they had all returned to bed, he woke them yet again. While it was likely that none regretted being woken the second time given what followed, it was also likely that they did not appreciate the unnatural means that led to Devlyn's discovery of the shadow elves threatening Gwilnor.

Sulking as he sat on the bench among his friends, Devlyn did not feel like talking to them, but neither did he feel like leaving the dining hall to be alone. A shadow elf was living in the castle and no one knew whether that was the only one.

"What if they're right, what if I am supposed to become an ei'ceuril?" Devlyn blurted out.

Surprised by his outburst, the others at the table looked at him, but it was Kevn who answered his question. "Don't get carried away. Prophecy is a tricky thing; just as soon as you think you understand it, the meaning changes. It's as if it's living. If you want to become an ei'ceuril, that's one thing, but you can't simply join because you think you're forced to. It doesn't work that way. The desire to join must be genuine, and it's impossible to be inauthentic while inside the Chamber of Light."

"What of the prophecy? It's not like it leaves many options. Either I join the Ei'ceuril, I die, or I doom everyone. No offense, but I feel pretty genuine about not choosing the last two options." Devlyn's rising tone reflected his growing anxiety.

"If that's what you decide. Just know that it must be your choice, it can't be out of force or from fear. It must derive from freedom," said Kevn. A few moments passed where no one spoke, but Kevn looked thoughtful, as if he was contemplating something he wasn't ready to share with Devlyn.

"I can't speak for myself on becoming an ei'ceuril; I've never considered it, let alone looked into it. But what I can tell you is, don't make any rash decisions." Andrew broke the uncomfortable silence. "Just make sure to give it enough thought before you decide anything. Rash choices typically end poorly, especially when fueled by fear."

Devlyn sunk his head between his arms on the table and closed his eyes. He wanted to close his ears but since that was impossible, he could hear everyone else talking in the dining hall.

It was still dark outside when a few of the female students began coming in for an early breakfast. It was clear that they found it peculiar that the entire boy's dormitory was already crowded into the dining hall at such an early hour. In no time, they heard about all the night's events, a tale that had one girl not staying to eat breakfast but leaving almost as soon as she had entered.

Abbie was one of the early risers among the girls. She looked about as she paused in the entrance, then headed straight for Devlyn's table. Assuming that she wanted to duel with Andrew before classes started, Devlyn was caught by surprise when, without wasting time on niceties, she stopped next to him and demanded, "How did you know? Was it a dream?"

Stunned by her intensity, Devlyn had to think back. "What? No, my dream had nothing to do with it. And hold on, how do you know?" he asked.

"How do I know? The whole castle is gossiping about you. Don't tell me those pointy ears of yours are filled with only wax!" she said and hit Devlyn over the head. "If it wasn't a dream, then how?"

"I wielded. I couldn't get back to sleep after a bad dream. So, I wielded aerys through the city. I was curious about what Ceurenyl was like at night. Seeing as we're not permitted out of the castle after dusk, I couldn't think of a better way of finding out than wielding the air through the streets," Devlyn explained, aware that his friends now also heard exactly how he had known.

Abbie thought to herself a bit, chewing her lower lip as though the action mirrored her chewing thoughts. "But you dreamt, right? What was it like?"

Unsure of what motivated Abbie's curiosity, he looked at her and was caught up in her green eyes. "I saw my sister. In the dream that is, although, there was no white or black in her eyes; no iris nor pupil. They were completely blue." At that, Abbie's eyes widened slightly. "But, it was just a dream."

"There is no such thing as 'just a dream,'" Abbie mocked. "Stay out of trouble, dreamer." Without so much as a farewell, she turned on her heel and left the dining hall.

The four remaining at the table looked to one another, equally confused by Abbie's appearance and disposition.

"I swear, she's an absolute loon!" said Andrew as he brushed one hand through his hair. "She has me crazy, she does. If I don't watch myself, we'll end up wed with her carrying our babe one day!"

Alex and Kevn burst out laughing at Andrew's confession, and Devlyn managed a weak chuckle.

"A bloke like you could have any girl you wanted, and you're falling for Abbie Wintyr! Do you need to visit a Crimsyn? They would be more than willing to offer a good healing. I'm not sure if they can fix mental delusions though," Alex chided.

Not at all pleased by the jibe, Andrew landed a hard punch on his upper arm, almost throwing Alex clear off the bench and to the floor. Alex rubbed his arm trying to make the pain go away while pretending it didn't hurt. Sunlight began to wash through the large east-facing windows on the side of the dining hall, its beams blinding anyone foolish enough to sit across from them. Beginning to feel restless, Devlyn rose from the bench.

"How about a go in the practice yard?" he asked the others at the table.

Alex and Andrew quickly agreed, and to Devlyn's surprise, even Kevn was eager to hit something with a sword. The four walked out the dining hall and through the mostly vacant corridors. They were nearly at the courtyard where the Septyl knights and pupils practiced when Velaria appeared from an intersecting corridor.

"There you are, Devlyn; I need you to come with me," she said before any of them had the chance to greet her; she looked just as tired as Devlyn felt.

Devlyn apologized to his friends before joining Velaria with no little regret; for the first time since arriving at Gwilnor, he had actually been looking forward to a faux sword fight.

Neither spoke as they walked swiftly through the corridors. Devlyn did not ask where they were going, assuming that it was to her quarters for a private conversation about the shadow elves and their joined wielding. He quickly realized that this request for his presence was related to something else, since they descended every stairway they came to.

Soon, they were far beneath the castle, in dark, windowless passages lit only by the small globe of light that sat just above Velaria's palm. Although he couldn't see much at the pace Velaria was setting as she strode beside him, he could tell that these corridors were rarely used. The floor had a thick coat of dust that showed very few footprints. Cobwebs claimed the corners of the ceilings, and Devlyn had a hunch that more than just spiders crawled around down here.

At one point, they passed through a nondescript door, and the formerly straight path they followed now curved ever so slightly, so slightly that Devlyn would not have noticed without the shadows from Velaria's globe revealing the slight curve along the corridor.

A dim light appeared ahead. Devlyn was aware that they had walked quite a distance, which meant that they were likely no longer beneath the castle, despite Gwilnor's expansive footprint. The light in the distance was unstable, and its flickering drew Devlyn's curiosity. Just as he was on the point of asking about it, a restrained voice called out.

"Velaria, is that you? Did you bring him?" the voice sounded familiar.

Velaria waited until they drew closer before responding, but not before her globe of light extinguished without warning.

"Yes, Therril, he's safe."

"Oh good; very good indeed. The two have been separated since the knights brought them in. One won't stop yelling for the traitorous witch, which I assume is you." Therril spoke flatly.

As they turned to go on, Therril in the lead, Devlyn realized that they were not in a corridor; it was a tunnel, probably somewhere beneath the Temple of Ceur. And that would explain why Velaria's globe had gone out: the temple prevented wielding. A very small archway appeared before them. The poor lighting from Therril's flickering torch made it difficult to see beyond.

Therril walked through first, and Devlyn was glad that Therril had turned back toward him to provide light, since there was an unexpected drop that meant he had to step down into a small ordinary office. He looked back to watch Velaria step through the archway and could not believe his eyes! Behind Velaria, Devlyn saw the first rays of a new day through a window. Baffled by the phenomenon before him, he looked to both Therril and Velaria for an explanation.

Therril chuckled in his throaty laugh. "Surely this doesn't still astonish you."

"But…how? I thought no one could wield in the temple," said Devlyn.

"Huh, huh, huh. Just because *we* can't, does not mean the architects were incapable of it!" Therril was delighted despite the circumstances. "This temple was wielded from stones from every crevice of Teraeniel, including all four Skylands! The first ei'ceuril of the distant past wielded this temple into existence."

"How old is this place?" Devlyn asked in newfound awe.

"Much older than I am, I assure you! But it was built long before the elves even considered departing their beloved Skylands," Therril said pensively. "Now, we do have some business to see to," he added, and led them into the corridor beyond, where Devlyn was surprised to find that hundreds of men walked past in both directions.

None of them wore the ei'ceuril robes, so their finely made clothing meant they had to be kien wielders. *Are there really this many kien wielders?* he wondered even as he tried not to stare.

"Welcome to the unfortunate, yet necessary holding cells of the Temple of Ceur." Velaria waved Devlyn into a less-traveled side corridor where Therril already hurried toward an iron-clad door at the end.

"We need you to identify whether these are the men you heard. They are, without a doubt, shadow elves, but we must be certain that they are the same ones; if they are not, then there could be more in the city. Beneath our very noses," Velaria said, her distress evident.

Devlyn nodded, but as he did he thought again of the third presence he had noted while wielding. They went through the door into yet another corridor; this one was lined with many doors, doors that Devlyn presumed were all securely bolted given that they were the holding cells. Therril led them through one of the doors into a small room beyond. About midway into the room, a thin barrier of light fell from the ceiling to the floor, separating them from a sickly-looking man who stood on the far side of the room.

Devlyn was shocked by the man's appearance: grey, diseased-looking skin, faded red hair lying in thin strings flat against his skull, and the most appalling eyes. Perhaps they had once been the silver eyes of the elves but now, their murky grey no longer gleamed, and reflected no light.

"There's no need to fear him, he can't pass the barrier," Therril explained. "These are the Cells of Justice. The innocent can walk freely through the light. However, those who are not are crushed to the ground, incapacitated.

"Do not frighten the boy, old fool! And remove this traitor from my sight." The shadow elf spat at Velaria, before moving his gaze to Devlyn. "I remember hearing tales of the Phaedryn as a boy. But know that you will die, just as the others did; on your death, the memory of your brothers and sisters will be wiped from existence, and the world won't ever again have recourse to hope in your kind!" He stared directly into Devlyn's eyes.

As the shadow elf spoke, Devlyn paid careful attention. "It's him." There was no doubt in his mind but Devlyn's words sent the shadow elf into an even higher level of rage.

"The emperor will storm this city and bring every last one of you to your knees. You will worship the rightful Master!" With that, he again turned to Velaria, and spat through the barrier. "And you who call yourself an elf of Cyndinare! To think we share the same blood; you should be disgusted with yourself. Aiding these despicable mortals while deserting your own people! *We are gods next to them!*"

At that, Therril escorted them back into the corridor and resealed the door.

"It pains me that you had to go through that. I wish I could say it was the last time, but I cannot give such a guarantee." Therril rubbed Velaria's back comfortingly as he smiled benignly at Devlyn. They took a few moments in the corridor before entering the next holding cell.

Beyond its invisible barrier, a young man sat on the ground with his head on his knees. Devlyn thought he looked about Liam's age. Unlike the shadow elf in the previous cell, this elf looked far healthier. Not only was his skin a more usual fleshy color, but his hair was a rich vibrant red, more like Velaria's, almost flame-hued. Noting their entrance, he looked up to his visitors, allowing Devlyn to catch a glimpse of his eyes; they were the brilliant silver proper to elves.

Velaria walked to the barrier and beckoned the elf to stand. He rose slowly and crossed the small space to the barrier.

"I saw you in Gneal," said Velaria. "Who are you?"

The prisoner first looked into her eyes, and then cast his down to the floor before speaking. "Who do you believe me to be?" he asked quietly. He looked up once again, locking his eyes firmly with Velaria's before continuing. "My name is Jaerol Solaris and I am no shadow elf. Like you, my only crime is being a Cyndinari." He took another step closer to the barrier.

Recognizing the voice as the other he had heard, Devlyn backed away, but Therril and Velaria stood their ground. To Devlyn's horror, Jaerol easily walked through the barrier.

"Tell me," Therril said gravely, "how is it possible for one such as yourself to dupe the Erynien Empire? Surely such an attempt would result in death."

"If I had stayed among them much longer, I would have been found out and a shadow elf would have fed on my spirit to elongate his own life. I am still young, and young shadow elves retain a youthful appearance. The greyness does not set in for decades; slowly the body begins to decay, rejecting the unnatural means of survival. Among the shadow elves, those who have not begun to change are sent to human kingdoms as emissaries. I was sent to Gneal. I had heard of the atrocities that my people committed long before I arrived, but it was there that I first witnessed them. Dozens of Luminari from a small village in Parendior were tortured for information, their spirits extracted. Everyone was forced to watch. Different shadow elves came to feed on them. But they had not been taken and held because they had information; they were imprisoned as fodder for shadow elves needing their spirits." Jaerol spoke calmly, numb to the horror evoked in his audience.

Devlyn was not just horrified; he was furious. His family had been used as food, locked in dungeons for shadow elves to greedily feast on their spirits to lengthen their own.

"How could you just watch it happen? Why didn't you stop them?" Devlyn bellowed, tears stinging his eyes. "If you say you're not a shadow elf, then how could you stand by and watch my family have their lives sucked from them? You're a coward!" Devlyn's eyes blazed; he could not recall ever feeling so angry in his life. It was as though all the emotions he had bottled up over the past eleven years suddenly unleashed on this Cyndinari. An elf who was the first person, other than Lex, linked to the atrocities committed against his family. *Mother, where are you?*

Jaerol did not step back from the force of Devlyn's anger. Instead, he looked at Devlyn with what appeared to be an insincere attempt at sympathy. There was no empathy in those silver eyes, in that complacent face.

"Forgive my inaction; if there had been a chance to thwart their deaths, I would have. But the shadow elves never fully trusted me. Although they sent me to Gneal as an emissary, they still do not truly trust me." Jaerol spoke flatly as though he never felt any emotion.

"Why do they not trust you?" Therril asked curiously.

"The youth of the Cyndinari are forced to participate in a tournament. Training begins when they reach their eighth summer. The games are intended to make them strong and resilient. They learn to wield the erendinth and to use verathn."

Devlyn had never heard of a verathn before.

"Weapons of great power, wielded from shoots of the Tree of Life; however, the ones we used in training were butchered from the shoots, destroying them in the process," Jaerol explained, noticing Devlyn's confusion. "When we reach our sixteenth summer, we compete in the Grand

Tourney. There are four rounds, and we must duel our peers, often the ones we are closest to.

"The first three rounds are more general exercises, displaying our strength and endurance. The fourth round is to the death. The stronger combatant is expected to use tenebrys to take the life of the other, to extend their own and become a shadow elf. This is done before spectators, in the arena. When I fought, I defeated my closest and truest friend, wielding umbrys in a way that the spectators thought I was just being theatrical. But I could not steal his life for my own. I had no choice except to kill him, but I chose to not steal his life. I let his spirit pass to the World-Beyond, in peace. No one in the stadium, not the spectators nor the other participants, saw that I let his spirit go. They all assumed that I had acquired his life, elongating my own, as every other winning participant did. But, because the umbrys I wielded prevented everyone from witnessing my actions, some grew suspicious, and rumors followed."

Therril and Velaria did not seem to be the slightest bit surprised by the story, but Devlyn listened with disgust. He could not believe the gruesome nature of the Cyndinari. Half of their population murdered, so the other half might prove themselves stronger and thereby extend their own lives by consuming the spirits of their own people.

The story was horrible enough, but what was even more upsetting was that both male and female shadow elves wielded, and not just wielding the elemental erendinth, they could wield umbrys, one of the transcendental erendinth.

"How is it that male shadow elves wield with control? I thought it wasn't possible, even among them," said Velaria.

Devlyn could tell that she had wanted to ask that question for a very long time. It was no secret that the enemy wielded the erendinth, but no one knew how their kien wielders managed control.

"They can't control it and they don't. The only thing the emperor cares for is power; he wants nothing more than to eliminate any threat, regardless of its origin. Because of the catastrophic consequences caused by kien wielders when they lose control, the emperor encourages it."

Velaria and Therril both appeared concerned, but Therril also gave the impression that Jaerol had verified something Therril already suspected.

"There's something else you ought to know," Jaerol went on. "Umbrys was not wielded on the bridge. Since Erynor's return, many summers
before I was born, he saw to it that his strongest wielders acquired the ability to wield Darkness, to wield tenebrys. I also believe that the Deurghol,
those responsible for the Shroud, have returned to their Master's call, some
from as far away as Ogren and Daereneth."

28

CALL OF THE WOOD

The scent of autumn hung in the distant air as a cooling breeze brushed Velaria's face. Summer's warmth remained thick in the air but would not linger much longer. They were well into Kyrenth, the first month of the season, and the leaves had just begun to change.

The sound of powerful wings reverberated in her ears, beating against the empty light-blue sky; nothing affected her more than the dragon on which she rode. Yelaris was an incredible companion; the two had been loyal to one another for eleven years. Whenever they flew together, Velaria was always carried back to their first flight in and above the Illumined Wood. She had been terribly afraid of the offer from the dragon then, but stronger than her fear was the trust she held for Yelaris. Although they had only known each other for a short while at the time, they had made a lasting impression on each other, as though their pairing was meant to be.

Before she had entered the Illumined Wood as a novice, she had hoped she would encounter her guardian anadel, one of the lorendil, there. Only with the guidance of one's lorendil could a novice depart the Illumined Wood, with or without the novice's knowledge. Nearly a year had passed since she had entered the Illumined Wood, and during that time, Velaria had had many dreams about meeting her guardian anadel. When the day finally came where she glimpsed a blue figure flying overhead, she was startled. She had difficulty getting a clear view of it at first because the heavily leafed boughs of the trees above obscured much of the open sky.

Fear soon replaced her initial surprise when the great beast flew toward her. She had never been so terrified in her life. The various tapestries throughout the Azurelle Wing in Gwilnor told her exactly what the beast was. However, she did not need to recall those images to know the beast once the dragon's consciousness washed over her own, taking Velaria's fear away.

Instantly, she knew the dragon's name: Yelaris. The dragon's power and wisdom permeated her presence, and in that first instant of the bond, they knew everything about each other. In that shared exchange of identity, of memories, Velaria learned that Yelaris was not her guardian anadel, that as a spirit, a lorendil rarely revealed herself to an anacordel, a creature of both body and spirit. However, Yelaris *was* bound to Velaria.

Now, as they soared through the sky together, Velaria was again consoled by their bond. Every time she flew with Yelaris, Velaria's feelings of fatigue, anxiety, and worry faded. Today was a day to release the negativity and relish her special bond with Yelaris.

Velaria flew past the Temple of Ceur. She had always assumed that a mountain rose directly behind the temple, but the temple's foundation walls dropped hundreds of feet into the mountainous ravine. From above, she could see that the mountain rose much further behind the temple than it appeared from below. Unlike the side of the temple facing the city, which showed the full horizontal facade, the northern side displayed hundreds, perhaps thousands of windows poking through the curious stone below the main bulk of the temple. Velaria had always wondered where the ei'ceuril, temple knights, and kien wielders lived in the temple. She had presumed their accommodations lay below the Chamber of Light but could not imagine so many people living in a building without any windows, since she had thought the mountain rose from the far side of the temple.

The mountain the temple sat on concealed much of it from the city. Those in the city only saw a fifth of the structure. She knew the temple was immense beyond imagining, but the actuality of it was mind-boggling. Like the front of the temple, this side was seamless, as if the entire structure was woven from a single stone and melded flawlessly. Windows, doors, and balconies were all that penetrated the surface of the smooth cloudy surface.

Velaria wondered for a brief moment how the temple had been built but her exhaustion kept her from putting too much thought into it. Just seeing the temple brought back her sense of responsibility. Several weeks had passed since the incident at the bridge. The captured shadow elf remained in his cell, but Jaerol had been given an apartment in the temple with the other kien wielders. Velaria trusted Jaerol, but he was still a kien wielder incapable of controlling the erendinth. Her trust was based only on his word and his ability to walk through the barrier unimpeded, which admittedly was not much to go by.

Velaria had attended several meetings with the Ceurtriarch and the wise ones about whether it was safe to allow a shadow elf to roam free through the temple. Since none of them had ever met a shadow elf, at every meeting, Velaria had to insist that Jaerol was no more a shadow elf than the Ceurtriarch himself, to which he did not respond favorably, nor did the many wise ones present.

Jaerol had had to display his innocence before dozens of archstewards and wise ones by walking through the Chamber of Light. If he had been dedicated to the Darkness, he would have been crushed to the ground and incapacitated, rather than just walking through unscathed. While he did not float in the center of the domed chamber—a frequent phenomenon for those spiritually more attuned to the Light—Ceurtriarch Ealyndol had finally permitted him a degree of freedom, but only within the temple. Despite the meagerness of supporting evidence for his innocence, oddly enough, Velaria's trust was strong enough that she fought on his behalf in her meetings with the ei'ceuril.

While her meetings concerning Jaerol were frustrating, the meetings regarding Devlyn had been even more so.

She knew the prophecy as well as any other, but she had issues with forcing Devlyn toward the path laid out for him, forcing him to become an ei'ceuril. It seemed that she was the only one in favor of letting Devlyn choose freely; even the other Chairs began to side with the ei'ceuril. But with the capture of the shadow elf, the ei'ceuril pushed harder than ever to enlist Devlyn into their order. Velaria doubted she could refuse them for much longer, particularly since she had no clear reason to support letting Devlyn make the choice, beyond an unease about prophetic and ambiguous wording.

After all the heated discussions, and on top of her increased responsibilities as Chair of Azurelle, she badly needed to get away from Ceurenyl. She had looked forward to flying with Yelaris for over a month now, but never had the opportunity until today. There was nothing she enjoyed more than being with Yelaris, especially when they flew together.

Abbie Wintyr hounded Devlyn. A day had not passed without her inquiring about his dreams. The night after the shadow elf had been captured, he had dreamt of his sister again. Fortunately, he had not disturbed the entire dormitory this time. He thought nothing of the dream, so when Abbie asked him about it, he had spoken truthfully, telling Abbie about Leilyn's all-blue eyes. An onslaught of questions followed, and he soon began to worry about Abbie's wellbeing; to Devlyn, she seemed ill. Her hair was frizzier than usual—quite a sight considering its typical volume—her face had taken on a grey cast, and her voice cracked with sharp pitches.

While his dreams involving Leilyn and the forest she lived in kept occurring, he refrained from mentioning it to Abbie. In fact, he went out of his way to avoid Abbie altogether. He especially had no intention of revealing his other, more sinister, dreams. If hearing about Devlyn walking through woods and catching sight of his sister caused Abbie such grief, he could only imagine how she would react to the dreams that had menacing clouds threatening Ceurenyl. Abbie's condition seemed to deteriorate every day that passed; rumors said that she had stopped sleeping and washing, which Devlyn thought was true.

With his avoidance measures, nine days had passed since he had last spoken with Abbie, but her persistence won out after Kai's politics class. Devlyn left the class as usual, but as he did, Abbie came from the side and stopped him in his tracks. Sometimes, it seemed that she knew his class schedule better than he did.

"Listen, I don't care if you've been avoiding me, and I know this sounds ridiculous, but you *must* heed your dreams." Abbie's distress showed in her appearance as much as in her words.

"What's so important about these dreams? So what if I've had the same dream every night for nearly a month?" Devlyn snapped, his patience deteriorating.

"You said they'd stopped! Do you have any idea what it means?" She was beyond shock, a shock that quickly moved to ferocious irritation. "Of course, you don't. Why did I even ask? Listen, those dreams aren't your imagination; they're real. You are getting a glimpse into the future. It's rare, but for those who have the gift, the more often it happens, the sooner it will come to pass."

"I would love to see my sister again, in fact, the sooner the better." Devlyn dared not mention his other dream now, even though it occurred more frequently.

"You don't see her *here*. You're in the Illumined Wood when you dream of her. The trees you described are found nowhere else. I'm not sure what it means Devlyn, but I don't think you'll be here much longer. Have any of the magisters said anything about beginning your novitiate?"

"No, nothing of the sort; I haven't even been here for a year yet." Abbie was beginning to trouble him; he knew she meant well, but she stirred more thoughts than he cared to consider. "I'm sorry Abbie, but I really need to get to my private lesson with Oreste before the afternoon block of classes. I'll see you around." It was still early in the week, only Thenaen and after three hours of listening to Kai talk about the political climate in Eklean, Devlyn was scheduled for additional instruction in wielding aerys, which was better than politics, not to mention his private lesson with Velari in the evening.

Devlyn waved as he quickened his pace and left Abbie in the corridor outside the classroom. He had been giving some thought as to what those dreams could mean; although they reminded him of the phoenix dreams he had grown accustomed to, they weren't quite the same. An unsettling feeling swelled in the pit of his stomach; it had been there since he'd felt the darkness, the unseen presence among the others, the night he had overheard the shadow elves. Devlyn had tried to explain it to Emdian yesterday during his private lesson, but the old ei'ceuril had dismissed it quickly and had Devlyn return to his meditation.

With no idea as to who else he could go to, Devlyn walked mindlessly through the castle. He was too tired for a private lesson with Oreste and had no intention of searching anyone out as he walked through the corridors. He focused on the stone floor as he ruminated on his troubles and came to an abrupt stop as the corridor ended. A large, clear window stood before him, overlooking the side of the mountain on which Ceurenyl rested. Devlyn recognized the broad river at the base of the mountain surrounding the city; several other mountains prevented him from seeing further, which meant that he looked east.

Devlyn remained where he stood, with no inclination toward moving away from the window. Gazing east, he recalled a map he had recently seen, compliments of Ethyl's history class. It was much larger and more detailed than any map he had ever seen in Cor'lera. If he remembered correctly, the Illumined Wood sprawled far to the east. He remembered the Illumined Wood well. He had lived in walking distance from its nearest boughs his entire life, until the past seven months.

He had never gone into the Illumined Wood, and neither had anyone in Cor'lera. Every child, from a very early age, was told stories of villagers going in and never returning. A fear of the wood was bred into the children of Cor'lera. However, Devlyn had always longed to disregard the tales and explore what lay beyond the edge of the forest.

Although the Illumined Wood sprawled far from where he now stood, he continued to gaze out the window, lingering, half expecting something remarkable to occur. Several minutes passed, and the view beyond the window endured, never changing. Deciding he had had enough of the unchanging scenery, Devlyn shook himself out of his trance-like state, turned, and walked away.

Incapable of understanding his restlessness, Devlyn continued to walk aimlessly through the castle. Images from his dreams played through his mind as he walked, the gold and silver leaves swaying in the warm breeze, the forest floor green and alive with small animals scurrying about. Lost in the images, and purposeless, Devlyn unfortunately collided with someone.

Sister Lillianna's dismay at being bumped quickly turned to delight at seeing Devlyn, a much-appalled and apologetic Devlyn. Her delight quickly became concern.

"Something tells me you are deeply troubled. What worries you, dearie?"

Since Devlyn had not seen Lillianna in the castle before—in fact, he had only met her that one time in the temple with Kevn—for an instant, he considered telling her that he was fine, nothing was wrong. So he was surprised when he heard words flowing right out of his mouth, telling her everything that plagued his thoughts, even as they stood in the middle of a corridor. The words spilled forth as he confessed the fears brought on by the prophecy and what was expected of him. The ei'ceuril listened attentively.

Pausing to catch his breath, a final question escaped. "What's the life of an ei'ceuril like?"

"Oh, it's delightful." She grinned widely but did not provide further details. "Pay close attention to the Light; allow it to guide your steps. May your heart be filled with peace as you discern what comes next."

"Do you think I would make a good ei'ceuril?" Devlyn asked. A thoughtful look crossed Lillianna's face as she considered Devlyn's question.

He was about to take the question back when she spoke at last. "I believe that if you are called to become an ei'ceuril, you will be a good one, as would anyone who is called. But knowing with certainty whether you are called is beyond my telling. Have faith and trust in Anaweh's Light. It shines on us all; we simply need to incline ourselves in its direction."

Feeling more at ease, Devlyn thanked Lilliana for her kind words and went on his way. Surprisingly, his current thoughts about joining the ei'ceuril brought a sense of peace washing over him. The anxiety that had built up simply dissipated in a single breath, replaced by a slight warmth. Whether it was intended as an affirmation or that he no longer needed to worry over the choice set before him was not clear, but he felt at peace.

Once again, the image of the Illumined Wood came to his mind, and with it, a pull, a longing in his heart. He could not describe what the longing was for, but the desire persisted, and it yearned for something beyond his reach. *Is this what it feels like to be called? To have another pull you into another form of life, different, but the same?*

Changes in the Wind

The sun had not broken through the dense autumn clouds since the full moon of Kyrenth and the Vespenth moon was still young. There was no rain, but the ominous clouds above Ceurenyl threatened a storm beyond compare. The ei'ana spoke cryptically of the clouds, even as they closely studied the foreboding weather. Some spoke of it as an omen, others predicted the future weather to come, and still others claimed it was the work of Erynor.

Arguments and heated discussions became common occurrences in Gwilnor the longer the restrictions on leaving the castle grounds held. There was little opportunity for exchanging news with the outside citizens as well, since the restrictions extended to entering the castle. The Septyl knights intensified the castle guard, and while none of the students could see it for themselves, the number of knights barring the city gates was said to be no less than a hundred.

Only the entrance into the largest courtyard, better known among the students as the quad, remained unbarred; the ei'ana and Septyl knights claimed it was more defensible than the entrance hall. The quad was enclosed on four sides with only one arched opening leading to a narrow bridge, with the Dragon Tower rooted in the corner adjacent to it, looming high above. The wall opposite the arched opening belonged to the largest of Gwilnor's halls. Devlyn had a strong suspicion, one he had not shared with anyone, that behind the wall, on one of the upper floors, the girls' dormitory lay hidden.

The courtyard mesmerized Devlyn; its architecture drew his eyes upward as he stood in the large-scale space. Nothing about the quad was small; it was grand and intimidating. Devlyn did not know whether the castle had been constructed during a single period but easily imagined that if each of the three main sections of the castle had been built at different times, this part was definitely the final piece, the castle's crowning jewel.

Knights and ei'ana remained vigilant from the parapets which encased the entire courtyard. As the days went by, the students' awareness of the heightened security wore off and the additional knights were soon forgotten. However, the students remained very aware of, and curious about, the hundreds of women who filled the castle of Gwilnor. The ei'ana possessed power beyond compare, certainly above ordinary swords, and while they would never wield to attack an enemy unless provoked, they would also never hesitate to defend themselves and those in need of protection, particularly the students of Gwilnor.

All Eklean knew the strength of the Ei'ana of Septyl; kingdoms far and wide respected them and sought their counsel, but so too did they fear the Ei'ana. Wars and battles were no strangers to Eklean, but never had they touched the walls of Ceurenyl. Only Erynor had ever dared bring war against Septyl, and whether it was through the element of surprise or brute force, the city had fallen, and with it the stability and Balance between kien and kiara.

The boys in Devlyn's dormitory spoke in whispers of the power of the ei'ana, almost hoping to witness it. While they considered Devlyn a freak of nature, the women capable of wielding kiara were anything but. The students greatly admired the abilities of the ei'ana. It was only on one occasion that he had felt compelled to confront one of his peers. In the common room, just as Devlyn was walking past, Trethien had loudly proclaimed his desire to watch ei'ana battle shadow elves, especially the reckless kien wielder shadow elves. Better to just kill them all this time around than lock them up in the temple, he declared, eyeing Devlyn.

Devlyn had only just held himself back from wielding terys or aerys against Trethien. The other pupils cared little for Devlyn as it stood, and if he wielded against Trethien, it would only confirm their prior judgments of him; kien wielders had no place in the world. Devlyn forced himself to walk on without comment even though he wanted nothing more than to punch Trethien in the face. Later, Alex, Andrew, and Kevn all agreed that he should have given Trethien a nice bruise, one large enough to match his ego, but not large enough to get him expelled from school.

———————————————

Leaning on the balustrade of the Dragon Tower's uppermost balcony, Devlyn allowed his mind to wander. His anger toward Trethien faded as his concern about the phoenix grew. Devlyn had ventured to the Dragon Tower's rooftop balcony on several occasions since the capture of the shadow elf, hoping to link with the phoenix. Each time, he pushed his consciousness into the vastness, but he never felt the phoenix's presence; his invitation went unanswered. The first time he had tried, he had stayed in the cool cloudy air for over an hour, but since there never was a response, he devoted less time on each successive occasion. This time, he had only stayed five minutes in the cold air before deciding to find someone else to spend time with.

It had been over a month since Devlyn had last seen Liam, and he really would have liked to visit his brother now. But with the heightened security, Liam was restricted to the Temple of Ceur, along with everyone else who resided there. With the city on high alert, he knew Liam was training tirelessly with the temple knights. Although there was no credible threat, everyone feared the worst.

Cut off from Liam, Devlyn had found himself spending more time with Ellendren. He enjoyed her company, even beyond their training sessions. It pained him that he could not grow closer to her, but he also doubted that his feelings were reciprocal, and to confuse matters even more, he also felt as if he was being called to become an ei'ceuril. Romantic companionship would be forever sacrificed when he did. Regardless, he still intended to seek out the Lucillian princess as he descended the winding stairs of the Dragon Tower.

Corridor after corridor, he searched for her. He knew the girls' dormitory was near the Dragon Tower, but he had never discovered its exact location. The castle was large and complex, and no one had bothered to explain to the boys where the girls slept. Devlyn believed it was intentional, especially since the girls knew precisely where the boys' dormitory was.

He thought about going to the library but if Ellendren was not there, he'd have to search for a book to check out, and right now, he didn't feel like researching his next assignment regarding the fallen kingdom of Gestoria. So, he wandered on through another corridor.

It happened, after much fruitless searching and aimless walking, that he finally found Ellendren speaking with one of her tutors. Devlyn waited some ways off; he knew Ellendren had seen him, so there was no need to intrude on her conversation.

It was another ten minutes before Ellendren skipped over to him, a huge grin lighting her face.

"Oh, I have wonderful news, Devlyn!" Ellendren could barely keep both feet planted on the floor as she bobbed up and down. "I was just speaking with one of my tutors, she's a Crimsyn you know, anyway, she just informed me that I have been accepted to study with other Crimsyns at Erithel! I did not expect to be accepted when I applied; they rarely take anyone who has not completed their novitiate and gone through the Choosing ceremony. But I was! I leave at the end of the month. Can you believe it? I'm actually going to heal the sick at Erithel this Orenth. I've been dreaming of this since I first passed through Erithel."

Taken slightly aback as Ellendren's words poured out, Devlyn didn't know how to respond. He supposed he was excited for her, but it would mean she would leave Gwilnor for a while. "That's great, Elle," he managed at last, hoping that he sounded happy and forcing a smile. "I couldn't be happier for you."

At least you'll be away from Trethien. The thought brought an authentic smile to his face.

"I know this will disrupt our meetings, but it will only be for a short while."

The sudden news of Ellendren's departure made Devlyn forget why he had been looking for her in the first place, not that there had been a real reason aside from wanting to spend time with her. Ellendren continued to talk enthusiastically of her news and the wonders of Erithel as Devlyn tried to remember why he had spent quite a bit of time looking for her. When she mentioned their assignments due at the end of the week, he guiltily remembered the book she had loaned him.

Devlyn had made little progress on his essay on the southern Eklean kingdoms and city states. He knew very little about Yanil and Tiel, let alone the city states that had declared independence from their mother-land. From what Devlyn remembered, wars were common occurrences to the south.

The stronger countries endlessly attacked to reclaim their lost lands, while the smaller city states fought to keep their aggressive neighbors at bay. Ellendren was very knowledgeable about the situation to the south, quickly correcting Devlyn whenever he confused a city state for a kingdom, and then going into detail, not just over the current monarchs and rulers but assorted persons of importance as well.

Yanil's capital city, Lankor, intrigued Devlyn. The first time that he had heard that an entire city floated on top of the water, he had thought it too incredible to be true. However, he was alone in his fascination with the floating city. When he continued to ask questions, the other students stared at him with disbelief at his curiosity, one student even suggesting that he visit Lankor and see if he still felt the same toward it after the visit. It was only then that Devlyn had remembered that Yanil was the kingdom that had banished wielding and imprisoned wielders, the city his uncle, General Lex, had mentioned all those months ago in his speech to stir the blood of Cor'lerans.

Ellendren happened to have a book covering the history of Yanil and had given it to him following that particularly embarrassing lesson. Since then, he had only glanced over the first pages. It was a boring book that included many foreign and unfamiliar names and each page contained several dates linked to historical events. If she was going away soon, he'd have to make a big effort to read some of it before returning it to her.

By now, it was late in the afternoon and Ellendren asked whether he cared to join her for dinner, which he quickly accepted. By the time they reached the dining hall, it was already filled with students satisfying their hunger and Ellendren led him to the table where she and her friends typ-ically sat. The others had not yet arrived, but Devlyn doubted it would be long until they showed up. Ellendren went off to get the two of them something to eat, while he waited for the others.

They must be able to speak telepathically; how else could they always know where each other are? Devlyn looked around but did not see her friends and constant companions.

It was only the thirteenth hour of the day with dusk at least another hour or two off, but the threatening clouds kept the sunlight from pouring through the large windows of the dining hall. In fact, it looked as if it was the middle of the night, not early evening.

A warm plate filled with aromatic herbs sprinkled on vegetables and chicken hovered before Devlyn. He took it from Ellendren, glancing over at hers, which looked much the same, except that she had opted against the meat. Devlyn had noticed that she rarely ate it, often mentioning that the elves of old had never allowed slaughtered meat to pass through their lips. Not interested in arguing over something as silly as poultry, Devlyn accepted that Ellendren most likely spoke knowledgeably on the subject, even though he couldn't see the sense of it.

"Will you be able to meet tonight? I know you don't meet with any of your tutors on Saraen or Karaen, but since I'll be leaving soon, I was hoping we could take advantage of the time we have. I spend most of my weekends on schoolwork anyway."

"Sure. You are getting stronger, Elle. You almost wielded all four elemental erendinth the other night. It won't be long before you won't need my help anymore." Devlyn suddenly realized what that meant and grew depressed over the possibility of not meeting with Ellendren on a regular basis. Since he wasn't sure that she shared his feelings, he decided it best to avoid talking about it, and smiled encouragingly instead. It was not long until others joined them.

Abbie Wintyr was among the new arrivals; her recent disheveled appearance had only worsened. She shot Devlyn a glare, but said nothing, which did not upset him. Instead, he ate his meal, pleasantly chatting with the others about homework. No need to mention dreams.

The noise in the dining hall grew to its usual rowdy evening level. What was different though, was the high number of ei'ana present. While the hall could comfortably seat every resident in the castle, that normally only happened on feast days. Lately though, the ei'ana seemed to have acquired a fondness for the company of the students. That, or they were present as protection for the students if required.

Wind howled against the window panes, and high-pitched whistles screamed through small cracks in the casings. Devlyn imagined a storm would break any moment. No sooner than thinking it, lightning flashed, producing light far greater than the candles littered throughout, and making everyone pause to look toward the windows turned dark again.

Several seconds passed before the lightning was followed by a crash of thunder. The sound of it reverberated off the glass, but the walls of solid stone swallowed it. What perplexed Devlyn though, was that not a single drop of rain fell against the window panes.

What kind of a storm doesn't have rain?

The lightning and thunder became fairly regular, and those in the dining hall lost interest in the weather. After all, the castle did keep the storm outside.

The entire city had waited weeks for the brewing storm to break, waited while it loomed threateningly over Ceurenyl for days on end without following its normal course of heavy rain, wind, thunder, and lightning. Now that it finally broke, no one eating dinner in the dining hall was surprised despite its substantial intensity.

Boom. BOOM.

Devlyn looked to the windows, expecting to see another flash of light, then realized that the horrific sound had not been preceded by any lightning. Lightning always came before thunder. Silence reigned in the normally noisy hall as not a single person moved a muscle, no one spoke as they waited, listening for a clue, for anything that would tell them what could have caused such a crash.

Just as hushed murmurings began to fill the hall again, a girl rushed through the massive doors. She ran toward one of the older ei'ana sitting near the front, Mother Agnelle Phanstienne, Chair of Auburnis.

The girl handed Mother Agnelle a note and the entire room looked toward the Chair of Auburnis. As she read the note, the kind lines of her face sank, and she seemed to grow older. It was a short note, but Devlyn noticed that Mother Agnelle took a while to read it, holding it before her face for several moments longer than needed, saying nothing. At last she stood, hugged the frightened girl who had brought the note and spoke in a surprisingly loud voice.

"Students, return to your dormitories at once. No one is permitted to leave his or her dormitory until notified; any students who need to cross a bridge must be escorted by an ei'ana. Ei'ana, report to your assigned stations," Mother Agnelle bellowed through the dining hall. She paused for another moment and took a quick glance at the note clutched in her hand before speaking again. "Ceurenyl is under attack. Be at peace, children, he cannot reach us here. We are safe."

As soon as she finished speaking, the entire dining hall erupted in panic; students flew for the exits while ei'ana remained composed and tried to maintain an orderly exit of students, to no avail. The noise level rose again as everyone rushed to the doors, pushing and screaming. Devlyn heard Erynor's name repeated on many lips and wondered whether there was any truth in the rumor.

Who else would dare attack Ceurenyl? he thought as he followed the stream of students and ei'ana out of the dining hall. *Who else could?*

A hand grasped Devlyn's shoulder, and he turned, surprised to find that the strong grip belonged to Mother Agnelle. He would never have expected a woman her age to possess such a fierce grip. Devlyn noticed that she held a curious-looking, translucent stick in her other hand; it was about as big around as an angot, about the length of his forearm, and it had a golden hue. She gripped it confidently at her side. Devlyn thought it an odd object for one to be holding at such a time.

Does she intend to poke someone's eyes out?

"Have you made your decision, my child?" Agnelle's question was pitched for his ears alone.

There was no need for Devlyn to ask which decision; he understood what she wanted to know. There was no time to consider it any longer; he had spent the past month going back and forth and not once had he come closer to a decision. At last, he nodded.

"Very well. Do you know where you are needed?"

The temple, he thought. Again, he nodded to the elderly Chair who still grasped his shoulder, her fingers pressed firmly into the little muscle there.

A moment of quiet passed between them, Agnelle looking intently into his eyes, before her hand moved from his shoulder to tenderly cup the side of his face. "Believe in yourself, child, and follow the Light; much depends on you."

Without another word, Agnelle darted through the crowd of students and beyond the doors, her brown robes flying behind her, leaving Devlyn alone in the dining hall.

He had lost track of his friends in the panic, and though he wanted to tell them where he was going, he also knew that time was of the essence. The girls rushed off in one direction while the boys clogged the corridor by the North Tower's stair hall. Devlyn turned along a vacant corridor, headed to the stairway he had gone down with Velaria not so long ago. Steadily and swiftly, he descended into the depths of the castle; he wielded a globe to light his path along the dark corridor. He walked cautiously, aware that he could not take a wrong turn or miss the nondescript door that would open to the tunnel, not a corridor, buried under the castle and city.

His light went out and his connection with the erendinth severed abruptly. It was an awful feeling; he felt terribly vulnerable. This time, there was no lit torch to greet him at the end of the tunnel. Only darkness.

He walked on slowly and warily, hands extended before him in caution.

I don't remember it being this far off, he thought just before his foot caught a ledge, causing him to trip and fall into Therril's office in the temple. He grimaced slightly and was about to push himself upright when he realized that he was not alone.

Jaerol sat on the couch, his legs crossed. Although the Cells of Justice had proven his innocence, seeing the Cyndinari free to roam the temple still startled Devlyn. In the candlelight, his face held its usual blankness, but he also seemed to have been concentrating deeply, solemnly. Devlyn opened his mouth to speak, but Jaerol shook his head and gestured him to remain silent, before closing his eyes to continue with his meditation.

THUNDERING

Velaria Treyven, Chair of Azurelle, stood atop the rooftop balcony of the Dragon Tower among her sister Azurelles. She and several other ei'ana were linked together to better enhance their wielding. She wished Devlyn was still in the castle but knew he had made his decision and was making his way for the Temple of Ceur. She supported him, but still wished that he had remained at Gwilnor, if only to protect it from the shadow elves now sieging Ceurenyl.

It was difficult to believe that Devlyn was capable of wielding two of the transcendental erendinth, an ability lost and long forgotten. Yet he had managed it through instinct. When they had linked together to overcome the shadow elf and Jaerol, she had felt an incredible presence in Devlyn, a presence that she had never experienced. She had noticed nothing sinister in the erendinth umbrys he had been wielding. Aware of the transcendental erendinth, she had refrained from wielding umbrys herself out of a long-standing fear of its capabilities, and its alleged connection to Erynor and his shadow elves, even though Jaerol insisted that they wielded tenebrys, not umbrys. She also feared that she could never manage the power on her own. Animys and umbrys were so different from the elemental powers; they even behaved differently.

The attack on Ceurenyl left no doubt as to its author; his style was imprinted on the siege. There was no need to destroy the city gate with such theatrics. She had reached her post just before the explosion and had watched as stone blocks exploded hundreds of feet into the air. More terrifying than the actual destruction was that she could not sense the wielding that caused the damage. It was certainly a great distance off, but normally distance was of no concern for Velaria; few in the castle matched her ability.

Not only was Velaria stronger than most kiara wielders, she also held one of the verathn, an ancient weapon of power. The ei'ana had managed to conceal a handful after the city of Septyl was lost and secretly passed them on until the ei'ana reestablished themselves following the Luminari's courageous self-liberation, starting with Lucillia's gentle, weaponless unchaining. Each Chair had personal possession of one verathn; the others were divided among select ei'ana, chosen individually by the Seven Chairs collectively. The names associated with the verathn they now possessed were long forgotten; the ones they held had the appearance of short sticks of varying lengths and widths. Velaria did not know when they came to be known as wands, but it was a name she found appropriate.

Not intended to be substitutes for the erendinth, but rather intensifiers, the wands allowed their wielders to refine their use of the erendinth and extend their strength tenfold. Since Velaria was the only ei'ana on the Dragon Tower's rooftop balcony with a wand, and with her authority as a Chair, she led their link.

As they held their position on the balcony, every so often, she wielded aerys so she could observe the events at the gate. The vast majority of the Septyl knights posted there had perished in the explosion, and while she was saddened by that, she did not permit herself to mourn; that would have to wait. Hundreds of knights and several ei'ana had been stationed there.

Just before the attack had started, the ei'ana who had been securing the gate with the Septyl knights managed to send a message that a force approached the city. Velaria had rushed to the uppermost reaches of the Dragon Tower just in time to witness an explosion beyond reckoning. A curious and brave girl, one of Gwilnor's younger students, had joined her there. Velaria gave the girl a hastily scrawled note for Agnelle, stationed in the dining hall.

Aware that they fought with little hope of success, the ei'ana and Septyl knights at the gate had fought hard nevertheless. Grossly outnumbered, they had battled shadow elves, both kiara and kien wielders, who wreaked havoc on Ceurenyl. She wondered whether the explosion was a consequence of the kien wielders among the shadow elves losing control.

Was it necessary; did they all have to die?

The counter-wields by Velaria and the ei'ana on the balcony did little to stem the attack. The attackers now forcing their way through the rubble at the gate were incredibly strong; even the women among them were far stronger than Velaria and the ei'ana in the castle. She thought they might possess verathn of their own; Jaerol had made it abundantly clear that the shadow elves possessed a number of corrupted verathn; there was no other way to explain their strength.

Velaria spared a glimpse to the tower's foundations and saw a stream of students rush across. The girls ran for their dormitory and several ei'ana led them across the bridge, while others remained stationed on the bridge.

The storm raged outside. Deep into the mountain and under the Temple of Ceur, Devlyn now sat on one of two wooden chairs in Therril's office next to the window that wasn't a window, with Jaerol and Liam. When Devlyn first tried to leave to find the Ceurtriarch, Jaerol told him he had to wait in the office for further instruction. Even here, they could hear the thunder without lightning. Shortly after he had made his rather undignified entrance, Liam came in and joined the two, repeating that Devlyn must wait for further instruction. Since Jaerol still occupied the couch, Liam had taken a seat on the remaining chair. Devlyn could almost touch the tension in the room between Liam and Jaerol.

Liam knew that Velaria trusted Jaerol but his own opinion was that Jaerol had managed to fool her, the Ceurtriarch, and the wise ones. That, or Jaerol bought off the lot of them with more golden crowns than they could carry without help. Imprisoned in Gneal, Liam had seen Jaerol often and although Liam had never seen Jaerol suck the spirit of other elves or humans, neither had Jaerol ever tried to prevent it.

Devlyn had discovered quickly enough that Jaerol was the Cyndinari in the castle of Gneal on the day Velaria had liberated Liam, the same elf who had seen them escape. Devlyn assumed that his brother was still bitter that Velaria had not dealt with Jaerol all those months ago.

Jaerol was aware of Liam's distrust and did not blame him for it. He'd had to play his role well enough to deceive the shadow elves into believing that he was one of them. Naturally, anyone on the opposite side of the conflict would also think Jaerol was the evil sort he pretended to be.

Ignoring Jaerol's request for silence, Devlyn now asked Liam many questions in hushed tones, but Liam had nothing to share, and didn't know whether anyone in the temple was aware of the attack in the city. Several times since he'd made his way into Therril's temple office, Devlyn had reached out to the phoenix with no success. He worried greatly for the phoenix, remembering the captured shadow elf's threat.

Aside from everything that was happening, Devlyn had a task at hand; he had made his decision and now had to seek out the Ceurtriarch. He had no idea where to find the man he had heard so much about. Despite all the tales he had heard, he had never met Ceurtriarch Ealyndol and had no idea what he looked like. If he ever managed to leave the office to search for him, he could easily pass him in a corridor without even knowing, not that he expected the leader of the Ei'ceuril to walk about the Temple of Ceur inconspicuously.

All he knew was that the Ceurtriarch was old—very old by most accounts—and that he had a long wispy white beard. It didn't strike Devlyn that the beard or the advanced age were useful bits of information, since many of the ei'ceuril were old and had beards.

Devlyn lost track of time as the hours stretched on, and still no news reached the office with the curious window.

Liam and Jaerol sat pensively with their eyes closed. Liam had moved his chair as far from Jaerol as possible, but not so far that he could not sit between the Cyndinari and Devlyn.

Growing restless, Devlyn asked Liam and Jaerol if they thought it was safe to search for the Ceurtriarch.

"We must wait here. The temple is large beyond imagining; if one of the ei'ceuril were to search for us, they would have no way of finding us, unless we remain in the place where they know us to be." Even with all that was happening, Jaerol's tone remained curiously flat.

Devlyn sat back in his seat, both resigned and annoyed. Aside from the incessant thunder, the office grew quiet once again. Devlyn noticed that both Liam and Jaerol had closed their eyes.

All I need to do is to get out the door without making a sound.

Keeping his eyes on the other two, Devlyn ever so slowly rose from his chair, relieved that it did not creak, and took a single step away from the chair toward the door, paused, then took another step, then another.

He was halfway across the office when Liam said, "You do know we're not asleep, right?"

"How did you hear me? I didn't make a sound." Devlyn could not believe his brother's perception.

"I was kept in a dark cell for eleven years; I can hear a mouse scrape against the floor five rooms away," Liam explained dryly. "However, we have been waiting here for quite some time, and the thunder without light continues. I'm coming with you. I'm eager for some news as well."

Jaerol did not appreciate the veiled reference to his role in Liam's confinement, but followed Devlyn and Liam out of the office without comment.

Liam was most familiar with the temple's layout and took the lead. Devlyn expected the Ceurtriarch's office to be closest to the Chamber of Light, remembering that Kevn had said something along those lines. The higher one was in the Ei'ceuril hierarchy, the closer they were to the Chamber of Light. And since the Ceurtriarch was the highest, he most likely occupied the quarters closest to the Chamber of Light.

They passed hundreds of men clustered together in the corridors, gossiping about what could possibly be happening outside the Temple of Ceur. Kien wielders all, they had no way of going out to see for themselves. The ability to wield was all that was needed to justify being kept in the temple, despite most of them not having wielded before and likely having no idea where to begin. Rumors of fighting in the streets were spreading through the crowds and some talked of an invasion, but it was clear that no one knew for certain.

The crowd thinned as they followed a staircase up, leaving the kien wielders behind and now walking among men consecrated to the Light. Some ei'ceuril huddled in small groups, but most went about their nightly business as usual, only a quickened pace indicating an urgency not typical for contemplative men.

Emdian stood in one of the small groups, hunched over his cane and peering at the others.

"Devlyn my boy, what in the blessed name of Anaweh are you doing here? Are you not aware of what is plaguing our streets? Now is not the time for a private lesson." Devlyn considered telling the old ei'ceuril steward about the tunnel but decided otherwise.

"I need to find Ceurtriarch Ealyndol. I've decided to become an ei'ceuril." It was the first time Devlyn voiced his decision. He felt relieved to have finally declared it, as if a weight was lifted from his shoulders. Even so, he could not say whether the choice was his own.

Emdian looked into his eyes, considering the authenticity of Devlyn's words. "Very well, my boy. I hope this choice is from inner peace and not due to this evening's events." Emdian gestured for Devlyn, Liam, and Jaerol to follow him.

Emdian spoke sparingly as they walked through the corridors; he seemed to have little breath for conversation, wheezing all the way. Their pace was considerably slower than before Emdian joined them and came to a near halt when they reached the grand stair hall.

The storm continued to rage outside and the walls shook with tremors from the thunder. Did the crashes come from the storm, or were they like the boom unaccompanied by lightning the students had heard in Gwilnor's dining hall?

If they are shadow elves, how powerful can they be to make sounds such as that? The thought plagued him as he followed Emdian.

Devlyn recognized this particular corridor from previous visits. A pair of doors of great proportions would stand at the end, with the Chamber of Light sprawling behind them. Emdian led them unhesitatingly past all the doors and intersections directly to the entrance of the Chamber of Light where, tonight, four temple knights stood guard. Two of them opened the doors for Emdian and his companions after each recited the entrance petition. Light washed across their faces as the doors opened.

Staying near the edge of the chamber, Emdian walked along about a quarter of the perimeter, halting before another set of doors, identical to the chamber's entrance doors.

Four more temple knights stood guard. One demanded that Emdian state their business. Why did they seek an audience with the Ceurtriarch? In Devlyn's previous encounters with temple knights, they had been much less authoritative, but considering the current circumstances, it was understandable. How many others had come to these doors this evening seeking answers?

Emdian replied, and one knight went in leaving the rest where they stood.

No less than an hour passed before the temple knight returned. Devlyn's little group advanced toward the doors, but the knight permitted only Devlyn to pass through.

Devlyn looked to Liam. A knowing look passed between them, a farewell of sorts, and Devlyn went in alone as the doors sealed behind him.

He stood in a large foyer where several doors led to other rooms in the Ceurtriarch's semi-private chambers. There was no telling how extensive the quarters were; a large house could easily lie behind any of those doors, a mansion tucked within the temple. Straight ahead, a pair of opened doors offered a view into a large office, and Devlyn went in.

A very old man stood in the room, and at first, Devlyn did not notice him. When he did though, he was surprised.

Next to this man, Emdian could be called a youth. But this man's back was straight, his posture flawless, hands clasped in front. Pointed ears poked through long white hair and a wispy beard nearly reached his waist. Silver eyes shifting to green just around the iris looked at Devlyn with kindness and question.

"My son," the Ceurtriarch broke the brief silence, "I am Ceurtriarch Ealyndol Roendryn. Is there something you wish to ask of me, Child of Light?"

Registering his last name, Devlyn wondered how the Ceurtriarch, the Chair of Vyoletryn, and Ellendren were related. The formalities were beyond anything he was accustomed to.

Since no one ever expected that Devlyn might one day meet the Ceurtriarch, no one had bothered to instruct him in the proper manner of addressing the Ceurtriarch. Ordinarily, he'd be quite nervous about being in this august presence, and tonight's events and his decision to come to the temple further heightened his anxiety.

"Ceurtriarch Ealyndol, Arbiter of the Light," he started, recalling some of the titles applied to the man before him. "I desire to join your order and live the way of the Ei'ceuril."

As he spoke, the Ceurtriarch approached and Devlyn was incredibly grateful that Ealyndol had a kind face. No longer on opposite sides of the vast room, Devlyn could almost count the many wrinkles on the older man's face if he wished.

Ealyndol extended his hands to Devlyn, placing them first on his brow and next before his chest. Dashing lights emanated from his hands as he did so.

"I send you forth to the Illumined Wood with my blessing." Ealyndol smiled, his wrinkles multiplied, and his eyes gleamed. "No less than a year shall pass before you depart from a way you came not. You are to go to Lucillia immediately. From there you shall enter beneath the boughs of the Illumined Wood to begin your novitiate. Before you enter, you must speak with the Aryl of Lucillia. I wish that the time before your departure could be prolonged, but the result of this attack on Ceurenyl remains unknown."

Devlyn stood before the Ceurtriarch, his decision made, and his fate sealed by the proclamation, on his way to the Illumined Wood as an ei'ceuril novice. *Was he expected to respond?* A single question crossed his mind.

"How am I to get to Lucillia? There's only one way in or out of Ceurenyl, and I imagine it's not accessible." Perhaps there was a minum nearby.

Ealyndol smiled weakly, and he led Devlyn through one of the arched doors into a spacious sitting room where, on the far side and behind an elegantly woven, drawn back curtain, doors to a balcony stood ajar. Devlyn caught a glimpse of movement on it as the first rays of a new sun began to rise above the Laudien Mountains. Clouds and smoke hung above the city but did not stretch to the horizon.

WORDS OF SHADOW

Ealyndol waved Devlyn on toward the balcony. Just a few steps away from it, Devlyn's mind flooded with familiar images of greeting and welcome, followed by images of himself riding on a blue dragon.

Pushing the door wide open, he was greeted by the incredible sight of Yelaris standing alertly on an extensive curved balcony that ballooned outward from the temple. Although her wings were folded, Devlyn had no doubt that she could unfurl them and leap into the dawning sky at a second's notice.

"My child, you must reach Lucillia with all haste to warn the Aryl of Lucillia about the attack on Ceurenyl. Tell them that I believe their only hope is to enact the Protection of the Wood. The faith of one will protect their people. The events spoken of in the prophecy are unfolding, and there is no stopping them. Go now, Child of Light, but with caution. I know not what perils you might encounter as you flee from here. If the Light wills, I hope to welcome you on your return." The weight of his position as Ceurtriarch Ealyndol Roendryn, High Archsteward and Arbiter of the Light carried in Ealyndol's soft voice.

Yelaris twitched impatiently, sending images of urgency tainted with anxiety coursing through Devlyn's mind.

Understanding, he gave a last nod to Ealyndol, resisting a strong urge to hug the Ceurtriarch, even though he had only just met the elderly elf. Devlyn stifled a yawn—he had been awake the entire night—before climbing onto Yelaris' back. He was not yet seated properly when she bounded from the balcony and plummeted over the edge, following the shear drop of the temple before she leveled off and maneuvered through a canyon.

Yelaris flew northward, staying clear of the city and out of sight of possible watchers. Devlyn desperately wanted to know what was taking place in Ceurenyl, but Yelaris stayed on her course, soaring along the bottom of the canyon. Behind them, smoke rose from the far side of the temple, the scent of it filling their nostrils.

Loud crashes drummed unabated. Devlyn hoped to see some lightning. Lightning and thunder went together; the absence of the eye-blinding flashes was troubling. The loud crashes were unnatural and wreaked havoc below.

Devlyn desperately wanted to help the sieged city. Yelaris remained resistant to turning back. The troubled images came from her as well. While she too wanted to help the besieged, especially Velaria, she was fixed on the plan to take Devlyn as far from Ceurenyl as possible.

They were not in the air for more than five minutes when a screech filled their ears. More screeches followed and a roar fiercer than anything Devlyn had ever heard nearly stopped his heart. Devlyn's shock increased when he realized that he felt Yelaris' do the same. Turning to look did not improve things; the sight of a dragon bearing down on them paralyzed him. Larger than any beast Devlyn had ever seen or imagined, its scales were darker than he had ever thought possible, so dark that Devlyn thought the smoke and sinister clouds hanging over Ceurenyl looked bright in comparison.

Shadow enshrouded the beast, covering much of its body. It flew directly toward them on wings so powerful that they rarely beat. The massive head of the dragon pierced through the shadowy veil, a head so large that it looked as if the beast could swallow Yelaris whole.

On a straight path, it could easily outfly Yelaris too, so the smaller dragon took advantage of her size and maneuvered in swift, nearly acrobatic movements that Devlyn did not think possible of a dragon, especially with him on her back. Yelaris might be smaller than the other beast, but she was still a dragon of considerable girth. She dove from the sky toward the lower reaches of the mountainous slopes, flying close to the canyon's hazardous mountain wall.

Devlyn held on for his life, keeping his seat with difficulty as he hugged her sinuous neck. Whenever the colossal dragon drew near, Yelaris abruptly veered up at an angle that made Devlyn's hair stand on end. Her evasive maneuvers brought them near the city gate, or rather, where the city gate once stood.

The sight was horrifying. Flames engulfed all the buildings near the gate, smoke billowing heavily above the inferno. Several had already collapsed, leaving burning debris where once magnificent structures stood. The gate itself lay in rubble, with only the bridge leading to it providing a clue to its previous location.

The city was breached, and the mystery behind the loud crashes resolved. The gate and nearby wall lay in ruins, beyond repair with shadow elves climbing over the rubble to wreak further havoc beyond.

Wider than most houses in Cor'lera, the gate section of the once magnificent defensive wall had exploded, reduced to boulders and rough-cut stone. The rest of the wall encircling the city was undamaged; the attackers had concentrated their efforts on the gate.

Dozens of dark beams pierced the sky. After the capture of Jaerol and the shadow elf, Devlyn had asked Therril about them during one of their private lessons. Therril explained that the beams were a forbidden product of tenebrys: Darkness manifested, a cursed form of wielding which corrupts and dominates the erendinth, its only power to destroy.

Now, the shrieks continued above and behind them, and Yelaris' maneuvers avoided the malicious wielding. No longer flying along the slopes of the mountain, they now soared above the city away from the shadow elves at the gate.

Suddenly, a force fell over Devlyn from behind.

Darkness pressed against him. It fell on his mind and tried to strangle him, stirring great fear in him. Desperately calling on his inner strength, Devlyn wielded kien—pressing himself into the erendinth—and battled the colossal force away. He felt as if he was drowning, as if a fast-flowing river tried to drag him beneath the veil of the living.

In a panic, aware that the reprieve would be brief, he called on the incredible strength and power that was his, pressing further into the erendinth to wield all four elemental erendinth simultaneously and directly at the dragon. His wielding was sloppy and unrefined, but even so, nothing could stop him. All that mattered was that he must be stronger than his pursuer.

He felt the water, air, stone, and fire form, each balanced as they united, complementing and magnifying the others. Relying on instinct, and without knowing what the effects of such a wield might be, Devlyn waited for the right time to launch the extraordinary power he held; it continued to grow stronger, taking more of his strength into the energy.

The dragon was closing in. Devlyn discharged the beam of pure energy manifested of aquaeys, aerys, terys, and ignys toward the giant beast, its resonating power lingering in his grasp and he held his breath as it exploded on the dragon. A sigh of relief escaped when he felt it strike.

It was a momentary victory, for the dragon soared on through the sky, unfazed.

Laughter came from whoever rode the dragon.

Crushed by his failure, Devlyn despaired, but stayed pressed into the erendinth, ready for the next assault.

A massive force pushed against him, seeming to want to either encase or penetrate him. He wielded the erendinth and shot through the attack, but he could feel his strength waning with every attempt he made to beat back the all-encompassing tide.

It was as if he attacked gas; every time he penetrated it, it reformed and continued to squeeze against him.

Whispers in an unfamiliar language danced in his mind with each attack, delving into his thoughts like tendrils, searching out what might be hidden within. Desperately, he tried to wield the transcendental erendinth, but every time he tried, his link to the elemental erendinth was severed, leaving him to press into them anew to fight off another attack. How had he done it before? He couldn't think past the fog over his mind.

It seemed like a distant memory, a dream almost. In desperation, Devlyn wielded the four elemental erendinth again, but rather than trying to pierce through the attack, he formed a globe around himself and Yelaris, holding the spherical shield in place, allowing it to build.

The whispers ceased and Devlyn pushed the globe outward in a burst of energy that shattered the dark force.

An intimidating roar escaped the colossal dragon's maw, immediately reminding Devlyn that dragons breathed fire. The beast was close enough that, if it wished, it could incinerate both him and Yelaris to cinders with a single breath.

Yelaris feared the possibility as well, no stranger to the tales from her kind about this ruthless dragon and sent Devlyn an image of a shaft of air beneath one of the dragon's wings. Devlyn quickly wielded aerys to strike one of the dragon's wings from below, pushing it off course and giving Yelaris precious time to flee.

A thunderous voice boomed through the city, a voice so immense that it pained his ears and caused Yelaris to moan in response.

"DOES THE BOY RUN FROM HIS FATE? ON ONE OF MY OWN? NONETHELESS, BE ASSURED, YELARIS, YOU SHALL PERISH FROM A DEATH FAR WORSE THAN WHAT I WILL INFLICT ON OTHERS OF YOUR KIND STILL IN HIDING, FOR I *WILL* FIND YOU. NOW, FLEE, RACE AWAY, FOR WHEN YOU LEAVE THAT WRETCHED WOOD, YOU WILL NOT RECOGNIZE THE WORLD YOU ABANDON THIS DAY. JOIN WITH THE LAST LIVING PHOENIX IF YOU CAN, FOR I LOOK FORWARD TO EXTINGUISHING YOU BOTH. LEARN THE WAYS OF THE PHAEDRYN ALONE, FOOL BOY, BUT REMEMBER THIS, THOUSANDS OF YOUR ANCESTORS DIED AT MY HAND, THE HAND OF EMPEROR ERYNOR MERIDEN OF THE ERYNIEN EMPIRE. YOUR PEOPLE WILL ONCE AGAIN BE IN CHAINS AND YOU AND THE PHOENIX WILL ALSO DIE BY MY HAND. NO ONE IN THIS LAND IS SAFE, NOT EVEN THE WRETCHES IN THE CITY BELOW, THE CITY THAT I ALLOWED TO ELUDE AND ENDURE THROUGH MY PREVIOUS REIGN. FOR NOW, I WITHDRAW FROM THIS PITIFUL SHADOW OF WHAT ONCE WAS. KEEP MY PETS, EVEN THE TRAITOR YOU CAPTURED! FLEE, COWARD, FOR WE WILL MEET AGAIN."

The voice stopped and a sickening silence fell. Devlyn's ears still rang. He wiped at a trickle near his ear and saw blood on his fingers. Overwhelming sadness filled him as he looked at the city below. Erynor's strength was beyond anything he had known. Attacking him directly was impossible; the best he had been capable of was redirecting the dragon's path with a force of aerys, and even that he had barely managed.

Yelaris hovered above the destroyed city. From below, hundreds of shrieks filled the air, the same screeches he had heard just before Erynor and his dragon hunted them down. Were they meant to frighten the people of Ceurenyl?

An image entered his mind, that of a high-pitched screech emanating from a shadowy figure, a shadow elf. Hundreds of shadow elves flooded the city. Bad enough when there had been only two, it would now be impossible to know whether all the shadow elves had departed with their emperor.

There was no doubting it, Ceurenyl was no longer a safe haven for the people of Eklean. Thought the safest city; it had managed to survive the fall of Krysenthiel to endure Emperor Erynor's dark reign over a thousand years ago, always serving as a sanctuary. Erynor had never dared attack the city before.

Yelaris beat her powerful wings, taking them toward the river beyond Ceurenyl and followed it north and east away from the city and the Shroud. Devlyn tried to locate the patch he and the phoenix had cleared, but it was too difficult to see such a minuscule hole in the massive Shroud.

The landscape below was impossible to discern. As they flew, Devlyn regretted that he had not been able to tell his friends at Gwilnor of his decision to become an ei'ceuril. Too late now. He'd had his opportunity to tell them but now, Ceurenyl was behind him.

SON OF FEOLYN

The city of Lucillia was beyond anything Devlyn had ever expected. The elves of his village had spoken of it with awe. Many longed to visit the mysterious and great Pilgrim City of their people. All the Luminari living in Cor'lera held a desire to pay homage to Lucillia.

While many of the buildings reminded Devlyn of the Cor Inn, these looked to have been welded from the very trees. Although every building was of wood, not a single tree had been harmed in the process. Devlyn had never concerned himself about the lumbering of trees, so had also never minded a house or building constructed of felled wood. However, this city stirred him to regret such methods, as if this was the proper manner of construction.

With no idea how such buildings came about, Devlyn felt a rightness about them. Trees intertwined with others to form majestic buildings. Twigs and vines supplied ornamentation with leaves and flowers flowing from them, making the buildings appear alive, and reminding Devlyn of Velaria's dress.

Most incredible, though, was the palace. The largest building in the entire city, it sat atop a hill in the center, poised on the edge of the Illumined Wood and visible from every street. Devlyn had grown accustomed to magnificent castles of stone and marble, but none surpassed the royal palace of Lucillia. Unlike the others, it had no towers or spires to pierce the sky. A single drum formed of the tallest trees sprouted from the center of the palace, but it appeared to be more of a domed chamber than a tower. Not tall like the other castles Devlyn had seen, this one sprawled across the hill it rested on. The palace had a natural balance, nestled in the elven city against the Illumined Wood.

Arches were in no short supply, formed by vines with flowers. The detailed ornamentation of the palace filled Devlyn's eyes. Vines with leaves displaying patterned carvings wrapped around columns woven from trees that themselves flourished with fine carvings in spectacular patterns. What truly surprised Devlyn, was that none of the windows had a single pane of glass. Vines and branches melded from the trees to form openings along the walls, but nothing prevented the elements from passing through.

Devlyn and Yelaris had arrived the day before, flying over the intricate city walls directly toward the palace. Yelaris left him there before soaring off again, presumably back to Ceurenyl. The palace attendants who greeted him insisted that he rest before his audience with the Aryl of Lucillia, Vernal and Harnyl Roendryn, queen and king of Lucillia and Ellendren's parents. He told the person who welcomed him about the attack on Ceurenyl and pleaded that they take proper precautions to prevent the same fate from reaching Lucillia.

When Devlyn woke the following day, the page temporarily assigned to see to Devlyn's needs shocked him with the news that he had slept more than twelve hours. Despite being awake well over twenty-four hours, Devlyn should have immediately reported his urgent news to the Aryl on his arrival, and here he was slumbering away. The events at Ceurenyl haunted his thoughts. Smoke and destruction were seared into his mind, coming to the forefront whenever his eyes closed. The awful scent of burning and death still tormented his nostrils, and his ears still rung with the screeches and that awful booming voice belonging to Erynor.

When Devlyn sprang from bed to ready himself, the page led him to a wardrobe and offered to help him dress. Stunned, Devlyn refused and gently pushed the young man aside before reaching in for his grey robe. However, the robe hanging in the wardrobe was of white linen, not grey. It was also of a different cut and fabric, similar to the grey robe he had grown accustomed to, but without a doubt different.

"What happened to my robe?" asked Devlyn.

"Beg your pardon, my lord, but you are no longer a student at Gwilnor Academy. Ei'ceuril students wear these robes." The page pointed into the wardrobe. Distracted, Devlyn stared at the man.

"Lord? Why are you calling me that?"

"Because, my lord, you are of the Line of Feolyn, Aryl of Cor'lera," the page replied.

"I'm no lord of Cor'lera, there's a mayor there, appointed by the Council of Perrien."

"I beg your pardon, my lord, but that mayor is not the rightful ruler of Cor'lera. King Roendryn appointed your ancestor, Feolyn and his wife, Gwendolyn, as Aryl of Cor'lera, and all who follow their line; Perrien has no authority over Cor'lera."

Devlyn still wanted to argue with the page that he was no lord, but decided not to press the point, especially since the page had countered each of his arguments.

After the eventful waking, the page insisted that Devlyn take time to eat breakfast. Deciding it best to not challenge him again, and besides, he was hungry, Devlyn shoved a piece of buttered bread with jam into his mouth.

Next, the page led Devlyn from the room and into a corridor, much the same as the room he slept in. Evenly spaced bare tree trunks lined the way with vines entwining between them, forming walls of leaves and flowers. Light flooded the corridors through the eastern windows. Because there was no glass in the windows, Devlyn felt as if he stood outside. The fresh air gently wafting into the corridor was reviving.

The palace had few stairs; in fact, Devlyn wondered if there was more than a single story in the entire structure, and better yet, how could that happen, since he walked on a grassy floor, the softest grass his feet had ever walked on. He wanted to walk barefoot but thought it might be indecent in the royal palace, especially since he had an audience with the Aryl of Lucillia.

The page stopped at a grand archway that left Devlyn with mouth agape. Thick and thin vines intertwined to form a large pointed arch, not as steep as the pointed arches in Gwilnor but quite majestic. Silver and gold flowers and leaves hung from the branches, glistening as if a spring rain had just fallen, even though winter was only two months away.

The room beyond the archway was round, and there, slender trees extended toward a domed ceiling. Devlyn's eyes followed the slender trunks upward and was astonished to see branches also clad in silver and gold leaves interlacing to form a dome open to the elements. The floor of this room wasn't covered in grass; instead flower petals reflected the light from the sun.

Devlyn walked carefully across the petalled floor toward the royal couple who sat on two thrones of equal beauty, bound together as one, complementing one another. He stopped before the Aryl of Lucillia and bowed before them as they rose to greet him. The queen of Lucillia reminded him very much of Ellendren, the same light brown, nearly blond hair and silver-melding-with-green eyes as her daughter's. The two were almost identical, bearing the same features, only the age difference marking them mother and daughter.

"Too many suns have risen and set since a son of Feolyn last walked beneath this dome. Devlyn, I am Queen Vernal Roendryn of Lucillia, descendent of Roendryn, son of Lucillia, and I welcome you to the Pilgrim City of Lucillia. May your visit be restful and disperse the anxiety burdening your heart."

Devlyn bowed once again and thanked the elven queen for her generosity.

"We were informed of the strife terrorizing Eklean. Do you bring news of this?" King Harnyl spoke with a robust voice.

"Yes, Your Majesties. I'm sorry to bring such news, but I came from Ceurenyl on Yelaris, one of the free blue dragons, to warn you that hundreds of shadow elves, led by Erynor, attacked Ceurenyl. They obliterated Ceurenyl's gate, leaving the city vulnerable to future attacks. I tried to wield against Erynor, but he was too strong. There was nothing I could do." Devlyn bowed his head. The images and smells returned; he did not trust himself to speak about them and stood silently.

Only then did Devlyn notice that the queen and king held hands.

"You are aware of the prophecy, yes?" Queen Vernal asked. Devlyn nodded and she continued in her graceful tone. "Part of the prophecy alludes to the elves of Luminare returning to Arenthyl. When they do, Lucillia will fade and return to the Illumined Wood. We do not know when this will occur, but it was said, long ago, that when our pilgrimage among the boughs of the Illumined Wood begins to fade, a gift must be given to the one named by Lucillia herself." Vernal stared into Devlyn's eyes. She released her husband's hand and stepped gently from the dais before holding her hand out to Devlyn.

He took her hand in his and felt something pass between them, as though some of the queen's power passed from her to him.

The connection was brief, and the queen then led Devlyn away from the domed chamber. They walked through the grand archway and re-traced some of his earlier path. Queen Vernal seemed to glide rather than walk, like a swan on a glassy lake, majestically erect, head held high, back straight, shoulders squared, arms swinging loosely at her sides.

They came at last to another archway, similar to but smaller than the one leading to the throne room and opening to a chamber at the far end.

"We stand in the heart of the palace. From this spot, the palace grew, and by extension, the entire city," Vernal explained.

Devlyn noticed that several arches led into the room from different parts of the palace. A path ran from each archway to join a broader one around a circular pond in the middle of the large room. Three people could easily walk abreast around the pond. At its center rose a wooden statue of a beautiful woman holding aloft a small violet jewel. From the jewel, a resplendent light cast the room with a violet glow.

"She holds the jewel of faith. She brought it to the slave camp when our people were still in Erynor's chains. We do not know where she retrieved the jewel. It's one of seven that form Ceurendol, the Jewel of Life. You must take it with you and join it with the others; only then will our gift of life immortal be reclaimed," Vernal said. She stretched one hand toward the jewel in the center of the pond, and the other to Devlyn.

"I could not, and even if I dared, how would I cross the water to retrieve it?" Devlyn looked into the surprisingly deep pond. He would have to plunge in and swim across and back.

"The statue sprouted from the place of Lucillia's sacrifice. Just before she gave birth to Roendryn and Feolyn, Erynor had threatened to kill her and the children she bore. Her faith was strong, though, and a bright light filled this area. It filled the Luminari with wonder and seared Erynor and his shadow elves. When the light faded, Lucillia's body was gone, leaving this jewel and two infants in her place, our common ancestors." Vernal's smile was warm. "To cross the water, all you need is faith, a small task compared to what is yet to come. Take my hand, I can go with you this small way."

Hesitantly, Devlyn held her hand. Whatever had passed between them before did not happen again, but now, he saw the woman standing before him differently, as if they were equals, descendants of the same royal Lucillian line. Her august titles of queen and Aryl of Lucillia faded as he looked at her. He didn't even think of her as Ellendren's mother, she was simply Vernal.

She took the first step, and to Devlyn's amazement, she did not sink, but stood atop the still water, gentle ripples flowing from the touch of her feet.

Devlyn followed with a wavering step onto the water and was left in awe that he did not sink. Together, they took another step, followed by another. Halfway to the statue, Devlyn took his eyes from the jewel to look into the water, as he did, his feet began to sink. Vernal stood steady while Devlyn began to panic.

"Fix your gaze, Devlyn," she gently encouraged. "Accept the gift freely given."

At once Devlyn looked up at Vernal, and then to the jewel held aloft by the statue of Lucillia and continued to the statue with Vernal at his side.

"Mother..." he gasped before trailing off before her beauty.

"Truly, she is a mother to us all."

Devlyn stood entranced. The statue held the violet jewel, offering it to anyone who looked on it. Devlyn felt an odd sensation. Joy mixed with desire; wonder with truth; mystery with confidence. He knew he looked into something much greater than himself. He looked into the faith of the Luminari, poured forth to form a jewel, given freely to anyone who looked on it.

Devlyn took the jewel from the statue's hands; it came free without a struggle. A rush of incredible energy flew from the jewel into Devlyn. It felt similar to the erendinth, as if the same forces were involved, yet wholly different. As he clasped the jewel, he grew lightheaded and the circular room began to spin. The tune ever in his heart filled his being and for the first time he could remember, words sprang from his lips.

"With an unheard song upon thy heart,
Might light steps ever mark thy start.

"Endless were the days of bliss, when elven folk sang on lighted ray of sun and star.
Then, Darkness neared; Mount Cyngol, outlawed source, forced the elven kin withdraw,
But in Aldinare, exemplar of the Skylands, proud kindred refused and remained above and far.
To save his brethren from misery did Aren go, falling beneath a dark'ning claw.
Mar'anathyl, Mar'anathyl, oh ancient Lorenthien home, ever shall Aren long for thee, thy noblest son.

"Upon Eklean's surface, anon three elven realms begun,
Rejoicing as others passed beyond, for reason of their defining choice.
Golden meadows of morning light, shady glades of silent night, and islands bright of midday sun.
To a whisper did one listen, from whence spoke the heinous voice.
Ramiel, Ramiel, oh wretched ancient foe, reject and wring thy corrupting tongue.

"An age by human minds came and went, whilst the elven era was still young,
Teraeniel was joined in purpose found, Anacordel of every race were bound.
To Arenthyl clung every people, as hymns of joy were sung,
For the Exalted Lorenthien Aryl had resound, Life again ought be found.
Krysenthiel, Krysenthiel, oh blessed realm of flowers gold, untouched–unstained by olden strife.

"Poured into a jewel did the Luminari invest their Life,
As dawn stretched wide her open arms and filled every heart with awe.
Jealous ire claimed the Cyndinari as they employed the assassin's knife.

With darkened hearts and plots renewed, they paid heed to a silenced and buried maw.

Erynor, Erynor, oh of forsaken worth, blot thy ears and quit thy course henceforth.

"Red turned the land, blood and vice poured forth,
Eklean wept as war returned, their dreams set aflame and burnt.
Septyl fallen, beseiged in the night from south, east, west, and north.
The Balance of kien and kiara broken; the Erendinth unlearnt.
Ei'ana, Ei'ana, oh wielder maimed, reclaim thy powers and regain thy early frame.

"Despairing, an elven queen, Ithendryl was her name,
Her husband king she grieved; elf stolen by death; phoenix eaten by draconic fiend.
She proclaimed the Phaedryn lost as such, her fate she knew the same.
Away she sent an egg with a hundred Guardian Knights, a phoenix unborn—unseen.
Ithendryl, Ithendryl, oh beloved queen, was ever an elf so keen, to hath foreseen the abject aftermath.

"Forsaken the present, forgotten the past, whilst the future held but a single path.
Death's kiss found those of Dawn and Day, creators of the Jewel and Shroud,
Unforesought, the elves of Luminare and Cyndinare felt an unknown mortal wrath.
Dark the days when shadow fell across the land; lament the lonely sound.
Ceurendol, Ceurendol, oh blessed Jewel of Life, return erelong that we may know thy song.

"Mis'ry and slav'ry belonged to those of Dawn, their toil spanning ever long.
Bruised in face and body, clad in tattered rags, a gravid elf appeared,
Torture and pain familiar fellows among the throng, yet her faith stayed ever strong.
From olden days, the lucilliae's gleaming shell seen once more, now manifest quite clear.
Lucillia, Lucillia, oh faithful true, might the love you refused to sell, be ever left unfelled.

"Softened hearts admired her steadfast amity, as fear and dread dispelled.
Swayed the Cyndinari set to guard; rueful, loathe to remain untrue.
Intent on freedom, awaiting a child, Lucillia blossomed and swelled.
Once learnt, the precious secret was soon sent to their emperor's view.
Auriel, Auriel, oh Anadel among the stars, wouldst thou save us from Ramiel's lech'rous knave.

"Brutal the discovery, depraved the Empire's stave,

In force the Empire did band, once but a shadow when first held command.
Into the Illumined Wood as one, fled former captor and former slave.
Behind the Erynien force pursued, to wooded land they dare not stand.
Luminare, Luminare, oh dwelling aloft in cloud, if only we were with thee; unspurred into fir.

"Slowed by broken water, Lucillia fell behind, whilst Erynor lunged upon her.
A vow flew from his cursed lips, that no free child shall this slave bear.
Unencumbered did his blade sing death, screeching through severed leaves astir.
A prayer flew from her blessed lips, her silent heart of light to share.
Anaweh, Anaweh, oh Creating Light, nourish and prepare my sons, so the least may give his life untarnished.

"A purifying Light curtailed the malicious ones, brought solace to the anguished.
Where Lucillia fell beneath the blade, alone lay two babes as the sun bowed down.
Roendryn and Feolyn were they named; their ravished mother, from Teraeniel, vanished.
All creation flocked as one to the newborn cry to lift each blessed crown.
Roendryn, Roendryn, oh just and kingly elf, Aryl to set the Luminari free.

"Thrones blossomed beneath to reign, whilst budding city was sung from tree.
Where Lucillia passed, her likeness gazed west, the wooded city off'ring rest.
Roendryn now Aryl with his wife, the Erynien Empire brought to broken knee.
North, Feolyn went in peace, beneath the forest eaves he stayed, a pilgrim like the rest.
Feolyn, Feolyn, oh father mine, ever shall Cor'lera's treasure be, the cradle of an unborn king."

Queen Vernal stared at Devlyn, her eyes widened. "Where did you learn that?"

"I don't know." Devlyn's head still spun, but the room did begin to steady. "I've always known the tune, but never the words."

"Your mother must have sung it to you. A similar song was passed to me as a child." Vernal paused a thoughtful moment.

"I ever so wish you could remain here with us Devlyn, but you must leave for the Illumined Wood and begin your novitiate. Once you cross, Harnyl and I must enact the Protection of the Wood. No one will be able to enter or leave the city while the shield stands. When you see my daughter again, please tell her she will always have my love." Vernal paused, the affection for her daughter evident. "It pains me that none of my children will benefit from this protection."

Devlyn impulsively embraced the queen of Lucillia, which she returned warmly.

Vernal led Devlyn from the room and through the palace to the gardens in the back where Harnyl waited. The Illumined Wood sprawled beyond the palace gardens, the trees stretching high over Devlyn's head, much higher than any of the buildings in the city, even higher than the palace's dome. Devlyn took one last look at Vernal and Harnyl, the Aryl of Lucillia, and bowed his head as both gave him their blessing.

He turned and left the world.

Not ten paces into the thick trees, he saw the barrier of greenish light fall between him and Lucillia; the Protection of the Wood was in place. Although he knew it would not take long before he would lose himself in the majestic forest, he did not know what he would come across while in the Illumined Wood. He desperately hoped the time would pass swiftly, aware that his friends and the entire world remained in grave danger.

Erynor had revealed himself once again, proclaiming war on those who lived freely outside the Erynien Empire, and casting great fear on them all.

Despondent and nearly despairing, Devlyn clutched the violet jewel and was filled with consolation. The Darkness which tempted to claim his heart fled and, in its stead, came a simple concept: this year was a gift. The sun still rose to the east; dawn was still fresh in the air and the promise of life rested on his heart.

Here ends the First Part of
The Jewel of Life:

Splendor of Dawn

Look for the second part of

The Jewel of Life:

Hidden Within

Appendix A

Glossary of Terms

Abbey School

The preferred system of education for children throughout Eklean. Those deemed capable are sent to higher studies, preferably at Gwilnor Academy.

Aelish

Native language of the elves. Largely forgotten, only used in academic circles.

Aerys

An elemental erendinth. The essence of air.

Albien

One of the seven Schools of Septyl. Albiens focus on truth and care for many of Eklean's libraries. Motto: Truth is discoverable. Emblem: A naked male and female elf holding unraveled scrolls with an owl perched behind, cast in gold on a white field. The chair of Albien is known as the Seeker.

Aldinare

Western Skyland of the Aldinari, one of the four elven kindreds. Lost to the Darkness. Only a hundred Aldinari escaped the Skyland with their lives.

Alicorn

A legendary beast native to the Skyland of Aldinare. A winged unicorn.

Anadel

Spiritual creatures that predate Teraeniel and Somnaeniel. Their native home is Lumaeniel. There are four known classifications of anadel: irythil, enthiel, lorendil, and naril.

Anacordel

Creatures of both body and spirit.

Anaweh

The Creating Light.

ANIMYS

A transcendental erendinth. The essence of spirit.

AQUAEYS

An elemental erendinth. The essence of water.

ARANTIULYN

One of the seven Schools of Septyl. Arantiulyns focus on strength and protection and oversee the Knights of Septyl. Motto: With fortitude, we will protect. Emblem: A naked male and female elf in a fighting stance with swords in hand with a lion prowling cast in gold on an orange field. The Chair of Arantiulyn is known as the General.

ARCHSTEWARD

Part of the Ei'ceuril hierarchy, they are elevated wise ones. Before kien wielders were restricted to the Temple of Ceur, archstewards lived in every major city of Eklean tending to those faithful to Anaweh, the Creating Light.

ARYL

The united head of an elven house composed of a king and queen or lord and lady.

AUBURNIS

One of the seven Schools of Septyl. Auburnises focus on inner peace. Motto: To love is our gift. Emblem: A naked male and female elf offering a garland with larks flying above, cast in gold on a brown field. The Chair of Auburnis is known as the Pilgrim.

AUREPHAEN

Feast day of the Luminari, commemorating Auriel and the dawning sun. Celebrated on the 15th of Aurenth, the spring equinox.

AZURELLE

One of the seven Schools of Septyl. Azurelles focus on the advancement and training of the erendinth. Motto: The zealous soul must be temperate. Emblem: A naked male and female elf wielding the powers with a dragon behind, cast in gold on a blue field. The Chair of Azurelle is known as the Blue Dragon.

Belin's Watch

An Evellion city in the Vespien Mountains comprised of humans and dwarves. Named for Belin, the dwarf who sheltered Thellion refugees in their greatest hour of need.

Borephaen

Feast day of the Eldinari, commemorating Boriel and the sleeping sun. Celebrated on the 15th of Borenth, the winter solstice.

Bowl of Theniel

Sea set apart by the merpeople as sacred. The place where Theniel brought the waters to Teraeniel.

Centaur

Anacordel dedicated to protecting the forests of Eklean, particularly the Illumined Wood. The upper body is like an elf's but broader and more rugged while the lower body looks much like a four-legged horse.

Ceurendol

The Jewel of Life. Created by the Luminari by placing their life essence within seven jewels of incredible brilliance which allowed them to share their immortality with every race in 1.3a (7085.3E). Also known as the Light Diamond, the Lieben Stone, and the Heart of Hearts.

Ceurendol War, the

A cataclysmic war instigated by the Erynien Empire which began over a philosophical difference over the Jewel of Life and whether immortal life was proper for the 'lesser races.' The war divided Eklean in two factions, those faithful to the Luminari and those subjugated by the Erynien Empire. As the fate of the war grew clear, emissaries and merchants from other continents withdrew from Eklean, fearing the Erynien Empire. 322-500.3a (7407-7585.3E).

Ceurenyl

City founded by the ei'ceuril. Home of the Temple of Ceur and Gwilnor Academy. The only city not to fall into Erynor's control when Krysenthiel was lost to the Shroud.

Ceurtriarch

Leader of the ei'ceuril, known as High Archsteward and Arbiter of the Light.

Chancellor

The head of Gwilnor Academy under the authority of and appointed by the Seven Chairs.

Children

When capitalized, refers to the proto-race.

Cor'lera

A small village in eastern Parendior and in disputed territory claimed by both Lucillia and Perrien. The vineyards of Cor'lera produce the coveted ice wine, the Cor'leran Blue.

Crimsyn

One of the seven Schools of Septyl. Crimsyns focus on healing and run many hospitals and infirmaries throughout Eklean. Motto: Through healing, hope is given. Emblem: A naked male and female elf dancing with a dog, cast in gold on a red field. The chair of Crimsyn is known as the Physician.

Cyndinare

Southern Skyland of the Cyndinari, one of the four elven kindreds. Lost to the Darkness.

Daereneth

Continent south of Ogren and west of Ja'Horan. Tropical continent.

Deurghol

The Cyndinari directly responsible for the Shroud. They are neither living nor dead. Also known as the Deathless.

Dragon

Legendary creatures bound to the erendinth.

Druids of Kweil Aitch, the

Secluded faction of humans who learned to walk Somnaeniel, the World-in-Between, early on.

Dwarf

Anacordel who sought the deep roots of the mountains.

Ei'ana

An organized group of wielders. Since the Balance was lost during the Ceurendol War, there are only kiara wielders among the ei'ana. There has not been a kien wielder among the ei'ana for over a thousand years.

Ei'ana Counsels

A series of norms ei'ana are to follow in regards to wielding. The counsels prohibit men from becoming ei'ana due to their inability to wield safely after the Balance was lost. The counsels also require ei'ana to bring kien wielders to the Temple of Ceur for their own protection and the protection of their communities.

Ei'ceuril

A religious order, currently a majority of men, focused on serving Anaweh, the Creating Light. Because a kien wielder is not capable of wielding with control, every male ei'ceuril capable of wielding is confined to the Temple of Ceur.

Eklean

Continent where the anacordel first stirred as Children.

Eldin Wood, the

Home of the Eldinari.

Eldinare

Northern Skyland of the Eldinari, one of the four elven kindreds. Lost to the Darkness. The Eldinari were the first to evacuate their Skyland for the lands below.

Elemental Erendinth, the

Forces wielded to influence the elements. *See Erendinth.*

Elf

Anacordel who changed little when the different races were created. Because they wished to retain their original form, their immortality remained, and they were gifted the Skylands. There are four elven kindreds, the Luminari, Cyndinari, Aldinari, and Eldinari.

ELYA

Powerful wielders born of any race who learn to wield instinctively and are not limited to the restrictions common to normal kien and kiara wielders.

EMRADIEL

One of the seven Schools of Septyl. Emradiels focus on beauty and life. Motto: Only the prudent thrive. Emblem: A naked male and female elf gesturing with open palms toward the beauty around them with a stag behind, cast in gold on a green field. The chair of Emradiel is known as the Tender.

ENTHIEL

Anadel dedicated to one of the seven irythil. The enthiel are very involved with the anacordel. A single enthiel guides an entire people.

ERENDINTH, THE

The erendinth are the wielded powers believed to have created Teraeniel. Tradition says that there are seven powers, three transcendental: lumenys, animys, and umbrys; and four elemental: aquaeys, aerys, terys, and ignys. Much is forgotten or unknown about the full extent of the erendinth which are dependent on inner spiritual and emotional workings.

ERENDINTH GAMES, THE

A game of wielding created at Gwilnor Academy, involving the wielding of all seven erendinth.

FAUN

Short nocturnal anacordel with the hind legs of a goat from the navel down. Some fauns have horns.

GIANT

Anacordel that were drawn to the frozen north. During the Great Blessing, their physical features became capable of withstanding the harsh tundra of Glacien.

GLACIEN

Northern frozen continent spanning the northern pole. Connects Eklean and Ogren.

GOBLIN

Anacordel native to the Kinzdol Islands. Known for their monetary shrewdness.

GOBLIN GUILD

Infamous bank and guild of Eklean. Regulates the majority of Eklean's currency. The Goblin Guild is based in the Kinzdol Islands with branches in every city and most villages.

GREAT BLESSING, THE

Event recorded in the Theseryn where Anaweh blessed the growing differences among the anacordel and solidified their choices by making each their own distinct race.

GUARDIAN KNIGHTS

Order of knights once based in Krysenthiel that served and protected all the land from injustice. The Guardian Knights were largely composed of Luminari and were defeated during the Ceurendol War.

GUARDIAN SENATE, THE

An international body, crossing countries and continents to ensure the wellbeing of Teraeniel. Disbanded toward the end of the Ceurendol War.

GWILNOR ACADEMY

The foremost school dedicated to the education of wielders, located in Ceurenyl.

HOLY TOMES

Volumes recorded by various ei'ceuril, some being prophets, and from which the ei'ceuril base their beliefs and practices.

HUMAN

Anacordel that differ among themselves more than any other race. They traveled the furthest from the Valley of Saeryndol, migrating across the entirety of Teraeniel.

Ignys

An elemental erendinth. The essence of fire.

Illumined Wood, the

A vast forest with mysterious qualities and inhabitants.

Irythil

The seven anadel who, under Anaweh's guidance, introduced the erendinth, thereby creating Teraeniel.

Ja'horan

Continent south of Eklean. Inhabited largely by nomadic peoples.

Jahro Islands

Island chain in the Unarian Sea. Believed to be the home of pirates.

Keeper

Head of the time wardens and possessor of the time key.

Kiara Wielder

A female wielder. Kiara wielders learn to control the erendinth easily but require a kien wielder to reach their potential strength. Because the Balance was lost, kiara wielders are not able to reach their potential strength.

Kien Wielder

A male wielder. Kien wielders reach their potential strength easily but require a kiara wielder to learn control of the erendinth. Because the Balance was lost, kien wielders are not able to wield safely, and if any male begins to show an aptitude to wield, he is sent to the Temple of Ceur where wielding is impossible.

Kinzdol Islands

An archipelago in southern Eklean, homeland to the goblins and Cyndinari.

Kweil Aitch

Island east of the Illumined Wood. The place where the veil is thin between Teraeniel and Somnaeniel.

Lorendil

Anadel that guard and protect individual anacordel. Some anacordel are known to communicate with their lorendil.

Lucillian Alliance, the

An alliance of the Eklean kingdoms established to return peace and order to Eklean following Emperor Erynor's disappearance.

Lumaeniel

The World-Beyond. Dwelling of Anaweh, the anadel, and those anacordel who have passed beyond.

Lumenys

A transcendental erendinth. The essence of light.

Luminare

Eastern Skyland of the Luminari, one of the four elven kindreds. Lost to the Darkness. The Luminari evacuated their Skyland for the lands below where they established Krysenthiel.

Masters, the (Seven Masters, the)

Vigyl Vyoletryn, Cyrelle Azurelle, Lanielle Emradiel, Lyon Arantiulyn, Mainor Auburnis, Caelyn Crimsyn, and Saeyrn Albien are the founders of the Seven Schools of Septyl and Gwilnor Academy.

Meridean Conclave

Governing council of the merpeople.

Meridephaen

Feast day of the Cyndinari, commemorating Meridiel and the noon sun. Celebrated on the 15th of Meridenth, the summer solstice.

Merpeople

Anacordel who longed for the depths of Teraeniel's oceans.

Miervae

Anacordel who longed to nurture Teraeniel's forests. Miervae are also referred to as Great Trees and begin their life as Settlings.

MINUM

The least of Eklean's races. A short half-bred creature of goblin and human origins. Before the elves migrated to Eklean, they were enslaved, sold by goblins to humans.

NARIL

Anadel reminiscent of the seven erendinth. There are seven types of narils and they are commonly known as nymphs.

NYMPHS

See Naril.

OBSERVANT

Non-wielders who have dedicated themselves to one of the Seven Schools of Septyl.

OGRE

Brutish anacordel covering the vast majority of Ogren. Half-bred creature of giant and human origins.

OGREN

Continent east of Eklean and west of Qien. Mountainous land with a mixture of forests and deserts. Inhabited by giants, humans, and ogres.

PHAEDRYN

Those bound with a phoenix.

PURGED DESERT OF DWONIA, THE

A vast wasteland in western Eklean that was rumored to have at one point been fertile. Home of the Twelve Tribes of Dwonia.

RETURN

The final stage of formation of an ei'ceuril toward becoming a steward. Often occurring in the Illumined Wood.

SCHTACH

Language of the dwarves.

SCHTAM

(1) A dwarven people. (2) The dwellings of the dwarves.

SCHTAMITE

The eight dwarven Schtams.

SEGUIAN

A portal created to traverse space and time. Traversing time is restricted and only the keeper can use the time key to traverse time.

SEPTYL

(1) The Order of Ei'ana composing the Seven Schools of Septyl. (2) The city of the ei'ana in Krysenthiel and now lost in the Shroud.

SEPTYL KNIGHTS

Order of knights dedicated to Septyl. The knights receive their training at Gwilnor Academy and vow to serve one of the Seven Schools of Septyl.

SERVANTS OF SHADOW

Secret organization carrying out the orders of shadow elves and, in some instances, the orders of the Deurghol.

SETTLING

Tree-like creatures that wander about in their youth until finding an appropriate place to settle their roots and grow into a Miervae, also known as a Great Tree. Settlings have unique vitality qualities.

SEVEN CHAIRS OF SEPTYL, THE

The leaders of the Ei'ana. Each of the Seven Schools elects its own Chair who leads his or her particular School and participates in the leadership of Septyl. Responsible for admitting student wielders into Gwilnor Academy and selecting a chancellor.

SEVEN SCHOOLS OF SEPTYL, THE

The order of Ei'ana, composed of Albien, Arantiulyn, Auburnis, Azurelle, Crimsyn, Emradiel, and Vyoletryn Schools.

SHADOW ELVES

Cyndinari who consume the spirit of others to prolong their own life.

Shroud, the

A diseased-looking fog placed by the Cyndinari over the entirety of Krysenthiel. It severed the Luminari from the Jewel of Life, cutting them off from their life essence and making them mortal, as well as any others who had benefited from it. An unanticipated result was that the Cyndinari also lost their immortality with that placement of the Shroud over the Jewel of Life. The Shroud's mysterious origin is one reason no one has been able to remove it.

Skylands, the

Four island countries, Aldinare, Cyndinare, Eldinare, and Luminare, floating in the clouds thousands of feet above the ground. The dwelling places of the elves before they were forced to evacuate to the land below.

Sojourners

The exiled of Dwonia who sought reentrance after forming an allegiance with the Erynien Empire.

Somnaeniel

The World-in-Between. A realm visited by dreamers. Gateway between Lumaeniel and Teraeniel.

Steward

A clerical class of ei'ceuril with the ability to wield.

Temple of Ceur, the

Home to the ei'ceuril and pilgrimage site for the faithful. It is impossible to wield within the temple walls. All kien wielders are confined to the Temple of Ceur.

Temple Knights

Order of knights dedicated to protecting the Temple of Ceur and the city of Ceurenyl. Some of the temple knights are men who were brought to the temple when it was discovered that they could wield. These temple knights are prohibited from leaving the temple.

Tenebrys

A corrupted form of the erendinth, unrecognized by the Ei'ana of Septyl as one of the erendinth and absolutely forbidden to wield. The essence of Darkness.

TERAENIEL

The World-Below.

TERYS

An elemental erendinth. The essence of stone.

THESERYN

Holy tome recording the creation of Teraeniel and the anacordel, written by the first Ceurtriarch of the Ei'ceuril. The Theseryn states that seven irythil, under Anaweh's guidance, introduced the erendinth thereby creating Teraeniel.

TIME KEY

An artifact created by the Luminari to restrict the ability to traverse space and time. It was entrusted to the minums, the least of Eklean's races.

TIME WARDENS

A select group of minums entrusted by the Luminari with the ability to create seguians, allowing them to travel to any place and any time.

TRANSCENDENTAL ERENDINTH, THE

Wielded forces to influence the ethereal realities of lumenys, animys, and umbrys. The ability to wield the transcendental erendinth is forgotten.

TREE SPIRITS

Narils who agreed to bond with the trees under Sariel's guidance.

UMBRYS

A transcendental erendinth. The essence of shadow.

VALLEY OF SAERYNDOL

Birthplace of the Children, the first anacordel.

VERAKRYL

A crystalline tree within Mount Verinien which brought life to the world and is connected to Anaweh. Also known as the Tree of Life.

Verathel

Sprouts of Verakryl, the Tree of Life.

Verathn

Weapons of power.

Vespephaen

Feast day of the Aldinari, commemorating Vespiel and the setting sun. Celebrated on the 15th of Vespenth, the autumn equinox.

Vyoletryn

One of the seven Schools of Septyl. Vyoletryns focus on justice and diplomacy. Motto: With justice, peace. Emblem: A naked male and female elf holding a staff with an eagle soaring above, cast in gold on a violet field. The chair of Vyoletryn is known as the Watcher.

Wielders

Anacordel capable of wielding the erendinth.

Wise Ones

(1) Part of the Ei'ceuril hierarchy. There is no certainty how many are among the ei'ceuril. (2) Part of the Ei'ana hierarchy. There are seven wise ones for every School of Septyl.

Yanilean, the

The undisputed monarch of Yanil, always male. Used both as the monarch's title and as his name during his reign.

Days of the Week

(Based on the seven anadel involved in the creation of Teraeniel)

Gwynthaen–Thenaen–Uraen–Ramaen–Lerenaen–Saraen–Karaen

Months/Moons

(Based on the anadel attached to the elves)

Spring – Marenth, Aurenth, Delenth

Summer – Dynenth, Meridenth, Reventh

Autumn – Kyrenth, Vespenth, Orenth

Winter – Estlenth, Borenth, Lierenth

Currency

Goblin Guild currency – 16 iron angots for a copper lewt. 9 copper lewts for a silver jent. 13 silver jents for a gold crown. 3 golden crowns for a lumol.

Luminari currency – 8 kenols for a narol. 4 narols for a lumol.

Appendix B

Dramatis Personae

Abbie Wintyr

Human with emerald eyes. Student at Gwilnor Academy.

Agnelle Phanstienne

Luminari. Ei'ana and Chair of Auburnis.

Alexander (Alex) Vaerin

Human from Perrien, whose family migrated to Cor'lera. Devlyn's cousin on his father's side.

Amry Thellion

King of Evellion. Married to Queen Lara.

Andrew

Human from Sudern. Student knight at Gwilnor Academy.

Arbol

A faun searching for settlings.

Aren Lorenthien

Luminari. Led a rescue party to Aldinare and did not return.

Arlyn

Ei'ceuril steward from Cor'lera. Devlyn's uncle on his mother's side.

Bernard

Human from Perrien. Ei'ceuril, librarian, and magister at the abbey school of Cor'lera.

Danielle Aequin

Luminari of House Aerquin. Student wielder at Gwilnor Academy.

Devlyn Telvin

Ward of Cor'lera's abbey school. Physical features indicate Lucillian ancestry.

Dolan Telvin

Father of Devlyn, Leilyn, and Liam. Husband of Evellyn.

Ealyndol Roendryn

Luminari. Ceurtriarch.

Ellendren Roendryn

Luminari. Princess of Lucillia. Student wielder at Gwilnor Academy.

Emdian

Human from Sudern. Ei'ceuril steward.

Entiel Telvin

Human from Perrien. Ei'ceuril, steward, and abbot of the abbey school of Cor'lera. Devlyn's uncle on his father's side.

Erynor Meriden

Emperor of the Erynien Empire. Disappeared after Lucillia gave birth to the twins, Roendryn and Feolyn in 7857.3E. First Cyndinari born on Eklean.

Evellyn Telvin

Luminari from Cor'lera. Mother of Leilyn and Devlyn. Wife of Dolan.

Fyona Orendi

Luminari. Student wielder at Gwilnor Academy.

Hannah Torin

Human from Mindale. Azurelle ei'ana and magister of the Art of Wielding at Gwilnor Academy.

Harnyl Roendryn

Luminari. Aryl of Lucillia. Married to Queen Vernal. Father of Prince Aaron, Princess Kaela, and Princess Ellendren.

Jaerol Solaris

Cyndinari. Erynien emissary.

Kai

Human with physical features that suggest an origin other than Eklean. Azurelle ei'ana and magister of politics at Gwilnor Academy.

KARL

Human from Perrien. Observant of Vyoletryn.

KEVN WEYVIEN

Luminari. Student at Gwilnor Academy. Previously studied to become an ei'ceuril.

KIARA

A mythical woman believed to be the first female wielder.

KIEN

A mythical man believed to be the first male wielder.

LARA THELLION

Queen of Evellion. Married to King Amry. Azurelle ei'ana.

LEILYN TELVIN

Sister of Devlyn, believed to be living in the Illumined Wood. Daughter of Evellyn and Dolan.

LENORA HANARYLD

Human from Ceurenyl. Ei'ana and Chair of Arantiulyn.

LEX TELVIN

General from Perrien, key player in events surrounding Devlyn's family. Devlyn's uncle on his father's side.

LIAM TELVIN

Son of Dolan. Half-brother to Devlyn and Leilyn.

LILLIANNA

Human from Mindale. Ei'ceuril and formerly an Emradiel ei'ana.

LORETTA JAVIE

Human of Sorenthil. Ei'ana and Chair of Crimsyn.

LUCILLIA

The woman who gave birth to the twins, Roendryn and Feolyn.

MYRANDA LARIVIERE

Princess of Sorenthyl. Student wielder at Gwilnor Academy.

OMA

Dwarf of the Oern Schtam. Stone seer.

ORANNA

Luminari. Azurelle ei'ana and chancellor of Gwilnor Academy.

PAUREL ROENDRYN

Luminari. Ei'ana and Chair of Azurelle.

SAENDRE

Luminari. Student wielder at Gwilnor Academy.

SELENYA WAEYN

Luminari. Ei'ana and Chair of Albien.

SKIMP

Minum and time warden.

THERRIL

Ei'ceuril magister of theoreticals at Gwilnor Academy.

TIERA WELDON

Luminari. Ei'ana and Chair of Emradiel.

TRETHIEN NARIELLE

Luminari of House Narielle. Student knight at Gwilnor Academy.

VELARIA TREYVEN

Cyndinari born in Lucillia. Azurelle ei'ana.

VERNAL ROENDRYN

Luminari. Aryl of Lucillia. Married to King Harnyl. Mother of Prince Aaron, Princess Kaela, and Princess Ellendren. Direct descendant of Lucillia.

VINE VAERIN

Human from Perrien. Mother of Alex. Devlyn's aunt on his father's side.

Waleisius

Merchant in Cor'lera, more commonly known as Walei.

Yelaris

A free blue dragon bound to Velaria.

The Seven Irythil and their Associated Enthiel

Uriel – Lord of the Stars, whose name means Anaweh is my Light. Irythil who brought Anaweh's Light to Teraeniel.

> **Auriel** – The Dawn Star. Guardian of the elves of Luminare.
>
> **Meridiel** – The Noon Star. Guardian of the elves of Cyndinare.
>
> **Vespiel** – The Evening Star. Guardian of the elves of Aldinare.
>
> **Boriel** – The Night Star. Guardian of the elves of Eldinare.

Gwynthiel – Lady of the Lorendil, whose name means Strength of Anaweh. Irythil who brought Anaweh's spirit to Teraeniel.

Ramiel – Lord of Death, whose name means Arrogant toward Anaweh. Betrayed Anaweh and all creation. Irythil who brought shadow to Teraeniel.

Theniel – Lady of the Seas, whose name means Anaweh Heals. Irythil who brought water to Teraeniel.

> **Nauto** – Guardian of all humans living along the coasts.
>
> **Aquae** – Guardian of the merpeople.

Sariel – Lord of the Land, whose name means Command of Anaweh. Irythil who brought substance to Teraeniel.

> **Tera** – Patroness of harvest and nourishment. Often referred to as Mother Tera.
>
> **Mundi** – Guardian of the dwarves.

Lereniel – Lady of the Winds, whose name means Friend of Anaweh. Irythil who brought air to Teraeniel.

Kariel – Lord of Peace, whose name means Who is Like Anaweh. Irythil who brought fire to Teraeniel.

Appendix C

Civilizations of Teraeniel

Aldinare

Remnant of Aldinari rescued from the Skyland Aldinare by Aren and accompanying Phaedryn. They are considered part of Krysenthiel.

Race: Elf

House/Aryl: Avign, Eraen, Kenoril, Threilen

Audun

One of the eight Schtams composing the Schtamite. Situated at the westernmost edge of the Laudien Mountains.

Head of State: Patriarch Dridn IV, son of Dridn III

Race: Dwarf

Briel

River valley kingdom situated between two rivers forming the River Reifen and the slopes of the Dead Wood.

Capital: Briel

Head of State: King Irvienne of the Royal House Haert

Motto: Seek the message

Sigil: Black raven on a yellow field

Race: Human

Brunst

One of the eight Schtams composing the Schtamite. Situated within the Vespien Mountains. Close friends with the Eldinari.

Head of State: Patriarch Thraen, son of Anuun

Race: Dwarf

Charren

A kingdom spanning across two continents, Ogren and Daereneth.

Capital: Karithel

Head of State: King Sanhir of the Royal House Irithru

Race: Human

Daer Empire

Oldest continuous human empire in Teraeniel and advocate of slavery and colonialism. Situated on the continent of Daereneth.

Capital: Daer

Head of State: Body of the Daer Senate

Race: Human

Dwonia

Desert country once controlled by the Twelve Tribes of Dwonia. Only two tribes refused to ally with Erynor and remained in the desert.

Heads of State: Chief Kodin of Tribe Fendur and Chief Genin of Tribe Vadir

Capital: Nynev

Sigil: Red lion on a yellow field

Race: Human

Eldinare

Eldinari society secreted away in the Eldin Wood.

Head of State: Aryl Fendryl and Dalenya of House Lierafen

Capital: Stellantis

Houses/Aryls: Aeris, Allandis, Glaeda, Illia, Jamsyl, Lenwyn, Lierafen, Nyen, Oreleste, Shendielle, Rudyn, Taureh

Sigil: White tree on a green field

Race: Elf

Erynien

Cyndinari empire founded by Erynor Meriden, its sole emperor. Responsible for the Ceurendol War and enslavement of the Luminari.

Capital: Broid

Head of State: Emperor Erynor Meriden

Sigil: Bronze sun on a red field

Race: Elf

EVELLION

The mountain kingdom where the Laudien and Vespien mountain ranges meet. Original inhabitants were the refugees of Thellion.

Capital: Everin

Head of State: King Amry and Queen Lara of the Royal House Thellion

Motto: The pure will soar

Sigil: White eagle on a blue field

Race: Human

FRIETON

The free city-state of Frieton. Given to the minums on their release from slavery.

Capital: Frieton

Head of State: The Keeper (identity unknown)

Race: Minum

GESTORIA

Fallen kingdom situated on the Plains of Orithil. Once great allies to Thellion and Krysenthiel. Obliterated during the Ceurendol War.

Capital: Quellion

Motto: Will triumphs pride

Sigil: White gold winged lion on a blue field

Race: Human

GLYOL

One of the eight Schtams composing the Schtamite. Easternmost and only schtam in the Illumined Wood.

Head of State: Matriarch Vylma, daughter of Toreldn

Race: Dwarf

Harol

One of the eight Schtams composing the Schtamite. Situated in the Laudien Mountains.

Head of State: Matriarch Loewn, daughter of Brenola

Race: Dwarf

Ja'horan, Tribes of

Nomadic civilization on the continent of Ja'horan.

Race: Human

Ja'nalihn

Short lived kingdom covering all of Ja'horan.

Race: Human

Jopht Schtam

One of the eight Schtams composing the Schtamite. Southernmost Schtam in the Vespien Mountains and staunch defenders against the Shadow Schtams from northern infiltration.

Head of State: Patriarch Oerth III, son of Oerth II

Race: Dwarf

Krysenthiel

The kingdom of the Luminari. Currently lost within the Shroud. Translates to land of the golden flowers, named by a human trying to speak Aelish, the language of the elves, to describe the countryside.

Capital: Arenthyl

Head of State: Exalted Lorenthien Aryl

Houses/Aryls: Aerquin, Clarion, Ginielle, Lauriel, Lorenthien, Narielle, Reyndien, Taerinior

Sigil: Seven golden kryseniels blossoming from a larger central kryseniel on a white field.

Race: Elf

Lucillia

Kingdom of the Luminari after gaining their freedom from the Erynien Empire. Named after Lucillia, the woman who gave birth to the twins, Roendryn and Feolyn.

Capital: Lucillia

Head of State: Aryl Vernal and Harnyl of House Roendryn

Race: Elf

Mindale

A kingdom east of the southern Vespien Mountains.

Capital: Binton

Head of State: King Lawrence of the Royal House Maroven

Motto: Mind over body

Sigil: Brown ox on a green field

Race: Human

Nunstol

Shadow Schtam that was cast off by the Schtamite for their actions in Mount Cyngol.

Head of State: Patriarch Uriden, son of Urodrn

Race: Dwarf

Oern

One of the eight Schtams composing the Schtamite. Belin belonged to Oern Schtam and sheltered Evellion and his people as they fled Elothkar.

Head of State: Patriarch Forvl VIII, son of Forvl VII

Race: Dwarf

Parendior

A hilly country north of the Laudien Mountains and west of the Illumined Wood. Most Parendians are farming folk, and when Perrien invaded, they had no means of defending their land.

Capital: Gneal

Head of State: Perrien Council

Motto: Protect the harmony

Sigil: Purple doe on a beige field

Race: Human

PERRIEN

A kingdom north of the Laudien Mountains where the citizens over-threw their monarchy and replaced it with a council and doubled their territory by invading Parendior.

Capital: Gneal

Head of State: Perrien Council

Motto: Swift to action

Sigil: Grey rider and horse on a white field

Race: Human

QIEN EMPIRE, THE

Empire of the Hundred Kingdoms on the continent of Qien, west of Eklean.

Capital: Zhongshi

Auxiliary Capitals: Beishi, Dongshi, Nanshi, and Xishi

Head of State: Empress Qien Wei

Race: Human

SORENTHIL

A kingdom along the River Meyien.

Capital: Myrium

Head of State: Queen Karina of the Royal House Lariviere

Motto: Flow with the waters

Sigil: Blue dolphin on a light blue field
Race: Human

SUDERN

A city state on the Dagger's Point peninsula. After a bloody civil war with Josque, the inhabitants declared themselves independent.

Capital: Sudern

Motto: Hidden daggers

Sigil: Red ship and dagger on a white field

Race: Human

THELLION

The fallen Eklean kingdom covering all the lands east of the Vespien Mountains. Met its downfall through a civil war relating to succession.

Capital: Elothkar

Motto: Eternal wisdom

Sigil: Silver winged horse on a white field

TIEL

A southern kingdom bordering the Erynien Bay and the Unarian Sea.

Capital: Josque

Head of State: Queen Alesei of the Royal House Ziera

Motto: Eternal wisdom

Sigil: Orange serpent on a blue field

Race: Human

TORSIL

A weak kingdom with little influence on its neighbors.

Capital: Trest

Head of State: King Gordon of the Royal House Carvil

Motto: Stronger together

Sigil: Grey wolf on a red field

Race: Human

UNDOL SCHTAM

One of the eight Schtams composing the Schtamite. Deeply religious and situated in the Laudien Mountains surrounding Lake Saeryndol. They have strong ties to the Luminari.

Head of State: Matriarch Miurel IV, daughter of Miurel III

Race: Dwarf

VORN SCHTAM

One of the eight Schtams composing the Schtamite. Situated at the northernmost edge of the Vespien Mountains.

Head of State: Matriarch Tiltha, daughter of Tilma

Race: Dwarf

YANIL

Southern kingdom along Erynien Bay. Yanil was once jointly ruled by the Yanilean and the Judges of Yanil.

Capital: Lankor

Head of State: The Yanilean

Motto: Deep as justice

Sigil: Black castle on a blue field

Race: Human

ZORIK

Shadow Schtam that was cast off by the Schtamite for their actions in Mount Cyngol.

Head of State: Matriarch Jiora, daughter of Jiorza

Race: Dwarf

About the Author

Ryan D Gebhart first started writing the Jewel of Life series in 2012 in Philadelphia, PA, shortly after concluding his undergraduate studies in philosophy. This unexpected passion evolved over the years and has remained a constant companion through his career changes, from a Capuchin Friar, to a Claims Processor, and finally in his current endeavor as an Architectural Graduate Student in Washington, DC. Ryan D Gebhart is originally from Wilmington, DE.

Keep up with Ryan D Gebhart at www.RyanDGebhart.com